POISON FLOWER

A DARK HIGH SCHOOL BULLY ROMANCE

STEFFANIE HOLMES

Cover design: Ever After Cover Designs

ISBN: 978-1-99-104612-3

❀ Created with Vellum

POISON IVY

Beware the wrath of a broken blind girl.

Victor. Torsten. Cassius – the jock, the artist, the stepbrother.
They made me theirs – body, heart, and soul.
They got inside my head.
They broke down my defenses and made me trust them
... maybe even *love* them.

They betrayed me.

They think they're untouchable,
but they forget that I'm one of them.
I'm the poison flower in their garden,
beautiful and deadly,
hiding in plain sight.

I know all their secrets,
Their weaknesses,
Their darkest desires,
And I'm going to make them *pay*.

Poison Kiss is a new adult, dark contemporary romance with three hot, dangerous guys and the blind girl who rules them. It is intended for 18+ readers.

Victor, Cas, and Torsten think they know everything that goes on in Emerald Beach, but do they? Find out when you sign up to Steffanie Holmes' newsletter and get a bonus scene in your free copy of *Cabinet of Curiosities* – a compendium of short stories and bonus scenes – when you sign up for updates with the Steffanie Holmes newsletter.

JOIN THE NEWSLETTER FOR UPDATES

Victor, Cas, and Torsten think they know everything that goes on in Emerald Beach, but do they? Find out when you sign up to Steffanie Holmes' newsletter and get a bonus scene from *Poison Ivy* inside your free copy of *Cabinet of Curiosities* – a compendium of short stories and bonus scenes. Sign up for updates with the Steffanie Holmes newsletter.

https://www.steffanieholmes.com/newsletter

Every week in my newsletter I talk about the true-life hauntings, strange happenings, crumbling ruins, and creepy facts that inspire my stories. You'll also get newsletter-exclusive bonus scenes and updates. I love to talk to my readers, so come join us for some spooky fun :)

A NOTE ON DARK CONTENT

I'm writing this note because I want you a heads up about some of the content in this book. Reading should be fun, so I want to make sure you don't get any nasty surprises. If you're cool with anything and you don't want spoilers, then skip this note and dive in.

Keep reading if you like a bit of warning about what to expect in this series.

- There is some bullying in the first and second books, but our heroine holds her own. No heroes in this story threaten or are involved in sexual assault of the heroine.

- Cassius' language is violence, and twice in this book he exhibits violence toward Fergie - once in a fight between the two of them in the arena (which she wins), and once when he believes he has to kill her, but can't go through with it.

- Fergie experiences revenge porn - both in her past and present.

- Fergie is sexually assaulted by a teacher in the first book.

- The Poison Ivy guys are part of a dark criminal underworld in Emerald Beach. There is some murder, violence, torture, and other crimes in this book, including a crucifixion scene.

- There is some discussion of suicide.

I'd definitely call this book 'dark', and it's for readers who like their heroes a little psychotic and their heroines badass. If that's not your jam, that's totally cool. I suggest you pick up my Nevermore Bookshop Mysteries series – all of the mystery without the gore and violence.

Enjoy, you beautiful depraved human, you :) Steff

To James
For being my lighthouse

"Nitimur in vetitum.
We strive for the forbidden."

– Ovid's 'Amores'

PROLOGUE
CASSIUS (THREE YEARS AGO)

"You're doing great, little bro." Gaius watches from his lookout high in the branches of a jacaranda tree, his face hidden in a canopy of violently purple flowers. I finish emptying a gas can over the dilapidated building, and reach for another. "All you have to do is light the match, and you'll avenge Gemma."

Through the edges of the red mist over my eyes, I stare down at the gas can in my hands as I slosh the liquid over the wooden porch and around the old classroom, making sure to get lots of it on the hatch that leads down to the basement. I feel as though I'm watching a movie with a red filter over the lens. These aren't my hands. This isn't my body moving through the old horticulture building, leaving a trail of gas and broken dreams in my wake.

Gaius has been calling me 'little bro' ever since we were kids, even though I've been twice his size since I was nine years old. We look nothing alike – our two different dads mean that he's wiry and green-eyed with an aquiline nose and Mediterranean skin, and I'm a giant with a voice made of gravel and skin as black as obsidian, like our mother. The old nickname reassures me; it makes me feel like I belong with him, like it's us against the world.

Especially when he says it in the same confident voice he used when he got me to sneak extra cookies from under Milo's nose, or when he handed out the next job to the Poison Ivy Club. That voice says, 'everything is going to be okay. I'm on your side, and nothing can touch us.'

But even with the rage sizzling in my veins, I know this time it's different. I'm playing for more than just an extra chocolate chip crunch.

I'm playing for a life, and I can't fuck this up. Not this time.

"I light the fire, and Gemma is safe," I murmur as I move deeper into the building, making sure gas drips from every surface.

My heart hardens to stone as I picture Gemma the last time I saw her, two nights ago. She's lying in my bed, the sheets tangled around her naked legs as her whole body trembles with heart-wrenching sobs. That prick Konrad went to the school administration about her grades, and now there's a fucking investigation. Her parents forbade her from seeing me and Victor, but Gemma escaped that prison they call a home and came to me.

Me. Not Victor.

She came to my house, crawled into *my* bed, and she begged me to hold her in my arms while she popped several pills and fell into a fitful, nightmarish sleep that she hasn't woken from in two days. Every time I try to touch her she screams, and I'm so fucking angry that they did this to her that I've been systematically destroying Cali's house from the inside out.

Gaius watched me punch a hole in the kitchen wall, and he knew exactly what I needed to do. "Instead of taking out your anger on our home, little bro, you should direct it at the people who deserve it."

"How can I do that?" I growl.

Gaius had an answer for me. I shouldn't have been surprised. He always has an answer for everything.

What Gaius proposed was more devious than anything I could ever come up with, and I loved him for it. My brother always did have a creative mind and a true capacity for leadership. He told me what to say on the phone calls. He found me all the equipment I needed. He chose the perfect place – the ideal sepulcher for the rot in Gemma's life.

I'm going to cut the cancer right out of the world for her, because that's what love is. Love is burning the world to see someone smile.

I finish the second can and head back outside. Gaius' gloved hand appears amongst the purple flowers. He tosses a lighter down to me. "All you have to do is flick that lighter and Gemma is free."

Free.

It was all she's ever wanted, all she talks about in the rare moments between partying and fucking when we do talk. She doesn't think I can listen, but I do. All I want to do is listen to her, because girls like Gemma – bright and kind and quiet and so, so perfect – aren't supposed to want a brute like me. When I hold her, its like clutching a delicate flower in my hands. As hard as I try, I know that at any moment, without even meaning to, I might tear off her petals or crush her in my fist.

I know that she is not for me. I know that she will choose Vic in the end. But Vic – with his moral code and his Harvard career to think about – can't put her back together after they've torn her apart.

But I can.

I step closer to the old horticulture lab. The school used to run classes here, back before Victor August took an interest in the subject and his mother donated the money to build state-of-the-art greenhouses nearer the main buildings. It's hidden in amongst a small woods so students could study some weird fungus that grows between the roots of the acacia trees or some such shit.

All I know is that they built a concrete basement underneath for storing all the chemicals and compost. Gaius and his friends have been coming here for years to smoke weed and drink and play cards, so he knew that the thick door in the basement could be locked tight.

He knew it would be perfect.

I toss aside the second gas can. It bounces off the first and skids into a tree, shaking loose some of the bright flowers. They rain down on me, tiny purple trumpets clinging to my shirt. Gemma used to play trumpet in band, although she gave it up this year to hang out with me and Vic. She said she always hated the harshness of it, but her parents wanted her to learn an instrument, so she picked the trumpet so she could torture them with her practice. They think I'm the one who turned her against them, but she hated them well before I started fucking her.

I can hear them now – Mr. Shaw's indignant baritone, Mrs. Shaw's screeching soprano. Another voice joins them. That's Konrad's annoying broken English. All three of them scream at me from beneath the floor. They pound on the basement ceiling. I hear cracking that I think might be them breaking furniture, looking for something they can use to break down the door. Mrs. Shaw's sickening wail rises above the others. The only person she despises more than me is her own daughter.

Gemma doesn't need that kind of negative bitch in her life.

They want to change Gemma, even though she's perfect already. They want to mold her into this silent porcelain doll. A frozen plaything, pretty to look at but unable to move or think for herself.

Parents aren't supposed to do that. Parents should encourage their kids to be themselves and let their natural talents shine, the way our mother does. To Gaius, the one with the brain, the one born to lead, she's given lessons on the inner workings of the organization, how to deal with the clients and arrange every part of a job. And for me, her little monster... she lets me sit in the corner of her private lair. She lets me watch her at work. Sometimes, she even lets me lop off a toe or burn her *sacer* into a victim's skin.

As far as I know, she's never let Gaius into the lair. That's our special place – just Cali and me.

Gemma's parents never even tried to have that kind of relationship with their daughter. They were so critical of her, even though she was so smart and perfect and amazing. They made her feel stupid and ugly and disappointing, and I *hate* them for it. I've hated them so long that the hatred has wormed its way beneath my skin. It comes to life now, wriggling and writhing just below the surface, ready to burst out of my pores.

Finally, I have a way to make Gemma see that she's as wonderful as I've always told her she is, and that they were wrong, and wrong people deserve to be punished.

I flick my finger on the lighter. The tiny, perfect flame dances in the gloom.

I toss the lighter onto the wooden porch, right inside the old classroom doors.

With a *whoosh*, the flames leap to life.

When a fire takes hold, it's like watching a ballet dancer leap across the stage – a living, breathing specimen of grace and beauty, dancing to a tune only it can hear.

Smoke billows from the windows and through cracks in the crumbling facade – white at first, but darkening to sooty black as it consumes the plastics, paint, and chemicals still left inside. The building creaks and groans as the timbers contract, and the acrid smell reaches my nostrils. Up in the tree behind me, Gaius coughs.

I know I should stand back, but I want to feel it. I let a solid wall of heat roll over me, feeling my vengeance, my love for Gemma, in my *bones*. My cheeks burn and my eyeballs dry up inside my skull. Gaius jumps down from the tree. He moves quickly away from the blaze, but I can't tear my eyes from the building. I need to see. I need to *feel* them suffer.

I float above myself and watch from a spot just beyond my shoulder as the fire tears through the upper level of the classroom. Glass shatters as windows blow out. Above it all, the screams of Gemma's parents and that ungrateful little Russian shit rise like a soprano – the fire's swan song, its majestic finale.

The fire hasn't reached them yet, but they can smell the smoke. They can feel the heat pressing in on them, like an Edgar Allen Poe punishment descending on them.

Their screams fizz in my veins. I feel like someone has pumped soda into my bloodstream. I dart around the structure, watching the fire from every angle, burning the memory of it into my retinas.

"Good boy, Cassius," my brother's voice coos from behind me. I tear my eyes away to look at him. He stands further back in the trees, his arms folded, staring at me with an expression that can only be described as *triumphant*. "You're such a good boyfriend. Gemma will want you now. After this, she won't even look at that Victor again."

Victor.

For a moment, my best friend's face flickers in the flames, and I think that I wish I'd told him about tonight. All my life, we've told each other everything, me and Vic and Torsten – all our darkest secrets laid bare for each other. A friendship must be forged in blood. I don't want to leave them out of something so momentous, especially not when Victor loves Gemma as much as I do.

Gaius must sense my hesitation because he moves closer and squeezes his hand on my shoulder. "You can't share a girl with Victor August," he says, "because you'll always be second-best, brother. He's clever and attractive and confident – a leader. A winner. And you're a monster. But sometimes the world needs monsters."

And he's right. He's always right. I can't compete with Victor's perfection. If I want to keep Gemma, I have to show her that I will go to lengths that Victor August wouldn't even dream of.

The red mist fades from the corners of my eyes, and I hear the screams change. They no longer cry for fear of what's coming. Each piercing wail carries the immediacy of pain. Maybe the floor has caved in on top of them. Maybe one of them has collapsed from smoke inhalation. Maybe the flames are burning off Mrs. Shaw's skin, turning her disapproving glare and cruel tongue into ash and soot.

Beside me, Gaius shifts. He grabs my hand and presses something into it. It's his phone.

"It's Gemma." Gaius shoves my hand toward my ear. "I called her for you. She deserves to be part of this. Tell her what you've done for her."

I take his phone and raise it to my face. Gaius has put it on speaker. "Gemma, can you hear me?"

"Cas, what's going on?" Her voice trembles. I can barely hear her over the roar of the fire, the crack of the roof timbers caving in. "What's the noise in the background?"

"It's the sound of freedom."

"What do you mean, Cas? You sound strange. You're scaring me."

"I'm at the old horticulture classroom. I've got your mother and father and that Konrad fucker locked in the basement, and

I've lit the building on fire. It's so beautiful, Gemma, I wish you could see it. I'll take a video and send it to you—"

"Cas, you... what?" Gemma's voice wavers. "Please tell me that you're not serious. This is a joke, right?"

"Of course not. This is a gift – my gift to you. I want you to know what you mean to me—"

"Cas, you have to let them out!" she screams. "You can't do this. You can't kill my parents! How could you do this?"

"I've done what you wanted. I got rid of them for you. Now they won't be able to stop us from being together. They won't put you through any more hell about your grades. They won't make you cry ever again."

"No, Cas, no," she screams into the phone. "How could you think this is what I wanted? Get them out of there. You've got to save them. Cas, if you kill them, then you kill me. Do you hear me?"

She sounds so... final. So decisive. I haven't heard that kind of certainty in her voice for a long time. The section of the porch sags and collapses, spraying sparks into the purple blooms of the jacaranda trees. "Baby, I *have* to do this for you. I have to show you how much I love you."

"This isn't love, Cas. You don't know what love is. Don't make me responsible for their deaths. Please... I've already done so much to hurt them. If you take them away, I have nothing else to live for."

"What are you talking about? You have me. And Victor. We'll look after you."

"I can't love you," she sobs. "I can't love the person who killed my parents."

The roof above the door collapses, and the house yawns and groans as the fire consumes it. Inside my chest, her words eat away at my stone heart until there is nothing left.

"Gemma, don't say that. I'll—"

But the call cuts off as the phone blasts out a shrill ring. It's the tune of an annoying ringtone Gaius has for certain numbers. I've been hearing it a lot lately. The screen flashes with a name – BOB THE BUILDER.

I drop the phone. It lands in the scraps of porch wood and rings and rings, that name flashing across the screen.

Who the fuck is that? Why are they calling now? Where's Gemma? I have to talk to Gemma.

Beside me, Gaius' jaw sets. He scrambles after the phone and manages to grab it out of the burning rubble with a stick. He brings it to his ear, wincing as his gloved hand touches the hot metal. "What? I'm a little busy right now. You won't believe..."

He trails off as whoever it is on the other end says something. "That doesn't make any sense," he snaps. "Are you sure he's there?"

The screaming abruptly cuts off.

"Fuck," Gaius yells. He hurls the phone into the fire. It hits the front door and drops to the flames to be consumed by the dancer's fiery skirts.

"What's wrong?"

"Nothing," Gaius says, his jaw set as police and fire sirens careen down the road toward us. "Nothing for you to worry about, little bro. Everything is fine. But we have to get out of here."

"DIO. STEP AWAY FROM THE DOOR."

I don't move from my bunk as the door to my cell swings open. The fuck I'm going to jump to attention just because Detective Stone deigns to grace me with his presence.

Stone enters the cell with his usual swagger, followed by a

uniformed officer jangling a set of keys. "On your feet, Dio. You're free to go."

I smirk.

Detective Stone is new to Emerald Beach, and he hasn't learned the way things work around here. You can't send a Dio to prison. Not unless you want to come home from work one day to find bullet holes in your windows and a horse head in your bed.

I'd been so sure of that fact that I hadn't even kicked up a fuss when the police rolled up to the house and arrested me because they had some bullshit eyewitness account. I called Cali when they first arrested me and she blew up, said it was my fault for going stupid over a girl and killing someone without covering my tracks. She said she wouldn't lift a finger to help me, but I knew she wouldn't let me rot in here. She must've cooled down and called in a favor.

I hum a Metallica song as I follow the officer out of the cell. But the tune dies on my lips as they push another guy inside. Our eyes meet on the threshold, and my brother flashes me his signature grin.

"Gaius, what are you—"

"I'll see you on the other side, little bro," he says. "Look after Mom for me."

1

VICTOR

I walk out of practice whistling Nick Cave's 'Red Right Hand.' Torsten's dreary goth music has finally got inside my head, and I'm too damn happy to care.

My muscles burn from the punishing practice drills Coach Chaney put us through, and my balls and thighs ache from the pounding we gave Fergie last night.

Fergie. Just her name makes me smile wider. *My Duchess.*

Our Duchess.

She knows the truth about us. It's all out in the open, and she doesn't just accept us and what our families represent, she *craves* us.

Cas has worked through his shit, and he no longer feels the need to win her against me. We can share her without all the macho bullshit.

And Torsten... I've never seen my friend so happy. She just *gets* him.

She gets us.

Fergie's wormed her way under our skin, and I know that one day she won't just be my Duchess. She'll be my Queen.

Everything is perfect.

Almost perfect. There's only one small niggle in the back of my mind – a thread I can't stop tugging on, even though I don't like how it unravels me. The secret Torsten and I discovered about Fergie and her father's fake identities.

I keep telling myself that it's a coincidence. There are so many reasons why they might choose to forget their old lives that have nothing to do with the Triumvirate, but when I look at the timing of her arrival in Emerald Beach, I see only red flags flapping in the breeze.

I know what I have to do. I have to confront Fergie about it. I need answers, and I need them before Cas gets wind of what we know. Because Cas won't think. If he believes for a moment that his mother's in danger, he'll strike first, and not even Fergie Munroe can survive the rampaging bear that is Cassius Dio's hatred—

"There you are, big brother."

Juliet throws her arms around me and nearly knocks me off-balance.

"Are you okay?" she whispers, squeezing me so tight I hear things in my spine *crack*.

"I'm better than okay." I plaster a grin back on my face. "Everything is falling perfectly into place."

"Interesting take on things, but sure." Juliet pulls back and studies my face as she falls in step beside me, her aristocratic features twisting in concern. Looking at Juliet is like looking at a funhouse mirror – I see my own sharp cheekbones, dark wavy hair, and icicle eyes reflected back at me, only twisted and contorted. My face but not my face. A crease appears between her eyes. "I didn't expect you to be so chipper about this disaster, but maybe you've been listening to Gabe's positive affirmation tapes."

I stop in my tracks. My gym bag crashes against my side. I wrap my fingers around Juliet's arm, squeezing a little harder than I intended. Something about her expression sends alarm bells jangling in my brain. A squirrelly feeling wriggles in my stomach. "What disaster?"

"You know, what that bitch Fergie did."

"Excuse me?"

What the fuck did she just say?

Juliet steps back, her pink lips twisting into a frown. "You don't know?"

My stomach sinks into my knees. "Don't know what? Juliet, has something happened to Fergie?"

The fear crushes me into the ground. It's the same fear that took me the day Gemma refused to pick up her phone, or the day I waited outside school to walk Juliet home and she never came out.

I'm too late. I can't save the people I love.

Juliet huffs. "Can you *get* any more behind? Fergie and her father aren't who they say they are. They have fake names, fake identities. They're connected to all this shit that's been going down with the Triumvirate. I bet she even sent that parcel bomb—"

"Fergie wouldn't send a bomb in the mail. She..." I trail off as understanding dawns in my sister's eyes.

"You knew, didn't you?" Juliet digs her fingers into my shoulders. Her nails bite my skin, but I can barely feel it, I'm so fucking worried. "Don't lie to me, Victor August. You fucking *knew* about this. That's why you're not surprised. She's been in my house, in my *room*. How could you know and keep this from me, from Mom?"

"Torsten and I know about their fake identities, but that doesn't mean she's connected to anything," I say weakly. "We're doing some more digging to get to the truth—"

"More digging? Jesus H. Christ, if you two amateur gumshoes would stop thinking with your dicks for one second, you'd see that you're *digging* your own fucking grave. Think about it." Juliet ticks reasons off on her fingers. "One, they show up in town just as shit hits the fan with our parents. Two, Fergie has martial arts training. What use is that to a blind girl? Your answer is Three – she's an excellent actress. Pretending to be blind is the perfect cover. Think of everything she might've seen simply because we didn't think she could see it. Four—"

Rage bubbles in my veins. "None of that is evidence. And Fergie *is* blind, and don't you ever imply otherwise. As for the rest of it, Torsten and I are investigating. *We've got this.* But in the meantime, you can't tell Cassius because he'll go full Bear and do something stupid. Innocent people change their identities all the time—"

"Innocent people don't get *this* kind of fake identity – the kind you can only get from someone in our business. But you don't have to worry, big brother," she beams her sunshine smile up at me. "I'm taking care of you for a change."

"Jules, what are you talking about? How do you know about this anyway?"

"Cas found out. He found her old IDs and put it all together. He's not as dumb as you all seem to think. He couldn't find either of you this morning, so he came to me." She pats my arm. "We fixed it. Fergie won't ever betray you again."

"Fixed what—" Before I can get another word out, Xavier steps out in our path, waving his phone in his hand, a big grin on his stupid face.

"Hey Vic, looking good," Xavier yells. "Why'd you never tell me about that swing of yours? Your teammates would love to try it out if your girlfriend's up for it."

"Did you get a go in her ass, too?" Miles calls out. "Or is that Cas' territory? Because if he's suddenly open to sharing..."

A cold, dark feeling settles in my stomach. "Juliet. What did you do?"

Juliet hands me her phone. "You can thank me with an extravagant present. I prefer diamonds."

I stare down at the screen as she starts a video playing. The post already has thousands of views, hundreds of comments. A familiar moan fills my ears as I stare down at my Duchess in my arms as I stroke her hair and tell her exactly what we're going to do to her.

It's security footage from the library, zoomed right in so that Fergie's face is clearly visible as we tie her into the swing and lower her down on Torsten's waiting cock.

For a brief moment, I think about the footage that's leaked from our phones, the security breach Torsten is still trying to pinpoint, and a glimmer of hope flickers inside me. That maybe one of our enemies did this. That someone evil is responsible for the hurt this will cause Fergie, and all I have to do is punish them and everything will be okay.

That hope withers and dies.

Because Cas did this. Cas and Juliet.

My sister and my best friend might as well have taken a knife to Fergie's skin in front of me, that's how much this fucking hurts.

I squeeze my eyes shut and shove the phone back to Juliet.

"Turn it off."

"Why?" She dials up the volume. Now Fergie's moans echo, followed by my grunts and the hot *SLAP* of Cas' hand against her ass. "Everyone needs to see that she's nothing but a slutty gold-digger."

"I can't believe Cas did this."

She snorts. "Do you think that ape is clever enough to think of a way to put her in her place? No, he ranted to me, and I asked him what the worst thing he could possibly do to her would be, and he said that she'd had a sex tape released once before and it ruined her life..."

...and it ruined her life...

Oh, Cas.

In that moment, I understood everything – why Fergie had hidden her identity from us, and why she was so determined to get into an Ivy League without us digging into her past. The only thing that makes no sense is why she trusted Cas with that secret. She had to know that he'd use it to destroy her.

"Jules, I'm begging you to turn that video off."

"What's wrong, Victor? You can't handle the truth? Your pretty little plaything is a spy. She's trying to destroy everything our parents fought for, everything our mother sacrificed to build." Juliet's lip wobbles – a classic sign that she's about to blow. "I know you don't see it now, but I did this for *you*. You're supposed to rule Mom's empire one day, Vic, and you can't rule if you're weak."

Fuck.

Fuck.

Is that what she thinks? Is that truly what she fucking thinks?

When this is over, you'll be begging for my weakness, little sister.

I square my shoulders and allow every atom of my anger to appear on my face. Juliet cowers from me as I grab her wrist and snap, "Take me to Cas."

"That's not a good idea. I've got him locked away. He can't—"

"Thank you for your concern," I hiss through gritted teeth. "I know *exactly* what my friend must be like right now. Take me to him, *sister dearest*, before I do something I regret."

2

VICTOR

Juliet leads me around the back of the art building, toward the small woods that borders the far end of the athletic fields. Xavier and my other teammates try to follow me, but I must look pretty murderous because one glare from me and they scatter. She stomps down a narrow path through overgrown oleander bushes and towering jacarandas, their leaves giving way to bursts of bright purple flowers. I know exactly where we're going.

The old horticulture suite.

A cold lump forms in my stomach as I duck under the chain-link fence and stare up at the blackened shell of a building sitting atop a patch of barren earth. In my first semester at Stonehurst Prep, I had horticulture and biology classes here – it was a wonderful space, the only remaining section of a much older wing of the school that was demolished to make way for more modern facilities. My mom was so impressed with my horticulture project that she gave the school a bunch of money to build a more modern horticulture department, and this building fell out of use. But that's not why it's been seared in my memory.

"You brought him *here?*"

How could she? Doesn't she know what that must be doing to him?

"It's the only room at school that has a basement," Juliet says. "I needed to keep him secure so he didn't hurt anyone."

It's a bit fucking late for that. What about the hurt you've done to him?

We pick our way carefully over the collapsed porch and step inside. Ever since the fire gutted the place, kids have been daring themselves to come here at night. They have parties here some-times, but we never go. Cas can't even hear talk about that night without losing his shit. How my sister even got him inside...

I know how. If Cas found out about the fake identities, if he thinks Fergie is after his family, he'll descend into his rage state. He describes it as a red mist that forms on the edges of his brain and slowly closes in, squeezing and squeezing until he's shrouded with a blanket of pure hate. He can't see, can't feel, can't experience *anything* in the outside world. All he becomes is a vessel for his rage.

When Cas gets like that, he becomes the perfect weapon. You can point him at anything you want destroyed and he won't stop until he's picking bone chips from between his teeth. If Juliet told him that the answer to his rage lay in that basement, he would have walked in without even knowing where he was.

As we near the building, I can hear him – not even the thick concrete walls of the basement can muffle Cas' roar. As much as I hurt for Fergie right now, I know that she's strong enough to survive this. But Cas... he needs me...

I follow Juliet deeper into the ruin. Wood hangs from the giant charred hole in the ceiling, and bits of old furniture and posters are given back to nature. Birds nest in the rafters, their feces dribbling down the walls like some kind of disgusting Jackson Pollock painting. My throat closes. I hate being here. I hate remembering what happened that night, how it turned our lives upside down, how it shaped my closest friend into the perfect killing machine, and how once again I couldn't do anything to save—

Juliet kicks aside a piece of rotting wood and shows me the gaping hole in the floor with the steel ladder someone's left there for easy access. Cas' cries increase in volume. I follow her down the ladder onto a dirt floor. The basement is made from concrete and cinder block, which is how it survived the fire mostly intact. I notice some beanbags and a table covered with empty beer cans, and a hookah pipe stashed in the corner. Graffiti crowds every available surface – some is clever artwork, but most of it is just scrawled names and rude doodles.

Juliet hurries me past the party room to a room at the back, the door blocked by a wooden bookcase. It's obvious from the noise that Cas is on the other side.

"If you want to see him, you'll have to move that." She frowns at the bookcase. "I chipped a nail putting it in place."

I shove the bookcase out of the way, marveling at my sister's strength to move it in the first place. I feel disoriented, like I don't know my twin at all.

The door behind is held shut with several bolts.

"Jason Greer was running his drug empire out of the basement for a while," Jules says. "He locked up his lab and supplies in here. When he found out I was going to lock Cas in here, the cyclops was all-too-willing to give me the codes."

"Of course he was." I lean my ear against the door.

The animal on the other side slams into the wood, smashing the door against my head. I reel, clutching my throbbing ear.

"Cas?" I call out. "It's me. It's Victor. Can you hear me?"

The only reply is the sound of something heavy thumping the door.

Juliet wrinkles her nose. "All this over a blind girl."

"Jules, just *go*," I snarl at her. "I have to focus on Cas, and I can't even bear to look at you right now."

She puffs out her lower lip. "Aw, don't be such a sulk. You're acting like I'm the bad guy here. I'm not the one who lied to you."

"No. You're the one who broke our mother's cardinal rule and used a woman's sexuality against her. Even if we forget about Fergie – who's been nothing but nice to you – why would you do this to *me*? Harvard's going to see this video. I'm not invincible. I could get in serious trouble for this."

"Please," she rolls her eyes. "You're Victor August. If you want to go to Harvard, a little sex swing action isn't going to stop you. Those old pervs on the admissions board are probably watching it on repeat right now—"

"Get out!" I yell. In the room behind me, something smashes. It sounds like glass. Who the fuck left something glass in that room? Cas could hurt himself and not even notice. I rub my temples as a headache flares.

Juliet's lip trembles. Normally, if I saw that look, I'd immediately scoop her into my arms and tell her that everything will be okay. I'd take her pain away, because I'm Victor August and that's what I do. But how can I do that when she's the one who caused the pain?

Who will heal my scars?

"I don't know you anymore," I say, my voice cracking.

That does it. Juliet turns on her heel and storms off, leaving me alone with Cas and his rage.

Back in the party room, I locate an old janitor's closet with some old mops and rusty solvent cans. I dust the cobwebs and dead beetles out of a bucket and head over to the broken old sinks we used to use for potting. I try the taps and, surprisingly, they still work. I fill the steel bucket with ice-cold water and carry it back to the door.

"Hi, friend. I'm right outside the door. I'm not going anywhere," I lean against the door and pull out my phone. "I'm going to wait here until you're finished acting like a tool."

I tune out the sounds of growling and smashing behind me, and focus on scrolling through my social feeds, getting a sense of the damage Cas and my sister have done.

My stomach churns when I see still shots of the video being posted on every social media channel. Fergie gets the brunt of the commentary – because the world is a fucking cruel place to be when you're female and you like sex – but Torsten and Cas and I are not immune. I've never been called so many imaginative names in my life.

At least the school seems to be onto it. Every time I click on a link, it's been pulled down for content violations, but this thing will spread. And they can't get it down off the revenge porn website where Juliet originally posted it.

Dru's name pops up in my feed, and against my better judgment, I click on her profile pic. My stomach sinks into my knees as I read her status.

"I'm not going to give this thing any more life by posting the video. You all know what I'm talking about. You've all seen what the Poison Ivy Club will do to anyone who crosses them.

Victor August claims that they're changed since the days of Gaius Dio, but it's a lie. They may be better dressed, but they're still a bunch of thugs who prey on desperate people and ruin lives for fun.

Well, you know what, bitches? California has revenge porn laws, and not even Dio, August, and Lucian are immune. I for one won't stand silent while another woman has her privacy violated because of male greed. Who's with me?"

At least half the school, by the looks of her comments.

I think back to the fight at my party, when Dru looked me in the eyes and promised she'd make the Poison Ivy Club pay for every crime we've committed. Well, she's got her chance, and she doesn't even have to get her hands dirty. Cas and Juliet made sure the evidence of their crime is out there for everyone to see, and we learned from what Cas did that our families aren't always immune to the law...

I can't even blame Drusilla for wanting vengeance. What we did to her wasn't great, but if I could go back now, I'd do it again.

I have to look after my family, and Cas is my family.

But I don't know what to do when my family implodes.

I emerge from the cesspool of humanity that is the internet after a sex tape, to find the banging and screaming have subsided.

"Cas?" I call out.

No reply.

"Please, Cas. Just make a sound or something so I know you're still alive."

Nothing.

I sigh. He's probably hit his head and knocked himself out. That's often how these bouts of rage end. I don't want to go anywhere near him in case he gets a second wind, but I need to check that he's not bleeding to death.

Shoving the phone into my pocket, I crawl to my feet, pick up my bucket, unbolt the door, and fling it open.

Cassius lies in the middle of the floor, atop a pile of debris, his face and knuckles bloody. There are several holes punched in the walls, and even the concrete pillars holding the building up look a little dented.

"Victor August," he slurs. He's always like this when he comes down from one of his rages – it's like babysitting the guy at the party who knocks back ten Jäger shots in the first hour.

I tip the bucket over his head. He gets a mouthful of water, and for a blissful moment he looks too stunned to do anything. But then he jerks to his feet, shaking himself like a dog.

"What the fuck was that for?" He squeezes water out of his torn shirt. He looks around the room, his eyes glazed over.

"What the fuck was that for?" I yell. "I can't believe you did this to Fergie. *Our* Fergie."

"That bitch was never ours," he spits. "She betrayed us. I found evidence that she's been lying about who she is—"

"And so instead of, I don't know, talking to *her* about it, or hell, waiting for me to talk to you about it, you go to my sister and the two of you concoct this rotten plan? What the actual *fuck?*"

"Didn't you hear me?" he growls. "She's lying. She's not who she says she is. She has a wallet full of fake IDs, and she and that dentist have infiltrated my *house*. I bet she's not even blind—"

"I don't want to hear another word of that horseshit. You insult her, and you insult your own intelligence... what little is fucking left. We've been hanging out with Fergie for weeks. *Of course she is blind.* Did it ever occur to you that maybe Fergie's name has nothing to do with Cali or the Triumvirate? That maybe she changed her name because some bastard put revenge porn of her online and she had to burn her life down and start again? Come on, Cas, I know she told you that, so why shouldn't you put those two things together—"

He towers over me. "You knew about this?"

Fuck. I probably shouldn't have said all that.

Cas stares at me with eyes like granite. Behind them is *nothing* – no pain. No hurt. No brotherhood. It's as if I've flipped a switch in his brain, and suddenly he can't recognize me.

Which is very, very dangerous.

"Torsten and I wanted to investigate first," I say quickly. "We wanted to clear Fergie's name before we told you. We didn't want something like this to happen—"

"Because we've been friends," he hisses through gritted teeth, "I'll give you a five-second head start before I come after you and rip your head off."

"Cas—"

"Four seconds."

He cracks his knuckles.

I run.

3

FERGIE

"What are you going to do now?" Euri says, as if she's reading my thoughts.

"*We* are going to get even," I growl. "We're bringing down the Poison Ivy Club."

I close my fist around my phone as it beeps wildly, as messages from gross men flood my inbox and social feeds. Because that's the thing about revenge porn, isn't it? It's not just that images of you are *out there* for everyone to see, but they make it so that every horrible incel can seek you out to make their rape threats and send you dick pics of their tiny choads and tear your body apart to build up their fragile egos. And all the while you're drowning in their keyboard-spew and you don't have the power to go around the world to every one of their seedy little bedrooms and punch them all in the face. There's nothing you can do to make it stop, so you curl up in a corner and wish you were dead.

Sometimes you do more than wish...

I had to change my name to escape it all last time, and now, thanks to my stepbrother, it's beginning all over again. I suck in breath after breath, trying to force my lungs to work, as I grip that phone so hard that I think my knuckles might break.

If I have to go through this again, I'm going to drag all three of them into this hell with me.

"How are you going to bring them down, though?" Euri says. "They're rich, they have teachers and officials and probably the police in their pockets, and their parents... well, you know there are rumors. They're untouchable. Victor August has made sure of it."

"They're not untouchable," I say. "Trust me. When I made my deal with them, their price was that I became one of them. And that means I know their secrets. I know enough that I can make their lives a living hell. The bigger you are, the harder you fall."

Outside the office door, the bell rings. Students file past, calling out to each other as they head to homeroom. The beeping of my notifications becomes one long, shrill drone. I wait for Euri to get up, but she remains on the floor beside me.

"You're going to ruin your perfect attendance record," I say.

"Fuck attendance."

"I've made you into a bad girl, Euri Jones."

I hear her opening a drawer in her desk. A package crinkles, and something heavy rolls inside. A moment later, Euri presses a plastic cup into my hand. "Then we might as well add drinking on school property to my list of deviant behavior," she says with the hint of a grin.

I take a sip. It's a whisky, and a bad one – the kind that burns all the way down. "I have never loved a person more than I love you in this moment."

"It's nothing on the top shelf stuff you're used to drinking at Casa Dio," Euri says. "But sometimes when I'm here alone at night, I need a little something to get me through."

"Would you believe Cas has this collection of ancient

whiskies he's adorably proud of? Each bottle is worth tens of thousands of dollars," I say as I clink the plastic cup against hers. "Actually, that gives me a revenge idea..."

The alcohol burns so good. Euri opens the package, which turns out to be Tootsie Rolls. I unwrap one and we chew in silence while my phone goes wild on the floor. I turn it off and toss it against the wall, enjoying the satisfying *CLANK* as it hit and bounces to the ground.

"Wait." I turn to Euri. "It's ED Day. What about you? What schools did you get into?"

"I got into Brown," she says with a sigh. "I don't want to go to Brown. But we don't have to talk about me."

But I want to talk about Euri. I want to talk about how Brown is inferior to Harvard in all the ways (sorry Brown, but my loyalties go way back), and I want her to knit me another lopsided scarf because I need to think about something other than the video that's making its way around the entire school right now.

My whole body shudders.

Everyone is watching it. Right now, teachers are chasing their tails, frantically trying to take down the videos, but as quickly as they have them removed, more will appear. The principal will be on the phone with the police, but no one will be able to trace who put it up, and irate parents are probably already calling the school, threatening to remove kids or funding if the problem doesn't disappear.

Everyone will know who's responsible, but not one of those boys will face any consequences. But I'll be told that it's in my best interests to find a new school, to lie low, to avoid going out. For my own protection.

That word sticks in my mouth. That word that Victor is so fond of. "I'll protect you," he swore, over and over and over. And I trusted him. I trusted *all* of them, those fuckers.

"This is what we do for family," Cas said before we threw Coach Franklin into the pit. "We protect our own."

How could I be so stupid?

Before long, the media will descend like vultures to pick over the carcass of my new life, to wonder who could have driven a perfectly mediocre good girl like me to such wanton depravity. Soon, Dad will find out that I've ruined our second chance at happiness. What will he do with me?

It nearly broke him last time, but that was when I was his innocent little girl. That was when he still loved me and didn't keep secrets from me and didn't have his new crime family to take my place. Now he'll see me having perverted sex on a swing. With three guys. One of whom is my stepbrother. And he'll know that we can't ever go back. That this nightmare is our life now.

At that thought, I crumble.

The tears break free of their dam and flow down my cheeks. I let them come. I fucking *embrace* them. I melt into a puddle on the floor in front of Euri's desk.

I'm no longer aware of my personhood. I become this vessel for pain, for sorrow. I cry until crying has no meaning. I think Euri is still there. I think she's rubbing my back, saying something to me. But I can't hear or feel her. I've gone somewhere else.

Sometime later, I become aware of my body again, and I feel two tiny warm arms around me, and a soft hand stroking my hair. Euri whispers that everything is going to be okay. They're empty useless words, but hearing them makes my tears flow anew.

"You know, usually I don't let people who've screwed me out of my dream college snot all over my shoulder," Euri says. "But I'm making an exception for you."

I laugh, and the laughing makes me cry harder.

"I'm so, so sorry," I sob into her shoulder. "I don't deserve you. I'm a terrible friend. I knew what it would do to you, and I didn't care."

"I get it, Fergie. Believe me, I understand the hunger for an elite school."

"But that's just it – you *don't* get it. How could you? Even in my position, even if you were faced with the same choice, you wouldn't make the decision I made. Because you're a good person." I sniff. "I think something's seriously wrong with me. I'm addicted to them, even after everything they did to me. They filled a place inside me that I never even realized was empty. And they had me convinced that they felt the same. When he first met me, Cas said that he didn't want me in his house, that he'd find a way to get rid of me. This was his plan all along and I can't—I can't—"

"Victor August has his rules," Euri says. "I don't know why they broke them for you."

"Because Cassius knew," I say. "He knew that this happened to me before. He knew that this is what it would take to break me."

"What do you mean?"

In between breathless sobs, I tell Euri everything. I tell her what Dawson did to me, how we tried to fight it in court but we couldn't, how I found myself standing on the edge of a bridge one night, willing myself to jump, how I couldn't do it because I didn't want to hurt Dad any more than I already had, but I thought about it all the time until Dad moved us here and got Cali to change our identities. And how I'd been struggling with school ever since I got here, knowing that it's all pointless, that I'll never get to have the life I worked for.

"I guess I felt like... after everything I'd been through, why shouldn't I get to go to Harvard? Why should I play by the rules when no one else does? But I wasn't thinking that you're the me at this school, and when I hired the Poison Ivy Club, I'd be screwing over another version of myself."

"It's okay," Euri breathes. "It's really okay. I understand, Fergie. I'll help you. We'll contact Harvard immediately, take control of the narrative—"

"No, Euri, there's more. There's so much more."

She refills our cups. I tell her about the Triumvirate, about what we did to Coach Franklin, and about attending Saturnalia at the Colosseum and finding out that my dad's been aware of it all this time. By the time I'm done, she's downed two more cups of whisky. This is good, because I did just tell her I murdered a guy, and if she gets drunk enough, she might convince herself that I made it up.

"You... fed him to a lion?" she slurs. "For serious, you killed him?"

Or maybe not.

"Yeah. He made me..." I can't say the words again. Not today. Not after the video.

Euri downs another cup of whisky in one gulp.

"Fergie, this is... a lot," she says. "I should turn you into the police."

"You should. I helped kill a guy, Euri. I don't even feel guilty about it. I'm as fucked-up as the Poison Ivy Club. If you want to turn us in, I won't fight it. Maybe the world is safer if I'm behind bars."

"Or maybe to stand up to something like the Poison Ivy Club and the Triumvirate, you need to become like them." She squeezes my hand. "I'm not going to narc on you. This is girl-code shit right here. Coach Franklin was scum. I don't think you're the first girl at this school he's done something like that to. The world is better off without him. And as for the guys, I'm not exactly surprised. I've heard rumors. Everyone has. But I didn't realize quite how high up in that world they are."

"I'm sorry to load all this on you, after everything I've already taken from you—"

Euri sighs. "I'm just a girl who likes to knit scarves and search for the truth. But you, Fergie, you're a force of nature. You remind me of all of them in different ways. I think you can be their mirror. We hold you up to them, and we force them to see the truth about themselves."

A slow grin spreads over my face. "I like it."

"And then, maybe we feed them to this lion."

I clink my plastic cup against hers. "Even better."

4

TORSTEN

I'm in the shower when my phone rings. I know it's Victor because I assigned him the song, "God is in the House."

I step out of the shower and dry my hands so I can pick up the phone. I think that maybe he's calling about last night.

Last night...

I never thought I'd be part of something so... beautiful. Being with Fergie is like living inside a painting. It's like seeing the colors of Monet for the first time every single day. But it's even better because I understand. And I *am* understood.

Every time I step outside, I feel as though I'm stepping into an elaborate game that everyone else understands, but I'm just learning for the first time. Livvie always expected me to know the rules, and she'd get so angry when I messed them up. I hated that I made her angry. I just wanted to understand. I just wanted her to love me the way she loved all her other children.

Vic and Torsten have been my friends for long enough that they can see when I'm confused. They try to help me with the rules. "They're not smiling because they're happy, Torsten. They're laughing at you," and "you can't ask that question,

Torsten." But there are so many rules, and they seem to change all the time, and I find it so much easier if I hide in my sketchbook, or if I just don't go outside at all.

I like to help. I like to do things on the computer that Victor needs. I like the Poison Ivy Club because we help people get into the right college, and that makes them happy. I used to like to paint for Livvie, because she'd smile at me. Her smile is so pretty. She wants me to call her Mother, but she's not my mother. She's not like mothers in books or on TV. Maybe I had one of those mothers, once, back in Norway. A mother with an apron, offering me a spoon of cake batter to lick.

I just want to *understand*.

But Fergie... Fergie is like no one I've ever met before. She doesn't stare at me in that way people do, the way I don't understand but Victor says is them trying to figure out what's wrong with me. She doesn't seem to care if I don't follow the rules. Half the time she doesn't seem to be following the rules herself.

When I'm with her, I don't feel like there's anything wrong with me at all.

And I thought that if she could have Victor or Cas, she would never, ever choose me. Because who would? But she did. She chose all of us. And I get to keep Fergie Munroe and my two friends.

I can't stop smiling. I'm smiling because I've never been so happy.

I'm smiling as I pick up the phone.

"I'm in the parking lot," Victor barks the moment I answer. This is unusual behavior. Normally, Victor begins a phone call by lecturing me about the social niceties of answering with some kind of greeting. I don't know if I should be smiling anymore. "Get down here, now."

I hang up, grab my keys and sketchbook off the bathroom counter, and run out of the room.

There's a woman in the elevator when I get in. She presses herself into the corner, as far away from me as it's possible to get inside a four-foot cube. I know I should smile and say, "hello." That's what Victor says I should try doing to strangers. But I'm too worried about his phone call. He isn't acting like Victor.

The elevator doors open onto the lobby. The woman lurches out and sprints into the crowded restaurant. I head in the opposite direction, across the marble lobby toward the enormous glass front doors.

"Mr. Lucien, *sir*." One of the concierges runs after me. "Wait, please, let me get you a robe—"

It's not Robert, who always appears at my door whenever I call and makes sure I get the dinner I like, but Tony, the snooty one who smiles at me because he's laughing at me. So even though I know that Victor wouldn't like it, I shove past him and walk straight out into the parking lot.

Victor's in the turning circle. He leans across and shoves open the door for me. I'm not even fully in my seat before he pulls away. Another very non-Victor thing to do. I slam the door shut as he careens into the street.

"You were allowed to put some clothes on," he says.

"I didn't know that." I slick my wet, matted hair out of my eyes.

"Of course you didn't."

I watch Victor as he drives. He's definitely not his usual self. He's still wearing his basketball uniform, and there are sweat patches under his arms. Victor always changes back into his designer clothes after practice. And his driving is wild, erratic, more like the way Cas drives. I'm about to ask him why he's different, but he gets there first.

"Cas found out that Fergie and her dad have fake identities."

I know this is bad. I cannot guess how bad, but I don't have to guess, because Victor reveals the whole story while he dips and swerves between lanes, breaking all kinds of traffic laws. I can't bear to look at him when he's like this. It makes me feel like the ground has come out from underneath me. So I flip open my sketchbook and work on the shading on Fergie's cheek.

"Torsten, did you hear me? Do you understand? There's a video of Fergie and the three of us on the internet *right now*. And the school is blowing up – not literally, I mean, everyone is going crazy over it – and Cas hates us because we knew and didn't tell him, and I need to find my mother so I can find out once and for all if their fake identities are a threat."

My body jolts as I'm struck by the force of the *wrongness*. An awful sick feeling swirls in my stomach. Last night was just for us. It was beautiful and special. They wouldn't understand. They would look at Fergie the way they look at me, like she's wrong. And Fergie is not wrong. She is the most right thing in the universe.

I glance over at Victor, and that squirmy wrong feeling inside me grows stronger. This is about Fergie, and she's not here. She should be in the car with us. Why isn't she here?

Where is she? Is she okay?

We pull into the parking lot of the Emerald Beach Museum of Art and Antiquities. The museum is closed to the public today, and the parking lot is empty save for our mothers' cars and drivers, and a row of armed men guarding the entrances. Livvie, Claudia, and Cali are inside at their annual Saturnalia Council meeting, where they share information and plan the Triumvirate's activities for the next year.

Fergie isn't here.

Why are we here?

Victor pulls in beside his mother's Porsche. I fling open my door and jump out. It's bitterly cold, and I shiver. I take off in a run, heading in the direction of Stonehurst Prep.

"Torsten, where are you going?" Victor yells after me.

"To find Fergie."

Isn't it obvious?

Why hasn't he found her? Why isn't she here with us?

"She's not going to want to see us after what Cas did," Vic cries as he jogs after me. "She has no idea why he did it. I promise we'll find her as soon as I talk to Mom and Cali. But we need to know what's going on so we—"

He grabs my arm, but I shove him off and pour on speed. "You do what you think is right, Victor. And so will I. I'm going to find her."

5

VICTOR

Torsten's ass wiggles as he stomps off, his naked skin glistening in the sun. I stare after him, the swirling feeling in my gut confirming that I should go after him. I should find Fergie. My heart is fucking breaking for her.

But I can't afford to think with my heart right now. I have to be the leader, and right now we need information. We need answers. And *then* we can figure out what to do.

I pull out my phone and dial my mother's number, but it goes straight to voicemail again. I know she won't have her phone on during a Council meeting, but I was hoping she might've turned it on during a bathroom break or something and seen my dozens of messages.

Back when the Triumvirate consisted of three warring families vying for control of the city, they held a Council every year during Saturnalia to divide territories, hash out contracts, settle disputes, and arrange the marriages of their offspring and loyal soldiers. The meeting would change location every year to prevent the Feds or one of their enemies from finding them.

Outside of these Council meetings, the three families ran their empires separately with their own distinct flair. Their relationships were usually antagonistic, built on flimsy alliances that could be severed in a moment. They thought nothing of lopping each other's heads off if it meant furthering their aims.

Our mothers changed all that. They work together and share resources for the good of all our families. They meet most weeks for cocktails and scheming, but they still keep the annual Council meetings for the sake of tradition, although they always hold them in the Emerald Beach Museum of Art and Antiquities – Mom's greatest achievement.

I know this year the topic on all of their minds is the parcel bomb and the escalating attempts by City Hall and the mysterious Zack Lionel Sommesnay to squeeze them out of the city.

Normally I'd never consider barging into their sacred space, especially during a war council, but I need to get Fergie's situation straight in my head, and that means going to the person who knows.

Sighing, I lock the car and head for the entrance of the building. One of my mother's security guards steps forward. "You can't go in there, Mr. August. They don't want to be disturbed."

"It's an emergency." I elbow him in the gut as I shove past him. He makes an angry sound but doesn't come after me. I'm Victor August. I'm fucking untouchable.

I stalk through the empty lobby, my basketball trainers squeaking on the marble tiles. My gaze sweeps upward, as it always does when I'm confronted with this place. The towering Doric columns lead up to the carved pediment displaying replica Roman sculptures and a Latin inscription.

Alea eacta est.

Let the die be cast.

My family motto. Our legacy to this city.

"Mom?" I yell. My voice echoes in the cavernous space,

bouncing back on me, sounding impossibly hollow and small. "Where are you? I need to talk to Cali."

Their voices carry from the August Gallery – the largest of the three vast galleries in the museum. My mom started the museum's collection with a cache of priceless scrolls she found stashed in her home by the previous owner, Howard Malloy. The cache once belonged to her father, Julian August, but he traded it for one of Howard's twin daughters, who he raised as his own. It's not a known secret that Claudia August isn't born of August blood, but since my mothers changed the rules about who can become an Imperator, it doesn't matter so much anymore.

The scrolls are displayed in the long, ornate August Gallery along with more statues and artifacts recovered from the ruined estate of Livvie's father, Nero Lucian. Opposite this gallery is the Lucian wing, where a changing array of art exhibits are displayed. At the rear is the Dio gallery – that displays weaponry and armor from across the world, because of course it does.

To Cali and Livvie, the museum serves a practical purpose – it's an institution that allows them to funnel insane amounts of wealth overseas through the acquisition and sale of artworks and artifacts. But for my mother, this place is so much more.

I hover in the entrance of the gallery, listening to my mother and her two friends laughing and chatting. You'd think they were enjoying a tea party and not discussing the management of one of the largest criminal empires in the world. But that's why they're so good at what they do. They show that with trust and friendship, you truly can rule the world.

They're old friends, but they're also badass bitches. Just seeing them sitting around a table in the center of the gallery, cocktail glasses filled, laptops and ledgers spread out between them, I'm filled with a sense that everything is going to be okay. We are still untouchable.

I take another step into the room. "Mom? I have to—"

Only, my foot doesn't hit the floor. The marble tile kind of... wobbles out from beneath me. A deep rumble tears through the building, and I'm aware, dimly, of a trembling scream rising from deep within me. I trip and fall into a statue of Caesar. I throw my arms around the dictator to stop myself from falling over.

"What's—"

Then everything goes black.

6

FERGIE

E uri flops down on my bed. I pace across the fluffy rug, too agitated to sit. Spartacus thinks we're playing some kind of game, and winds himself around my feet, trying to catch my toes.

We snuck out of school between third and fourth periods and came back to Cali's house. I needed to check that Cassius hadn't hurt Spartacus to further destroy me. Luckily, the only people who were home were Seymour and Milo, and I was able to get Euri upstairs and into my room without incident.

The minute I held my kitty in my arms, I felt a little better. But now that I'm back in this horrid house where my father betrayed me and Cassius broke me, I realize that I cannot stay here. I need to find a hotel or something. I open my drawer to find the cash I keep there for emergencies, and as I turn around I kick something on the floor – it's my old purse, the one that contains all the evidence of my old life.

I hurriedly shove it under the bed before Euri sees. But what's it doing there? Spartacus must've dragged it out from the hiding place. The straps definitely feel a little chewed.

"What happened to these locks?" Euri asks. I hear a clink as she raises a broken end of one of the bathroom locks and lets it fall back against the door.

"Cassius doesn't like to be locked out."

"He's insane," she breathes. "Maybe you should move in with me for a bit."

"That's not a bad idea. I don't think I'll ever be able to close my eyes in this room again. But will your parents be okay with the girl who screwed you out of Princeton and Harvard crashing on your sofa?"

"Are you kidding? They'll be thrilled that I have a real friend to invite over." Euri's voice cracks a little. "I haven't told them my ED results yet. Having you around might make it easier when I break the news about Brown."

"It's not over yet. You've still got regular decision schools." If you don't get accepted into your first choice school Early Decision, you can apply Regular Decision. Those applications were usually due between January and March, and you would hear by April 1st if you had a place. I was confident that Euri would have her pick of great schools in April.

"Come on, Fergie. I have to face facts. Brown is the best school I can hope to get into. It's a good school. I should be grateful."

"I have ideas. I think we can—"

I'm interrupted by a crash downstairs.

"Fergie, are you home?" Dad yells.

No.

My whole body freezes. I'm not ready for this. I'm not ready to break my father's heart all over again. I'm not ready to hear the horror in his voice when he finds out that I've been fucking my stepbrother and his two friends.

I swallow. "Wait here," I whisper to Euri. "I might need you."

"Fergie, please answer me!"

I grab my cane and walk out into the cavernous stairwell. My feet don't want to move. I feel like I'm walking to the gallows. I lean over the side of the balustrade and call down to him. "Dad, I'm here."

"Oh, thank god." His voice cracks, and I hear his footsteps taking the stairs two or three at a time. *Don't cry don't cry don't cry.* "I called the school and they said you'd left, and I swear my heart broke into a million pieces. Fergie..."

Dad appears beside me, puffing his lungs out. I cry out in surprise as he throws his arms around me, crushing me against himself.

He's holding me like he's afraid of losing me.

It's the hug I didn't realize I've been longing for ever since the day I stood on a bridge and decided that the world would be better off if I were dead. I bury my face in his shoulder. I thought I'd cried myself dry in the Sentinel offices, but fresh tears spring from my eyes.

"Dad, I'm so sorry you had to see that video," I sob. "I know it must've hurt you, especially after everything—"

He squeezes me so tight that he chokes the words from my lips.

"Oh, honey. We've put Dawson's evil video behind us. *I'm* the one who's sorry. This is supposed to be our new start, and I've gone about it all wrong and now..." he pulls back a little and wipes my hair out of my eyes. He kisses the tip of my nose, the way he used to do when I was a little girl. "I just needed to know that you were okay."

"Dad, what—"

"Cali had an important meeting today with the other women in the Triumvirate. It was at the Emerald Beach Museum downtown and someone..." he swallows. His whole body shudders. "Someone set off a bomb."

"A bomb?"

My whole body goes cold.

"Your stepmother is okay – a bit beaten up, but nothing she can't handle. The other two ladies also survived. But Claudia's son, your friend Victor... he was in the building at the time, and he's been badly hurt. They're not sure he'll make it."

7

FERGIE

Seymour drives all of us to the hospital. Dad sits in the front, and Euri and I hold hands in the back. The whole of the trip, I think about the party at Vic's place, when he took me to his mother's rage room and let me smash my way through a pile of antiques and then shoved me against the wall and told me he would own all of me.

I remember how his touch lit me up and made me *feel* again, in a completely different way to how Cas made me feel. I wish with my whole coal-black heart that I had the chance to truly give him everything – to have that kind of relationship with a person where they held your secrets close and guarded them with their life.

I didn't realize how much I wanted that until they ripped it away from me.

I wish that I could cry because Vic is hurt, and it feels as if a bomb has torn through my chest and left a gaping hole inside me.

But I won't cry for that bastard. I cried all my tears on Euri's shoulder, because of what he did.

I hate Victor because he's alive. I hate him because I'm terrified he might die. I'm a fucking mess.

As we roll over the bridge into Tartarus Oaks, I realize that I know where we're going. "Vic is with Galen?"

"Ah, so you've met Galen, then," Dad's voice cracks.

"Dad—"

"It's okay, Fergalish. I'm not angry. I'm just sad that you had to find out about these things from your brother and his friends. I know we need to have a talk about all the secrets I've kept from you. But not today, okay? Not while my wife is lying in a hospital bed."

The pain in his voice would break my heart if I had a heart left to break. "Okay, Dad."

He still hasn't mentioned the sex tape. But the knowledge of it is there inside my empty chest, and it burns and burns every time I think about Victor dying.

We travel the rest of the way in silence. Dad's silence is small, huddled, his mind with his new wife. My silence is a nuclear explosion burning the world – a thousand emotions pulsing through my body before I have a chance to process them.

Victor's hurt.

Victor might not survive.

Dad hasn't seen the video. He thought I was talking about Dawson's video.

Someone tried to blow up the Triumvirate.

Victor might not survive.

You'd better fucking survive, Victor August. I want to kill you myself.

We pull into the parking lot. Unlike the night that I came here with Cassius to help Spartacus, it's the middle of the day and the place is packed. Cars circle the parking lot, and the shops and businesses that occupy the old hospital building bustle with people. I don't know how we're going to get into the maintenance shed and the secret tunnel without anyone seeing us, but as I unfold my cane, Dad leads me right through the front doors of the old hospital building and into a shop. It reeks of mint and disinfectant. I can even smell the jar of lollipops on the counter for the kids who've been brave.

Dad tugs me past a boxy piece of furniture I assume is a receptionist's desk, but I stop in my tracks. "Hang on," I say. "This is your dental clinic, isn't it?"

"Yes."

Through the haze of pain and confusion, I remember Livvie Lucian talking about Dad over dinner, saying that she was taking Isabella to get a filling done. I read between the lines. "You...you *work* for the Triumvirate?"

This is next level. I thought he just knew about Cali's business, but he works for her? Is my mild-mannered father an *assassin*? What the fuck is my life?

Dad makes a squeaking sound. "It's not like that, Fergalish."

I know he wants to get to Cali, but I need some answers. I grip his arm. I don't let go. "It's not like what?"

"It's not how you're thinking. This *is* a dental clinic – it's not a front for drug smuggling or anything like that." Dad pulls me into a larger room – his examination room, I guess by the lighting and the heavy scent of disinfectant. Euri hangs back, letting us have this delightful family moment to ourselves. "Most of my clients are still ordinary people. I used to come to Emerald Beach all the time to do emergency surgery for Cali's soldiers, and sometimes for the fighters at Colosseum. That's what I do here when she needs me. I also make appointments for people who need to see Galen. Down here."

Dad grunts as he lifts a panel off the wall. He takes my hand and leads me inside. I find myself in another tunnel that extends between the walls. Dad helps me down a narrow set of stairs. Euri walks behind us, and she doesn't say a word about being led into the basement of the old hospital through a secret passage by my father the crime-syndicate dentist, because that's the kind of friend she is.

We enter the basement to find it bustling with activity. Galen runs past us, barking orders at his nurse. All around me, people yell over each other, and machines beep and hiss. Dad tucks my hand firmly into the crook of his elbow and leads me across the room and behind a curtain to a bed.

"Cali, sweetie, are you okay?" Dad settles into a seat, dropping my hand. I guess he's holding hers now. "I came as soon as I could, and I brought Fergie with me."

"I'm *fine*, John," my stepmother's voice croaks. She sounds... much the same as ever. A little raspy, chillingly cold, and annoyed with the world. But not like she's just been involved in a bomb attack. "Galen's not going to let me die, more's the pity. But I need you to get me out of these restraints. I can walk fine. I don't need to be here, but we have to get to the museum before the police swarm the place. I need to see my soldiers. Are they okay? Is anyone else hurt?"

Cali's restrained?

As casually as I can, I slide around the edge of the bed, feeling with my fingers for the straps that tie down her ankles and wrists. It's true, Galen has my stepmother literally strapped into her bed. But why?

"I'm not going to do that," Dad says. "And these restraints are here for your own good, since you keep trying to leave when you need to be here. Galen's trying to save your life, you know."

"I'm still alive, so his job is done," she snaps. "Get me out of this bed!"

The bed wobbles as she fights against the restraints. She's *terrifying*.

"Don't do that," Dad pleads.

"It's too late, anyway," Euri says. "We passed the museum on the way here. The building is swarming with cops."

"Who the fuck is this?" Cali screams. "Damnit. I need to—" Cali breaks off into a coughing fit.

"Darling, you have soldiers to handle all this. If you need me to relay orders, I'll make sure they get to the right people. But for now, you have to rest. You're no good to anyone if you bust your stitches."

Dad talks to her exactly the way he used to talk to me when I'd be laid up from a jiujitsu injury. I always hated lying around in bed. I want to do things. For the first time, I find myself feeling a little shred of empathy for Cali. It must be killing her to be cooped up in here when she knows someone's after her.

"Don't you dare let her move, John. She's just the sort of person who'll get up too soon and push a broken rib through her lung," Galen barks as he rushes past. "Hi, Fergie. How's that cat of yours?"

"He's a little terror. Thanks for all your help, Galen." At the thought of Spartacus and that night when Cas and I sat in this same clinic and waited to hear if he'd survive, a knife twists inside my empty chest.

"Cali, you have a broken rib?" Dad's voice trembles, drawing me back to the present. "You never told me that."

"It's nothing," Cali grunts. "It barely even hurts. There are other people here who need that bastard's mollycoddling more than me. Did you find out about Claudia and Livvie? And *what's this about a cat?*"

"I didn't hear anything about a cat," I say quickly. I'm still hiding Spartacus in my room back at Cali's house, and I don't want Cali to find him since she was the one who wanted Cas to get rid of him in the first place. "Dad, I think Cali might be hallucinating. It's probably the painkillers Galen has her on for her broken rib."

"I'm *not* hallucinating—"

"Darling, please don't get worked up. There are no cats. Claudia's fine. Noah shielded her from the brunt of the debris, but both of them have some cuts and abrasions. Livvie was closer to the blast. She's unconscious right now, but Galen says she'll be fine. It's Victor they're worried about."

My heart squeezes tight. I purse my lips shut. I can't bring myself to ask about him, even as I move my head, trying to listen for the sound of him in another bed in the clinic. I don't hear Vic's smooth voice demanding Galen try some specific treatment. If Victor August were conscious, you'd better believe he'd be trying to tell the doctors what to do. Which means...

"What happened to Victor?" Euri asks. She reaches over and squeezes my hand. "Why was he even there at all?"

Good old Euri.

"We don't know," Dad says. "I just heard that he's in a coma."

A coma.

I squeeze Euri's hand so hard that she yelps. I can't deal with just *sitting* here, twiddling my thumbs as if my life hasn't exploded and Victor isn't in a coma. I need to find him. I need to... I don't know what I need to do, but all I know is that if I have to sit here a moment longer, I'll start punching things.

Dad and Cali talk in low voices, forgetting I'm there. Euri manages to extract her fingers from mine. She disappears for a bit. When she returns, she tugs my sleeve and leans in close to whisper, "I've found Victor if you want to see him."

I nod and stand, and Euri leads me through the maze of people and machines and beds to another corner of the clinic. She pulls back a curtain. "There's no one else here. I asked them to step out for a minute so you two could be alone. He's lying in the bed." She leads me forward and shows me where the edge of the bed is. "There are a lot of machines attached to him. He looks peaceful – like he's sleeping."

The urge to fling myself at him courses through my body, but I manage to hold myself back. Tiny invisible insect legs crawl over my skin as I think that right now, that sex tape is doing the rounds at school. How long until some internet troll sends it to the Harvard admissions office? And Victor gets to check out of all of it because he's in a fucking coma?

The humiliation of it wraps around me like a fog obscuring everything it touches. My legs wobble. Euri pulls up a plastic chair for me, and I collapse into it. I reach out a trembling hand and graze his wrist – he feels warmer than I expect.

But he doesn't feel like the Victor I remember. He doesn't feel alive. He doesn't have that spark of vivacity crackling beneath his skin. The Victor I know would never do this to the people he cares about. He'd never lie here like a stone when I need him to hold me through this.

But the Victor I thought I knew is a lie.

"How dare you go and get yourself blown up, Victor August," I growl. "I need to hate you today."

I yank my hand back.

"I hope the bomb blew your dick off," I mutter.

Nothing. Nothing but the steady beep of the machines keeping him alive.

"Why did you do it?" I want to shake him. I want to hurl things at him, to poke my fingers into his eyes, to do something, anything to get him to wake up and speak to me. I want him to take it all back, to make it go away. I want him to save me from the pain of all of it because I'm so goddamned tired of having to save myself. "Why did you have to be just like everyone else? I hope you can hear me in there, Victor August. For once I get to talk and you have to listen. You made me feel so safe. You made me believe in my bones that anything in the world was possible for me, and I haven't felt that way for a long time. I've been working up the courage to tell you about what happened in

Massachusetts, but I'm guessing that Cas told you all anyway because this reeks of his cruelty. I think that... maybe... I was in love with you. With all three of you. And it's so hard for me to say those words, because I said them once to someone else and they betrayed me. Why did you have to betray me, too? Why did it have to be a fucking lie—"

"What the fuck is she doing here?"

A rough hand grabs me. I'm torn from the chair and slammed against the wall. My teeth clatter together.

Somewhere behind me, Euri screams.

"*You*," Cassius snarls, his lips right up close to my face. "How dare you show your face here?"

He shakes me so hard that something pops in my neck. He lifts me off the ground, shoving me into the wall and trapping me with his bulk so I can't maneuver my legs around him or get a good hold.

"What the fuck are you doing?" Galen yells as he rushes into the room. I can feel someone pulling at Cassius, trying to get him off me. But they might as well be playing tug of war on a freight train for all the effect it has on my stepbrother. "Put her down. I don't have time to deal with more broken bones today."

"Vic's here because of *her*." Cas' lips graze my cheek as he growls in a voice so dark and dangerous, I know the sex tape was just the beginning of the hell he plans to put me through. "I'm going to *kill* her."

He means it. His hand closes around my neck, his fingers digging into my skin. I gasp as he starts to squeeze. He's so strong he could crush my windpipe in a moment, but he's doing this slow. He wants me to feel it, wants me to know exactly what's coming. He licks my cheek. "I'm going to enjoy watching you wilt, little Sunflower."

"Do it," I choke out. I raise my chin so he's forced to look into my sightless eyes. As much as my body wants to fight him, I force myself to relax. "Kill me."

Maybe it's time.

Maybe it was always meant to end like this. Maybe Cas is supposed to finish what I started that day on the bridge.

What's the point? The world isn't made for people like me.

I don't think I'm strong enough to live with that video out there.

It's time to stop fighting. Let death come for me in the form of my monstrous stepbrother. Because right now, as his fingers press into me, I can't bear the thought of facing the world after what he did.

"You don't mean that," he growls, and his grip loosens a little, giving me just enough room that if I wanted to, I could twist my body and attempt to escape him. "You're not going to hang here like a sack of potatoes while I choke the life out of you. Go on, Fergie. Fight me. Kick me. Bite me. Use your martial arts training to break my arm. You know you want to, and it will make your death so much more fun to me."

I let my hands drop to my sides. "Kill me, Cassius. I'm done. I had to leave behind everything I was to come here, and I've got nothing left. I don't want to love someone who hates me. I give up. You won. Kill me."

A sound tears from Cas' mouth. It's so full of anguish that it doesn't even sound human. He tears his hands from around my throat and staggers back. I drop to the floor like... well, like a sack of potatoes.

I gasp for air while Cas lets out a guttural cry that threatens to tear a fresh wound through my empty chest.

The room erupts into chaos. I have no idea what's going on except that everyone is shouting and Euri screams and something smashes on the floor beside me and Cas' wail cuts off with a hateful curse.

Tiny hands pick me up. "Fergie, are you okay?" It's Euri, and she's shaking. She sounds terrified. But I'm not. I just asked my stepbrother to kill me, and I don't feel a thing. I'm *numb*.

Again.

The more things change, the more I stay the same.

"Perhaps it's best if you leave." Galen drags me and Euri away.

Euri tries to stop him as he marches us through the clinic. "But Victor—"

"Victor stands a much better chance of surviving if Cas doesn't destroy my clinic. And he seems to want to do that because you're here. I'm sorry, but you need to go." Galen shoves me and Euri into the tunnel and slams the panel behind us.

8

FERGIE

I still haven't registered the impact of Cas' wrath when I slide into the car. But Euri's a mess. As soon as Galen shut us in the tunnel and we couldn't see the others, she burst into tears. She's crying now as she does up her seat belt – fat silent tears that I can smell in the air.

Euri is a good person, the best person, and I've got her involved in this mess. I wish she didn't have to see that. I wish she didn't have to hear me tell Cas that I've given up. But I'm too numb to care.

The leather seats crunch as Seymour turns to us. "What's happening? Is She all right?"

Has Seymour seen the video?

"Fergie?" Euri asks. But I shake my head. Seymour isn't talking about me, and I can't speak. If I have to open my mouth, I'm going to scream.

"Fergie wasn't the one who had a building fall on top of her," Seymour says. "I want to know about Cali. Is she okay?"

"She has a broken rib and some cuts and bruises, but yeah, she's okay," Euri says with a sniffle. "Galen wants to keep her overnight for observation, in case she has internal injuries he can't see. Don't take Fergie back to the house. She's going to stay with me for a while."

I turn to Euri. "I don't think—"

"You can't live under the same roof as that monster, Fergie. You're staying with me." Euri's voice is surprisingly firm.

"I think that's wise," Seymour says as he pulls out onto the road.

Great. So Seymour knows. I try not to think about the kindly driver watching Cassius plow into my ass while I hang from a sex swing. I fail. Bile rises in my throat.

We drive in silence for a bit. I grip Euri's hand, crushing her fingers as I fight to gain control over my body. I need to fight against the numbness and find the anger that seized me at school. Because I'm not letting Cassius Dio rub me off the face of the earth. He wants a fight. I'll give him a fight.

Finally, I wrestle back some semblance of control. My fingers brush the spot on my neck where Cas grabbed me. I'm going to have mighty bruising there to match the welts on my ass from where he spanked me. Was that really only last night?

"Seymour, do you know who you work for?" I ask.

"If you mean, do I work for one of the finest assassins in the world and the leader of the Dio crime family, then yes, I do."

A gasp escapes Euri's throat. "Do you have to kill us now?"

He laughs harder. "No, no, Miss Jones. John and Cali informed me when they returned from Saturnalia that Fergie is now privy to our little secret, and I would presume she'd go straight to her best friend with the news. For what it's worth, Miss Fergie, I never liked that they were keeping it from you. I told Her that you were too clever – you would figure out the truth, but I must obey Her wishes, and She wanted you to be kept in the dark."

I have so many questions about all of it, but only one that

burns in my veins right now. "Do you know what Cassius did to me today?" I ask.

Please, please don't let Seymour have seen the tape. I don't think I can bear it for the kindly groundskeeper to see what went on in that library last night.

"Milo and I know more than anyone gives us credit for," Seymour says, and his voice is sad. "Cassius came downstairs in the morning, in the foulest mood I've seen him in since... well, since his brother went away. If he's hurt you, Miss Fergie, then Cali will see to him."

"I don't think I can wait for Cali for this one." I curl my hands into fists. "I need to have my own justice."

9

CASSIUS

After Galen kicks Fergie's pathetic ass out of the clinic, I try to get back to Victor, but an ice-eyed blonde bitch blocks my way.

"Get the fuck out." Claudia shoves me back through the curtain separating Victor's bed from the others. "You're not bringing your bullshit in here. Can't you see that Victor's in serious condition? If you start a fight and break one of those machines..."

Her voice trails off, and her whole body shudders. I want to laugh at the idea of seeing the Great Claudia August in a state of panic, but I can't. It shakes me a little. The world wobbles.

Nothing is as it should be.

"He's *my* friend," I say. "He needs me."

"He doesn't fucking need you!" she screeches, shoving me again. "You're the reason he's in this bed. Your stupid fucking club has made us all targets."

I laugh, because the idea is so fucking ludicrous. No one we've dealt with is blowing up museums because we didn't get them into the right college. But then Noah steps in front of Claudia, and that's no laughing matter. This close, he's almost the same size as me, and almost as dangerous. I know with between the anger blazing in his dark eyes and the weariness in my body from destroying the basement and seeing Fergie again, he'd probably break a few bones. "Get out, Cassius."

"I know who did this to him," I say, because I know that'll stop him in his tracks. "My stepsister and her father. They're fakes. She's not even really blind. She—"

I don't like the way he looks at me, like I'm a stupid little kid he wants to put over his knee. Beside him, Claudia closes her eyes, her shoulders shuddering.

"Cassius Dio, what the fuck have you done?"

At the sound of that sharp voice, every person in Galen's infirmary goes silent. I turn to see my mother swing herself out of her hospital bed in the bay opposite and stalk toward me, dragging an IV drip and a bunch of random medical devices behind her.

My lip curls back into a sneer. For the first time, Cali looks... vulnerable. It's a good thing I'm here, protecting this family just the way Gaius wanted me to, doing what has to be done when no one else can.

"Mother."

The word passes through her with a visible shudder. She hates being called Mother. She jabs a trembling finger at a hard plastic chair. "Sit down."

"I think I'll stand—"

SMACK.

A hand whips across my cheek. I hear the slap before I feel it – a biting sting that's more shock than pain. I stagger back into a perfectly-placed foot that sweeps me off-balance. I topple into the chair beside Vic's bed. My whole body aches from destroying that basement room. I stare down at my hand, which

I can barely feel, except for the tips of my fingers where they dug into Fergie's neck.

"That's better." Cali taps her nails against her IV drip. "Now, we can talk about the fucking diabolical mess you've made of our lives. First, you bring your stepsister to Saturnalia, against my direct orders, and then you start a fight with her here. You disrespect Galen's clinic and endanger the life of your oldest friend, and that's not even mentioning you laying a hand on your stepsister, a member of our family—"

"Where is he?" John rushes in, hands balled into fists at his sides, his head swollen and red. He strides right up to me and looms over me. I'll give the dentist credit – he has more balls than I thought. "You tried to *choke* my daughter. You want to explain yourself, son?"

"You're not my father," I shoot back, and the red mist dances on the edges of my vision that this guy dares try to talk like my fucking *father* when he's the one infiltrating our house. "I don't have to explain anything to you, John *Macintosh*."

He winces at the sound of his real name, but remains looming over me, one hand balled in a thin fist while the other snakes around my mother's shoulders, steadying her. I hate that steadying hand – it should be me helping my mother. Fergie and John have fucked everything up.

I shrug. "You want me to explain? Fine. I've been eating your daughter's sweet pussy and slapping her ass red for weeks. But then I found out that she's a liar and a spy and a fake, just like you. And I did what I have to do to protect my family. If you want to find out why she's got her panties in a knot, then check your phone."

John's face twists as he steps back and fumbles in his pocket for his phone. He pulls it out, and I can see hundreds of notifications already flashing on the screen. He pulls up the video file I text him earlier, and a moment later, Fergie's voice fills the room – that simpering tone begging for my cock, followed by the heavy smack of my palm on her plump little ass. John tosses the phone to Cali, and his face crumples.

"No." He sinks to the floor. "No. She can't go through this again. She *can't*."

Cali glances at the screen. She glances at me, then at the screen again.

Then she fucking *loses* it.

"You idiot," she screams at me, coming at me with decades of lethal martial arts training. "You're destroying the one good thing in our lives."

You break everything you love.

I don't have time to blink before Cali has me on the floor. She punches and kicks until bright, cold spots dance in front of my vision. She's wild, uncontrolled – this isn't my mother the trained assassin. She could knock me out with one punch, but she doesn't want me stunned. She wants to *hurt*.

My own mother wants me to bleed.

Cali gets her wish. I'm fucking hurt. I'm bleeding on the ground and I'm bleeding on the inside and the cold black void that is where my heart is collapsing beneath her onslaught. My mother – the woman I'd die to protect – hates me.

And all because of Fergie fucking Macintosh.

I'm too stunned to fight back, my body too weak from the rage I've expelled already today. I lie there and I let my mother pummel me. I hear the snap of things breaking and the dribble of blood on the tiles and the violent immolation of everything good left inside me burning away to ash.

"I know exactly what you wanted from the moment she walked into our house," Cali screams at me. She draws away, panting, clinging to John as he strokes her bloodied hair. "You think that you're so subtle, but you're as subtle as an ax to the head. People comment on how alike we are, on how proud I must be of you, and how good a successor you will make. But they don't see what I see. They don't see how much of my brutality I've always held back in order to be a leader. And now I see that I was right to stop you from becoming Imperator. You have no restraint, no sense of loyalty. You're a thug, Cassius, incapable of anything but base instinct. You care about nothing and no one, not even your own family. How can I leave my empire in the hands of a man who will betray his family like this?"

Every word cuts me. I ball my hands into fists, but the rage doesn't come. I've spent it all on Fergie. And this only makes me hate her more. It's because of her that my own mother has turned against me.

"I tried to protect you," I yell back. "I got rid of her for you!"

"No, Cassius. You looked for an excuse to hurt her because you are hurting. If you were protecting me, you would have come to me with that information, and I would have told you that I already knew that John and Fergie's identities were fake, because those identities were made by me."

This new information burns through me. All this time my mother knew their secret. All this time she had engineered their new lives in our house, and she never thought to tell me. I'm her *son,* and she let me humiliate myself at the feet of my fake stepsister.

Were they all laughing at me? Poor, stupid Cassius, who believes he's found true love with a girl whose name he doesn't even know.

Cali doesn't trust me. She doesn't want me to be Imperator.

With a cry of pain, I turn my head toward the hospital bed. I need Victor more than ever. He'd know exactly what to do. I grab the bed and try to pull myself to my feet, but Claudia and her husbands block the bed, their arms folded. Noah kicks me, sending me sprawling across the tiles. They're not letting me near Victor, and I don't blame him.

You break everything you love.

"Get out, Cassius. Get out of this clinic." Cali's jaw tightens as she points at the door. "You're a disgrace to the name of Dio. I don't want to see your face again."

I sleep over at Euri's house that night. Her sister, Artemis, has a shift at the hospital, so it's just the two of us and her parents. I want to hide in her room because I can't face the thought that Euri's parents might know about the tape, but Euri assures me that it wouldn't have had time to reach them, and delicious smells waft down the hallway and drag me out of her room to join them for dinner.

Euri's mother makes shepherd's pie and serves it with steamed broccoli and big slices of sourdough bread, while her dad tells us about the hilarious things some of his less-bright students try to get away with in their term papers.

As we're eating apple pie for dessert, someone touches my hand. The Poison Ivy Club has got me so frightened of my shadow that I nearly leap out of my seat. But it's only Mrs. Jones, reaching across the table to pat my arm in a motherly way. I wonder if they know something odd is going on, but don't want to say anything.

"It's so lovely to finally meet you, Fergie. Euri's told us a lot about you." Her words sound saccharine sweet.

Professor Jones adds in his booming voice, "Our girl here made you sound so interesting we half-thought that she made you up."

There's a hint of something in their voices that makes me think Euri's confided in them about some of my less-than-perfect qualities. I reach under the table with my free hand and jab her in the thigh. Hopefully, she'll be able to extract us from this table before they decide to stab me with a butter knife.

"Euri's wonderful," I say sincerely. "I'm lucky to have her as a friend. Moving across the country and starting a new school hasn't been easy, and I've made a few missteps. But I think I'm finally on the right path."

"Oh, you mean college?" Euri's mom's voice brightens even more, which should be impossible because she already sounds like a Mariah Carey song. "Where are you going to school?"

No, I mean the hellfire I'm going to rain down on my stepbrother and his two friends for what they did to me. Beneath the table, I squeeze Euri's leg so hard she yelps. "I got into Harvard."

"Harvard. Did you hear that, Allan? Fergie got into *Harvard*. That's wonderful! Congratulations, Fergie."

"Perhaps you can help Euri with her essays," Professor Jones suggests. "For some reason, she decided not to apply for her first choice schools, so she's had early acceptance to Brown, but we think she can do better with Regular Decision."

"Dad, please—"

"We had such high hopes for both our girls," Mrs. Jones coos. "Artemis had an accident in her senior year and it shot her confidence. We keep trying to put her on a plan toward college again, but—"

"Artie's happy where she is," Euri says with a strained voice. I sense her stiffening beside me.

"Artemis should be a doctor at that hospital, not an orderly," Professor Jones snaps, and I can hear the disappointment dripping from his voice. "I did not work hard all these years to have my daughters squander the gifts they've been given. Artemis might be a few years behind, but she *will* go to college next year. We will not accept anything less. And while Brown is a perfectly adequate school, Eurydice's always dreamed of going to Harvard or Princeton—"

"I'm not applying to Harvard or Princeton anymore," Euri says in a firm voice.

Her words are like a nuclear weapon landing on the table. I imagine I hear the *THWACK* as the professor's head flies off and his brains hit the ceiling. We sit in the burned-out silence of Euri's revelation for several excruciating moments, until Mrs. Jones rallies and says in an indulgent voice, "Don't be silly, Eurydice. Of course, you're getting into one of those schools. We're alumni, so we get precedence, and we've been working on your essays for months. Harvard is your dream school—"

"Yes, and dreams change. I've decided that I want to go to school overseas. Cambridge has a great English program. So does Blackfriars—"

"Yes, and they also had a secret cannibal society on campus." Professor Jones slams his fist on the table. "We're not sending our little girl there."

"That scandal was nearly twenty years ago! What school doesn't have a scandal? And it's not my only option, either. There's the University of Auckland in New Zealand—"

"Euri, honey," her dad sounds like he's fighting to control his temper. "We love that you're thinking outside the box, but those schools are too far away. We won't be able to run over if you need us. Look at your friend, Fergie. She's not trying to escape her parents—"

No, it's really my psychopathic stepbrother that has me running to the hills.

"—Fergie understands that she needs extra help because of

her eyesight. What if you have an accident or fall down the stairs or you can't see the slides—"

Oh hell no. They are not using Euri's eyesight as an excuse because they want to wrap her in cotton and send her to the same schools they went to—

"Then I will sort it out," Euri says firmly. I'm incensed on her behalf, and ready to jump in, but I can see this is a battle she's ready to fight herself. "I'm nineteen years old, and I want to be a journalist. I'm going to be reporting from foxholes in war-torn nations and from the front row at presidential rallies. I think I need to learn how to live without my mommy and daddy fighting my battles for me."

"I don't understand where this hostility is coming from," her mother says in a put-upon voice. "We've already discussed that there are plenty of jobs for journalists that don't involve being shot at. What about the summer internship you had at that arts magazine? Or working for the Home Shopping Channel? Or writing the column about the mayor's office—"

Euri shoves her chair back so violently it hits the wall behind her. "Excuse me, I've lost my appetite."

She storms off. I drop my fork on my half-eaten plate and wipe my hands on my napkin. "Thank you so much for dinner, Professor and Mrs. Jones. But I'm quite tired. I think I'll go to bed."

I grab my cane from where it rests on the back of my chair and head off in the direction of the hallway. As I move toward Euri's room, I hear Mrs. Jones whisper to her husband.

"Let her go. Perhaps she'll talk some sense into Eurydice."

Like fuck I will.

I manage to locate Euri's room at the end of the hall. I push open the door. "That was an interesting dinner."

"That's one way to describe it." Euri's on her bed. I hear a package crinkle. "Want a Mallomar? You'd better get in quick because I'm going to stuff myself with sugar until I explode and then I won't have to think about college ever again."

"Have I mentioned that I'm sorry lately?" Euri wouldn't be upset right now if it weren't for me. I sit gingerly on the corner of the bed.

"About a million times." Euri tosses me that package. "I'm fine. Well, not fine, but better than someone who's just had a sex tape released. I still hate the Poison Ivy Club, so don't ever tell them this, but I think they did me a favor. I've been so set on Harvard my entire life – because my dad went there – that it's become the safe option, and I don't want to be safe. I want adventure. I want to reinvent myself as someone more than Euri the dorky overachiever, and I need to put a decent-sized ocean between me and Emerald Beach. Being forced out of Princeton and Harvard has made me see possibilities I'd never considered before. Oxford, Blackfriars, Amsterdam, Melbourne, even Auckland looks pretty amazing. And New Zealand has the added bonus of being as far from here as it's possible to get without being on an iceberg."

"I think that sounds amazing."

"I know, right?" Euri's voice sings with excitement before turning pensive again. "I just wish I could get Mom and Dad to understand. I know they're worried about me being alone in a foreign country. Things will be harder because of my eyes and I don't make friends easily and, well, they know a bit about you so..."

"...so they know that I got the Harvard slot instead of you..." I finish.

"Yeah. And I get that they're just looking out for me, but it sticks in your gut, you know? That your own parents don't think you can hack it?"

I think of Dad keeping secrets from me. "I know exactly what that feels like."

Euri grabs the Mallomars from me. "I know part of their attitude is because of Artie. They think she panicked in her senior year and that's why she didn't apply to any colleges. They are really angry with her for not 'living up to her potential,' and it makes living in this house pretty hard."

"Mmmm. I couldn't help but notice that your parents don't know about the Poison Ivy Club and their connection to Artie's 'accident'."

The package crinkles as Euri stuffs my cookie into her mouth. She chews thoughtfully, then says, "My parents are bright and well-meaning, but they're pretty clueless. If we'd told them they would have fought for Artie against the school and tried to bring the Poison Ivy Club down, and they would have been eviscerated. We decided it's better not to tell them the full story." Euri shudders. "And I can still see a little, you know. I can see your mind whirring. Whatever you're plotting to get back at them, it can't hurt Artie or my parents. It's got to be directed. I don't want anyone else to get hurt."

"I think there's always a risk," I say. "The Poison Ivy Club has a lot of power in this town. We need to take that power away. That's the only way any of us will be safe. And I think we should start by—"

A knock at the door startles me out of my thoughts. "Hey, sis," Artie calls, cracking the door. "I'm home. I heard Fergie's staying with us."

"I am. Hi, Artie." I wave in the vague direction of the door.

Artemis steps inside the room and shuts the door, turning the lock. She smells like a hospital. She sits down on the bed between us.

"So, sister dearest, why is Mom slamming all the dishes and Dad outside smoking a cigarette with his serious face on?"

"They had a talk to me about my future," Euri mumbles. "They want me to apply for Harvard or Princeton. They don't want me to study overseas."

"You can't see me, Fergie, but I'm rolling my eyes so far back in my head I can see my own brain matter," Artie says with a smile in her voice. "Only our parents would hear their daughter got into Brown, or that she intends to go to Cambridge or Black-friars, and consider that a disappointment."

"They want you to go to college next year," Euri says.

"I know exactly what they want me to do," Artie says. "But it's not their life, it's mine. The Poison Ivy Club helped me to see that. I don't think I want to go to college anymore. At least, not next year. Not on their terms. But that's not what I came here to talk to you about. I heard what happened with the video."

No. Fuck.

No.

Her words bring it all back with a rush – the fear, the humili-ation, the acid taste of bile in my mouth at the thought of what Artie's seen.

Artie pats my knee. "I'm so sorry, Fergie."

Her words grate against my psyche. I'd been so preoccupied with Euri's problems that for ten minutes I hadn't thought about Victor lying unconscious in that hospital bed or the three of them making our night on the sex swing public, and now I'm back to feeling sick to my stomach, so... yay?

I don't need her pity. I need to put my stepbrother's head through a wall.

"How do you know about the video?" Euri demands.

"Are you kidding? It's all over social media. Plus, my manag-er's daughter goes to Stonehurst Prep, and all the parents got a message about it. It's all everyone's talking about in the break room. And I know what it is to be a victim of the Poison Ivy Club and to desperately want justice, but those boys were always so untouchable." Artie's nails dig into my skin. "But they're not untouchable anymore, are they? They *cared* about you. I can see it in their eyes. That's why they did this to you. And I get the feeling you're not the type to roll over and take it, so I want to know how you plan to retaliate."

I grin at her. "I'm going to *burn* them. Why?"

"I have an idea for something you could do to Cassius. It's cruel, but he deserves a little cruelty." She presses a vial into my hand. "Take this."

"What is it?"

"Pure evil in a tube." With a relish for devilry I never thought her capable of, Euri's sister describes a prank that has me grinning. I pocket the tube and promise her that we'll get the results on video for her.

After Euri and I shower and brush our teeth, I settle in her trundle bed with an audiobook, and Euri sits down to start on her homework. She taps my foot. "Hey, Fergie?"

"Yeah?"

"What are you going to do? I mean, really? If someone is targeting your stepmother and her Triumvirate with bombs, are you in danger, too? Should we be going after the Poison Ivy Club?"

A lump rises in my throat as I think about my dad's panicked voice and Victor lying in that hospital bed. "I am worried about the bomb. From what the guys said, their families have been targets for a while, and they don't know who's responsible. But it's all tied in together, isn't it? Cas and Victor and Torsten think they can get away with ruining lives because they've seen their parents do it. Cali snaps her fingers and she can literally have people *killed*, which is all the more reason for me to find my own means of revenge. The police can't touch them, but I can—"

I'm interrupted by a crash and a shout from Mrs. Jones. Euri rushes to the door. "Mom, what's going on?"

Mrs. Jones shouts. Euri yelps as someone barrels into the room, throwing her into her desk.

"What the fuck is going on?"

A rough hand grabs my arm. "Come with me. *Now.*"

11

FERGIE

I'd recognize that smooth, liquid voice anywhere.

Only he doesn't sound like his usual self as he shakes my arm roughly – he sounds angry, which is terrifying and confusing and a million other things I don't want to feel right now.

"Torsten?"

He yanks my arm. "Come on."

"What are you doing?"

"You're coming with me. I'm going to help you."

"The fuck I am." I break his grip and step back into the relative safety of Euri's room. "You can't just walk into Euri's house and drag me around, not after what you did."

"Get away from my daughter and her friend right now," Mrs. Jones shrieks. "Fergie, he's stark naked."

"He is?"

"He is." Euri tries to push herself in front of me. "Go away, Torsten. You can't talk to her, especially not with your dick waving in her face."

"You'd better get out of this house right now, young man,"

Professor Jones says from behind him. "Or I will be forced to call the police."

"I'm not leaving without Fergie."

The cold certainly in his voice breaks something inside me. I've had a long, hellish day, and I thought I'd found a safe place to rest my head for the night. I thought that maybe I'd finally get the chance to close my eyes and forget for a few blissful hours that the three guys I'd come to care for more than anyone had betrayed me. But nooooo, a naked Torsten *has* to drag me away to some fresh hell.

"It's bad enough that you released that video." Tears escape my eyes and flow down my cheeks. I don't bother to stop them. Let him see what he's done to me. "But you have to come here and torture me? Fuck off. I don't want to see you."

"I didn't release the video and I'm not torturing you." Torsten can't deal with my hyperbole. "All I did was hold your arm, and I did it because—"

The tears stream down my face, hot and wet and humiliating. "Torsten, I need you to listen very carefully. Whether you had something to do with it or not, there is a video of me having sex with you on the internet. I feel like my body has been violated. I can't bear to have you touch me, and no way can I trust you."

I didn't release the video.

They are the words I so desperately want to hear, and he spoke them with such ferocity that I almost dare to believe him.

He's Torsten. He doesn't lie.

But the idea of it, the *hope* of it, spreads in my chest, and *that's* the real mistake. I want to trust him so badly, but I can't. Torsten *would* lie to protect Victor or Cassius. He'd lie if they told him to.

That's the only reason he's here.

He's just as guilty and just as dangerous.

Torsten grabs my wrist again. He raises my hand to his cheek and presses my fingers into his skin. "Look at me. *Look at me,* Fergie. Tell me if I'm lying to you."

My breath hitches as I draw my fingers over him, as I feel the familiar ridges of his face, his full lips, his impossibly sharp cheekbones, his eyelashes that feather my skin so softly. I feel the tears that run in rivers down his cheeks, and the corners of his mouth are turned down with a sadness that rivals my own.

I feel *him*. Torsten. My Torsten.

And I *know* the truth.

I know in my bones.

I know in the shattered pieces of my coal-heart.

He didn't have anything to do with it. He's not here to hurt me. He's here to save me.

I draw back. "Go outside and wait for me. I'll be out in a second."

And he does. He pushes past the Joneses and leaves. He trusts me to keep my word. I turn to the trundle bed and start shoving my things into my backpack.

"You're going with him?" Euri squeaks. "But what about the video? What about everything?"

"Torsten didn't have anything to do with releasing the video."

"You don't know that."

"I do." I snap my backpack shut. "Euri, I know you're a profoundly good person, and it probably looks to you like I'm walking back to one of my abusers, and you're going to try and stop me. But Torsten didn't do this. And I need him right now. I need him to get through this."

"So the plan is off? You're not going after Poison Ivy?"

"The plan is *on*. We're meeting tomorrow, at school, in the Sentinel offices, to draw up our battle plan. But we leave Torsten out of it. We might even be able to get his help. But you have to let me go with him now."

Euri makes a choking sound as she wraps her arms around me, squeezing me tight. I know she wants to tie me down so I don't leave, but she pulls away. She lets me go. "I want you to text me exactly where you are. If you don't show up at school tomorrow, I'm stringing Torsten to the rafters in the art suite by his testicles, with piano wire."

I laugh. "That's fair."

I didn't have much stuff with me – only what was in my backpack. I hoist it over one shoulder and walk outside. Torsten takes my bag from me and loops my arm in his. He doesn't say a word as he leads me to the end of the driveway and opens a car door for me. I'm surprised to hear Seymour's voice.

"Seymour, what are you doing here? I thought you'd go back to be with Cali."

"I did, but then I saw this guy's white, naked ass running down the street, and I thought he might need me more. He's been running around the city all day, butt naked, trying to find you. I wouldn't have told him where you were, but he was starting to worry me. And he's not the only one desperate to find you."

"Mew!" a tiny but determined voice admonishes me from the seat.

"Spartacus." I lean over and poke my finger through the mesh on the cat carrier. Big mistake. Spartacus bites down on my skin, and I yelp.

"Seymour, thank you for bringing me Spartacus. And Torsten. You made the right decision."

"This is a good man you have here, Fergie," Seymour says as Torsten settles into the seat next to me and reaches across to squeeze my hand. "This boy has been coming to our house since he was a wee lad. He knows that he can call me anytime he needs. All the boys can. And you, too."

My heart aches. I remember Milo making all that food for Victor and Juliet's party, and the way he still packs Cas' snacks for school like he's a little kid. They really are a family, all of them. I thought I could be part of that, too. I've never had that kind of thing – it's been me and Dad for as long as I can remember.

But Cas and Victor had to ruin it.

Torsten squeezes my arm. "I trust Seymour," he says simply. And I know it's that simple for him. It doesn't matter that Seymour works for the Dios – Seymour understands Torsten. He feels safe in this car. Seymour won't make judgments about Torsten or try to initiate small talk, the way a taxi driver might.

We drive across town and turn into a space with other cars beeping and moving around us. Someone flings open the car door and a snooty voice says, "Welcome back to the Elysium Hotel, Mr. Lucian. Is there anything I can help you with?"

"Yes, thank you. Fergie will be staying in my suite with me," Torsten says. "Can you send up her bag? And some food?"

"Certainly. And would Sir like me to launder him some fresh clothing?"

"No, that's fine." Torsten slides out of the car, completely oblivious to the fact that he's still naked.

As the concierge helps me out of the car, he murmurs, "Do you have any requests for dinner, ma'am? Mr. Lucian has a specific menu he prefers us to follow, but you might like something more... adventurous."

I left Euri's table without finishing my dinner, so I'm still starving. "Thank you. Please bring me something delicious. And something with chocolate for dessert. And I promise I'll get him to put on some pants."

"Bless you, ma'am."

I grip Spartacus' cage in one hand and my cane in the other, and Seymour and Torsten flank me as we walk into the hotel. I turn to the driver and throw my arms around him. It's strange – last time when Dawson released the video, I felt so utterly alone. It was only me and my dad, and it wasn't easy to talk to him about the horror of it. But this time, I feel as though I'm surrounded by people who have my back – Torsten, Euri, Seymour, Milo, Artie...

I've lost so much, but I've gained something important, too. I have true friends in my corner. I don't have to fight the world on my own anymore. And that makes me even more determined that I'll make Victor and Cassius pay.

I squeeze Seymour extra hard and say, "Thank you for everything. Could you do one more thing for me?"

"Anything, Miss Fergie."

Please don't tell Cali or Cassius where I am. But if my dad asks, tell him I'm safe."

"Of course."

He drives off, and Torsten and I walk inside. The tip of my cane rolls over the marble, and I lay my head on his shoulder and breathe in his vanilla and honeycomb scent, and his love warms the chill in my veins, and I realize that for the first time in a long time, I am truly safe in his arms.

Tonight, I rest. Tomorrow – *revenge*.

Torsten leads me into an enormous elevator. "What floor?" I ask, running my fingers over the braille buttons.

"Thirteen."

"The penthouse suite," I grin. "Would a Lucian have anything less?"

"My mother doesn't own this hotel," Torsten says. "That's why I'm staying here."

That wasn't what I meant, but I appreciate his explanation. At the mention of his mother, the horror of Galen's clinic comes rushing back. "Torsten, do you know what happened today? A bomb went off at the museum. Your mother is with Galen now; she has some injuries, and Victor is—"

"I know," he whispers. "Victor drove me to the museum. He wanted to find Cali. He wanted to ask her about your name, Fergie Macintosh. But I didn't go inside with him because I had to find you."

Torsten's words sting. Victor went to Cali. *Why didn't he ask me?*

And why is he going to Cali after they released the video? I can't even ask him because he's in a coma and he might not wake up and I don't want to ask him because he did it... he did this to me...

Now I'm thinking about the video again. The sickness rolls in my stomach, and the threads of my thoughts of Victor unravel as the tears crowd my eyes again.

All those things we did and said to each other in private, and now it's out there. Everyone has seen it. Has the concierge seen it? Is that why he's being so nice... I can't stand it. I can't...

I cling to Torsten as my body shudders in revulsion. The elevator dings and Torsten holds me close as he leads me down a wide hallway. I can hear water running – some kind of indoor water feature. It's probably supposed to make the place feel tranquil, but it just makes me want to pee.

Torsten swipes a keycard and the door opens. I can tell the space beyond is vast, the echoes uncluttered. I click my tongue and listen, sensing a wall dividing the room in front of me. The left side feels bright, metallic – a kitchen. The right side is more muffled and cozy. I sweep my cane to the right and find a sofa. I set down Spartacus' cage and unlock the door so he can jump out, and flop down on the cushions. The cat leaps onto my lap and digs his needle claws into my school blazer.

"Pets aren't allowed in the hotel," Torsten says. He's still hovering in the doorway, suddenly a stranger in his own space.

I kick off my boots. Spartacus leaps after them to attack the laces. "I was hoping the fact that you're a Lucian might mean that they don't kick us out over it. Your concierge friend didn't seem to mind." I pat the sofa beside me. "Please, come and sit. I need you to hold me right now. Can you do that?"

The door clicks shut. Torsten slips off his own shoes, and I hear him stack them neatly beside the door. A moment later, he sinks down beside me. His arm goes around me – it's a little stiff, but it feels so warm and so good that I sink against him. Spartacus senses a lap has been created and leaps onto me, settling on my legs and starting his buzz-saw purr.

"Is this okay?" Torsten asks.

"It's perfect," I say, nuzzling into Torsten's shoulder and enjoying this brief moment of physical closeness, because I know this isn't normal for him and it might become too much at any moment. I stroke Spartacus' soft fur. "Now, I need you to tell me exactly what happened this morning. When I woke up, I was alone, and your note was on my forehead. And then I got to school and found out about the video, and then the bomb... I'm missing lots of pieces. When you tell me, I might cry and get upset, but I want you to keep talking, okay? Don't stop. I need to know everything."

Torsten threads his fingers through my hair. His rare touch means everything to me. My nose fills with vanilla and honeycomb, and I lie on his strong chest and let the tears fall again. Out there, thousands of people are watching me fuck three guys on a sex swing, but in here, with him, I'm safe.

"I left Cas' house with Victor," Torsten says, his Scandinavian accent coming through stronger because he's distressed. "Victor dropped me off here at the hotel and went to basketball practice. Cas was still asleep with you when we left. I don't know what happened at school because I wasn't there."

"I know," I try not to be impatient with him. "I mean later, when Victor picked you up. Did he say anything about what happened?"

Torsten remains silent. He seizes me by the shoulders and pulls me up so I'm facing him. His finger touches the tear rolling down my cheek, and lets out a shuddering breath, his whole body trembling.

"Torsten. I *need* to know. Remember what I said, even if I'm crying, you have to keep talking."

Torsten's fingers stroke my hair again, and I think he's trying to calm himself. I think I understand what he's feeling – he can count the number of people who've cared about him on one hand and still have fingers to spare, and the idea I'm hurt and they caused it rips him right through his too-big heart. "Victor was wearing his basketball uniform. He was sweating, so he'd come from practice, even though practice should have ended thirty minutes before. He told me that he'd seen Cas in the basement of the old horticulture building, and he was so angry he'd compromised the structural integrity of the building. Cas found out that your name is Fergie Macintosh. Cas thinks that you and your father are spies or assassins or maybe that you work for the government. He thinks you're pretending to be blind."

Cas thinks I'm… *pretending?*

Jumping to a stupid fucking conclusion about me I can *almost* understand. After all, Cas has been taught to gouge first, ask questions never.

But after *everything* we've been through together, after the way he touched me and made my whole body sing, after he gave me the best birthday present and brought Spartacus home to cheer me up, after he made all those promises about being there for me, he thinks I'm *faking* being blind?

Everything unravels. Even though I no longer see color, I understand what Cas means when he says that a red mist descends on him. I'm so angry that I *feel* red – I can feel the fire of it, the passion, the raw, unadulterated, pulsing hatred of it bubbling over inside me.

I grit my teeth. "If Cassius Dio thinks that about me, he can fuck off into the sun."

"The sun is ninety-three million miles away. He wouldn't be able to reach it before he froze in space."

"I know, Torsten. Thank you."

Torsten's fingers are in my hair again. When he speaks, his voice sounds worried, but he doesn't stop. "Cas was upset because he believes you lied to him and that you're trying to hurt Cali. When Cas is upset, he stretches people on a rack or cuts out their tongues or feeds them to Clarence—"

"Yes, yes, I get the idea," I mumble. On my lap, Spartacus senses the mood shifting, and he jumps up to go explore the rest of the room.

Torsten swallows. "Victor and I already knew that your name is Fergie Macintosh. We found that out while we were investigating you. But we didn't tell Cas because Victor thought he might react like this. I didn't like keeping it a secret. I wanted to ask you about it. I was going to ask you last night, in the library, but..."

...but then I opened my legs and my mouth and let the three of them have my body... and my heart.

All this time, I'd been beating myself up about the secrets I was keeping from them, and they already *knew*.

"I was going to tell you that night," I say. "I guess it's too late now. My old boyfriend released a video of me, naked, touching myself the way I did for you back in my room. Dad and I went after him in court but he hadn't broken any law, and he sent the pictures to the Harvard admissions board so I couldn't apply there anymore. So Dad got Cali to make us the fake identities, and he married Cali and we moved here."

I wish it felt good to get the full truth of it out, finally. But all I feel is numb and red-raw and flayed alive.

"I know," Torsten says. "I know all of it, but it doesn't matter. Do you want me to go on with the story?"

"Yes, please."

"So, Victor found Cas in the building. Victor usually calms down angry Cas or locks him away where he can't hurt anyone. But Victor was busy at practice and Cas knows I can't help him, so he went to Juliet."

"Juliet?" So Victor had nothing to do with the video. Relief floods me, but it's short lived, because then I remember that the video is out there, and I'm seized again by a wave of powerful nausea that leaves me heaving.

"Yes, Juliet. Cassius told her about your fake name. He told her that he had to protect his family from you, and also that someone once released a sex tape about you. Victor thinks that's why they decided to pull the security tape from the library and post it online."

I ball my hands into fists and beat them against the sofa cushions. Cassius is the only one of them I told about Dawson, and only because of that moment we had together with Spartacus. Because of all three of them, I expected my stepbrother to hold that secret close, because he alone understood what it cost me. I didn't tell him that we'd changed our name because of the fallout from Dawson's video, but could he honestly not put that together? Is being a spy faking blindness *so much more plausible* than the truth? Fuck that shit.

In my most vulnerable moment, I gave Cassius the ammunition he needed to destroy me.

"When Victor picked me up, I thought he was coming to find you," Torsten's voice wavers. He knows something's wrong inside me, but he doesn't know how to fix it. But I asked him to tell me what happened, so he's going to keep going no matter how much it upsets both of us. "But he only wanted to talk to Cali and his mother. Victor's mother always has the answers. He said he needed to hear the truth from Cali before he could decide what to do next."

He did?

I thought I was relieved to hear that Victor had nothing to do with posting the video, but I'm *incensed*. After everything we've been through together, he needs to hear from my fucking evil bitch stepmother?

Every sugar-coated word he said to me these last months tastes like a lie.

You were supposed to protect me, Victor August. You were supposed to put me back together again.

Cas' betrayal I understand on some deep, primordial level. Cas has been made into a monster by his mother, by the way people expect him to behave, and so he knows only one response when he's hurt.

But Victor... Victor's hurt cuts deepest of all.

Cas says that he doesn't believe I'm blind, and Victor has to talk to his fucking *mother*.

Fuck them both.

Fuck them with a rusty hatchet.

"Thank you, Torsten," I breathe as I let the hatred soak over me, as I let it seep into every pore, infect every vein until it strips away the last pieces of humanity I have left.

"I don't care what your name is." Torsten slips his fingers through mine and squeezes.

"I know. That's why I'd like to stay here with you, if that's okay?"

"This is what you want? To stay with me?" Torsten stiffens.

"Very much so. And Spartacus, too. But if that's too scary—"

"But... why would you want that? I'm not normal, Fergie. I'm not a fun person to live with."

"So? I'm not normal, either. What the fuck is normal, anyway? Have you ever known me to do anything I don't want to do?"

"No. But I've only known you for a few months, so—"

I sigh. "That was a rhetorical question, but you're right. We've only known each other a few months, and I feel more comfortable with you than I do with anyone else in the world. I'd love to stay with you, and please keep being your wonderful not-normal self, because that's the Torsten I'm madly in love with."

His fingers crush mine. "You... are in love with me?"

"Madly in love with you," I correct him. "The 'madly' part is important."

"Oh, well then, I'm madly in love with you, too."

Those words are exactly what I need to hear right now. They're the words I need to cling to if I'm going to survive this. I lean in and kiss Torsten on the lips, letting my tongue explore his mouth a little as he kisses me back with his shy possessiveness. And I feel fucking sorry for everyone who has passed over Torsten's love, because it's so beautiful it could shatter the world.

There's a knock at our door. Reluctantly, I pull away, and Torsten gets up to answer it. My lips burn with the ghost of him.

It's the concierge with our food. He sets it out on a small table for us, and slips me a folder. "Our room service menu in Braille, ma'am," he says.

This is my kind of hotel.

I slip the concierge – who tells me that his name is Robert – a couple of bills for his trouble, and he closes the door with a promise that he'll return later with some dessert.

We sit down to eat. I ask Torsten to explain what's on my plate. He's not very good at naming the foods, but he's great at precise instructions. He moves clockwise around my plate and even counts the exact number of meatballs. No one's ever told me that my water glass is 'two-and-three-quarter inches' from my fork before.

The food tastes amazing – the chef of the Elysium deserves his own TV show. My meatballs are dripping with some sweet, rich sauce, and the pesto and ricotta pasta is out-of-this-world good. There's grilled eggplant smothered in chili and garlic, and a small antipasto platter of cheeses and cured meats with slices of fresh bread. He's even brought a platter of salmon for Spartacus.

I wash my food down with a glass of red wine, and I'm not even certain I'll have room left for dessert, although I'll give it my best shot.

"What are you eating?" I ask Torsten.

"Steamed fish. Tomato and cucumber salad. A glass of apple juice. I usually have the same thing. I don't like having to make decisions."

"I get that. Decisions are stressful. Let's make a rule – no decisions in this hotel room. We just do what we want, and fuck the consequences."

"I like this rule."

When we've finished our food, I find my eyes fluttering shut. It's hard to believe everything that's happened to me today. "I'm really tired," I say. "I'd like to go to sleep now."

"If that's what you feel like doing," Torsten says with a smile in his voice. "I'll show you the bedroom."

He leads me through a door at the end of the kitchen into a large room with a high ceiling. I click my tongue and can sense the bed in the center, facing an entire wall of glass that looks out over the city lights below. It feels warm and safe and cozy, and my body responds with weariness. I raise my hand to touch the wall and find my way to the bathroom door, but my fingers brush something odd. It feels like a big sheet of paper loose on the wall, like wallpaper that hasn't been properly hung.

"What's this crinkling noise?" I ask, feeling around the edges with both hands. Spartacus leaps up onto the nightstand and bats at it enthusiastically.

"I covered all the walls with paper," Torsten says. "So I can draw on them."

"Every single wall?"

"Yes. I even covered up the TV."

I'm surrounded by Torsten's artwork. For some reason, that makes me feel even safer. "What are you drawing?"

"People," he says. I know there's more to it than that, but he's being deliberately vague so he can avoid telling me the full truth. A memory flashes in my mind. It was the night of my birthday, when they took me to Everlasting Hart farm and fed Coach Franklin to Clarence. I remember Torsten's pencil scratching across paper as he drew me while Victor thrust balls-deep inside me. He normally only draws famous artworks from memory, but that night he'd only wanted to draw me.

And that makes me even more curious about what my dark, brooding artist is drawing now. But he *is* taking me in, even though it's probably incurring the wrath of my stepbrother and the Dio and August families, so I'm not going to press the point.

Torsten flicks on the light in the bathroom for me, and I can see the outline of the door on the wall. I move inside and he helps me find the sink and the shower controls and the free bath products. I try not to flashback to the day at the Olympus Club when Victor and Cas had me in the shower. But I can't help it. The memory burns through me, only to be replaced by the sound of my own moans being playing through Juliet's phone speakers.

How could all of it mean so little to them? I *trusted* them. I believed I was one of them. How could they have thrown it away because they were too afraid to trust me?

Torsten shuffles back into the sitting room to work on his paintings. Spartacus chases a balled-up paper around the bedroom. I turn on the shower water and step under a piping hot stream. I let the water wash over me, imagining it washing away my feelings for them. I have Torsten now. I don't need them. And I can't allow myself to feel anything for them because I'm going to *destroy* them.

I have to be strong. Stronger than last time. I let Dawson get inside my head. I let him make me believe that I was worthless. He took away my chance at Harvard, so I let him take away my last name, my history. Not this time. I am a fucking queen, and by the time this is over, I will make sure they know it.

I step out of the shower, wrap myself in every warm, fluffy towel on the rack, and shuffle Egyptian-mummy style back into the bedroom. I flop down on the bed. My head swims. I smell acrylic paint and the sharp tang of charcoal. Torsten's in the corner of the room, hard at work on his art.

"Can I join you?" he asks, and I hear him washing his brushes in a tub of water. From the sound of things, Spartacus has cornered his ball of paper and is busy tearing it to pieces.

"It's your bed," I answer Torsten.

"No, it's not. I gave it to you."

I hold out my hand to him. "You did. That's because you're amazing. And I'm inviting you to join me."

Torsten lays down beside me on top of the duvet. He doesn't touch me, but I can sense every inch of him as if he were pressed up hard against me. The distance between us sizzles with unspoken things.

"I got into Harvard," I blurt out, remembering the email on my phone. Today was supposed to be a happy day, the culmination of everything I worked for. The words don't taste real.

"Of course you did," he says simply.

I squeeze my eyes shut, trying to keep the tears inside that are once again threatening to escape. I wish I'd been able to get into Harvard on my own merit. I wish I'd never run to Poison Ivy for help. I wish my dad never met Cali fucking Dio so Cassius would have ruined someone else's life instead of mine. But we don't always get what we wish for, and now I have to decide what I'm going to do with the dregs of a life that have been left for me.

"I wish we could go back to last night," I say with all the

hope and bitterness my empty heart cavity can muster. "I wish everything was the way it's supposed to be."

I don't know what I expect Torsten to do, but it's not what he does – he leans in close and touches the very tip of his nose to mine. It's so beautiful and so intimate, and I don't think I've ever felt so loved in my whole life.

"Last night was the happiest night of my life," Torsten says. "Cassius ruined that."

"He did." I blink, and the tears cascade down my cheeks. *Will I ever stop crying?* "And Victor, too."

"Victor didn't release the video," Torsten says.

"No, he didn't. But Victor made me a promise. He promised that he'd be there to take the pain away when Cassius tried to ruin me. But when he's forced to choose between the girl he supposedly worships and his bitter, monstrous friend, he chose Cas." I hug the towels tighter around myself. "And maybe I'm not surprised. But if he's going to be on Cas' side, then he's my enemy, too."

"Am I your enemy?" Torsten's voice shatters. "I couldn't stop them. I—"

"Torsten, you saved me. You came to find me when *no one else* except Euri – not my dad, not the school, not either of the guys who swore they would protect me – wanted my side of the story. I know you're risking everything and everyone you care about to keep me here." I reach out a hand and tentatively touch his cheek, running my hand over the curve of his lips.

"You're everything I care about," he whispers.

I trail my hand down his neck, over the curve of his shoulder blades and down his bare arm, across the hard planes of his abs and into the elastic of his boxer shorts. I wrap my fingers around his cock and stroke him until he hardens, and an exquisite gasp escapes his lips.

"Fergie, you don't have to—"

"I know," I grin as I pump him harder. "But I want to. I think I need to remember what it feels like to care about someone. And to have them care for me."

"I can care for you," Torsten says. He reaches out and knits his fingers in my free hand. He leans over and kisses me.

The only parts of us that touch are our clasped hands, my fingers sliding down his dick, and our lips. But somehow it's the sweetest, most intimate kiss. It promises so much, and makes a warmth pool in my chest that's not about hate.

Fresh tears spring in my eyes. Torsten pulls back.

"I've upset you. I'm so sorry."

He tries to yank his hand away, but I hold tight.

"Torsten Lucian, don't you dare leave this bed," I say. I run the tip of my finger around the tip of his cock, and he shudders with pleasure. "Not all tears are for sadness. I'm crying because I haven't felt safe in a very long time the way I feel safe here in this bed with you."

Before he can protest, I lean in and kiss him, a little more hungrily this time. I search the edges of my bruised and blackened soul for all the feelings I want to show him, and I pour them into that kiss. I need him to see how much he means to me.

This time, when Torsten pulls away, the heat between us lingers, and it's tinged with longing and with need.

"Will you..." he struggles to find the words. "Will you take off the towels for me? I want to watch you unwrap yourself."

"Okay, but I'm going to need my hands back."

Reluctantly, he slides his fingers from mine, and I pull my hand from his boxers. I flip down the edge of my towel, revealing my naked shoulder and the curve of one breast. Torsten's breath hitches, and he reaches over and grazes his finger over my nipple, playing with it until it stands in a stiff, needy peak and goosebumps trickle down my arms.

"You're cold," he says. "My skin always does that when I'm cold."

"Then kiss me until I'm warm all over."

"But kissing doesn't—"

I muffle his protest with another kiss, searing my soul to his as I unfold the rest of the towels, revealing my naked body one limb at a time. His fingers brush my skin lightly – it almost feels as if he's painting me with his touch, tracing the lines and shapes of me, breaking me down into my constituent parts.

His soft kisses turn possessive as he grabs my hips and rolls me over so that I'm facing away from him, my back pressing against his hard chest. He wraps the duvet around us, cocooning me in thousand-count Egyptian cotton. Under the blankets, he pushes me away slightly, so that the only part of us touching is my hips nestled into his, and his shaft rubbing between my ass cheeks. He reaches down between my legs and finds my clit.

He works diligently, mimicking the method I showed him, copying it almost exactly from memory – slow at first, then harder, dipping and swirling and using my own juices to slicken it. And dammit if it doesn't drive me wild. Mewling cries fall from my lips as my body floods with pleasure.

The orgasm starts in the soles of my feet and roars through my veins, washing away Old Fergie for good and issuing forth someone new. Someone baptized in fire and blood. I've been cleansed of the last pieces of hope that what happened last night will ever happen again.

For one glorious night, I surrendered to the power of the Poison Ivy Club. I gave them everything, and they spat on my gift. With Torsten's magical tongue and fingers and cock, he'll draw their poison from my veins so all that's left is him.

And he is enough for me.

He turns me over and I straddle him, driving myself down on his cock, keeping my arms on the bed and not touching him any more than necessary so he can feel his way through the sensations the way he needs to.

And I fuck him. I fuck him hard and fast and messily and beautifully. I fuck him until the bed squeals in protest and Spartacus flees in terror and the city lights flicker and dim until only the moon is left. I fuck him until I forget myself, because when I'm riding his glorious cock, I don't have to think about what's waiting out there for me – about the video on display for the world to see, the monstrous stepbrother who wants to kill me so he doesn't have to see himself reflected in my eyes, and the larger-than-life King lying still and silent in a hospital bed.

I fuck him until I'm so filled with him that he is everything, and I am nothing.

We come together, shattering to pieces so that parts of him become mixed up with me and I don't know where I stop and he begins. And then and only then, I can close my eyes against the horrors of today, and find some semblance of peace.

13

TORSTEN

I lie in bed and watch Fergie as her eyelids flicker closed. It's taken her a long time to fall asleep. She kept opening her eyes and clenching her fists in the blankets. I asked her why, and she said she almost falls asleep, and then she remembers the video is out there and it makes her feel afraid and violated.

I understand feeling afraid. I remember the way I used to feel when Livvie would yell at me. I never understood what I did wrong. She would come afterward and try to hug me and apologize, but I still remembered the yelling and the sick, plunging feeling in my stomach. I don't want Fergie to feel like that.

Now she's asleep. Her red hair falls over her face, and she makes little whistling noises through her nose.

I think she's the most beautiful thing that I've ever seen.

It's so wrong that she's here with me. It's wrong that I'm all that she has. I think about Victor in that hospital bed, and Cas raging in his big, silent house, and I'm sad. Sadder than I've ever been. The one thing in my life that's always been constant has broken.

But in its place is her. I think if we're sad together, her and me, then maybe we won't feel so alone, so *violated*.

When I'm certain that Fergie's memories won't wake her, I slide myself out from beneath her and move to the corner of the room, where I've been painting the wall. I sit down, pick up my palette, and paint.

I've been painting this picture of Fergie ever since we went to visit Clarence. I've always painted because I want to understand why people act the way they do, why they seem to have this secret language of symbols and cues and expressions that I don't understand. But that night I realized that the only person I cared about understanding is *her*.

So I've been painting her on every surface of the room, her body curling around the light fixtures and reclining across the TV screen, and every time I paint her I think I see her a little more clearly.

I work on the precise angle of her lips until my fingers cramp, until other thoughts start to creep in at the edges. I know that I can't spend all night painting – there's work I need to do, work that Victor would expect me to do. Just because he's in a coma doesn't mean I should be slacking off.

I set down my palette, and clean my brushes and knife in the bathroom sink. Then I head out to the sitting room and sit down behind my laptop. With a few keystrokes, I've logged in to my VPN and made certain the hotel has no record of the sites I visit or the keystrokes I make, and then I get to work.

My art is about trying to understand the world. But I don't have to worry about understanding computers. They aren't confusing like people. You tell them to do a thing, and they will do the thing – it's so simple I don't consider it a special skill the way Victor and Cas seem to.

My homepage is filled with articles about the museum

explosion, but I can't read those articles. They're filled with too many assumptions and lies, too much emotional language that makes no sense to me. Instead, I flip back to the security logs and continue where I left off.

I know that Fergie has to hurt Victor and Cas. When she first moved here, Cas would talk about how he'd break her. I've seen Cas break people several times, but I've never felt it *inside* my chest like I did with Fergie. As if he'd broken me, too. And then when Victor wouldn't go to Fergie for the answers…

I know that she has to have her revenge. I know that I've been so entwined with them for years that when she hurts them, it will hurt me too. I'm okay with that. My life doesn't matter.

But Fergie's not the only one out to get the Poison Ivy Club. And we have to know who's behind these attacks. I don't want anyone else to get hurt.

Videos were leaked from the Poison Ivy server, undermining our hold on the school. A parcel bomb was sent to Victor's house. Those people in City Hall, making sure our mothers can't expand their territories. Us getting kicked out of the Olympus Club.

Then, today, the bomb at the museum.

Victor and Cas don't believe this is a coincidence. But I don't care what they believe. I need to *see*. Because a computer won't lie.

I need to figure out who broke through my defenses and lifted those videos of Coach Franklin and Sierra from our server and shared them with everyone. I need to know who else has access to the years of favors and collateral we keep on our server. I peel back the layers of encryption around our logs and search lines of code until I see what I need to see.

But what I see makes no sense.

Computers don't lie. But this…

...this *has* to be a lie.

It can't be the truth. It *can't*.

The videos of Coach Franklin and Sierra were shared from Victor's phone.

14

FERGIE

BANG BANG BANG.

What the fuck is that?

I raise my head off the pillow as I'm pulled rudely back into the land of the living. It took me hours to get to sleep because I kept freaking out about the video, and now some fucker is doing construction at... I slam my finger onto my phone... 4:32AM. Well, he can fuck off into the sun.

"Mew," Spartacus agrees from his snuggly position in the crook of my arm. He doesn't like his sleep being disturbed, either.

The banging is coming from the direction of the sitting room. I throw my hand across the bed and feel a gaping coldness where Torsten's body should be. My stomach twists with fear.

"Torsten, are you okay?" I call out, wishing I'd thought to leave a weapon beside the bed. "Where are you?"

"I'm here."

He falls across the bed and his arms go around me, and I'm so grateful that he does it just because he knows I need it.

BANG. BANG.

All I can think about is that bomb tearing through the museum, and Victor lying in a hospital bed.

Where the fuck is that banging coming from?

"Someone is at the door," Torsten says. "No one is supposed to be able to come up here. I don't know who—"

"Torsten, open this door," Cas' gravelly voice booms through the night. "I need to talk to you."

Ah. I guess we know who's found us.

My fucking stepbrother. Of course.

Torsten doesn't move. He just keeps holding me while Cassius bellows his name over and over. I nudge him gently. "Talk to him through the wall. He's not going to go away."

I wrap the duvet around us, and we creep into the sitting room. I settle on the sofa, pulling the duvet around my naked body and cradling Spartacus in my arms, while Torsten leans against the door.

I mouth the words at Torsten.

"Who is it?" he calls out in his deep, quiet voice.

"Who do you think? The tooth fairy? It's fucking Cassius. I need somewhere to stay. Cali kicked me out, and no one at the gym wants to incur her wrath so they won't let me stay there." He kicks the door again. "Will you hurry up and open this?"

Cali kicked him out? That's interesting. I'm not sure I even believe him.

"I'm not letting you in."

I stand up and move to the door. I feel for Torsten's hand and find it gripping the door handle, the knuckles stretched from the strain of indecision. Cassius has been his friend for so long – it must be killing him to see everything disintegrating.

That's Cassius' fault, not mine.

"What the fuck are you talking about? *Open this door.* You

owe me. I took you in when you couldn't live with Livvie anymore. I let you sleep in my room, in my fucking bed, and I lied to my mother and told her you'd left so you didn't get into even more trouble. You are opening this door *right now*."

I feel Torsten's body tense. He's thinking that Cassius is right, that he did do this for Torsten, and above all else, Torsten believes in doing what's fair. He touches my arm, and I know that I have to save this or that monster will find his way inside.

"We're not interested in what you have to say," I yell.

"That's my sister," Cassius growls. "Fergie's in there with you? What the fuck is she doing here?"

"I'm staying here," I shout back. "So get your own crash pad, because Torsten and I don't want you here."

"Torsten, you can't do this. She's completely fucked up our lives. She made Victor walk into a *bomb*. She lied to us about who she is. The last time I checked, you hate liars."

Cassius hits the door again, and I feel the whole wall rattle. He must be slamming his body into the door, because only the full bulk of an angry grizzly bear could make the hinges groan with the effort of holding on. Any minute now the whole thing is going to cave in.

"I have an idea," I say. "Step out of the way."

Cassius roars and slams into the door again. I let him do it a couple more times, getting a sense for his pattern, and then just as I sense him launching himself at it again, I whip off the security lock and fling the door open.

Cas' roar of outrage turns into one of surprise when he loses control and barrels into the room. He slams into the kitchen unit, knocking over shelves of plates and wine glasses. Shattering sounds fill my ears as crockery and glassware hit the floor.

"You'll pay for this, you bitch," Cas howls from the middle of the chaos.

"Get out," Torsten says, his voice ice.

"Make me," Cas cackles. I hear more glass breaking as he rolls over and drags himself through the suite into the bedroom. We follow him, Torsten helping me around the broken glass decorating the floor.

"Oh, this is a laugh," Cas says. I hear the bed creak as he flops down on it, and there's a cruel smirk in his voice. "This is an absolute fucking comedy of errors."

"You're getting glass in our bed," I say. "And I know you don't give a shit about me, but you're scaring Torsten. Don't think I'm above pushing you out this window, because I'll do it—"

"Oh, Sunflower, you're so naive. You think you're in a safe little cave here with lover boy. But he can hide all sorts of things from you. Do you know what he's painted all over the walls?"

"You know I can't see the walls," I say.

"That so?" I hear the accusation in his voice. "So you have no idea that there's an eight-foot high painting covering this entire wall. It's a painting of *you*. You're naked, and you're smiling, and there's a gaping hole in your chest where your heart should be."

"You're making that up," I mutter. "You and I both know that Torsten only paints famous paintings."

Torsten's body stiffens. His hand flaps frantically – I hear the fabric of his sleeve moving, feel the air shifting. And I remember that he asked me at the ranch if he could draw me. That was unusual, too, but there's a difference between a sketch in a journal and a mural on the wall of a hotel room.

"You painted me?" I ask him.

He makes a choking sound. He wants to speak, but it's too hard for him. I hate that Cassius is causing him distress.

He painted me.

I think it's beautiful, but what do I know? I can't see the painting. I know that's why Torsten didn't tell me – he doesn't want me to feel sad. But now Cas has seen it, and he's determined to ruin this expression of the way Torsten feels about me.

I didn't think it was possible to hate my stepbrother any more than I do, but I was wrong.

"You're his muse, isn't that sweet?" Cassius snarls. "Too bad he thinks you're a cold, heartless bitch, just like everyone else—ow, what the fuck, dude? You stuck a palette knife in my *arm*."

Go, Torsten.

He moves so swiftly from my side that I can't stop him, and I don't want to. I hear them tussle on the bed, and Torsten cries out and Cassius yells, and my chest clenches in fear that Cas might do something to hurt Torsten, so even though I know it's stupid, I hurl myself at them. Cas catches me in midair and slams me into the ground.

Pain shudders through my body. I try to get up, but Cas plants his boot in my back and I'm done for. I know I'm about to draw my last breath, but all I care about is making sure Torsten gets away.

"Run," I gasp out. "Get out now!"

Cassius grinds his boot down on my back with another gleeful cackle, and I feel things popping and grating inside me. Why did I let him in here? I should have known that crashing him into the kitchen wouldn't slow him down. I should have—

But I don't have time to finish the thought because the boot is torn from my spine. I hear a thud, and Cas lets out a grunt. Torsten makes a sound that's almost inhuman, and I don't know what the fuck is going on, but I hear them move into the living room and toward the door. I roll over and crawl to my hands and knees to follow them.

"Don't you ever threaten Fergie ever again," Torsten growls, and his voice is so different, so dark and fucking angry, that chills run down my spine. They fight through the sitting room, over the broken glass in the kitchen, and I hear Torsten howl again as he shoves Cas back into the hallway.

I slam the door in my stepbrother's face just as he crashes into it. In this particular instance, the heavy security door wins against Cas. I hear him grunt again as he bounces off and slides to the floor.

I don't hear him get up again for a long, long time.

We call security.

Torsten and I pull off the top comforter in case it's filled with glass, and we crawl into bed. He turns up the stereo. Nick Cave sings "Stagger Lee" while an entire team of security guys carries my stepbrother off the premises.

Silence stretches between us as we both wrestle with the violation of our safe cocoon.

"Is there really a portrait of me on that wall?" I ask when my heart has stopped thundering against my ribs.

"Yes."

"And I have a piece of coal for a heart?"

"Yes."

"Why?"

Torsten doesn't speak for a long time. I almost think that he's retreated into himself, or that he doesn't understand the question, but finally, he says, "I've always copied the masters because when you peel back the layers, they're all made of the same materials – the same pigments and layers and techniques – but they have so many different things to say if you look carefully. Copying them is like opening up the computer code and seeing how it works. And you're such a beautiful mystery to me that I guess I…"

"You wanted to peel back the layers?"

"Yes."

I swallow the lump that's rising in my throat. "Why is my heart made of coal?"

"It is, isn't it?" His fingers brush my cheek. "That's what you said to me once."

"I thought you didn't understand metaphors."

"No, but I always listen." He wraps his fingers around my wrist, pulling me out of bed. I let him, trusting with my whole body that he means me no harm. He walks me gingerly over the broken things on the floor until I'm standing in front of the wall where he's painted me. He presses my hand against the paper.

I *feel*.

My fingers brush a rough surface – cold and gritty and not like any paint I've ever heard of before.

"Is this my heart?" I ask him.

"I mixed the paint with ground-up coal. And look," Torsten sweeps my hand over the painting. "This is a special medium I mix with the paint. It gives the paint these ridges. Can you feel them?"

"I can." I can feel the sweep and swirl of the lines, the love that he's dedicated to each stroke of the brush. He's made his painting into a sculpture so that I can see it, too.

"Torsten, this is..." I can't even get the words out.

"I wanted you to see yourself the way I see you."

This is how he sees me? My eyes fill with tears as I trace the lines of my own body, looking at myself through Torsten's eyes, curving my fingers around the dip between my breasts and touching the sharp corner of my elbow.

"Oh, Torsten, it's..." I struggle to breathe. "Thank you. Just... thank you."

It's the most beautiful thing that anyone's ever done for me.

He pulls me back from the wall. "I'm not finished yet. I want to work on it more, but you should try to sleep some more. It's almost time for us to leave for school."

School.

Stonehurst Prep.

In just a couple of hours, I have to leave the hotel and walk the halls of that fucking hellhole with my head held high, as hundreds of kids talk shit about the sex video and speculate about Victor's coma. It's enough to make me want to throw myself out that window.

But I'll do it. I'll do it because I'm Fergie Munroe, and I won't let this destroy me.

15

FERGIE

The last thing in the world I want to do is face Stonehurst Prep again, and when I open my eyes an hour later, I debate skipping. But Torsten is agitated and I know it's because I've interrupted his routine, so I decide to give him some space. My only other alternative is to go back to Cali's house, and that doesn't exactly feel safe between the psycho trying to blow up my stepmother and the psycho stepbrother who will happily gut me like a fish.

Besides, Euri and I need the computers in the Sentinel office to begin work on phase one of our revenge plan. And I'm not wasting a single day getting even with Victor and Cas and Juliet.

"You don't have to come with me," I say to Torsten as I help him tie the tie on his school uniform. "I know you'd rather be here."

"Victor would want someone to watch out for you," he says.

"I don't care what Victor wants anymore," I say. "He's dead to me. Do you understand?"

"He's in a coma, which is technically not dead—"

"I know that. I mean that I don't want him in my life

anymore. He didn't fight for me, for us, and that's as bad, or worse, as what Cas did."

Seymour arrives at the hotel to drive us to school. We pick up Euri on the way, and the three of us stroll through the front gates, my arms in theirs, my chin held high. Torsten's stony silence reassures me. I am a rock. Whatever they say about me, it's just words. They might batter me around a bit, but I'll stand strong against a storm.

It's awful. Just walking to my locker through their taunts and whispers is the hardest thing I've ever had to do.

But I do it.

Euri has a study period first thing, and I decide to skip English Lit because what does any of it matter anymore? Torsten refuses to go to his art class, even after I remind him what we're doing.

"I know you still care about them. I know you secretly hope that somehow everything is going to go back to how it was before Saturnalia. But I have to burn it all down. I have to draw a line so I can never go back to what we had before, and that means destroying Cas and Victor and Juliet. I have to *ruin* them. I don't think you want to be part of that."

Torsten squeezes my hand. "If you have to burn it all down, then let me light the match for you."

"That's not all," I say. "You guys have done a lot of bad things as Poison Ivy. I can't go after Vic and Cas without something sticking to you."

"I need to be with you," he says. "What Cas did is wrong. You deserve justice, and if this is how you get justice, then I will help you. I don't matter."

"You do matter. You matter very much."

He walks me to the Sentinel offices. Euri greets us. If she's surprised to see him there, she doesn't say anything. "Have a seat, both of you. I've emptied the vending machine of every remotely delicious food, so we can hole up in here for hours if we need to."

(The vending machines at Stonehurst Prep are filled with weird-ass stuff like kale jerky and nutritional dust. Welcome to California, I guess.)

"Good. I'm starving." I'd been too freaked out to have breakfast at the hotel. I plop down into the chair opposite hers and reach for a rhubarb and carob bar. A seat creaks as Torsten lowers himself into the desk that he usually uses, right at the end of the row, far away from us.

"Okay, so revenge," Euri taps a pen on her notebook. "I can't believe I'm saying this with a straight face, but how do we plan on fucking up Poison Ivy?"

"I'm imagining two phases," I say. "Phase one – we write this article you want to write. An exposé to take down Poison Ivy once and for all. We break the story of the high school club where students pay to lie, cheat, bribe, and beat their way into Ivy League colleges."

Behind me, Torsten's pen scratches across his notepad. He has to know what an article like that would mean for him, but he doesn't say a word.

"Three things I'd like to point out," Euri says. "One, you're aware what an article like this might do to Torsten?"

At least *someone* has noticed.

"Yes. I want to try and leave him out of it as much as possible. He does what Victor and Cas tell him to do, but..."

Euri asks, "Is he aware?"

"I'm aware," Torsten says from across the room. His pencil never stops scratching. "I did wrong things, and I will accept punishment for those. I want to do whatever makes Fergie feel safe again."

"Okay." Euri takes a moment to suck in a breath. "Thing number two – if everything you told me yesterday is true, about your stepmother being some kind of assassin and the club being involved with organized crime... is it dangerous to print something? I want to stop the club from getting people into Ivies who don't deserve it, not put a hit out on my family."

"Didn't you know all of this already when you suggested the article," I ask with a lift of my eyebrow. "You were the one who first hinted to me that something sinister was going on with my stepmother and the club."

"It was all rumors, dark whispers in the corridors. I didn't know any of it for real. I assumed it was all exaggerated to give Poison Ivy street cred – I thought crime families only existed in movies."

"Our parents told us we had to stop the club," Torsten pipes up. "After the parcel bomb."

"Excuse me, what parcel bomb?"

"The one Victor got in the mail."

I spin around in my chair. "Torsten, what are you talking about?"

He makes an exasperated noise in the back of his throat. "Someone sent Victor a parcel bomb. A couple of weeks ago. Claudia's security caught it before it went off. Our parents think it's the same person who has been trying to disrupt their operations. They don't want any extra attention, so they told us that we couldn't have the club anymore."

"And now Cas has released the video of us," I say. "It's going to bring a world of trouble down on their heads, ask me how I know. Do you think that's why Cali kicked him out?"

Torsten doesn't reply.

"Okay," I turn back to Euri. "So it seems as though the only people who are going to get in trouble if this comes out are the ones who deserve it."

"All the same, can you talk to your stepmother and make sure?" Euri's voice pleads. "I can't publish this anonymously. I need my name on it – otherwise, I can't use it for my college application."

"Have you decided where you're applying?"

"Yes. I'm going for an overseas school. Blackfriars, Oxford, Auckland, Melbourne," she says shyly. "Mom and Dad don't have to know until I get my acceptance."

"Good. I heartily approve. And I'll find a way to guarantee our safety before we publish."

"Okay. Good. Thing the third. If we print this article and can get it to make a splash, it's likely that every student connected to Poison Ivy will lose their college place. And that includes you."

There it is – in black and white. The jewel I give up for vengeance.

"I'm okay with that," I say. "This time, I didn't earn my place at Harvard. I won't take it from someone who did."

"Are you sure? Because it's *Harvard*. I don't want you to hate me because I took that away from you."

I am sure. The more I think about it, the more sure I am.

I think a big part of me didn't really believe the boys could get me in. That I'd fucked up my life so badly that not even the Poison Ivy Club could save me. And they swooped in and saved me in all the ways I didn't know I needed saving.

If I'm brutally honest with myself, my Harvard dream died when Coach Franklin assaulted me. I buried it when I listened with glee to a lion tearing him to pieces. I can't peek behind the curtain of the Triumvirate and go back to dreaming of picturesque quads and crowded lecture halls.

My thirst for vengeance is my new desire, and I'll pursue it with all the tenacity I'd reserved for college applications. The Poison Ivy boys are in my bloodstream, and I won't stop until I've made them pay.

"Harvard is dead to me," I say, and I mean every word. "We've burning it all down, Euri. I don't care what happens to my life, because it's already ashes and dust. Got it? And Torsten feels the same way. If you need to reconsider your involvement, then—"

"I'm in this, Fergie. I've got your back. I just wanted to check you've got your eyes wide open, pardon the metaphor." Euri writes something down. "We write the article. And what's phase two?"

"I'm not going to wait until we print the article to get back at Cassius, not while he's still acting like he's perfectly justified in what he did. I'm going after all three of them. Juliet, Victor, and my dear, darling stepbrother. I've been making a list."

I pull my Braille note out of my bag and start reading off my revenge ideas. Euri bursts out laughing when I get to some of the more creative ones, and she can barely contain herself when I add Artie's idea to the list.

"You're diabolical, you know that?"

I grin. "We are going to have so much fun—"

BANG.

I jump at the sound.

"That's someone at the door," Euri says. "Did you invite anyone else to our revenge party?"

"No."

BANG BANG BANG.

Euri stands up, but I grab her arm. "Don't get it, it's probably Cas here to kill me."

"If I get closer..." she slips her arm out of my grasp, "...I can see through the glass in the door. It's Drusilla Hargreaves."

Drusilla? I remember her chilling words at the party. She has her own reasons for wanting Poison Ivy to suffer. You know what they say – the enemy of your enemy is your friend...

"Let her in."

Euri moves around the desk and flings open the door. Drusilla's heels clacks on the tiled floor as she storms over to our little war council.

"Hey, Euri, Fergie. I came looking for you as soon as I saw... Oh, hello, Torsten."

I can hear the credulity in her voice.

"Drusilla." Her name comes out like a hiss.

"You seriously want him here?"

"He had nothing to do with the video being released," I say.

"So?" Drusilla sinks into Euri's chair. "He's their trained lapdog."

"Don't call him that."

"I'll call him what I like. Torsten never says boo to a goose, but he's just as dangerous as the other two because he can hack into any computer system, can't you, doll? If Victor demands it, this guy will change your grades, and if you hurt his friends, he'll give you a record that means no college will ever want to touch you."

"You hurt Cassius," Torsten says with surprising conviction. I know the words are the truth as Torsten sees them. Drusilla hurt his friend, so whatever they did to her was justice.

Drusilla sounds as though she doesn't give a shit about anything anymore. And I can very much relate to that sentiment.

"You're here to hurt Cassius, too," I remind him.

"That's different."

"All I'm saying is that I find it hard to believe he's not behind the video," Drusilla says with a smirk in her voice. "I mean, you *were* behind Fergie at one point."

"Dru," Euri barks. But I just laugh. Torsten keeps on scribbling and doesn't say a word. I take his silence for his trust. He's doing exactly what he promised. He's letting me do what I need to do, even if it means listening to Drusilla.

"All right, fine. Chill out, Jones. I didn't come to pick a fight." The office chair creaks as she wheels herself closer. "Fergie, my offer to you still stands. My sole purpose in returning to this school is to take down Poison Ivy, and I'm guessing that now you understand why. If you want to join forces with me, I'm all for it."

"I'm interested," I say. "But I need answers first. I need to know what they did to you."

"I assumed you already knew."

"All I've been given are vague hints that are something to do with their old girlfriend, Gemma, and Gaius Dio." I set my Braille note on the desk and lean forward in my chair. "But I think we both know Victor and Cassius have a way of twisting the truth, of making themselves into the heroes when really they're the villains. So I want to hear it from you."

"She's not—" Torsten starts, but I hold up my hand.

"I think you need to hear it from Drusilla, too," I say. "We listen, and then we decide what we believe."

Drusilla reaches across the table and grabs one of our carob bars. The wrapper crinkles as she opens it. I let her chew, my nails digging into the arm of my chair. Beside me, Euri sits on the edge of the desk, tapping her pen on her notebook. I know she's as intrigued as I am.

Torsten draws, but I can feel the tension rolling off him. He doesn't like this, doesn't like being close to someone he feels justified in hating.

"Our story begins in freshman year at Stonehurst Prep," Drusilla says in a deep voice, like she's narrating a fairy tale. "Gemma and I are best friends – we have been since first grade. Our families live on the same street. We holiday on the Amalfi Coast together. We borrow each other's clothes and paint our nails the same color. You get the idea. Anyway, Gaius Dio is a senior, and he's king of the school. All the girls want to fuck him, and all the guys want to be part of his group. He has this reputation as a kind of school vigilante – a Robin Hood with a Porsche 911. The rumor goes that Gaius has this secret club made up of some other senior boys and some shady people from the wrong side of town, and if you give him what he asks for, he'd beat up, threaten, or extort whoever was making trouble for you. A lot of girls say they hire him to get rid of creepo boyfriends or handsy stepfathers, and they happily pay in pussy. Gaius is good at choosing the jobs that increase his social status and make him even more popular and beloved. He might be a brute, but that boy could play the game. He was decent to look at, too." Drusilla smacks her lips together. "He should have been a politician. He certainly reminds me of my mother."

I rest my elbows on my knees, more interested than I'd like to admit in this part of Cas' life that I've never been privy to. This is the most anyone has ever told me about Gaius Dio. All I know about him is that he used to sleep in my bedroom, and he's currently in jail. I thought I was getting closer to Cas trusting me enough to open up about him, but now that bridge is razed to the ground, I can get what I need from Drusilla.

"What was Cas like with his brother?" I ask before I can stop myself. I'm so used to him as the muscle of Poison Ivy. I want to understand him as someone's little brother, since he never acted like a brother to me.

"Even at thirteen, Cas was enormous. And tough. He kind of acted as Gaius' bodyguard, the same way he is around Victor and Torsten. He idolized Gaius, of course. He'd throw himself at anyone who even questioned his older brother's word. It's weird, because most people are pretty sure that they're not blood brothers."

That got my attention. "What?"

"Oh, right, you might not have noticed," Dru says. "Cas looks like Cali – it's obvious from his bone structure and his skin that he shares her Ghanian heritage. But Gaius was as white as a ghost. Was he even Cali's son? There were rumors, but you don't say that to a Dio unless you want to end up six feet under."

Euri furiously scribbles notes beside me. I lean back in my chair, taking that in. I had an inkling from things he's said that Torsten isn't Livvie's biological son, either. In crime families, blood means everything. I wonder if Gaius' paternity is a reason for that bomb at the museum, although that wouldn't explain the parcel bomb sent to Victor.

For that matter, who the fuck *is* Cas' father? My vicious stepbrother never mentions him, and neither does Cali. She appears to have sole custody of Cas. Is this an angle we've considered—

No. *No.*

I don't care about Cas' Daddy issues, and the Triumvirate's problems are no longer my concern. The only thing I care about is making them *pay.* I tune back into what Drusilla's saying.

"—It was an open secret that Cas was one of the guys who did the dirty work for his brother's little club. He once beat up a senior lacrosse player so bad that the guy had permanent brain damage – but he did drug and date-rape a girl, so no one gave Cas up. The guy's parents even convinced the police that he'd accidentally fallen down the stairs. That was the power of Gaius Dio."

"I remember that," Euri says. "The girl he assaulted was a friend of Artie's."

"Exactly. At the time, we thought Gaius was doing a good thing. And because Cas was Gaius' brother, he and Victor and Torsten were automatically part of their group. Cas loved being the thug, but you could see Victor found the whole thing a bit uncouth. Victor August walked around like he was the Prince of fucking Persia, above all of it, above Stonehurst Prep, above all Gaius' nonsense. He was going to be valedictorian, go to Harvard, and I think he was nervous about Gaius fucking up his plans. But he wouldn't leave Cas' side, so if Cas hung out with Gaius, then so did Vic."

"How did Gemma become part of all this?"

I've heard her name come up before, but none of them want to talk about her. And that makes me even more interested in who she is and what she meant to them. I've never been jealous of the idea of Gemma, but I'm intrigued by how she made them into who they are.

"My poor best friend got tangled up in their mess," Dru says. "Gemma's parents are... they're *cruel*. They're both high court judges, and they expected Gemma to be their perfect little angel. Anything less than perfect grades wasn't acceptable. She was president of every club, on the junior varsity field hockey team, captain of the swim team, in the debate society, and the Model UN. Her schedule was *insane*, and she was always stressed about a test or a meet or a tournament. I think that's why she liked hanging out with me – don't get me wrong, I care about school-work. I wanted to go to a fancy school and get as far away from this shithole and my mother as I could, but I also know how to have fun."

The more Drusilla talks, the more I think that if I'd met her and Gemma in freshman year, I would have liked them both a lot.

"So Gemma's facing all this pressure at home, and her work is piling up, and I guess she's starting to feel overwhelmed. But I didn't know that. She never talked about any of it. I was trying to get her to loosen up a bit, so I dragged her to a party at Vic's house, and she got talking to Vic and they hit it off. They were both intense and competitive. I thought it was good for her, you know, to see that guys like him also had a social life. Only what happened is that he told Gemma that he could fix all her problems for her, and she jumped on it.

"Gemma goes to Gaius on Vic's advice, and she says that she needs to be top of the class list. And Gaius hands it over to Cas to take care of. So Cas starts hanging out with Gemma, trying to figure out how to make her top of the class, because it's not exactly his specialty. And somewhere in there, the two of them start dating her."

"I remember," Euri says. "The three of them would walk down the hallway, and everyone had to jump out of their way. And they'd make out all over that table in the library. It was so gross."

I don't say a thing. My body still burns with the memory of what it means to be owned by Vic and Cassius. I can imagine Gemma was having a hell of a lot of fun.

"For a while, everything was good. We'd go to their parties on the weekends, and because Gemma was dating both of them, we'd sit at their table in the special glass fishbowl. And Gemma's grades were consistently perfect, even though she was spending all her time with the two of them and none of it studying.

"At first, I thought she'd just learned to relax more. I was so naive. I didn't see all the warning signs until it was far too late. I liked the popularity I earned by association, and I let my own shit get in the way. I was a bad friend, and I own that."

"Too late for what?"

"Gemma started ditching classes. She stopped paying attention to her coursework. Her grades were still perfect, but I knew there was no way she was keeping up. And it wasn't long before other people noticed, too – this is an ultra-competitive school, after all. I know now that Cas and Victor were doing it all behind the scenes, making sure the teachers knew that Gemma had to pass. But at the time it made no sense. I thought she was using study drugs.

"There was this new kid in our class, Konrad. He was an exchange student from Russia. He didn't understand the way American schools worked, all the cliques and things. He had to keep top grades or he'd lose his scholarship and he wouldn't be able to stay in America, so he was kind of annoying and competitive. He was in a lot of the same clubs as Gemma, and he started making noise about her not being as good as her grades implied. To teachers. To the staff. When his complaints fell on deaf ears, he went to Gemma's parents."

Behind me, Torsten's scribbles grow more urgent.

"He told them that he was a friend of Gemma's, and he was worried about her, that he thought she was struggling under the pressure. He brought up study drugs, too. And so Gemma's parents take a closer look at their precious daughter, and they find cocaine in her bedroom. They're terrified of what all their rich, perfect friends will say when they find out that their daughter has become a wild, uncontrollable animal. So they threaten to pull Gemma out of Stonehurst Prep and send her to an all-girls convent school, far far away, if she doesn't get her act together.

"Gemma doesn't want to leave Emerald Beach. She cries to me, but all I can do is rant and swear about how awful her parents are. So she cries to Victor and Cas. And Cas had his orders – Gemma will top the Stonehurst Prep freshman class, no matter what.

"So he calls up Konrad and Gemma's parents and tells them that he's from the school, that they're having a meeting about Gemma's grades and Konrad's complaints. He tells them it'll be in the old horticulture building down at the end of campus. I don't know if you've seen it, but it's kind of hidden away in the trees. It's a weird place for a meeting, but no one questions it.

Gemma's parents show up there for the meeting dressed in their finest clothing, ready to lay down the law on this Konrad kid. And as soon as they step inside, Cassius locks the door behind them. And he lights a fire."

"Shit," I say.

Drusilla keeps going, her dusky voice wavering a little. "Gemma's parents managed to break a basement window and get out, but Konrad wasn't so lucky. He was trapped under a fallen beam. He died in the fire."

Drusilla grabs another candy bar and opens it with more force than is necessary.

"The funny thing is, despite all the evidence that the fire was deliberately set and that the three of them had been lured there by these phone calls from someone pretending to be from the school, and even though Cas was *arrested* at the site and taken to jail, the police determined that the fire was accidental."

It's... a lot to take in. I know my stepbrother has done terrible things. What he's just done to me feels like the most awful thing in the universe, but this is... next level.

Killing Coach Franklin is one thing – no one will miss that scumbag – but Konrad was a kid. He came to this country looking for a better life, and because he crossed the path of Cassius Dio, he ends up worm food. It's sick.

"Where was Vic in all this?" I ask. "And Torsten?"

"I didn't know about it," Torsten says. I hear a ping as his pencil lead snaps and flings against the desk.

"Vic didn't know, either. This was all Cas trying to impress his brother. But Vic is the one who stepped in and arranged everything with the police and the school. Even back then he was smoothing over Cas' mistakes."

"So Cas just got away with this?"

"Almost." There's a cruel smile in her voice. "I was there that night. I have a video of Cas lighting the fire. I was just so angry about Konrad that I leaked the video on social media. Then the cops *had* to do something. They had Cassius in custody, but Gaius was the one who went to jail for it."

"How did that happen? If the police saw Cas in the video..."

"That's just the thing – you see Cas walk around one side of the building, and then come back with a hoodie on that's covering his face. I know it's him because I saw him, but in the video, it could be anyone. Which is what his lawyer argued. And Gaius confessed that he'd been the one wearing the hoodie, the one who set the fire."

"What did you say in court?" I ask. "Surely your eyewitness testimony counts for something?"

Dru snorts. "It was made *very clear* to me by Cali Dio when she climbed in my window one night and held a knife to my throat, that I would explain to the police that I'd been mistaken, that I *could* have seen Gaius that night. She must've known Gaius was lying, but she wanted him in jail instead of Cas. But the thing is, if Cas had gone down for it, he'd have been tried as a juvenile and got a smaller sentence, but Gaius was eighteen. An adult. He's serving a long sentence. And he was definitely the more clever of the two brothers. So why would Cali want to send him away?"

I imagine my stepmother wearing a white fishtail dress and kissing my father while a buck-toothed Elvis impersonator leers in the background. "I have no idea why my stepmother does anything she does."

"Both Cali and Victor August made it clear that after I gave my testimony, I'd be leaving Stonehurst Prep, and that I could not ever return or have any contact with her boys ever again. And so I enrolled at Acheron. The next year, Victor takes over Poison Ivy from Gaius and completely changes the way it operates because Victor August has *standards*. But has it changed, really? It's still Cassius Dio doing the dirty work. No matter how good my grades are, my transcript never shows as being good enough for the colleges I want. That's Victor August's standards. I did everything he wanted and I'm still punished for it."

"And Gemma?" I ask, dreading the answer. "What happened to her?"

"She heard about the fire, and she knew exactly who was responsible. She sent me this voice message." Drusilla clicks on a file on her phone and lays it on my knees, speaker pointing up.

"Hey... Dru?" A girl's voice crackles through the speaker. She sounds distressed. "I just heard that Konrad's dead. Konrad *died*. He was in a fire at the old horticulture building with my parents and... I've been at the hospital but they won't let me see Mom and Dad. No one will tell me anything, but I know Konrad died because of what I asked Gaius to help me top the class, and my parents... they've been right all along. They're better off without me screwing up their lives. So are you, Dru. So is everyone. I've been thinking about this for a while – I can't fight who I am. I'm evil, and bad things happen to people because of me. You're all better off without me. I just wanted to say that I love you, that you're the best friend I could ever ask for, and that I'm so so sorry."

Well, *shit*.

"Gemma jumped off the Tartarus Bridge," Dru says. "She hit the water so hard it crushed her bones. She died instantly."

She jumped off a bridge.

My body reacts to this with a jolt that nearly knocks me out of my chair. Gemma killed herself and I just listened to her suicide note, and it's exactly the same way I intended to—

The world spins. My stomach lurches as bile rises in my throat. I feel my body kind of... melt, but I don't feel anything else until a warm arm goes around me.

"Fergie?" Torsten sounds so worried. "You slid off your chair. I don't understand."

But I can't answer him. I'm somewhere else. I'm standing on the Witchwood Falls bridge, my arms wrapped around my freezing body as the water rushed beneath me. I throw my arms wide and picture myself leaping off the edge and flying like a bird before dropping into the waters – a baptism to cleanse me of my sins.

It's a terrible coincidence that the last girl Victor and Cassius shared killed herself in the same way I'd contemplated...

I *feel* her in my bones and sinews and veins, this girl whose one mistake was falling for the wrong guys. And I'm more determined than ever that for her, for Gemma, we will bring down Poison Ivy.

I shake my head. "I'm not okay, but it's nothing to do with you. I want our vengeance to be for Gemma, too."

"And for Konrad," Dru adds. "I've kept my end of the bargain. I've stayed away from Stonehurst Prep and tried to forget, but Poison Ivy never lets you forget. Konrad's screams haunt me. That guy should be the one getting his Ivy League acceptance, not Victor fucking August. My best friend should be Harvard-bound, not you, Fergie. Poison Ivy is *evil*. And I'm not going to stop until the whole world knows that."

"What's changed?" I ask. "If you're in danger here, why did you come back? I heard you at their party. Why aren't you afraid of them anymore?"

"I met someone," she says. "Someone who has a secret that can destroy not only the Poison Ivy Club but bring down the entire Triumvirate. I assume you know what the Triumvirate is?"

Dru knows about the Triumvirate? This can't be good.

"We know," Euri says. "And I assume they're not your mother's biggest fans."

"Don't you worry your pretty little head about the mayor's office, Eurydice. They won't touch or my mother while we're under *his* protection. And that means that I can protect you, too. But fair's fair – we're going to need some help from Fergie."

"Who's this guy?" I snap. I'm sick of knowing half the truth about things. "And what's this big secret?"

"His name is Zack Lionel Sommesnay," she says. "And his secret belongs to him."

16

FERGIE

Behind me, Torsten drops his pencil.

"Huh, that's a weird name," I say.

"He's a weird guy," she says. "He's German. Kinky, too. I've got bruises on my ass you wouldn't *believe*. I saw the video, so I know you can relate."

Euri chokes on her Mallomar. My cheeks flush with heat.

I hear Torsten's notebook clatter on the floor, and a moment later Dru cries out as he grabs her chair.

"You know Zack Lionel Sommesnay?" he rasps.

"Torsten, back off." I fix him with a sightless glare. "How do *you* know this guy?"

"His name's come up in my research. He's been buying up real estate my mother had earmarked for new clubs, and he's been blocking other things that Claudia and Cali want to do, through City Hall and other official means. He's deliberately making trouble for the Triumvirate, but no one knows why or who he is. Cali has been trying to ferret him out for months. And Drusilla has walked in here and given him to us." His voice turns cold. "I don't like lies."

"There's no lie here," Dru says with a smirk in her voice. "I'm an open book."

Are you, or are you the book of Satanic Verses?

Ooof, Victor would have liked that one.

"Okay," I say slowly, trying to give myself time to draw myself away from thoughts about Vic lying in a hospital bed, about him choosing his relationship with Cas and his mother over me. "Where did you meet this Zack Sommersby guy?"

"Sommes*ney*, and he's been helping my mother on her 'clean up Emerald Beach' campaign," Drusilla says. "I work in the mayor's office sometimes – it looks good on the college resume, not that it helped with early admissions. Despite perfect grades and top recommendations, I didn't get into my EA schools. I wonder why that could be?"

"You hurt Cassius," Torsten snarls, confirming what Drusilla clearly already figured out – that they sabotaged her, even after she did everything they asked.

"He hurt himself," she shoots back. "Anyway, Zack and I got talking in the office and realized we're united against the same enemy. And now we're offering our help to you, if you want it. You don't have to agree now. All you have to do is meet with him."

I turn in my chair to face Torsten. "Do you want to meet this guy?"

His pencil scratches across the page. I know that learning about Zack Lionel Sommesnay has upset him, and I think he's not going to answer me, but without stopping his sketch, he says, "I want to do what you want."

"What if I don't know what I want?" I say, only half-kidding.

"I'll tell you what, If you're in, meet me at my car after school on Thursday and I'll take you to meet Zack. If not..." Dru stands and pats my knee. "Good luck, Fergie. And happy hunting."

17

FERGIE

The next two days at school are about what you expect. People stop talking the moment I step into class. They whisper in the hall as I move things in my locker. The words I said to the guys haunt me through the pity, the silence, and the secret laughter the other students barely try to disguise.

I wouldn't survive it if it weren't for Torsten. He remains at my side every moment, even sitting with me in the classes that he's not in. No one will say a word while he's around, and insults roll off him like water off a duck's feathers, which is a silly thing Dad says sometimes.

The one blessing is that Cassius and Juliet aren't at school. I assume they're with Victor, but maybe they don't want to face the chaos they wrought. Cowards.

I hope Victor's okay, and then I catch myself hoping and I remember the video.

I hope he's fucking *dead*.

Victor August talks a big game about being the protector, the man with the impeccable moral code. But when I needed him most, he left me alone to deal with the most brutal, terrible thing that's ever happened to me because he values his mother's truth over mine.

Just because he's in a coma doesn't mean he's not culpable. They all deserve to pay.

On Thursday, Euri meets me and Torsten after my final class. "What have you decided about Drusilla?" she asks. "I'll go with whatever you think."

Torsten squeezes my hand. "I will stand with you."

"I think it's worth meeting this guy. If he's here to mess with the Triumvirate, then we can help each other. And it wouldn't hurt to know who your mother is up against." I squeeze Torsten's hand back. "Who knows? That might be leverage we can use in the future."

"It took you long enough. I was just about to leave," Drusilla huffs as she opens the door to her Bentley and gives me a shove inside. "I don't like hanging around this school. Too open."

"What are you afraid of?" I scoff as I struggle to pull on my safety belt. Beside me, Euri drops her bag on the seat, and Torsten folds his long legs into the front. "No one is going to put a bullet in your ass in the middle of the parking lot."

"You know that for a fact, do you?" She tears out of the parking space before I've even pulled my door shut. "Cassius Dio would love nothing more than to see me bleed out in front of everyone. Granted, Victor's more of a guns-drawn-at-dawn kind of guy, but I heard he's currently a vegetable, so…"

Dru must see my face, because she doesn't finish her sentence. Instead, she speeds through Harrington Hills, tearing around the corners with such reckless disregard for human life that Euri and I yell funeral plans at each other in case one of us doesn't survive.

At long fucking last, we pull into a sweeping driveway. I smell fragrant oleander bushes as Drusilla slows to a stop outside a large building I assume is her house. She ushers us inside, through a series of large rooms and halls onto a bright verandah enclosed on three sides by glass. The air smells fresh and heavy with moisture, and I hear birds twittering in the trees outside. I think it's lovely until it occurs to me how much Victor would love it, and then I want nothing more than to get the fuck away from all the fragrant plants and taunting birdies.

I sense another person with us, a stranger, waiting at the other end of the room.

A chair scrapes back from a table. A deep voice says, "Fergie Munroe. I've heard many things."

The voice is familiar. It takes me a few moments to remember where I've heard it before. "You were at the Olympus Club," I say. "When we got kicked out. You hide your German accent."

"This is true." He lets down the affected American, allowing his thick German accent to shine through. "It is sometimes not best to let people see who you really are."

"I couldn't agree more."

Behind me, the door closes with a click. "We can talk privately," Drusilla says as she turns a lock. "No one else is home, and Zack has already swept the room for bugs."

"I'll do my own check," Torsten says. He moves around the space, tapping away at an app on his phone that looks for secret recording devices. He returns to my side and announces that the space is clear.

I can't help but wonder why this guy we're seeing is so happy to have Torsten here if he knows that Torsten is Livvie's son. Won't he just assume Torsten will tell his mother everything?

"Would you like to sit down?" Zack Lionel Sommesnay says. He sounds older than us, maybe mid-twenties? His voice is deep and lyrical, and I see why Drusilla has a thing for him. "We have iced tea and pretzels. Drusilla thinks they make me feel at home, but truthfully they are nothing like the pretzels in Germany. At least those were made of bread." He bangs one on the table for emphasis. "These... these could be fired from a Civil War cannon."

I pull out a chair and sit down, leaning my cane against my leg and feeling for the edge of the table. Drusilla pushes a glass of iced tea into my hands. Torsten takes out his notebook and starts scribbling.

Euri floats over my shoulders, jiggling nervously. But I sense that her reporter's mind is storing every nugget of information for later.

"Drusilla showed me your video that went up on the internet yesterday," he says. "I did not watch it. It makes me angry to know men have treated you this way."

Him saying this makes my stomach lurch. Not because I don't believe him, but because it reminds me of all the people who *have* seen it. For the rest of my life, every time I walk into a room, every time I shake someone's hand or are introduced to a new person, I'll wonder if they've seen me screaming in a sex swing while my stepbrother grinds his cock into my ass.

I cut off that line of inquiry before he goes any further. "I know who's responsible – Cassius Dio. Juliet August, and Victor August. I will make them pay."

"I believe it," he says with a chuckle. "Dru warned me that you're a firecracker. I don't doubt that you will achieve what you set out to do. She's brought you to me because we're here for the same purpose. You wish to destroy the teenagers—"

"—not Torsten," I clarify, nodding in the direction of my scribbling artist. "He had nothing to do with it."

"—and I am here to destroy their parents." Bitterness mars his voice, making his German accent even more pronounced. "I believe we might be able to help each other, for our goals are intertwined."

"I'm not in the habit of asking for help," I say. "I believe in doing my own dirty work."

The wonderful chewing sound Clarence made when he devoured Coach Franklin flitters inside my skull, and I'm reminded of that one time when I let three men do my revenge for me, and how amazing it felt to be the one being taken care of. But that was a one-off, never-to-be-repeated.

"As do I, Fergie Munroe. I suspect you and I have more in common than you might believe. We both grew up with disadvantages, with things that made us different from others. And we both know exactly what we want from life, and are not afraid of what we have to do to get it."

"You know a lot about me." I lean back in my chair. "And I know nothing about you."

"There is not much to know. I was born and raised in Germany, in the Franconia region of Bavaria. My father was not in the picture, and my mother was a victim of the New Triumvirate's grab for power. They killed her before I was barely out of the womb and left me in the hands of the German care system, where I lived in violent, abusive care homes until I turned eighteen. I have spent every moment of my life building up a considerable fortune in the Bitcoin market and amassing a network of favors and contacts across the globe, and all of it for one reason – so that I might have the means to bring down the Triumvirate and save future kids the heartache I've experienced. It will be my mother's legacy. I think you can relate to this?"

His voice cracks. I can tell he loves her deeply, this mother he barely remembers. My coal-heart softens to him, just a tiny bit. I lost my mother too early, too, and I think about her as little as possible, because if I think too much it hurts more than I can bear.

Drusilla coos at Zack, nuzzling him, trying to build up the sympathy, and just like that, my suspicion radar is picking up enemy vessels. I'm about to leave, but Zack's attention has been diverted from me.

"You," he says, and it takes me a moment to realize that he's addressing Torsten. "I know who you are. You're the Little Artist."

"That's Torsten *Lucian*," Drusilla says. "As in, Livvie Lucian's son."

"He's not her son, though," Zack says. "Your friend here was a missing person's case in Norway a few years ago. It was on all the news channels in Europe. 'Young boy gone missing from his mother's hip Oslo apartment.' He'd been drawing in his bedroom when someone came into the house and abducted him. This is why the press dubbed him the Little Artist. A torn charcoal drawing was all that remained on the scene. It looked like a decently good render of a Constable. The police found a partial bootprint that matched boots owned by the mother's ex-husband, but the boots were a popular variety, and with nothing else to go on, the case was dropped. And so, you forgive my surprise to see the Little Artist here in California."

I whirl around. Torsten is still drawing furiously in his book as if he hasn't even heard what Zack said.

Is that his story? Did his father steal him from his mother? How did he end up here, in America, with Livvie?

What has it done to him to live with that knowledge?

I reach out to Torsten and close my hands over his whirring wrist, forcing him to put the pen down. "Torsten, I need you to talk to me. Is what Zack said true?"

"Yes."

He says it so flatly, as though it doesn't matter. To him, it probably doesn't. But it matters to me.

"Can you tell me, if you were taken from your mother, how come you ended up with Livvie?"

"Livvie Lucian won me from my father in a poker game," Torsten says, in a voice that's flat and bored and implies that he'd prefer to be left alone to his drawings. I think about all the times he's said that she's not his mother. I assumed he meant because he'd disowned her, but this is Torten we're talking about – he meant it as the literal truth.

Livvie took him from his family, and he knows that. He has a mother somewhere in Europe who never got to see this beautiful man grow up, and that is the worst fucking crime here. My mind burns with questions, but I don't want to push him to answer, especially not in front of Zack and Dru and Euri, so I drop my grip on him.

"That's it?" Zack asks. He sounds a little brassed-off. "You still trust him? How do you know he's loyal to you? How do *I* know that he won't go running straight to Mummy with everything we've shared today?"

"You should ask him yourself," I snap. "He can hear you just fine. And I'll ask you the same question. How do I know I can trust *you*? How do I know you aren't a spy for Cassius?"

He pushes something across the table to me. "Take this."

I pick it up. It's a bunch of papers tied together. "Obviously I can't read this. What is it?"

"It's a deed of sale. I've had Drusilla email it to your school address, so you can read it on your device. It gives you ownership of a Tartarus Oaks building that I purchased out from underneath Olivia Lucian. I'm giving it to you as a gesture of good faith."

"Wait, you're giving me a building?"

What the fuck is this guy's game?

"Chill out, it's not an exciting building," Dru says. "It's just a bunch of offices, mostly empty. There's also a Chinese takeout on the ground floor. They do an excellent kung pao chicken."

I'm not going to take their word for it. I hand the papers to Euri, lean back in the chair, cross my boots on the table, and pull up the email. As my screen reading software reads out the deed to me, my mind whirs.

I own a building? How the fuck did this happen?

And what will happen if Livvie finds out? I don't have Cas and Victor's protection any longer.

The reality of my current situation hits me. *I might be Cali's stepdaughter, but if anyone in the Triumvirate finds out I'm sitting here with Zack Lionel Sommesnay, and that he's given me a building that was supposed to belong to Livvie...*

"That document looks legitimate," Euri says as she flicks through the pages. "And I just did a property search on the City Hall website. The address is listed under your name. You own that building, Fergie."

I reach across and squeeze Torsten's hand. I wondered why Zack was so willing to allow him to be here, and now I know. He's made certain that Torsten can't talk.

It starts to sink in just how fucking dangerous this game is. I've been so caught up in thoughts of vengeance that I hadn't stopped to think about what teaming up with Drusilla might actually mean.

My fingers itch to throttle Sommesnay.

He's done this on purpose, the sneaky bastard. He's given me an expensive gift, sure, but he's also made sure that I'm tied to him now. If I tell anyone about this meeting or reveal what I know about him to the Triumvirate, he'll make sure that my stepmother knows whose name is on that deed, and why.

And doesn't even matter if I spit in his face and walk away right now – if Livvie finds out I own this building, I'm dead.

This building isn't a gift – it's a noose around my neck.

I decide that my best course of action is to feign the innocent blind girl. It's easy to do – people assume that because I'm blind, I'm also stupid, and in this instance I intend to play that to my advantage. I slip my phone back into my pocket and smile at the snake across the table, like I'm pleased with his fucking gift.

"Okay," I flick my long hair over my shoulder. "So you gave me a building. What now? Do I have to give you a lap dance in return?"

He laughs. "Nothing like that, Fergie. This building is simply my guarantee, is all. I truly do believe we can help each other."

I drum my fingers on my thigh. "If we could make this snappy, I have revenge plans to get back to. Tell me what you – a multi-billion-dollar international businessman – need from a blind nineteen-year-old Harvard wannabe in the midst of a sex-tape scandal?"

"We need someone inside Cali Dio's house," Zack says. "I have tried to place a spy on her domestic staff, but she's had the same live-in chef, valet, and cleaning lady forever, and they're fiercely loyal. But having her stepdaughter and her son's closest friend feeding us information would be even more valuable."

"Why her house? Why not the gym in Tartarus Oaks? That's where she runs the business, right?"

"Your stepmother is much too clever for that. Cali keeps that gym and its associated businesses squeaky clean. Her real enterprise is obviously carried out wherever a job needs to be done, but she requires a room where she can interrogate her marks, and where she stores her weapons and records. These hiding places exist in various locations all over the world, and my intelligence has led me to believe one is somewhere inside her Emerald Beach property."

I snort. "Right, my stepmother, the most notorious assassin in the world, brings her torturing home with her. That I believe. Do you think she does a little flagellation at the dinner table?

Pulls off people's tonsils while she's on the john? It's ridiculous. There's nothing like that going on in—"

"Three staff members in my mother's office have been subjected to a Cali Dio interrogation as the Triumvirate try to uncover intelligence about Lionel here," Drusilla says. "Thankfully, no one except for my mother and I have met him, so they couldn't tell her anything. Two of them will never regain the use of their voices, but from the scant details the third could give us, we know that these interrogations happened in Emerald Beach, in a residential building, most likely Cali's home."

Wait a second... "You mean Cali's bringing people back to her house to torture them? I've never heard anything like that going on."

"She will keep everything well hidden. Which is why we need you."

I tap my cane. "In case you haven't noticed, I'm *blind*. I'm not exactly great at ferreting out secret hideaways."

"I ask nothing so arduous," Zack says. "I simply need information. The layout of the rooms within her home, transcripts of conversations, descriptions of any strange behaviors—"

"Everything Cali does is strange."

"—her comings and goings. Who she visits. Who visits her. That kind of thing."

"But what will you use this information for? I mean, you're looking to take down a criminal organization, right? Well, good fucking luck. Cali isn't just going to hand you her empire. She's not going to go quietly into the good night. You and I both know this thing ends in bloodshed, so why would you think I'd want to put myself in the middle of that?"

My fingers itch as I remember the feel of Victor's warm skin beneath mine as he lies in that hospital bed, alive but not alive. I think of the revenge list sitting in a file on my Braille note.

I'm already in the middle of it.

"Your stepmother is an evil woman, Fergie. She kills people for money, and she enjoys it," Zack says. "Do you think she deserves to live? What about Claudia August? Or Livvie Lucian, the woman who stole a boy from his family?"

I don't know how to answer that question. I'm remembering Clarence again, how he crunched on Coach Franklin, and when he swallowed, he swallowed down all that rage I was holding inside. I never would have been able to pick myself up again after what Franklin did to me if it wasn't for the Poison Ivy boys and the Triumvirate.

Making Cas, Victor, and Juliet pay is one thing, but betraying Cali? My dad? Destroying the Triumvirate? I don't think I want to do that.

Somewhere along the way, my moral code got jammed. I'm in just as deep as all of them. And I have no desire to dig my way out.

I swing my feet off the table. "I'm sorry. We can't help you."

"I don't understand," Drusilla says angrily. "This is what you want!"

"Cali is my stepmother, and I'm not spying on her for you." I pick up my cane and fling my bookbag over my shoulder. "You can keep your building. Euri, Torsten, let's go."

"Wait."

A hand closes around my wrist. The fingers are large, masculine, but soft. I remember the way Cas' fingers felt against my bare skin, rough from the work he does for his mother, calloused and laced with scars from his hours in the ring. I hate how much my stomach twists with longing.

I break Sommesnay's grip with a flick of my wrist, but I keep facing him. "Why am I waiting?"

"You don't want to help me now. That's fine. You may change your mind. But let me prove to you that we're on the same side. Let me give you something that you need for your own ends, no strings attached." He lifts my hand, unfolding my fist so my palm lays flat. He traces his finger over my exposed palm. "There must be something that I can do to help you get your revenge."

Fuck it.

"Yes," I say. "Actually, there is."

18

VICTOR

"... Victor... brother... come back to me..."

My sister calls me.

Juliet? Juliet, are you okay?

I can't see her. All I can see and feel is darkness. The kind of darkness that's so complete it feels like a blanket weighing you down. I try to move my limbs, but they're pinned by the gloom.

"I had to leave behind everything I was to come here, and I've got nothing left," I hear Fergie say, but I don't think she's talking to me. I think this is a memory of a conversation we never had, but before I can grasp the memory and pull it close, it's consumed by my sister's wails.

Juliet, where are you?

She sounds so far away, and it's my job to look after her. Where is she? I can't let them take her again. I have to protect her. I can't fail her again.

My eyelids flutter. Bright light stabs through the darkness. My head explodes with pain. I cry out and shut them, but the bright light is still there. My sister keeps calling me, but this time she sounds closer. Someone pats my arm.

"Victor, you're in there! I know you're in there! Don't panic.

I'm right here, and so is Mommy and all our dads, and Galen, too. You're going to be okay. Galen says that you might not be able to move immediately, but you're awake. OMG, you're awake."

None of the words make any sense. I open my eyes again to splotches of colored light. The colors wiggle and coalesce into a fuzzy image. A corner of Galen's clinic with the curtain pulled around the bed, machines beeping crazily. And crowded around me, my parents and my sister. Juliet drapes herself over me, but I don't feel her weight, just this dull, numb sensation of something warm brushing my skin.

What's going on? What's happened?

I open my mouth to ask the thousands of questions pummeling my brain, but I can't seem to control my lips or make any sound happen. My mother throws her arms around me, and this time I feel her touch as a strange fire dancing over my skin.

"You're awake." She buries her head into my shoulder. "Victor August, don't you *ever* do that to us again."

Do what?

I try to remember, but my brain is made of cotton candy. I remember being in the museum, running through the hall of Roman statues. I remember a feeling of dread clenching my heart, the same feeling I had the day they took Juliet. I remember Fergie's peaceful face as I kissed her sleeping lips goodbye. But nothing else.

It's all blank.

Galen pushes through my family and starts fussing with the machines and the various needles stuck into me. "I know how emotional this must be, but you all need to step back and give him time. It might take him a few minutes or a few days to recover his voice. Victor, do you understand us? If you can hear me, but you can't answer, blink once."

Now that I can do. I blink once.

"You've been in a coma for three days. You've just woken up. Do you understand?"

One blink.

How did I end up in a coma? I try to ask, but all that comes out is a low croak and a wad of spit. I guess that's an improvement?

"I know it's scary, especially because I can see you're trying to speak and you can't, but you're fine. I think you'll make a full recovery, it just might take you some time, okay? In the meantime, I need to run some tests on you. Is that okay?"

One blink.

As Galen moves around me to the machines, I let my gaze focus on the faces around me. Mom, Noah, Eli, and even Gabriel – he would have had to cancel shows to be here with me. Juliet, her eyes shining with tears. But where's Fergie? And Cas and Torsten? Why isn't Fergie here?

"F-F-Fergieeeee—" I manage to choke out.

"He spoke!" Mom cries.

"He said that bitch's name," Juliet frowns.

"Yes, but he spoke. Galen, he spoke!" Mom grabs my shoulder, shaking me a little. "Say something else, Vic."

"Wheeeeere Fergie?"

"I don't know, love," Mom says. "I guess Torsten is out looking for her—"

"I won't let that betraying bitch anywhere near you, brother."

Mom's eyebrows shoot way up, but she steps back and the rest of them part to give me a view of the person who spoke. A monstrously huge figure looms at the end of the bed, twisting the curtains between his beefy hands.

"There's been some trouble, so I've only allowed Cas to see you with strict rules," Mom says. "He's not to touch you, and if he starts any shit I'm kicking him out. No one in this room is to tell Cali that he's here."

"Cas," I croak out.

He swallows.

"Hey, Vic. You look like shit."

My mother shoots him a warning look.

"Whaaaa—"

"What happened is that you ran into the museum just as some bastard set off a bomb," Noah says. "Your mother and I escaped, and so did Livvie and Cali. Yara is gone, and so is Livvie's tribune."

Yara.

No.

I close my eyes against the news. Yara is my mother's personal secretary, and she's been part of our family for as long as I can remember.

When I open my eyes again, I take in my mother's stricken face and Noah's grim frown. Eli is slumped in a plastic chair, his Ken-doll good looks marred by shock and grief. Gabriel leans against the wall, arms folded, dark eyes staring down at me as if he wishes hard enough he could swap places with me. Juliet sits on my bed, hugging her legs to her chest, her eyes huge and filled with tears, and I hate myself for putting her through this, because I remember how I felt when I thought she was gone, like a piece of me had been torn away and someone poured acid into the hole.

And Cas... Cas is the worst of all. My friend looks like he had a fight with a monster truck... and lost. Which has never, ever happened to Cas before. The orange flames in his irises have gone, and I see nothing in his eyes but cold, inky blackness. The last time he looked this shellshocked was after the police arrested Gaius.

Something niggles at me, something that I had to do, had to make right...

Fergie.

The memories slam into me. Walking across school with

Juliet as she brags about what she and Cas did. Finding Cas underneath the old horticulture building, wallowing in his own self-pity, driving with Torsten to the museum and watching him run naked across the city, and then searching the halls desperately to find Mom and Cali, to get answers so I can figure out what the fuck to do next...

Fergie.

Why didn't I go to her? Torsten was right – the truth doesn't matter when the girl I love is hurting. Fergie must've seen that video. She probably thinks all three of us are responsible for it. She's been all alone for days, facing the fallout of that video on her own. No wonder she's not here. She must hate me.

And I don't blame her. I fucking hate me, too.

No one is strong enough to live through that kind of violation. Not even Fergie fucking Munroe.

Why didn't I go to her? I got so caught up in trying to be a leader, to be the responsible one, the sensible one, that I let my girl down when she needed me most. And now she's out there, alone, living through the online hatred and the humiliation and the invasion of her privacy, and I'm can't stop any of it—

I hear someone wailing, as if they're in excruciating pain. It takes me a moment to realize that person is me.

"Vic, what's wrong?" Juliet crawls to me, placing her hand on my forehead. "Should I get Galen? What—"

I slap her hands away. I can't do this. I can't pretend that everything's okay just because they nearly lost me. As much as Cas needs me to hold him together, and Juliet needs me to protect her, and Mom's museum just got blown up, I can't be the one who fixes this for them. The weight of it bearing down on me is grinding my bones to ash. I can't help them if it hurts her.

I have to do what I should have done the moment I learned about the video. I have to find Fergie. I have to be there for her. I have to fix it.

With power I didn't realize I possess, I swing my legs off the bed.

"Victor, what are you doing?" Juliet tries to shove me down. "You just woke up out of a coma. You can't go anywhere. If you need the bathroom, Galen will get you a bedpan—"

"I have to see Fergie," I mumble. My mouth still won't work properly.

"Why?" Juliet scoffs. "I told you, Cas and I took care of that bitch."

She swipes at me again, but I duck under her arm and crash through the curtain. There's some machine on wheels still attached to me, and I shove it with both hands just as Galen barrels through the curtain after me. He goes flying and crashes into Juliet, knocking them both over and tearing the last needles from my arm.

"Victor," Mom screeches.

I don't stop to look. I bolt for the door. Eli throws himself in front of it, his chest heaving. "Son, you need to go back to bed. You're—"

"I need a ride somewhere," I say, knowing that if anyone will understand, it will be Eli, the one who loved my mother before he was old enough to even know what that meant. "Please, it's important. I have to get out of here before Juliet and Galen tie me back down to the bed."

It's a testament to the trust my parents have in me that Eli blinks once and then says, "Sure, let's go."

We duck into the tunnel and run, emerging into the parking lot a few moments later. Eli clicks his keyfob to unlock the car, and we dive inside just as Galen hits the parking lot, my sister, Cas, and Noah hot on his heels. "Victor, come back! It's not safe for you to—"

"Go, go, go!" I yell at Eli, who hits the gas. We squeal out of the parking lot. Honestly, Galen's right. I probably shouldn't have left. I don't feel great. I grip the front of the dash and fight a bout of wooziness.

"You don't look good, son." Eli's voice is thick with worry.

"Drive," I growl. "To the Olympus hotel."

If anyone knows where I can find Fergie, it'll be Torsten.

19

FERGIE

Drusilla drops me, Torsten, and Euri back at the Olympus in stony silence. Euri tries to say something as she exits the car, but Dru takes off before she can get the words out.

"Hey!" Euri yells after her. "You have my bookbag. I need that copy of the *Iliad* for my history essay!"

I take Euri's hand before she can run after Dru and get herself run over. "You've memorized that text, probably in the original Greek. You'll be fine. Are you okay?"

"I'm... something. I'm not sure fine is the word to describe it."

"I understand."

"I think you made the right decision." Euri squeezes my hand. "I feel for Dru, I really do. I remember when all of that went down, but spying on Cali for that Zack guy seems like a seriously bad idea. And what's with giving you a building?"

"It can be our new clubhouse," I grin. "Do you want me to call you a cab?"

"Nah, I've texted Artie. She's on her way."

We wait on the street for Artemis to arrive. "Hello again, Fergie. Hello, Torsten," she says as she flings open the car door for Euri. She tries to hide the incredulity in her voice and fails miserably. I know she's wondering why Euri and I are hanging out with Torsten. I'll let Euri explain – I don't have the energy.

Torsten and I head upstairs. He settles into the bedroom with his paints while I peruse the Braille menu, trying to decide what to have for dinner, when there's a knock on the door.

"Did you order dinner already?" I call out to Torsten.

"No."

He's too engrossed in his painting, so I lean against the door and call out, "If it's housekeeping, you can come back tomorr—"

"Fergggieeeee."

The voice reaches through the locked door and punches me in the chest. It's Victor, and he sounds like shit. But it can't be Victor, because Victor is lying in a hospital bed at Galen's clinic, in a coma.

"Ferrgggggie, opennnnn..."

It sounds *so much* like Victor.

"If that's you, Cassius, I don't care how much you fucking hate me. It's *sick* to come here pretending to be your friend in a coma, and it's not going to make me open this door—"

"Fergie, this is Eli," another voice calls out. "I'm Victor and Juliet's dad. I can assure you that Victor is out here, and he's not looking great, but he won't let me take him back to Galen until he's spoken to you. So I'd appreciate it if you could open the door."

Torsten's body weight presses against me. He cranes his head to see out the peephole. "It's Victor and Eli," he says. "Do you want them to come in?"

"Yes." Raw panic surges inside me. "Fuck yes!"

Torsten punches in the code and flings open the door. Victor must've been leaning against it, because he topples into me. I stagger back, hitting my hip on the edge of the table. I shove him and he rolls off me and hits the floor with a sickening *thud*.

I hate this and I hate *him,* but my body doesn't seem to remember that as I stand over Vic, trembling with fear that I might've killed him.

I hear grunting as Torsten and Eli pick him up off the floor and settle him onto the sofa. I don't know what to do, so I lean against the kitchen counter. At least he won't be able to see my trembling legs.

"I see you're out of your coma, Victor August," I say, keeping my voice cold and even. "Now get out of our room before I put you back in one."

"Fergieeeeeeeeee..." his words sound slurred, like he's a little drunk. "I had to see you. I'm so so sorry. You have to know that I didn't—"

"I know you didn't have anything to do with releasing the video," I say. "But what you did is so much worse."

"I know. I know that I—"

"No, Victor, you *don't* know. Because you're a guy. That video is never going to impact your life the same way it impacts mine. I've already been through this before. I've already—" the words catch in my throat, but I suck in a breath and keep going, "—I've already had a boyfriend release a sex video of me. He did it as revenge because he couldn't handle me rejecting him, and because of that, my dad and I took up Cali's offer to move to Emerald Beach and change our identities. And you knew about my false name, but instead of coming to me about it, you kept it hidden while you scurried around behind my back like the rat you are. I was going to tell you everything after Saturnalia, when I realized how much I... how much I *cared* about all of you."

Cared. Past tense.

The words taste like poison as my throat closes around them. My whole body trembles with rage as it all floods back to me, every awful moment of the last few days, every wretched regret caused by *him*. I bite back the tears that crowd my eyes. I find my strength.

"I wanted you to know the whole truth about me," I continue. "Even though it made me vulnerable. Well, joke's on me, right? I didn't even have to tell you, because Poison Ivy had all the fucking pieces it needed to destroy me completely."

"Please," Vic whimpers. "I'll do everything I can to make it up to you. I love you, Fergie. I've loved you since that night in the rage room. I'll get that video taken down. I'll talk to Cas—"

"Save your energy, Victor, it's over. It was over the moment you chose Cassius over me."

I love you, Fergie.

Why did he have to say that?

Why did he have to make it so hard to hate him?

The tears fall now, thick and heavy. I don't wipe them away. I let him see what he's done. "You told me that you'd protect me. You were the one who convinced me to trust Cas, but that was a lie. He releases that tape and instead of seeing if I'm okay, instead of treating me like someone you *love*, you decide that Cas' stupid need to be break shit is more important. You had to get *the truth* before you could even see if I was okay. That's not fucking love, Victor August."

"I made a mistake, and then I got blown up, but I'm here now, Fergie," his voice cracks with such raw emotion that I almost waver. "I came to see if you were okay."

"Well, I'm not okay. I'm very fucking far from okay. But I have Torsten and I have Euri, and that's all I need. Go away, Victor August. I'm not some broken doll you need to fix. You're not needed."

"Fergie, no, no." Another thump. Victor crawls along the floor, wrapping his arms around my legs. "This can't be it. This can't be over. I won't let it. Just give me a chance to—"

"Victor."

Torsten's voice booms through the room. I've never heard him sound like this before, so calm and possessed.

"You need to go."

"Torsten, I'm so happy you're looking after her," Victor blubbers. "You know that we can save this, right? We can have what we had the night of Saturnalia again. That's what you want, isn't it? Me and you and Cas and Fergie, we're written in the stars. All I have to do is fix it and—"

"Fergie wants you to leave."

"I'm not leaving, Torsten. Fergie and you and I are going to sit down and talk about this, and we're going to figure out what to do—"

"There's no *us* anymore." I kick my legs free of him. "There's me and Torsten. You chose your side, Vic."

"Please, you need to understand, Cas—"

"I *don't* need to understand jack or fucking shit about my sadistic stepbrother. Cas thinks I betrayed him, so he betrayed me right back, and he got Juliet to help him. He acted on instinct because he's an animal, but you... you were supposed to be so much more. You made me feel safe." I gulp back a fresh wave of tears. "Do you know how long it's been since I felt safe? But when it comes down to it, you didn't see me at all. None of us are people to the great Victor August – I'm just a pawn in the grand empire you're building."

"I thought..." Victor sobs. "I thought he needed me more than you."

"That's right. You thought about poor broken Cas who's so afraid of his feelings that when someone threatens to get too close he has to burn it all down. You thought about your sister, who needs drama to feel important. But you didn't think for one minute that maybe seeing the happiest night of my life broadcast for the world to see would break me? That maybe I'm not strong enough to survive something like this? That maybe I shouldn't have to be?"

"Victor, we should go," Eli says. He's already in the hallway outside.

"I'm not leaving until we talk this out." Victor hauls himself off the floor and collapses on the sofa. I move toward him, fists raised, ready to kick some August ass.

But Torsten gets there first.

"Fergie wants you to leave," he repeats. I can't see what he does, but there's a thump and Victor cries out, and then Torsten's moving across the room and the door slams shut behind him. I hear the lock click and Torsten plug in the security code.

Relief washes over me, taking out the remaining strength in my legs. I slide to the floor, my back against the kitchen island, and hug my knees to my chest.

Torsten slides down beside me. He doesn't touch me, but just his presence quiets the sobs wracking my body.

"I'm fine," I wheeze. "Thank you for getting rid of him."

He says nothing.

"If you're okay with it, Torsten, I could really use a hug."

His arms slide around me. He's a little stiff as he pulls me into him. Torsten still struggles with this kind of physical interaction, especially after facing the trauma of Victor showing up. I know he needs to go back to his painting, to perform those familiar movements that bring him back to himself.

But he tries his best to give me what I need. No matter what, he always puts me before himself.

"Thank you," I whisper, burrowing my head into his shoulder.

"For what?"

"For everything."

We stay like this, holding each other, until the trembling in both our limbs subsides a little. My phone rings, breaking the spell. I sniff and reach for it, assuming it was Victor trying to get through. But it's Dad's ringtone. A fresh wave of concern washes over me. Did whoever set that bomb come back to finish everyone off?

I wipe the tears from my cheeks and raise my phone to my ear. "Dad. Are you okay?"

"I'm fine, honey. I'm sorry for worrying you. I'm at home now with Cali. She's doing okay. She doesn't deal very well with being confined to bed. Anyway, I thought you might like to know that Victor's awake and he—"

"I already know," I snap. "He just showed up here."

"Fergie—"

"I don't want to talk about him. I wish he'd never woken up."

Dad sighs.

"Honey, I..." Dad's voice hitches. "I saw the video. Can we talk? I have so much I need to say, but I don't want to do it over the phone."

My chest cracks. I want so badly to talk to him. For months there's been this distance between us, and now... "I'd like that. But can you leave Cali?"

"Are you kidding? Seymour is fussing over her and Milo has made enough food to feed an army. She's fine without me for a bit." He swallows. "I miss you, kid. If I text you the name of a restaurant, can you get there? It's crowded and noisy, so we'll feel safe."

The text comes through. It's that Italian place he told me about when we first moved here, the one he and Cali go to on their dates. The one that he's never had any interest in taking me to before.

My heart thuds. "Sure, Dad. I'll call a cab and I'll see you there in twenty minutes."

≈

"HE'S YOUR STEPBROTHER. And you... you let him do that to you? You let the three of them treat you like that?"

I'm not even halfway into my seat when Dad's Judgement Express pulls in at Slut Shaming station. I slide right back out of the booth and grab my purse.

"Sorry," I say to the waitress. "I guess I'm not staying for dinner after all."

This is a mistake. I should never have come. He's too damaged, and I don't trust him. We can't come back from this.

"No, Fergie, wait. Please. I'm sorry."

The pain in his voice stops me in my tracks. I slump into the booth facing him and drop my cane on the floor, not even bothering to fold it up. "Fine. I'm here. But don't slut shame me. I can't handle it. Not now. It's not a crime to discover what I like in bed. The crime is that my stepbrother leaked a sex tape of me. Only, as we know, it's *not* a crime. But you're the one who married a mafia queen. You don't exactly get to claim the moral high ground."

"I know. I know." I hear his elbows hitting the table. He reaches across and touches his finger to mine, the way he's always done to make sure I'm okay. I jerk away, and I hear him cringe. "I shouldn't have kept Cali's work secret from you. She wanted to tell you, but after everything you've been through already this year, I didn't want to heap more onto your plate. I chose this for myself, love. I embraced Cali's life, her world, with my eyes wide open. I didn't want to take that choice away from you. That was why I decided to keep it secret until after you finished high school. After that, we were going to tell you everything and let you decide how much you wanted to be in our lives. I think I was just so afraid that you... that you wouldn't—"

"Dad, you know—" my voice croaks. "I was never going to disown you."

His finger wraps around mine. "My beautiful daughter. You

were always so headstrong. You do whatever you feel in your heart is right, consequences be damned. You're so much like your mother. You've got yourself into a bit of a pickle, haven't you?"

I try for a smile, but I don't quite make it. "I made a stupid mistake. I told Cas about what Dawson did. That's why he did this – because he knew it would hurt me the most."

"That boy has been causing trouble for Cali ever since he could walk," Dad says. "We were both happy when it seemed like the two of you were getting along well. Cas is the perfect soldier to have on your side, but if he feels betrayed, then... well, we know the lengths he'll go to assert himself. Your stepmother is sorry for not warning you about him – she's been distracted lately by work, and she didn't see this hatred of his brewing. She will deal with it now, though. Not only for releasing the video, but for disobeying Cali's orders. Cas wasn't supposed to tell you about the Triumvirate or invite you to Saturnalia. It showed a blatant disregard for her authority, and with the way things are right now, that could undermine Cali's leadership. She'll punish him for that."

"I figured a lot of it out myself, you know. I'm quite clever. I knew you were all hiding something from me. But yes, Cas and Vic and Torsten told me the truth on Saturnalia. And I *understand,* Dad. Really I do. I accept their choice, and although I wish you'd trusted me enough to tell me sooner, I accept your choice, too."

"Thank you, Fergalish. That means the world to me."

"I know. But that was *before,* when they were my... boyfriends. Now everything's a mess." I lay my head in my hands. "Jesus. I can't do this again. I'm not strong enough to survive it a second time."

"When Cali is on her feet, I'll talk to her. She'll know what to do. Maybe there's a Caribbean island somewhere we can move to with a decent school—"

I shake my head. "I can't start over again."

"But everyone in your school has seen this video. The principal assures me they're wiping it from school computers, but it's already up on various sites all over the internet—"

I lift my chin. "I'm not running this time. Dawson was bad enough – but those guys don't get to walk around that school like they own it while I'm the one who has my future destroyed."

"I don't want you to do anything rash. I'm angry too. I could rip their heads off." A napkin tears in his hands, and I realize that he's serious. "Things are different in California. They have actual revenge porn laws here. We have a legal case to go after people sharing the video. But Cas and Victor and Torsten are caught up in whatever's going on in the Triumvirate. They have targets on their backs, and you can't get mixed up in it—"

"Torsten had nothing to do with it," I assure him. "And as for the others, you don't have to worry about me. I'm not going anywhere near the Triumvirate or Victor August or Cassius fucking Dio ever again."

It's a lie, but it's the lie he needs to hear.

"What *are* you going to do?" he asks.

I shrug. "I'm going to graduate and go to college. The plan hasn't changed. It's just got layers now. So what if school is horrible? It's been horrible before and I survived. Cas hardly even goes to school anyway, and I have Torsten and Euri to look out for me if anyone causes trouble. And, Dad... before they did this to me, Poison Ivy got me into Harvard."

He sighs again. "Fergie, that's—"

"—cheating. I know. Don't worry, I'm not going to take the place. I got blinded by the promises they made me, that I could have my old life back, the life I felt I deserved. But I can see clearly now, pardon the puns. We can't ever go back, can we? Not getting into an Ivy is not the end of the world. There are lots of other colleges, and we live in the age of #metoo, so I might even be able to turn this experience into a winning college essay."

I try for a smile again. I know it looks a little wobbly, but it's the best I can do.

"Fergalish, are you *sure*?"

No. I'm going to burn it all down. I don't care if I end up in jail, or worse. I have to see those boys pay.

But I don't want him to know that when he's sitting with me and opening up to me. "I'm sure."

Our food arrives – two enormous pizzas dripping with sauce and meat and cheese. We both dig in, and we eat in contented silence. Dad finishes a bite and says, "Fergie, please come home."

"I can't. I'm not safe with him there."

"I'll make sure you are. Cas might not be afraid of much, but he's afraid of Cali, and if she—"

"I just *can't*. I'm fine. You don't have to worry about me. I'm staying in the Olympus with Torsten."

"You're my little girl. I'm always going to worry about you." He slides his hand across the table, and touches his sauce-covered finger to mine again. "But I don't want things to be this way with us. I want us to talk. Can we maybe meet here – every weekend, same time? And tell each other what's going on? I know you must have so many questions about Cali and her world. I'd be happy to answer them."

After everything that's happened, it's not much. It's not what I wanted from him. I want him to take me far away from here. I want him to choose me over his new family. But I know that's not fair of me, and what he's offering is the start of something. "Yes, we can do that."

"Good. You have no idea how happy that makes me. And if you're going to stay with Torsten, you should have your things.

I'll get your stepbrother out of the house so that you can raid your closet." He clears his throat. "Milo says your kitten has been missing you terribly."

"I missed Spartacus, too. He's happy at the hotel, but I want some of his toys."

"I think he'd like that. He's safer at the hotel. I can only check on him sometimes, and even in this enormous house. Cali would have discovered him hiding upstairs. For such a little guy, he's got quite a set of pipes on him."

I wrap my arms around him. "Thanks, Dad."

Over a dessert of tiramisu, we make arrangements for me to head over the next day to pick up my stuff. Dad calls Cali to discuss it as he hops in his taxi. I wave at him as his car pulls away, only feeling a tinge of guilt for lying.

Of course I want my clothes, and Spartacus needs his favorite blanket and some things to play with. But that's not the real reason I want access to Cali's house.

I'm ready to cross off the first item on my revenge list.

20

VICTOR

It can't be over. It *can't* be.

I stumble through the house, my mind reeling from everything Fergie said to me. Eli tries to help me, but I shove him away and crawl toward the stairs. All I want to do is get to my room so I can come up with a plan.

I can fix this.

I *have* to fix it.

"Victor, Eli, is that you?" Mom calls from her office. "Are you okay? You shouldn't have run off like that before Galen had a chance to check you over—"

"I'm fine," I yell downstairs as I slam my door shut. I'm not fine. My vision swirls and blurs, and every time I move my body I'm worried I'm going to throw up. But none of that's important.

I slide into my computer chair and unlock the screen. The icons wiggle in front of me, and I'm dimly aware that I probably shouldn't be trying to navigate a computer right now.

But I can't stop. Not until I've fixed everything.

I navigate (slowly) to an upscale Harrington Hills candy store and order the largest box of candy they have and ship it to Torsten's room. Then I order some French perfume with raspberry notes. I notice how Fergie recognizes things by how they smell, and I want to give her something pretty to smell since I turned her whole world to shit. An ad for the Fluevog shoe store pops up, and I'm browsing that when I feel a presence behind me.

"What are you doing?" Juliet plops down on my bed. "You should be resting, but if you've started shopping for my birthday present, what I'm *really* after is the new Gucci leather clutch—"

"I'm not shopping for you." I spy a purse with metal spikes studded through the top, and it looks like something my Duchess would love. Click. In the cart it goes.

"Those are for Fergie, aren't they?" she sighs. "Brother, I'm telling you this for your own good – you do not need that girl in your life."

"You've got it wrong," I say. "Fergie's fake name has nothing to do with our parents."

She shrugs. "So?"

"What do you mean, *so?* So, she's not trying to hurt us. So, there's no nefarious plan to overthrow the Triumvirate. So, you and Cas ruined her for nothing."

"Not for nothing, brother," Juliet says. "I figured Cas was blowing his gasket over nothing – as if Fergie had the brains to get some kind of secret identity past Cali and Livvie and Mom. I did it for you."

"How is this for me?" I slump on my desk. "I feel like my heart's been torn from my chest. I thought you liked Fergie."

My sister shrugs again. "I *did* like Fergie, but this isn't personal. It's politics. When Fergie first came here, I thought she'd be perfect for you, Vic. She made you so happy, and I could see you thought she'd make the perfect queen. But a girl like Fergie, she's not content to have a passive role in this family. I can see it in her, because it takes one to know one," Juliet grins. "Fergie would never be happy playing your obedient queen, Vic.

When Cas showed me that video, I saw something else, too. She's not going to choose between the three of you. She wants all of you, and Fergie is used to getting what she wants. It's fine for Mom to have three husbands, but those husbands aren't from Lucian or Dio. Fergie would keep you and Cas and Torsten for herself, and that would tie you down to the other families and weaken your power. There's only room for one woman to be in charge of the August family."

I stare at her in disbelief. "You? But you've never said anything about being Imperator."

"That's because it's going to be decades before Mom even considers giving up her crown, and I'm not going to sit around twiddling my thumbs." Juliet rolls her eyes. "Besides, I don't want to do what Mom does – put herself in the firing line every day because she's the face of our family. All that blood and violence is really quite disgusting. I don't want gore under my nails, thank you very much. But our family has assets that can help me build my fashion brand, and Mom refuses to allow me to use them. I don't see why, with all the power and influence we have, I should have to do everything the hard way." Juliet puffs out her lower lip. "When you're in charge of the August family, you'll let me do whatever I want. But not if Fergie's around, calling the shots. Like I said, it's just politics."

I stare at my sister as if seeing her for the first time. Has she always been this ruthless? Juliet defers to me, feigns disinterest in the business side of things, and even scorns Mom for her involvement in the Triumvirate. But when I think about it, she makes sure she's present at every Poison Ivy meeting, and every major Triumvirate event. She knows all the names written in the ledger, all the favors we accept, and the sacramentum that we're owed.

Do I really know my sister at all?

"Jesus fucking Christ, Jules. I would have given you everything you wanted. I got that house for you in Cambridge, didn't I?"

"You're telling me that if precious Fergie said to you that she didn't want you to negotiate a deal to get me a spot in Milan Fashion Week in exchange for a little inside information about the Caruso crime family, that you'd do it anyway?"

I glare at my sister. She's not wrong. If Fergie set her incredible mind to managing the August empire, and she told me something my sister wanted to do wouldn't work, then I'd listen.

Juliet shrugs as she stands. "Exactly. It's nothing personal, brother – you're pussy-whipped, and it doesn't serve my purpose, so she has to go. Plus, it's a hell of a lot of fun bringing down Fergie Macintosh."

I shove her toward the door and slam it in her face. I can't bear to look at her right now, knowing that everything she put Fergie through is all part of some master plan to make me dance for her amusement.

Am I really so easy to manipulate?

"This place gives me the creeps," Euri says. "It's so... sterile."

We're standing in the foyer of Cali's Harrington Hills mansion, the place Dad moved me into a few months ago but has never really felt like home. Dad assures me that Cali kicked Cas out, although he'd seen my stepbrother sneaking in a couple of times to use the shower. Apparently, Cas is coming back with Vic today to get some of his stuff, but if I show up before 1PM, I won't see him. Euri's with me because we have a lot to do and not a lot of time to do it.

"Cali's taste definitely lends itself to 'psychiatric ward chic,'" I say. "I'm trying not to read into this, but I did just find out that my stepmother is a famous assassin, so... hey, you want a snack? I hear Milo in the kitchen."

"I've heard nothing but amazing things about this chef of yours," says Euri. "So sure."

"Hey, Milo!" I call out as I lead Euri through the maze of rooms and into the airy kitchen. "I'm back and I smell something delicious—"

I'm cut off by the chef throwing his huge arms around me. We both burst out laughing as he nearly bowls me over.

"Fergie, it's so good to see you." Milo brushes my hair out of my face. He smells like flour and roasted coffee. "And now I've got flour all over you."

"It's worth it for a hug from you," I say. "This is so much nicer than the last time we spoke."

"I'm so sorry for how I treated you." His voice turns somber. "I was wrong to pay any heed to Cassius' nonsense. It's only that there's been some trouble lately and *She* told us to be on our guard, and all those things he said about you having a fake name—"

"Fergie is my name," I tell him firmly. "I'm never going to be anyone else. I had a false identity for a reason that had nothing to do with the Triumvirate. Cali helped me do it because of something rotten a boy did at my last school."

"I know. Your father explained everything." He sighs. "All this could've been avoided if we all knew about it from the start."

I shake my head. I think Cali knew that if Cas knew my secret, I'd eventually do something to piss him off, and then he'd use it against me.

Milo loosens his grip on me and reaches over to grab a plate from the counter. "I've been watching a lot of traditional British baking shows lately. Fancy some scones with jam and clotted cream? I've even got Earl Grey tea."

"Hell yes!" Euri pulls the plate toward her.

"So that's what the heavenly smell is. Can you do me a coffee instead of tea?" I ask. "I miss your coffee."

"It's hasn't even been a week."

"A week is enough when you need a caffeine fix."

"True." He starts the coffee machine. "How's the little guy doing?"

"Spartacus loves his new home. He's not technically

supposed to be living at the hotel, but Robert our concierge keeps slipping him salmon filets from the restaurant so I think he's won them over. Thank you so much for getting him that new feather toy. It's his new favorite."

We chat with Milo and polish off the plate of scones until I ask my phone to read out the time. "Argh. We need to get packing. Dad says we have to be out of here by one or we risk running into Cas."

"Yes. Go." Milo shoves us toward the door. "I'd offer to help, but Seymour and I need to take this second batch of scones over to his mother's house."

"Enjoy your time with your mother-in-law." I laugh as I kiss Milo's cheek, and I can feel his face crumple up with anticipation. At least half of his stories are about Seymour's cantankerous mother. "Euri and I have got this covered."

I lead Euri upstairs and down the familiar hallway to my room. I half expect to find the door smashed to pieces. It's surprisingly intact, but the series of locks I'd installed have been torn off. I kick one as I step inside my room.

"Stop gaping and come in," I call out to Euri. "He's not here."

"I can't believe Cas did this." One of the locks clicks in her hand as she inspects it. "Were you afraid all the time when you lived here?"

I shrug. "After everything that happened with Dawson, it was actually nice to have someone obsessed with me. For good or evil, I was Cas' whole world. It felt amazing to have his entire attention focused on me, like what I did mattered. Like I matter. Is that fucked up?"

"Completely. But at least he hasn't trashed your room. Hey, there are some dents in the carpet here." Euri clicks her fingers. "Oh, I bet that's where Gaius used to have his drumkit."

"Gaius played the drums?"

I add this nugget of information to the very short list of things I know about Cas' older brother.

"Yeah. It was one of the many reasons girls fell all over him – the hot musician thing. I think it's one of the reasons why he let his little brother and his friends have so much power. You know the twins' dad is some kind of musician, right? Gaius probably wanted some kind of introduction."

"I didn't know that about Vic's dad." I'd heard Vic say that his dad was on tour, but we'd never talked about it beyond that. I'm now curious. I wonder what kind of music he plays...

No.

I don't care.

I don't care about the August family and I don't care if Victor August loves music, because he's not going to taint my love for that, too.

"Well, now you do. Don't ask me the name of the band, though, because I can never remember. It's some weird heavy metal and classical music mashup thing. Not really my style, but you'd probably love it," Euri says, as if she's reading my mind. "Gaius had a band with some other seniors. They used to play a lot of the dances and parties and stuff. I thought they were shit, but what do I know? Speaking of shit music, your collection of t-shirts with demons and unpronounceable band names won't pack themselves."

"Do not mock my vintage heavy metal tees," I say as I throw open the closet doors. One thing I'm going to miss about Cali's house is this awesome walk-in closet with the shoe rack—

"Fergie..." Euri's voice strains. "Oh, no..."

"What?" I growl, my chest tightening. I thrust my arm into the closet, half-expecting to find a dead body. Instead, I touch fabric. My heart flutters with hope, but then I run my hand along the rack and I know something's wrong.

I pull out a hanger that holds my Iron Maiden tee. It's the

shirt I got at the very first concert I ever went to. Dad drove me down to Boston, and we sat in these horrible seats at the top of the stadium and listened to Bruce Dickinson run around the stage and yell, "Scream with me, Boston," and I screamed so much that I lost my voice for a week, and every time I wear this shirt, I remember how I felt that scream in my veins.

I can never wear the shirt again. Because it's no longer wearable. Ribbons of fabric fall through my fingers. It's been slashed. It looks like it's been attacked by a wild animal, which in a way is exactly what happened.

Cas did this.

I move down the rack, touching my clothing. Every piece is a memory I'd been desperately clinging to as a way to get through this horror.

Every single item of clothing has been slashed to pieces.

Tears spring in my eyes.

I *loved* my clothes. I love the way I can express something of who I am inside through them. I've spent years immersed in fashion and goth subculture online. Some of the shirts I owned were rare, impossible to replace. I pick up a Vivienne Westwood dress my dad brought me when I won the jiujitsu national championships, but it falls to pieces in my hands.

Cas did this, probably at Juliet's insistence. She knew what my clothes meant to me.

The growl rises from low in my chest. When I speak, I don't recognize my own voice.

"This is war."

Euri wraps her arms around me. "I'm so sorry, Fergie."

"Not as sorry as Cas will be."

Euri picks the dress from my arms. "I might be able to do something with this."

"Really?"

"Yeah. I'm not too bad with a needle and thread..." she laughs. "Don't look at me like that. I swear that I can sew a lot straighter than I can knit. Let's find some of your favorites and I'll see what I can do."

We hunt out a few of my favorite outfits and stuff them into a tote bag, then I collect my makeup and jewelry boxes. Thankfully, Cas hadn't destroyed that. My mother's jewelry is still safely inside. I hold the cold diamonds in my fingers, remembering the last time I got them out... to bargain with the Poison Ivy Club. *I'm so sorry, Mom.*

I add some of the toys Cas brought for Spartacus, and his bed, and the other things that Seymour left behind. As my fingers graze a fuzzy mouse, I remember the day that Cas brought him home to me. We sat on the bed, so close our legs touched, and Spartacus kept climbing onto my shoulders.

"I think he likes you," Cas said, and the awe in his voice almost broke my heart. I don't think he'd ever been close to a creature like that, ever known that unconditional love could be a thing. And then when he thought Spartacus was going to die...

I truly thought we'd made progress that day. My stepbrother almost opened up to me. Was it truly all a lie, a ploy to get me to spill my secrets so he could use them against me later? I don't think Cas is that good an actor.

But when it comes to my stepbrother, I can't trust my own judgment. I thought I could read him like a book. I thought we were cut from the same brutal mold, but I was wrong. And I fucking *hate* being wrong.

I reach into my pocket and wrap my fingers around the vial Artemis gave me. "Revenge time," I whisper.

"Okay," Euri's voice wavers. "If you really want to do this—"

"I do." I show Euri into the bathroom Cassius and I shared. I reach inside the enormous shower and unscrew the main head.

"I'll hold this, can you pour that inside? Don't get it on your fingers. Or mine."

"Okay... I think I can... oops," Euri giggles. "I put waaay too much in there."

"Oh no, too bad." I grin.

I manage to screw the head back on without spilling any of the liquid inside, and Euri checks it and says everything looks just as we found it. We move out of the bathroom, and we both break down into giggles as we gather up our tote bags filled with ruined clothes and cat toys and stack them by the front door.

Nothing like a little light revenge to make you feel better about life.

"What now?" Euri asks after we've stashed our stuff in the trunk of Seymour's car.

I dust off my hands. "Time for phase two."

"**W**hat are we doing here?" Euri asks as I punch in the code to the library that Torsten gave me. I'm hoping like hell Cas didn't think to change it, but my stepbrother is not imaginative enough to guess that I might try to get in here.

His loss.

"We're going to do some snooping for your article," I say as the panel chirps and the door clicks open.

"These doors are wild!" Euri's distracted now, running her fingers all over the wood. "Look, there's a little unicorn hidden in the vines..."

"Stop hugging the carvings and get in here." I shove the door open a crack and gesture to Euri. "After you, Lois Lane."

She breezes past me but stops in her tracks. I crash into her and get an elbow in my ribs for my trouble.

"Ow."

"Sorry, it's just..." she breathes. "This place is unreal."

"You saw it on the video."

"It was mostly in shadow," she swallows. "Apart from, you know..."

"Apart from my naked ass in a sex swing," I finish for her.

"Yeah. Sorry."

"Don't be sorry. It was fun while it lasted. But bringing them down is going to be fun, too."

"I can't believe Cassius hangs out here." Euri moves over to the bookshelves. I hear her pulling books out and flipping the pages. "This is... well, it's the library of my dreams. Look at all these beautiful books. And there are paintings on the walls. They look like Monet with the dappled light, but..."

"Torsten," I say.

"I figured. And the furniture looks expensive, but also cozy and comfortable. All it needs is a stormy night out the window and a hot vampire leaning against the mantlepiece and this is all my darkest fantasies come to life."

"Stop creaming yourself, Mina Harker – we have a mission to accomplish." I navigate my way around the sofa to the drinks cart and start pulling bottles from the racks. "Help me. Cas likes expensive, old Scotch. I want the oldest, fanciest bottles you can find."

Euri picks through the bottles. "Wow. This one is forty-five years old! I wasn't even alive when this was bottled."

"Perfect. What about this one?" I hold up a bottle with some fancy etched glass around the neck.

"I dunno. Hang on..." Euri taps her phone screen. "Fergie, you won't believe it, but that bottle is worth twenty-five *grand*."

"Excellent. It's coming with us."

We hunt out two more expensive bottles. I break the seals and take a swig from each, because I'm curious what forty-five-year-old whisky tastes like. The answer is: fucking amazing. I feel a little guilty about what we're about to do. It's not the whisky's fault that it's owned by a maniac. But needs must.

Bottles clink as Euri straightens up. "Right, we have the whisky. What now?"

I gesture around the room. "This is where Poison Ivy held its secret meetings. Victor also told me that Gaius built hidden compartments into the walls. Some of them hold sex swings, but I bet some..."

"...hold Poison Ivy Club secrets?" her voice brightens.

"Exactly. The information we need to make your *exposé* as deadly as possible is hidden in this room."

I think about Drusilla and Zack Lionel Sommesnay, and how they were asking about secret rooms in Cali's house. I know I did the right thing by not telling them about this library. I might be out to destroy the Poison Ivy Club, and I feel a real affinity with Dru, but I don't trust her creepy German boyfriend not to endanger my father, or Torsten, or Euri.

"What's this?" Euri drops something heavy on the table.

"I don't know. What is it?"

"It's a leatherbound book. I found it under a creaky floorboard. It looks like a ledger of some kind."

I drop down beside Euri, trying not to think about what I did the last time I sat on this sofa. But the memory of Cas bending me over and spanking me rears up, and for a moment I can practically feel his breath on my ear as he whispers, "That's for being a filthy girl who craves dirty, forbidden things." I press my thighs together as my skin prickles with the memory of my stepbrother's hand sliding into my cunt, making me scream and writhe, making me beg for him...

The leather spine creaks as Euri turns the pages of the ledger.

"It's a list of names, and beside each name is a list of colleges, and some notes I don't understand..." Euri turns another page. "Here's Bayleigh Laurent. She's the girl who hired Poison Ivy to destroy my sister."

I remember Victor showing me this book. "This is where

they keep the details of their clients. Victor says they don't keep electronic notes because it's too easy to hack."

"There's a column here I don't entirely understand," Euri says. "It's a list of items next to people's names. Here's Lucila's name. Next to her, it says, "Victor – the Cambridge house. Cassius – sacramentum. What's that?"

"No idea about sacramentum, but remember when we walked in on Victor and Juliet and Lucila in the bathroom? Victor told Lucila she had to arrange for her family to sell him a house in Cambridge. I think that column is the price their clients paid for Poison Ivy's services. Maybe sacramentum means a favor to cash in the future? Or it's some freaky sex thing?"

"Fergie, this is it." Euri snaps the ledger shut and starts opening the clasp of her bookbag. "This is what we need to write the article. This is every bad deed, every favor owed, every piece of the puzzle we need to take these guys down. We're taking it with us."

"No," I say. "They only have one copy. If we take it, they'll know we have it. They're going to figure out I got in here when they see what I plan to do to Cas' alcohol. But we want them to believe that their secrets are still safe. They probably don't think a blind girl can find that floorboard."

"They have security footage of us."

"No, they don't. Torsten controls the security system for the room. He looped the videos today so they won't even know we were here. They'll probably assume Torsten let us in or did this for us, and they'll assume he'd never turn them in."

"So we leave this behind?"

"Yes, but we take the information with us." I open the book out flat on her lap. "Take photos. As many as you need. Make sure they're in focus."

"Right. Of course."

Euri snaps away, which gives me far too much time alone with my memories. The library still smells like that night – the mingling of their distinctive scents clinging to the furniture, reminding me of all the delicious debauchery I thought could be mine. The way we came together felt so right, so perfect, but it was all a lie.

I need to burn it all down.

EURI FIGURES out how to work the Bluetooth speakers, and we put on Slayer's 'Reign in Blood' and go to town on the library. I tear into the leather sofa with the carving knife I took from the hotel, while Euri smashes objects from the shelves onto the floor. (She won't touch the books, because even in the midst of revenge, Euri is still Euri.)

"I've never understood heavy metal until this moment," Euri cries gleefully as she hurls glasses from the bar at the fireplace, where they break with a satisfying *SMASH*. "It's music to break shit to."

"Agreed. You can't hear a riff like that and not feel powerful." I finish with the couch and move on to the leather wingback chair Victor was so fond of. Slash, stab, slash, I imagine plunging my knife into Vic's smug face.

This is even more fun than the rage room in Victor's basement.

I cut and I stab and I smash until my muscles scream with pain, until every good memory, every thought that what we had that night might've been powerful enough to last, has been obliterated.

Euri and I collapse into a pile in the middle of our destruction. "I feel awful about the books," Euri says. "I tried to be careful, but a few on the lower shelves are covered in alcohol."

"It's for a good cause. I'm sure the books will forgive us." I help Euri to her feet, making sure to pick up the bottles we saved. "Come on. It's time for the next phase of our plan. Jell-O shots."

24

FERGIE

Euri and I are in the kitchen, dancing around to the Hu (Mongolian throat-singing metal. It's awesome) and pulling our trays of Jell-O shots from the fridge, when Cassius and Victor burst through the door.

My stepbrother's presence sucks all the air from the room, and not just because he smells from a workout. That plum and carnation scent of his swims inside my skull, driving out all other rational thought. I hope that one day I'll be able to be near him without the weight of everything between us crushing my bones to ash.

"What the fuck are you doing in my house?" Cas thunders.

"Last I heard, it's not your house anymore," I say sweetly, as if I hadn't timed this encounter exactly. "Besides, it's my house, too. Or have you forgotten, brother? I'm family, and you can't kill family, no matter what they do to you. Especially since I'm under your mother's protection."

Vic moves between us, his dark chocolate and hazelnut scent invading my nostrils as he uses his body to shield me from Cas' wrath. But it doesn't turn me to goo the way it used to. Now it just makes me more determined not to be his pawn.

"You should get out of here," Vic says, his voice calm and even, nothing like that broken guy who showed up at my door yesterday. "I can hold Cas back, but not for long."

"I'm done needing you to protect me, Victor August." I hold up a tray. "Jell-O shot? These ones are watermelon."

"Sure." Victor picks a few off the tray. I hear him toss his head back and lick the jelly out of the tiny cups. "Hey, these are good."

"They are, aren't they? The trick is to use decent alcohol. None of that blended crap. I went for the absolute top shelf whisky."

"What the—" Glass clinks as Cas swipes the empty bottle off the counter. "This is a Macallan Lalique seventy-two-year single malt. It's worth a couple hundred grand. Where did you get this? I have a bottle of this upstairs, but I haven't opened it yet..."

The room falls silent as his words sink in.

"Jell-O shot, brother dearest?" I hold out the tray.

The tray disappears from my hand. A moment later, I hear a *SMASH* and a hilarious popping sound as several Jell-O shots hit the wall behind us.

"That was a seventy-two-year-old Scotch?" Cassius growls. "You made my seventy-two-year-old Scotch into *Jell-O shots*?"

I toss my head back and suck out the jelly in one of the tiny cups. "Mmmm. This one is grape flavor. Are you sure you don't want one? We have plenty more where these came from."

I back up to the fridge and open the door, letting them have a good look at the trays of fruity shots lining the shelves inside. I keep telling myself that I'm safe, I'm safe, I have Cali's protection, but I can't bring myself to turn my back on Cassius, not when his hatred radiates through the room.

"Um, Cas..." Victor makes a choking noise. I hear him pulling more empty bottles of old, expensive single malt out of the recycling bin. "She's not kidding."

There are very few times in my life where I bother wishing that I can see. But I do wish on all the gods that I could have just a *peek* at my brother's face as it burns red with rage. But the wheezing sounds he's making as he realizes we've made hundreds of thousands of dollars of Scotch into fruit-flavored Jell-O shots is fucking worth it.

Cassius roars and storms upstairs. I hear the water running as he gets ready for a shower. Victor plucks the tiny shot from my hand and tosses it back.

"That was both incredibly stupid and incredibly hot, Duchess. I don't know what to say."

"You can say whatever you like because I don't give a shit about your opinion anymore." I pull off my apron and fold it on the chair. "It's almost time for us to leave."

Another roar from upstairs. Cas must've discovered the surprise we left in the shower head. Victor's hand lands on my shoulder. "I don't know what you did, Duchess, but you'd better run."

"Not quiiiite yet..."

I grab Euri's arm and we run into the foyer just as Cas leans over the railing above. I can hear his wet feet on the tiles and water dripping onto the floor in front of me. Euri's phone clicks as she starts her camera rolling.

"What the fuck did you do to me?" he yells. "I'm blue!"

Beside me, Vic chokes. "Cas, you're... you're..."

"I'm fucking blue!" Cas howls.

"If you're sad, perhaps you need Victor to come and give you a cuddle," I call up sweetly.

"No, you fucking bitch, you dyed my skin blue! And it won't wash out."

"No, it won't," I reply. "We used methylene blue. Hospitals use it as a dye to check connections. Get used to it, Papa Smurf, because you're going to be blue for months. You got that on video, Euri?"

"Yup." She grabs my hand. "Let's go."

We grab up our tote bags and make a run for the door. Cassius bellows, and I can hear him crashing down the stairs after us. I don't have my cane, so I have to trust that Euri won't let me hit anything. We make it out onto the street, where her sister is waiting for us.

"I've been so worried," she says as she throws the car doors open. "I saw Victor's car arrive and it suddenly occurs to me that I've let my younger sister walk into Cassius' Dio's home with only her blind friend for company."

"It was worth it." Euri taps her phone. "Want to see?"

She plays the video she took of a naked, dripping wet, blue Cassius Dio raging at the top of the stairs. Even though I can't see it, I can listen to his angry, panicked voice, and it warms my fucking coal heart.

Artie burns rubber away. I assume she's taking us home, but instead she climbs up the road toward the coast and parks. "We're at the old Harrington Hills cemetery," she says, turning around in the seat. "It's private here, and I'm not quite ready to go home yet. There's a bottle of Champagne in the trunk for you, Fergie. Give me that phone again, sister. I need to watch Papa Smurf Dio again. And again. And again."

25

FERGIE

By the time Artie drops me off at the hotel, Euri has already uploaded the video of naked, blue Cassius to social media. I do a victory dance in the elevator and skip into the hotel room as I fill Torsten in on the whole afternoon.

I don't expect him to get the joke, but I'm surprised that he's angry with me.

"Why would you encourage Cas' wrath? You know he's going to get you back for this, and it will be brutal."

I shrug. "He's already done the worst thing he could possibly do to me. I'm not afraid of Cassius Dio."

Torsten throws his brush across the room. It bounces off a wall and drops to the floor. I hear an excited yowl as Spartacus darts after it.

"I don't want you to go to school tomorrow," he growls.

"Well, that's too bad, because I'm going. By now the video is going to be circulating far and wide, and I want to bask in his misery the way he delighted in mine. You don't have to come, though, if it's hard for you—"

Torsten sighs. "I'll go with you. Maybe if he sees me, he'll go easy on you."

I think about Cas' animalistic cries as he chased us out of the house. "Don't count on it."

26

FERGIE

Torsten, Euri, and I walk into Stonehurst Prep with our heads held high. For the first time since Cas and Juliet leaked the video of me, I don't spend every second imagining that the people around me are watching it. I don't hear my name whispered on the breeze. I don't feel their eyes crawling over my skin.

Instead, all I hear is my brother's name and the sweet sound of their cruel laughter.

"Do you think that blue dye is really permanent?" someone says as we cross the courtyard toward the lockers.

"With his cheeks puffed up like that, he looks like a blueberry Gobstopper," a girl giggles with her friend as they come out of the library.

"He should make Papa Smurf his new stage name," chimes in Xavier, one of Victor's friends from the basketball team. His teammates chortle. "It'll sure put the fear of God into his opponents."

"He could take up the drums like his brother, and join the Blue Man Group," Bevan McManus, the captain of the lacrosse team, chortles.

Yes. Yes. *Yes*.

For the first time ever, Cassius Dio's name no longer strikes fear into the hearts of Stonehurst Prep students. He's gone from being the monster under our beds to the campus joke, and I am *here* for it.

I don't expect Cas to show up at school. It's not as if my stepbrother has any interest in classes. But when the whispers and muffled chortles of the student body intensify around me, taking on a nervous energy, I know that he's arrived in the building. This will be interesting.

I'm at Euri's locker, holding her books while she juggles her science project and the yearbook camera, when the entire hall falls immediately, eerily silent.

"Omigod," Euri whispers. "Cassius is walking down the corridor towards us *right now*. And he's still completely blue."

"Describe him to me," I say, loud enough that everyone around can hear it.

A girl behind us gasps at my audacity. Today I feel fucking untouchable.

"He's properly blue," Euri says, louder now. "Not a blue tinge, but his face, his hair, his arms – they're all dyed a deep, bright blue. And when you combine that with the sage green on his uniform, well...it's quite something."

"Yes," I grin, hoping he can see my face. "And the best news is, that dye won't wash out of his skin for *months*."

I hear the click of a camera. Beside me, Torsten says, "We need a picture for the yearbook."

CLICK CLICK.

From the other end of the corridor, Cassius *growls*. Students cry and scream and scramble out of the way, but I hold my ground.

Next thing I know, my back's against a locker, and my stepbrother's lips are pressing against mine.

He doesn't kiss me. He's just... there, breathing against me, letting me taste his rage, letting me *feel* the thin tendrils of his control slipping away. His hands grip my wrists, pushing my arms to my sides. His chest presses hard against mine, pinning me in and preventing me from getting a hold on him.

"You'd better fix this, Sunflower," he growls. "Find some soap or solvent that gets this dye off. I've got a fight on Friday, and I'm not showing up looking like a blueberry Popsicle."

"No can do," I say. My lips curl back into a saccharine smile. I enjoy the way his body quivers as he feels that smile, as he learns how deeply I find pleasure in his misery. "I wouldn't worry too much, brother dearest. After the video we took of you dancing around your house naked and blue does the rounds of the internet, your fighting career is *over*. Not even the hardest criminals will want to beat up on their childhood hero Papa Smurf."

"You're a fucking bitch!" he yells.

"No, Cas. I'm the girl who's getting even. *You're* the one who made a snap judgment about me, without even talking to me, and you did the one thing you knew would hurt me most. *You* acted like a little bitch because you're so afraid of intimacy that you can't talk to me about what really matters. You lost me, and when I'm done with you, you'll lose everything you ever cared about, and you'll have only yourself to blame."

"I haven't lost a damn thing except for a soon-to-be-dead stepsister I didn't even want," he growls.

"Wrong," I shoot back. "Where are your two best friends, huh? Where's the invincible, impenetrable Poison Ivy Club? In case you're so thick that you haven't noticed, Torsten's standing by my side, and Victor came to see me the other night, *begging* for me to forgive him. We had something great together, Cassius, something rare and bright and beautiful. *You* destroyed it, and in the process you did exactly what many in this school have wanted to do for years. You broke Poison Ivy. I've taken your best friends from you, and I've taken your fighting career, and your expensive whisky, and I'm coming for everything else you hold dear."

"You won't be able to do anything if I snap your neck right now," Cas yells.

His hand flies at my throat, his fingers scraping my skin. And that's exactly what I want him to do. His movement buys me the space I need to get leverage on him. As he squeezes his fingers into my neck, I draw on every ounce of strength and flip him.

His fingers fly from my throat as I slam him into the lockers. Students scream and duck for cover as he skids across the slippery tiles, howling with pain.

"I *dare* you to hurt me, Cassius Dio," I shout after him. "Do your worst. You've already betrayed me in the most perfect, evil way. Don't you get it, brother? Nothing you do can touch me now."

His breath wheezes as he struggles to get control of himself. "You betrayed *me*."

"No, Cas. I kept a secret from you because I'd been betrayed by someone I loved before and I didn't trust myself to fall in love again." I don't want to say the words, because they feel like tearing a hole through my own ribs, but I also know that only these words will have the power to cut him. "I *loved* you, Cassius Dio. I loved your strength and your brutality and your twisted sense of right and wrong. I would have died for you. *You're* the one who took that love and spat on it."

"You betrayed me!" Cas howls like an animal that's cornered and broken and alone. The sound shakes my very soul.

I hear his feet skid on the tiles as he drags himself to his feet and the roar of pure hatred that issues from his mouth as he charges at me. Euri screams. Torsten moves in front of me, blocking me with his body—

CLONK.

I don't know what's happening. All I know is that Cas doesn't hit us. Instead, there's a thump, and he moans with agony. There's a second clonk as someone sets down a hard metal object. It sounds like one of the large fire extinguishers kept in strategic locations around the school.

Someone hit Cas with a fire extinguisher.

I guess even the monstrous Cassius Dio can be stopped if you have enough hatred and metal behind you. But what brave soul would dare to step forward and risk his wrath—

"Cas."

It's Victor.

Of course it fucking is.

"Get up," Victor yells at his former friend, and I get the sense from the way people are shuffling that he's swinging around that fire extinguisher like a man possessed. His words still sound a little slurred. "Get up, you bastard. Face me. Face up to what you did."

"I told you that I don't need you to fucking save me, August." I curl my hands into fists. *No fucking way* does Victor get to steal this moment from me.

"You're right, Fergie. Everyone in this school can see you are the real Queen here," Victor puffs, every word dripping with sadness. "I'm not doing this for you. This is for me. Because you're right – the four of us had something amazing and Cas ruined it, and I let it happen. It may be too late for us, but it's not too late for me to stave his fucking skull in. I don't know if it will make this awful pain in my chest go away, but I'm willing to give it a go."

"Get out of my fucking face," Cas growls as he staggers to his feet. I hear Victor grunt as he hits the lockers. The blow must wind him because he starts making this horrible wheezing sound that makes me want to run to him.

But I don't. I root my feet in place, and I squeeze Torsten's hand so hard that he cries out. Cas' footsteps pound on the tiles as he shoves his way through the crowd.

"That's it, Papa Smurf. Run away!" I scream after him. "Run away from your mess just like you did with Gemma!"

"I hate you!" he screams back, and a moment later, a window shatters and he's gone.

CASSIUS

I run.

I run with shards of glass sticking out of my skin.

I run until my chest heaves and my monstrous heart feels like it's about to collapse into my chest.

I run until my legs give out and I collapse in a heap on the ground.

Only then do I look up and see where I am. I'm lying in the charred, packed earth outside the old horticulture building, staring up at the broken roof.

Nothing you do can touch me now.

Those words were so eerily similar to what Gemma said to me, all those years ago. I think about Fergie doing what Gemma did to herself, and my chest goes all tight and I can't fucking breathe.

When I was with Gemma, that was the first time I ever dared to believe I could be somebody more than this brute. If someone had killed her, I could have lived with it. I could have broken every neck in this fucking city until I made them pay, and in my vengeance, I might've eventually felt worthy of her love.

But *she* killed herself. She jumped and broke her body

because I broke her mind. Because she wanted to get away from me. And now I've done it again.

All I ever want is to keep my family close. My mother. Victor. Torsten. Gaius told me that he'd be my big brother always, no matter that we're not blood-related, no matter what I did or what happened. But then he left me. And he won't even talk to me. He won't accept my calls.

I *have* to do what I do, otherwise people leave and I'm alone. Victor and Torsten know what I'll do to them if they ever leave me.

But they left me anyway.

Fergie once said that she understood me, that she saw something of herself inside me. Today, when I stared down into those shattered emerald eyes, I saw a monster staring back at me. And I think she may be right – she might be the only person who understands how to love a monster, because she's a monster herself.

For the first time, I thought someone cared for me because of who I am, not *despite* who I am. But now she's dyed me fucking *blue.*

She dyed me blue and put it on the internet, and I have a fucking fight on Friday. When I step into the ring, my opponent isn't going to quake with fear. He's going to *laugh.*

And with the bomb at the museum, people are starting to question if the Triumvirate really holds the power in Emerald Beach. I can *feel* the shift in the air as the question on everyone's lips goes unanswered for days. Who's going after the Imperators? How did they nearly succeed? What will happen if Dio or August or Lucian falls?

Our soldiers are looking to us for guidance, for strength, and I'm on the internet throwing a fucking tantrum. No wonder my mother still won't take my calls, and Victor's swinging fire extinguishers at my head.

I wince as I press my fingers into the growing lump on the side of my skull.

She stole Victor and Torsten from me. The red mist creeps into the edges of my vision as I picture Torsten flinging himself in front of her, his eyes wide with fear. He was afraid of *me*. Torsten's always trusted everything I do. He's the one person I can count on not to question me or call me dumb or tiptoe around me because he doesn't want to set me off. Torsten's always treated me the same as he treats everyone else, and I didn't know how much I needed that until he threw himself in front of Fergie today.

We're in the middle of the most important power play in the entire history of the Triumvirate, and I should be leading our family at my mother's side, but Fergie fucking Macintosh made me look weak, and Cassius Dio is not fucking weak.

I'll show my stepsister. I'll show my ungrateful friends. I'll show them *all*.

Throughout the rest of the day, all anyone can talk about is my altercation with Cas and Victor. I find myself constantly pressing my fingers into my neck, running them over the bruises from where my stepbrother held me today, and the older one from Galen's place.

"I've been listening to this true crime podcast called *My Dad is a Gerbil*, and they talk about how strangulation indicates a highly personal and emotional attack," Euri says as we wait in line in the cafeteria. "It means that the perpetrator gets up close with their victim, they get to watch the life leave their eyes."

I consider this. Both of our physical altercations since the release of the video have ended in Cas' hands around my neck. My stepbrother could have shot me on the street, or even hired one of Cali's goons to take care of me. But he wants to do it himself.

And he could have done it today, in front of the whole school. I surprised him with that jiujitsu move and then Victor clonked him in the head, but he's Cassius fucking Dio. He's The Bear. He's a cold-blooded killing machine. And yet... the monstrous, dangerous Cassius Dio *ran*.

What I don't understand is why.

Did something I say get to him?

And why, after everything, do I *care*?

It doesn't take long for my stepbrother to have his revenge.

The next day, Euri and Torsten and I get to school early to do some work in the *Sentinel* offices. Only, when we turn the corner, Euri gasps. "Something's not right. Fergie. The door is kind of... distorted. The glass is smashed."

She steps forward and I hear her trying to open it, but she can't do it. Torsten manages to pull the door off its hinges, and the three of us enter the newsroom.

Euri sobs, and I know without seeing that everything is destroyed. I know by the acrid smell in the air. My stepbrother doesn't do things by halves. He fucking *commits*.

"Euri, are you okay? Tell me what you see," I breathe.

"Fergie..." Euri's voice wavers as she picks through the remnants of her office.

"Tell me."

"The computers are in bits on the floor. Their innards have been pulled out and someone has... has *pissed* on them. Cas' sacer is on the wall. He didn't just want to hurt us, he wanted to obliterate everything I've worked for." Her voice wobbles. "I've never done anything to him."

"You're friends with me, and that's enough. I'm sorry."

We back out of the room. Euri alerts the school office to the vandalism (not that they'll do anything – they won't risk angering the Triumvirate by going after one of their kids). We decide to head to the art suite, which is usually empty before school. Torsten can get us a private studio and we'll have some space to process this. But when we arrive at the art suite, it's in *uproar*. Kids are yelling and Mrs. Shelby, the head art teacher, is yelling down the phone.

"What happened?" I cry out.

"Cassius Dio is what fucking happened," Meredith growls as she brushes past us. "Someone's painted your name over every in-progress work on the easels, and all the finished pieces we've hung on the walls. Every piece of work we were submitting for our college portfolios is destroyed."

Torsten drops my arm. He bolts into an adjacent studio. A moment later I hear him unleash a sound that's so filled with anguish that it stops my coal heart.

Euri slips her arm through mine and leads me through to the private studio. Torsten's on the ground in front of us, making that noise that rends my soul. Euri gasps.

"It's a painting," she says. "Someone has torn it to pieces. But Fergie, it's a painting of you. You're... you were... *beautiful*. You're standing in a garden of what looks like Monet's flowers and water lilies, and there's paper and clay to make the flowers stand out. It's... it's..."

I drop to my knees beside him. "Torsten, I'm so sorry."

His hand reaches for mine. He's rocking back and forth, trembling, muttering nonsense under his breath. "I made this for you," he says to me. "I wanted to give it to you, to... to... show you how I feel... that I finally *understand*..."

I squeeze his hand back. "You show me how you feel every single day. I'm so lucky to have you, Torsten. It's going to be okay, I promise. Everything is going to be okay."

He shudders. "He's stabbed you right through the heart. He's cut up your face. He's obliterated you."

Torsten doesn't care that Cassius destroyed his artwork. All he sees is Cas' rage at me displayed ten feet high for everyone to see. Even in his darkest moments, all Torsten can think about is me.

"Come on." I drag him to his feet. "There's nothing we can do here. Let's get out of here before I'm lynched by angry artists."

"But Cas—"

"Cas still thinks he can destroy me by hurting the people I care about," I say. "He's only half wrong. When you bleed, I bleed. But if he thinks this will make me stop, he's a fool as well as a brute. He's not the only one who marks his victims for death – by the end of the week he'll be running scared."

29

FERGIE

E uri's afraid to sleep alone or even go back to her house in case Cassius follows her and hurts her family. I don't have the heart to tell her that if Cassius wants to find out where she lives, he can do that in an instant through his mother's connections.

Instead, Torsten and I take her back to the hotel.

If Robert the concierge is miffed about the gradually-increasing number of women living in Torsten's room, he says nothing about it. He does bring us a second room-service menu.

Euri and I spend the night drinking our way through the hotel's impressive cocktail list and pouring over our photographs of the ledger book. I try to ask Torsten about some of the notes, but he won't break the oath of silence he swore to Cas and Victor.

One of the first things I notice is how many times Juliet's name comes up in the payment column. Victor bargained away his morals to get his sister a summer internship with the NYC designer Marcus Ribald, tickets to high-profile events, and introductions to influential people. Juliet might not have been an official member of the club, but she certainly gained a lot from their business.

I store this information away for later. I have plans for Juliet. But first... I want the three of them to know that I'm coming for them. I want everyone at Stonehurst Prep to know that Poison Ivy is truly finished.

I'M SITTING in Chemistry class, diligently filling in the assignment for both me and Torsten, while he scribbles away in his sketchbook. My phone beeps with a text. I read it and quickly type a reply before Mr. Dallas can catch me, and resume my work.

A murmur shifts through the class – a faint shuffling, a few whispers, the usual sort of sounds, but the murmur grows and grows until it becomes loud exclamations and stools scraping as students flee to the windows.

"What is it?"

"Why is it glowing and hovering?"

"It... it looks like a flying saucer."

Never underestimate Californians when it comes to believing something ridiculous.

I can't see what they're all looking at, of course, but I *can* see lights flashing outside the window. Torsten and I move behind them so we can see. Even Mr. Dallas stops grading papers and joins us at the window.

A girl screams. "It's opening!"

There's a huge bright flash, and everyone screams. The warning bell rings. Mr. Dallas yells, "I've just got a message from the principal. Everyone out. We're evacuating."

Students cry out that we shouldn't evacuate, that we should be locking the school down, instead, but Mr. Dallas has his instructions and he won't falter. I join the throng of students crowding the doorway. Everyone runs in a different direction, heedless to the teachers trying to restore order. I'm separated from Torsten as the crowd pulls us along. As I round the corner of the corridor, an arm slips through mine.

"It's me," Euri whispers. "Torsten did an amazing job. I know what's going on, and even I believed that thing is real."

She yanks me into a supply closet and pulls the door closed behind us. I settle in behind a shelf of paints and cleaning supplies, listening to the hallways crowd with noise as the school evacuates. We don't have much time before this whole situation escalates.

The noise dies down. The door creaks as Euri pokes her head out. "The coast is clear," she says. "Come on."

I pick up the bag of supplies we stashed here earlier and follow Euri out, my cane rolling over the tiles. I don't need her to guide me – I've walked this path enough times this year. I know exactly where I'm going.

I stop in front of Cassius' locker. I rummage around in the bag and pull out the stencil Torsten made me last night and the can of spray paint. Euri helps me tape the stencil to the locker, and then I shake the can, uncap the lid, and spray.

It's a Death Lily.

My mark.

My sacer.

We finish Cassius' locker and move on to Victor's. I feel a stab of something like guilt, but I shove it down. He deserves this as much as the other two. I'm not going to forgive him just because he came groveling to my hotel room or tried to stick up for me in the corridor.

Euri tapes the stencil to the locker and presses the spray can in my hand. I laugh as I cover the stencil in paint, marking Victor as the next on my list.

The Death Lily is coming for him.

Finally, we hit Juliet's locker.

"You have to do this one," I tell Euri.

"It would be my pleasure."

Euri's hand trembles as she takes the can from me. This is probably the first time she's ever done anything like this, anything remotely illegal or against the rules. I'm proud as fuck of her. I hear the spray of the paint and breathe in the noxious fumes as she writes our final message on the wall:

THE POISON IVY CLUB IS OVER.
DEATH LILY WILL COME FOR YOU ALL.

30

VICTOR

After checking Juliet got out safely, I mill around with some of my basketball buddies, who are all talking about that crazy flying saucer, and phone my mother. After she hangs up, a hulking mass walks in front of me, blocking out the sun.

Cas.

"What the fuck was that?" he demands.

"How should I know?" I turn away from him. It's hard to look at his blue-stained face and not crack up laughing, and I can't laugh at him while he's got that dangerous glint in his eyes or I'll end up with my head through a window.

He shouldn't even be at school today. He's too dangerous, too unhinged. One wrong move and he'll start ripping heads off. I have to get him home...

No, Cas Dio is not my problem anymore, not since he's decided to destroy the woman I love.

But he doesn't get the message. He grabs my shoulder and whirls me around, dragging me up close to his scarred face. "It could be a bomb. Just like the one that nearly blew you up."

A *bomb*.

At that word, my knees wobble a little. I flashback to that sickening moment when I was running through the museum and the ground pitched out from beneath me and the edges of the world caved in.

I was *bombed*. I was in a coma for three days. My parents are running around in a panic that someone is after our family. My ex-best friend has me in a death grip and has a look in his eyes that suggests he might snap me in two any moment now.

But none of it feels real to me without Fergie.

I hold up my phone. "Of course it occurred to me. That's why Mom's sending soldiers over here right now. We need to make sure we catch this guy before he does any more damage. But that's all I can do from here. I'm not exactly going to walk up to a bomb and kick it."

"Is Torsten out?" he growls.

I glance around, searching for that familiar head of raven-dark hair. In the chaos of the evacuation and checking on Juliet and reporting to Mom, I hadn't found Torsten yet. I know he's at school today because I saw him with Fergie this morning, but I can't see him now—

Fergie.

Shit.

Where's Fergie?

I scan the crowd for her, but she's not here. Panic rises in my chest. Where is she?

I don't even care that she's not my girl anymore. I have to know that she's okay. I call her phone, but it goes straight to voicemail.

I glance back over my shoulder at the police swarming the school as a huge cloud of noxious gas spews from the 'flying saucer' site. I'm too skeptical to believe it's aliens, and looking at that lump of twisted metal, I start to wonder...

One of the officers, who is really Mom's soldier Marius

working undercover, gestures for me to step aside with him. He flips open a pad so that he appears to be taking my statement, and he leans in close and says, "The good news is, it's not a bomb."

My body slumps in relief. "And the bad news?"

"No bad news yet, just strange news. That device looks like a movie prop or some shit – it's just metal and wires, but it's got a computer inside it that's set to make lots of noise and smoke and a big flash. Best I can guess, it's one of your school buddies playing a prank – I'm guessing that the goal was to get everyone out of the building for some reason."

"Have you swept the building?"

"They're working on it." He nods to his colleagues. "We caught some kids sneaking out the back. One of them was that girl you were fucking in that video—"

Fergie. She's okay.

And she's behind this stunt, I'm sure of it. The flying saucer with the computer brain has an air of Torsten about it. But I can't fathom the purpose of it beyond getting everyone off class for a couple of hours.

I don't have to wait long to find out. After the police clear the building, we're allowed back inside. I wander across the court-yard with Xavier, heading toward my locker, and I see the mark.

Kids stand around staring at it, but no one dares to touch it. The paint is only just drying at the edges. It's the exact same thing we used to do to students who incurred our wrath.

A promise.

A warning.

A *sacer*.

Only, this isn't a Poison Ivy mark. It's an outline of a flower – a lily, by the looks of it.

"You got one, too." Juliet frowns as she taps her fingernails in the still-drying paint. "My locker is defaced, too, and there's a big crude message on the wall by the auditorium. Victor, you have to *do* something. We can't allow this to go unpunished."

"We did this to people all the time, and we were never punished."

I touch my finger to the edge of the paint, and the desperate, hopeful part of me imagines I smell the faint scent of raspberries lingering in the air.

Juliet grabs my shoulder. She shoves me – not hard enough to hurt, but I'm snapped back to reality. "Open your eyes, brother," she says. "Fergie's trying to take over this school. She actually thinks she can *bring us down*. Oooh, I'm going to make that bitch *pay*."

"You will not fucking touch her," I growl.

"You can't still have feelings for her—"

"Is your head buried that far up your ass that you don't know what's happening out there? This is bigger than me now, Juliet. That bomb made Mom appear weak. All three families lost huge deals and alliances – not to mention a considerable amount of our wealth – when that museum went up. Yara is *dead*. People believe the bomber is after Mom, and I think they're probably right. Lucian and Dio soldiers want her to stay out of the business until we catch this enemy. Things are precarious right now, and you and Fergie fighting this battle in public isn't helping."

"She started it by lying—"

"—and you're ending it. I don't care how much you hate Fergie – she's Cali Dio's stepdaughter. Like it or not, she is one of us now, and you put revenge porn of her on the internet. That's going to come back on our mother, on all of us. If you pursue this battle, it could break up the peace between our families. We have to be very careful, Juliet, or this could end in an all-out war."

My sister's face crumples, and she turns away in disgust. I

swipe my finger through the paint, and I bring it to my nose and sniff. Yes, definitely raspberries.

My chest flutters a little.

I'm in *love*.

The Jell-O shots, the blue paint in Cas' shower, and now this – Fergie has marked us as hers, the same way Cas marked her when she first came to school. She's doing to us exactly what we did to her, but she's doing it slowly, and publicly, drawing out the torture so we'll be looking over our shoulders for her next move.

When I first laid eyes on Fergie, I knew that she was anything but boring. I adored having her as a lover, but as an enemy, she's positively *intoxicating*. She's raised the stakes, and even though every public move she makes against us causes trouble for our families, I can't wait to see what she does next.

I *want* Fergie to punish me. I'll take anything she wants to give if it will keep her in my life.

THAT EVENING, I come home after practice to hear Juliet and Mom having a shouting match. I tiptoe down the hall and listen in at the door to the study.

"You have to do something," Juliet yells. "Talk to Cali – she should have her stepdaughter on a shorter lead. Fergie's turning the entire school against us. "

Mom slams a desk drawer. "I think you did that yourselves when you took over Gaius' little club and started manipulating college placements."

"That's Victor's thing. I have nothing to do with any of it because I know you didn't approve. *Fergie* is the one who hired them. She's the one who started sleeping with all three of them, playing them off against each other—"

"Juliet August, I sincerely hope you're not slut-shaming a

woman for having more than one partner," Mom's voice carries a warning tone.

"No, of course not," Juliet says quickly. "I just mean that she shouldn't be allowed to come after us like this. Our three families should be showing strength and solidarity right now, but she's turned Cas and Vic and Torsten against each other—"

"I've got hundreds of artifacts in need of a new home, creditors calling in their debts, contracts being canceled in every direction, and some dickweasel mailing parcel bombs to your brother," Mom snaps. She sounds tired. "I do *not* have time to adjudicate petty playground squabbles."

"It's not a petty squabble. Fergie is trying to destroy—"

"Fergie has a sex video she didn't consent to circulating around the internet. Honestly, I think she's handling things extremely well, given the circumstances. I hope she finds out who's responsible and gives them a bit of Dio justice."

Mom clearly doesn't know about Juliet's part in the video's release. She doesn't even seem to know that Cas is ultimately responsible, which is interesting. I believe Cali knows what Cas did and that's why she kicked him out of his house, but this means that Cali hasn't told my mom what she knows.

This is... not good. On the one hand, if anyone in our world found out that Juliet, an August, had tried to use a sex tape to bring down a Dio, retribution would be swift and bloody. Mom has strict rules about this, and I respect and abide by those rules. But on the other hand, our mothers tell each other everything. It's the basis of their entire system. For Cali to keep this secret...

...it means the Triumvirate is on shaky ground.

I'm too unnerved to listen to any more of it, so I slink away. After saying hi to Noah and Eli (who are hiding in the kitchen, eating takeout pizza), I head upstairs to my room and turn on my computer.

I have a mountain of schoolwork waiting for me, but I can't

think about any of that now. I've got my Harvard acceptance, so it doesn't matter anyway. The only thing that matters is making it right with Fergie. And I know where to begin. I need to get to know the girl I love. The *real* Fergie.

I have a name.

Fergie Macintosh.

I check that the door to my bedroom is closed, then log in to the VPN Torsten set up for me. We know that someone has been hacking our phones – that's how they got those videos of Sierra and Meredith. I don't want to lead whoever it is straight to Fergie's secrets.

With trembling fingers, I turn off safe search and type in Fergie's real name.

The first link is to a popular revenge porn site. It's Fergie's face in the thumbnail, those shattered emerald eyes focused on some spot to the left of the camera, her lips parted in a coy half-smile.

I can't bear to watch the video, but I click through to the page and read the comments of all the men who I'm going to kill.

It's exactly as bad as I suspected. Page after page of angry, microdick keyboard warriors making crude remarks about her body and her eyesight and listing all the unspeakable things they'd like to do to her. Dawson had provided her social media accounts and home address, and these shitstains talk gleefully about turning up at her house, following her at school and her after-school library job, and ringing Harvard admissions to tell them what a slut she is. By the time I've read through all eight pages of vile hatred, I'm ready to channel my inner Cas and start castrating some bitches. I'd be doing the world a favor.

I leave a link to the worst offenders in the chat for Torsten to see when he logs in, in case he can track them down or do anything about getting the video removed. I know he's not talking to me, but if it's for Fergie he'd probably be willing to help.

The next few articles are newspaper pieces from Fergie's hometown and state about her and her father trying to sue the school and the website to have the video taken down. I read a couple, but then I think about what Cas did, and I can't read anymore. We have revenge porn laws in California, but dragging Cas and Juliet through the courts would not go down well with our parents. I can see why Fergie's decided to go after her own justice.

A few pages into the search, I start to see other things come up with her name. There's a youtube video called "Death Lily: Jiujitsu Under-17 World Championships," with Fergie's name in the caption. I think of the lily Fergie stenciled on our lockers.

I click on the link.

The video starts playing. It's a montage of shots from several jiujitsu bouts – each with the same flame-haired girl fighting different opponents. The fight replays are interspersed with that same flame-haired girl bowing her head to receive medal after medal.

I don't know fighting the way Cas does, but I know enough to see that this girl is incredible. As soon as she has hold of her opponent, she can bring them down. Even when she looks beaten, she's able to power through and claim a win.

The girl is Fergie.

No wonder she was able to bring Cas down with those moves of hers. She's blind, fighting sighted opponents, and she's a jiujitsu *world champion*.

Whenever she finishes a bout, she looks surprised, like she'd forgotten she was taking part in a match. She goes to another place when she fights – somewhere inside her head where no one else can reach her.

She's never looked more beautiful to me.

"I had to give up everything when I came here," Fergie said to me when I was on Galen's bed. Looking at this video, I suddenly understand what she means.

I keep looking through the old links. There are numerous articles on jiujitsu websites and forums about Fergie. I read an article she wrote for a disability advocacy magazine about why jiujitsu is a great sport for blind and vision-impaired people, and see that she's spent summers teaching classes at camps for blind children all over Massachusetts. Another link directs me to articles she's written for her school newspaper, many of which have won journalism awards.

And like a complete numbnuts, I insisted on writing her Harvard essay for her.

For the first time since Juliet was taken, I feel the prick of tears welling in my eyes. No one's here to see, so I don't wipe them away. I let them fall in angry waterfalls down my cheeks.

Fergie Macintosh is a brilliant, accomplished woman who deserved a spot at Harvard. She deserved to have her old life. It's not fair that all she has in the world is us, and that Cas and I destroyed even that for her.

Well, maybe everyone in the world has forgotten Fergie Macintosh, but I haven't. And I will do whatever it takes to make sure that she has *everything* she deserves.

31

FERGIE

Torsten and I spend a few blissful days in his hotel suite, ignoring the rest of the world. Torsten paints and I listen to audiobooks (I'm onto this fun series by Steffanie Holmes about this blind girl who solves murder mysteries in a magical bookshop, and all her boyfriends are fictional characters).

I talk to Euri every day so she knows I'm still alive, but I don't bother going to school. I know that when the article comes out, I'll be saying goodbye to Harvard, and the idea of thinking about any kind of future for myself just makes me feel numb, and I don't want to ever feel numb again. Better to hold onto this all-consuming rage.

I keep waiting for the Harvard admissions to see the sex video and rescind my acceptance, but they don't. And that weirdly makes me even angrier. Perhaps if I'd known they didn't care about sex tapes, I wouldn't have given up my whole life to come to fucking Emerald Beach and meet the Poison Ivy Club and have my stepbrother completely fuck up my life.

I don't want to leave the safety of the hotel, but I know I'm going to have to face the real world at some point. Cas calls

Torsten repeatedly, but he refuses to pick up the phone, although he does spend a lot of time on his computer, clicking and typing and muttering to himself.

On Sunday morning, I'm sitting on the balcony of our room, sipping an espresso and pretending I'm in a Venice cafe instead of the fake plastic shithole that is Emerald Beach. Torsten sinks into the chair beside me. He doesn't say anything, but I can tell from the tension sizzling in the air between us that he wants to talk.

"Torsten," I say.

"I have to tell you something."

"Okay." I don't like his tone.

"I discovered that Sierra and Coach Franklin weren't lying. They were sent the videos taken as evidence by Poison Ivy. The videos were sent from Victor's phone."

"You're serious?"

"My information is accurate."

"But... Victor wouldn't do that." Everything I know about Victor August says that he would never undermine his own word.

Torsten doesn't say anything, but I hear his hand flapping and I know he's getting agitated. I hold up my hands. "I'm sorry. I wasn't questioning your research. I'm just finding it hard to believe that Victor would break his own rules like that. And for what purpose?"

"Other videos have been sent from his phone, too."

"Other videos?"

"Yes, Peaches O'Connor received the video of her bribing a teacher last week, while Victor was in his coma. This video was taken four years ago by Gaius Dio. I understand that because of that she pulled out of her place at the Ribald fashion showcase."

"Did she now?" Hmmmm. The pieces were starting to fit together in my head.

But before I had a chance to voice my theory, the intercom bleeped and Robert the concierge called out to us. "Miss Fergie, another package arrived for you. Would you like me to bring it in for you?"

I groan. Victor may have been obeying my demand to stay away, but he's been sending me things every day – chocolates and Harry and David fruit and expensive toiletries and purses...

"Sure, Robert. Bring them in."

The door clicks open, and Robert heads out onto the balcony and places something on the table in front of me. I assume it's a bunch of flowers because the air fills with a delicate floral scent. Robert hands me a card.

"This came with it, miss."

I'm about to give it to Torsten to read when I discover that it's written in Braille. I run my fingers over the words:

Duchess,

This is the last gift you'll get from me.

I'm sorry. I know I won't ever be able to say those words enough, but I have to say them one last time anyway.

I want you to know that I'm listening. You can't love me any longer, and I respect that. But I'll never stop loving you. I'm always going to watch out for you from afar. Things might get tough for a bit because of our families, but I want you to know that you have nothing to fear from me. Even though I don't deserve your forgiveness, I'll still do everything I can to keep you safe.

I wanted you to have this. I grew it in my greenhouse and it's always been one of my favorites. Now I know why.

– love, Victor

I reach out and grab the base of the gift. The wrapping crinkles under my fingers as I feel around the edges, up up up until the wrapping furls out. My fingers brush delicate petals.

Inside is a pot filled with flowers – leaves shaped like arrows with points so sharp they could cut skin.

Oh, Victor.

Tears spring to my eyes.

"What is it?" Torsten rests his chin on my shoulder as he studies the plant.

"It's a death lily," I whisper, and I try to say more, but Victor's gift has stolen my words.

Right now, I'm not ready to forgive him, but I like the idea of Victor August watching over me. My very own guardian angel. I hope he enjoys watching me burn his world down.

32

FERGIE

"Fergie, hey."

I grip the phone tight in my fingers. On the other end, Drusilla sounds surprised to hear from me. I move to the edge of the balcony, leaning over the edge so the sounds of cars zooming along the street reach up to me and the wind whips my words away before I can say them aloud.

Torsten's in the shower right now, and I don't know why I'm so afraid that he might overhear. He's made it clear that he wants me to do whatever I need to do to get the justice I seek, but somehow, I still feel as though I'm betraying something.

"I just want to say thanks again for helping me with that whole fake alien/evacuating the school thing," I say. "We couldn't have done it without you making the call to evacuate."

"It was my pleasure. The guys at City Hall thought it was the most fun they'd had in years." She laughs at the memory of it, and her laughter is a brassy, jarring thing. I don't think she's laughed genuinely in a long time. "It's a pity that you won't join forces with Zack. I think the two of you actually stand a chance of dismantling this entire criminal empire."

"I believe it, but I can't do that," I say. "Listen, Torsten's recently given me some information about the Poison Ivy videos that have been leaking. And I see that there are more injustices than mine that need to be put right. I was wondering if you'd like to help me."

"I'm listening."

I tell her what Torsten found out about the videos, and what I suspected. Drusilla whistles. "I'll check it out, but I'm positive you're right. And I'm guessing that you have a plan to right these terrible wrongs?"

"I do indeed." I outline the idea I had, and all the victims who might want to be part of it.

Dru whistles her approval. "You're *diabolical*, Fergie. I love it. Count me in, although I'm going to need Zack's help. Which means…"

"You don't have to spell it out. I know that I have to give him something in return."

"You've got something for me, you sneaky bitch." Dru can barely keep the delight out of her voice.

"I know very little about the Triumvirate that will be of use," I say. "Cali Dio doesn't exactly treat me like family."

Although she kicked Cassius out of the house. For me.

I'm still puzzling over that one.

"But I have one thing Zack might be able to use – the mark for Cali's next job. My dad let it slip during our last catch-up. I'll give you the name and details on the condition that no one gets killed, all right? Put my stepmother behind bars for her crimes if you want, but don't hurt her. And my dad is immune. Got it?"

"Got it." Dru clicks her tongue. "Now, give me that name. This is the beginning of a beautiful friendship."

33

VICTOR

"——It's getting worse out there," Mom's voice carries down the long table. "Three of my ships were sunk off the coast of Japan. We haven't got the full details yet, but from the footage we've been sent it looks like more explosives on board, possibly drone-activated—"

It's Thursday night, which is family dinner night. No matter what's going on in our lives, we don't miss a family dinner night upon pain of death. And our mother doesn't kid around – she'd follow through on her threat. Even when Gabriel is on tour he still has to sit down to family dinner via Zoom.

I wind spaghetti around my fork and listen with half an ear as Mom describes the disruption to her shipping timetable and the favors she's having to call in from the Yakuza to get the Japanese authorities off her back. And this is after she's spent a good twenty minutes ranting about all the problems within her ranks of soldiers – some of whom are using the bombing and the sex video as excuses to question her leadership.

I should be paying attention because everyone looks so serious, but all I can think about is Fergie. I've been checking my phone every ten seconds, just in case I have a message from her, even if it's just 'fuck off and die.' But there's nothing. She must have got my death lilies by now. I hoped they'd show her that I understood, but maybe I just scared her off.

My phone beeps. I'm not allowed to look at it during family dinner, but Mom's distracted by her ranting. I try to pull it out of my pocket to check it, but Mom snatches it away and places it in front of her setting.

"No phones at the table," she says.

So she wasn't *that* distracted. "Sorry."

"What's up with you, Vic?" Noah growls. "You're a million miles away. If you want to take over this empire one day, then now is a perfect time to step up and show us what we're getting for that expensive private school education. How would you stop our ships from being plundered by our enemies?"

"Easy," I say as I reach for my phone. "I'd buy planes."

Mom tosses my phone in the air. It sails across the room in a perfect arc and lands in the fishbowl with a *plop*.

"Next time you look at a phone during Thursday night dinner, I will ram it down your throat," she says in her sternest Mom voice.

This is what happens when your mother is a skilled knife-thrower – anything can become a projectile. Luckily, my phone has a waterproof case.

"I like Victor's solution," Juliet says, her mouth full of broccoli. "Planes are so much better. First class cabins, movies, all-night bar service—"

"Victor," Mom frowns. "I need you to be serious here. We're going to have to postpone our next shipments until we can increase fleet security, and that's going to drive up costs and may cause some tension with our partners in Japan and Eastern Europe. And all of this is going to be fodder for the growing faction within the August family to replace me as *Imperator*. And I need you to—"

She's interrupted by a furious buzzing from across the room. My phone is going nuts, vibrating under the water and making the fish dart around crazily. My message alert starts beeping and doesn't stop.

Something's going down.

I rise. Eli clamps his hand on my wrist, but I shrug him off. "I want to help, I *swear*. But I need to check my phone."

Before Mom can eviscerate me, I tear across the room and pluck my phone from the fishbowl. I wipe it off on my jeans and open the first of a long string of messages.

It's a video file sent from an anonymous source.

I assume it's spam, but as I go to delete it, the video starts playing. It fills the screen on my phone. Mom yells at me to get back to the table, but she must see something in my face because she stops and waves me out.

I squint at the video as I duck into the next room, not entirely sure what I'm seeing. It's a bulldozer tearing into the facade of a beautiful house while a building crew watches...

Hang on...

It can't be...

That's not just any house. It's a very *familiar* house...

It's *my* house. The house I brought for me and Juliet to live in next year. The cute, perfect little house with the shopfront that Juliet's had on her vision board since fourth grade. The house I hoped Fergie would live in while she went to Harvard, with the little attic room for Torsten to have his art studio, and the basement we can transform into a gym for Cas. I've already spent tens of thousands of dollars kitting out that house with high-tech security to keep them safe. To keep my family safe.

In minutes it's reduced to a pile of rubble.

"No," I whisper.

Juliet appears by my side and peers over my shoulder. It

takes her a couple of moments for the realization to dawn. "Fergie."

"I can only assume."

"How did she do this?" Juliet whips the phone from my hand. "This is a whole demolition crew. It would be insanely expensive to do this, and without the owner's consent? Where did she get the funds for this?"

"I don't know."

"Is it Cali's money? Because Mom's not going to be happy about that."

"I don't fucking know, okay?"

Juliet glares at me, and for a moment I think she's going to slap me. Instead, she wraps her arms around me.

I'm still pissed as hell at her right now, but I sink into her because she's my sister and she's the other half of me, and we both just lost a piece of our dreams.

"It's just a house, big brother," she says. "There are plenty of other houses in Cambridge."

But not that house. Not the house that Juliet has admired since she was a little girl, the house with the tiny shopfront downstairs where she was going to open her fashion boutique. Not the house that I got from Lucila especially for her. Not the house that I'd been having fitted with every security gadget on the market to keep her safe.

I pick up my phone with shaking hands and dial Fergie's number. I don't expect her to pick up, But it doesn't even ring twice before she picks up. She's laughing.

"You demolished the house."

"Yes, Victor. I did." She can't hide the satisfaction in her voice. "That's how this whole revenge thing works. You hurt me, I hurt you. And I'm not done yet, especially now that I know the truth. Torsten found the evidence, Victor. Those secret Poison Ivy videos that were supposed to be deleted? Your phone was used to leak them. After all your talk about Poison Ivy's moral code, you're full of fucking shit."

I stare at the phone in my hands as if it might explode at any moment. What does she mean, the videos were sent from my phone? How is this possible?

"Fergie, I swear to you that I didn't send those videos."

"They came from your phone. It's filled with Torsten's fancy security stuff, and he figured it out. You don't exactly let it out of your sight. Who else could have done this?"

A face immediately springs to mind. "I think I know. Fergie, please, whatever you're planning, can we just talk about it first?"

She laughs, and I know that she's already figured out exactly what I've just realized. She's been playing me all along.

"Please, Fergie. You wouldn't be doing this for me. I'm worried about you, about your safety. If you keep this up, you risk disrupting the peace of the Triumvirate. Things are already tense as it is, and you could—"

"I don't care. I hope you all rot in jail."

She hangs up.

34

FERGIE

"Hey, Sierra." I slide into the cafeteria table beside her and rest my cane against my chair. "My name is Fergie. I don't think we've ever talked."

"No, but I know who you are." Sierra's voice sounds wary. I don't blame her. After what the club took from her this year, I'd be wary of me, too.

"I figured." I lower my voice. "I heard about what Poison Ivy cost you, and I want to talk about revenge."

"I'm listening, but not here," she whispers. "There are too many eyes and ears that might report back. Follow me. Do you need me to take your arm?"

"Yeah, if you don't mind." The cafeteria is crowded, and these days students aren't so nice about getting out of my way. I may be another victim of Poison Ivy, but I'm also the one trying to bring down their kings. People are either too invested in Victor's scheme or too afraid of what Cassius might do to stand with me, so they ignore me. Suits me fine.

I loop my hand through Sierra's arm, and she weaves through the crowds in the cafeteria. I can't see behind the glass to know if any of the Poison Ivy Club or their hangers' on have seen us, but I'm not too worried if they do. I feel weirdly invincible.

They've already done the worst possible thing they can do to me, so I'm untouchable now.

We walk outside and across the fields to the art suite. "In here." Sierra leads me into a room and turns the light on. She pulls out a chair for me and closes and locks the door. "This is one of the fashion rooms. No one's using it at the moment because Cas destroyed all the student work. Well, everything except Juliet August's collection, of course. You know she's been chosen for the Ribald Showcase? It's this mega-prestigious event next week for up-and-coming designers."

"I heard about it." It's all over Juliet's social media. It's a massive black-tie affair with industry professionals and fashion houses from all over the world in attendance.

"I imagine it's her brother's doing, because she's not even that good. She wasn't even supposed to be in the running, but Peaches O'Connor pulled out at the last minute because of a family emergency."

"Somehow, I don't think Victor had much to do with this. He was in a coma at the time."

"True. Anyway," she slides the door shut behind us. "This one wall is glass so I can see if anyone is watching us. We're safe to talk here. You were saying something about revenge?"

I outline my plan. Sierra whistles. "Wow. That's... wow. It's a *lot*."

"So you won't help me."

"I didn't say that. I don't think you understand just how many people hate those guys. They've been manipulating the class rankings for years, and a lot of people have older siblings who were victims of Gaius' reign of terror. But I don't think anyone could guess the full extent of it. The problem is that as much as we all hate them, we're also terrified of them. Cas is...

well, unhinged, but Victor's the worst. He thinks he's on this great moral crusade, a Robin Hood righting wrongs and stealing from the rich to give to the deserving. He talks as if he's so much better than Gaius Dio, but he willfully refuses to see the damage he inflicts. A lot of families have been permanently scarred just so Victor August can move his pieces around the chessboard. You can see they might be afraid of opening old wounds."

"I can. So you don't think I'll get anyone else?" My plan relied on a lot of people having a thirst for vengeance as strong as mine.

"Can you guarantee that anyone involved won't suffer retaliation from Poison Ivy?'

"I can," I say. "I'm the stepdaughter of Cali Dio. I have power and I know how to make sure that they can't hurt you."

She's silent, and I know that she's considering if she can trust me. I don't know if I'd trust me. But finally, she steps forward and clasps my outstretched hand, shaking it firmly. "Okay. I'll help you, and I think I can bring in the others. Let's bring them all down."

"What do you think?" Eli twirls around. "Do I look like the father of a famous fashion designer?"

"You look like an accountant attending a pride parade," Gabriel grins as he runs his fingers through his hair. He's grown it even longer now, so it stretches halfway down his back. It looks epic when he's on stage tossing it around. I heard Mom tell him that if he ever cuts it short, she'll divorce him.

It's the night of Juliet's fashion showcase, and we're gathered in the foyer waiting for my sister to emerge from her room. It's the first time in months that our family has done anything fun.

What Fergie did to our Cambridge house has shaken her, especially with everything going on in Mom's world right now. It's shaken me, too. I didn't realize how much losing that house would shatter my sense of self. I'd promised myself that I'd make sure that my sister had everything she needed and that she'd never have to be part of this life. I didn't want her to ever be in danger again.

And now the house is gone and my promise feels flimsy and childish. And I can't even talk to Mom about it because she's got so much on her plate already. She didn't even know I owned the house. She'd ask where I got it and I'd have to tell her that it came from Poison Ivy, and that would just make her angry. I don't want to make anything worse for her now.

I want tonight to be perfect for Juliet, to be a chance for her to regain her feet. *Maybe* she'll be so distracted with her fashion aspirations that she'll forget all about Fergie.

Noah drives us all to the ballroom at the Lethe Hotel – one of Livvie Lucian's holdings. People mill in the street and on the lavish balcony. The paparazzi rush us as soon as we exit the van, eager to get their shots of Gabriel and his wife and their unconventional family. Our mother smiles for the camera, playing the role of the doting rockstar's wife, the public face she uses to hide her more nefarious reputation. I take Juliet's hand and guide her down the glittering red carpet. She turns to me, her eyes filled with adoration.

"This is your moment," I say, turning her chin back toward the cameras. "Enjoy it."

My sister smiles and waves to the cameras, striking a pose in her floor-length fishtail dress. She looks poised and glamorous and completely at home under the harsh flickering lights of the cameras. I can see why she craves this life for herself.

Mom has always told us that we couldn't expect to inherit the family business. She wants both of us to find our own way in the world, to cultivate our own talents and interests without fear of familial expectation. I've never wanted anything but to be her, but Juliet was always supposed to be free to pursue her dreams. I've fought for so many years to give my twin every chance to make her own mark outside of the family business, I didn't see that I'd dragged her deeper into our world.

My sister is destined for great things, for amazing things. And it's my job to make sure that she gets to live the life she deserves. It's my job to keep her safe. But have I gone too far?

How much of my sister's success did she actually earn?

I remain at her side as she glides inside. The ballroom glitters with hundreds of tiny lanterns hanging from the ceiling. I can't help thinking of Fergie and how much she'd love the lighting. Anything that sparkles delights her.

How many times have I imagined walking into events like this as Victor August, Imperator, with my Queen at my side?

But Fergie's made it clear that she doesn't ever want to see me again, and I can't blame her. I should have protected her from Cassius. I should have told him what I knew, or gone to her and got the full story. I should have trusted in what we had, but I didn't, and now it's broken and can never be repaired. Like the Cambridge house.

Like the Death Lily mark that still adorns my locker. The school swore they'd paint over it, but I forbid them. Every time I look at it I remember that I lost Fergie, but I still made a promise to her.

I'll protect her, no matter what.

We find our table, and I leave Juliet talking with some fashion industry peeps in garish outfits while I grab us both some drinks.

"Do you know who that is?" she whispers when I return, jabbing her finger at the man she's been talking to as he turns to address a colleague. "It's Marcus Ribald. He says he's been following me for some time, and he wants to talk to me about an internship. Can you believe it?"

"I can believe it," I smile down at her, even as my gut twists. "You deserve it, sis."

We take our seats at a table near the front of the room, and as our glasses are refilled and entrees served, the show begins. Three young designers are showing their collections tonight. The first is a guy from Acheron Academy whose collection has a space theme – lots of metallics with touches of military detail. His final model comes out in a silver leather jacket, and my chest constricts as I think of Fergie again. She'd love that jacket.

The second is a girl who was a contestant on *Runway Challenge*, and her collection reflects her Korean heritage with lots of sumptuous fabrics and complex embroidery.

We're served our main course – some kind of fish in a sauce so zesty it makes my lips sting. The room darkens. The crowd quiets. Juliet squirms excitedly in her seat. Her show is about to begin.

A dark industrial tune pumps from the stereo.

A single spotlight illuminates the first of Juliet's models as she moves through a cloud of fog and steps onto the runway.

I spit my drink down my shirt.

The model sashays her hips, her long legs unfurling as she shows off the shapeless garment she wears. It looks like a bedsheet with holes slashed in it for arms. Across the front in huge, angry red letters, someone has scrawled the message:

> *JULIET AUGUST ASKED MY SISTER TO STAY*
> *AFTER PRACTICE, AND MY SISTER FELL*
> *DOWN THE STAIRS.*

The model tilts her face toward our table, her features hardened with hatred. It's Eurydice Jones.

Beside me, Juliet spits out her Champagne. "What is this?" she chokes. "Get the fuck off my stage!"

Euri shimmies back down the runway as the next model makes it to the end. It's Sierra, and she's made her sheet into a kind of Roman toga. She strikes a pose so that everyone can read the message scrawled in red:

> *JULIET AUGUST SABOTAGED MY FASHION*

ASSIGNMENT SO THAT I WOULDN'T
BEAT HER.

Juliet leaps to her feet. She waves her arms at the stage manager who peers around the wings, looking completely flummoxed by the whole thing. More models shove past him to take to the stage.

"Stop it!" my sister yells. "Stop the show!"

But the show must go on. And on it goes – a line of models marching from the wings to take their turn in the spotlight. Every one of them is a girl Juliet has tormented or someone Poison Ivy has wronged. They each wear the same white sheets and the same pale, ghostly makeup. The same angry red letters spell out my sister's crimes.

JULIET AUGUST FORCED ME TO GO DOWN ON
HER OR SHE'D TELL MY PARENTS I'M GAY.

JULIET AUGUST MADE ME GIVE HER MY SPOT
IN THE FALL SHOWCASE.

JULIET TOLD HER BROTHER MY SECRET, AND
HE USED IT AGAINST ME.

"Victor," Juliet's nails dig into my arm. "Do something."

But I can't. I *can't*. Because I know exactly who's behind this, and I know in my heart of hearts that it *is* justice. This is revenge. Juliet has been manipulating everything behind the scenes to further her fashion career. She's been manipulating me. All those favors I got for her through Poison Ivy weren't enough – she stole secrets for her own ends. She stole *my phone* for her blackmail. She stole the very idea of what I wanted Poison Ivy to be.

And as much as I don't want my sister hurt or my family name sullied, I know when justice needs to be done.

She deserves this.

We deserve this.

This has been a long time coming. The stage fills with women who've been wronged in some way by the Poison Ivy Club. I dare a quick glance over to my family, and I can see from my mother's pursed lips that we're both in for a world of hurt.

The music reaches a crescendo as the final model takes her walk down the runway. Her flame-red hair has been piled on top of her head, and the ragged edge of her sheet cuts mid-thigh, revealing legs that go on forever. She looks like a giantess, a thousand stories high, a fairy queen whose touch will turn mortal men to stone.

She walks without her cane. She doesn't miss a single step.

She stops at the end of the runway, pausing long enough to ensure every eye in the room is on her, that the words scrawled across her white gown sink in.

JULIET AUGUST PUT AN INTIMATE VIDEO OF
ME ON THE INTERNET.

Fergie raises her arms to the lights, her whole face aglow. The beat drops and she spins around, revealing the words written on the back of her white tunic.

JULIET AUGUST CAN SUCK MY LADY BALLS.

36

FERGIE

The roar of the crowd washes over me as I hold my pose. The sheet's rising up at the back, and I'm slightly worried I might have my ass on display, but fuck it. It's nothing they haven't seen before.

I can't see Victor in the audience, obviously, but I *feel* him. His eyes rake over me, and I know that he understands why I did this. I can hear Juliet screaming at him to do something, but I'm not torn from the stage. A bullet doesn't pierce my chest.

Juliet August is nothing but a spoiled little bitch who expects her brother to swoop in and clean up her mess. And Victor August won't touch me.

I know he won't touch me because he sent me those death lilies. He knows who I am. He knows this is what he and his sister deserve.

This is as much revenge on him as it is on his sister. She may have been the mastermind behind all the hurt at Stonehurst Prep, but she never would have been able to do it without the Poison Ivy Club and the system Victor created.

Victor August needs to be in control, and he's just learned

that he can't control me. He's not safe, and neither is his perfect little family.

I'm the one with the power, and I like how that feels.

The music swells, and I start my slow walk back up the runway. Sierra skips up beside me and loops her arm through mine. She and Euri and Dru are the real masterminds behind tonight – Sierra wormed her way onto the committee decorating the showcase, and she had them place LED strip lighting down the sides of the runway, angled upward so it was bright enough that I could roughly see the edges. We'd done a couple of practices this afternoon, but I'm still shaking with nerves as I step off the runway. I can't believe I did it without walking off the edge.

"Fergie, you were amazing." Euri's arms wrap around me. "I'll never know how you did that without your cane."

"That was thanks to Sierra," I grin. "I was so terrified I'd walk off the end, but her lighting kept me in the center."

"I can see Juliet from here. She's at a table in the first row, just to the left of the catwalk. She's in tears. Victor's walking her out right now and the cameras are going wild. This is going to be all over the papers tomorrow. It's *perfect*."

It is. It's perfect.

So why do I feel like shit?

37

VICTOR

The car ride back to the house is silent – if you don't count Juliet's hysterical sobbing.

Every heaving breath she takes pierces my heart. But I don't comfort her. No one does. My mother stares straight ahead, her jaw working. Noah grips the wheel so hard his knuckles are white.

All those things written on the sheets were things I should have known about but didn't. All this time I thought my sister was uninterested in the Poison Ivy Club, but she's been using it for her own advantage. She's been cashing in our favors and taking files out of our secret cloud storage.

She's been doing this under my nose, and I had no fucking idea. I feel like a complete idiot.

Noah turns into the tunnel that leads to our house and parks the car in the underground driveway. My mother turns around and glares at both of us. "My study. Now."

"But Juliet—"

"Do *not* argue with me tonight, Victor. Go."

I help a still-sobbing Juliet out of the car. We follow our

parents into the study. Mom turns on the soft overhead lamp and points to the seat opposite her desk.

"Sit," she barks.

We sit.

Juliet buries her head in my shoulder, her tears making a damp circle on my Brooks Brothers shirt. I rub circles on her back, trying to comfort her but knowing that it's hopeless, knowing that we both deserve everything that's coming.

She may have been the one to orchestrate all that misery, but I allowed her to do it. I truly believed I could build Poison Ivy into something good, something that would help good, clever people – people like Gemma. And Euri. And Sierra – get all the good things they deserved. And along the way, I let the power go to my head, and I missed *everything* my deluded sister was doing.

Trust Fergie to bring this darkness into the light.

Mom sits on the edge of her desk, her arms folded. Our three dads flank her, wearing expressions that range from disappointment (Eli), to sadness (Gabe), to terrifying rage (Noah).

She stares down at me with those icicle eyes, and I feel a foot tall. "I've always believed we could keep the family business *and* be good parents. I thought that if we could teach you that even though we bend the rules sometimes, the Augusts have a code of honor that we *will not break*. But tonight, I've learned how mistaken I am. I see that my children have been so spoiled, so arrogant and fucking privileged, that they've grown into nothing but evil, manipulative bullies."

Juliet sniffs. "Mom, I can explain—"

"Don't you dare speak while your mother is talking."

Noah doesn't yell. His voice is very quiet and very dark. And that's when I know that we've really in trouble, that what we've done might be unforgivable.

Mom reaches over to Gabriel and squeezes his hand so hard

that he winces. "Victor August, you tell me straight. Is everything those women wrote on those placards true?"

Juliet kicks my shin. I swallow. "I think so. I... I didn't know about many of those things. I never did anything more than swap a favor for a favor."

"And the video of Fergie?"

Juliet stomps on me, grinding the heel of her stiletto into my foot.

I can't look at my sister.

I nod.

Mom turns to my twin. "Juliet August, you put *revenge porn on the internet.*"

"Fergie lied to Cassius!" Juliet cries. "She lied to everyone. She and her father aren't who they say they are. They have fake IDs—"

"Of course they fucking do," Mom snaps. "Cali is the one who arranged for Fergie's fake ID. She did it because at Fergie's last school her boyfriend put revenge porn on the internet and it cost Fergie everything, including her chance to apply to Harvard. Fergie and John came to Emerald Beach for a new beginning, and you've made sure that she can never have that."

I feel sick.

If we'd only told Cas sooner, if I'd actually *talked* to Fergie, asked her about why she left Massachusetts, I would have seen the truth written in her shattered-emerald eyes. I could have prevented this whole horrible mess.

"You both believe that you're untouchable because you carry the name of August," Mom snarls. "But you've never learned that kind of power cuts both ways. Let me tell you what your little stunt has achieved. Cali is pissed as fuck that her stepdaughter has been attacked – and no matter what you want to say, Juliet, this *is* an attack." Mom holds up her hand, cutting off Juliet's protest. "And you don't attack a member of the Dio family and walk away. Cali needs to show our people that she won't tolerate this behavior, which means someone's head needs to roll in the Colosseum. Now, I don't know if she knows that you're behind it, but I suspect she does because she's not returning my calls."

Shit shit *shit.*

But Mom isn't finished.

"And because Fergie and Torsten are being seen together in public, Livvie's not too thrilled, either. Their relationship is as good as an alliance between Dio and Lucian, *against* us. You have driven a wedge between our family and our closest allies, you've destabilized the Triumvirate at the one time when we needed unity, and you've made me look as if I can't control my own family. I told you that club of yours was a problem—"

"We've disbanded the Poison Ivy Club," I say. "I did exactly what you wanted."

"If you'd done what I wanted we wouldn't be in this mess, and I wouldn't be dealing with this instead of going after the bastard who put you in a coma for three days. You are *not* the leader of a criminal empire, Victor August. You are a nineteen-year-old boy who has no idea what the fuck you're playing with, and you, Juliet, you ruined an innocent girl's life and put your own selfish interests before your own family, and I don't know if I can ever forgive you for that."

"But that's not fair," Juliet sobs. "When you were nineteen, you—"

Noah cuts her off with a glare. "When we were your age, we didn't have a choice. We've raised you so that you have every opportunity available to you. If you can't top your class and get into a fashion showcase or a certain college on your own merits, then you don't deserve to go. There's enough trouble in our world without you bringing it right to our door."

"We can fix this," I say. "There must be a way to—"

"You won't be fixing anything."

"What are you going to do to us?" Juliet's chin wobbles. I know my sister well enough to know when she's putting on a brave face. She's terrified of Mom right now.

I'm fucking terrified, too.

Mom folds her arms and flashes us a cold smile. "Nothing. I'm doing absolutely nothing. I'm handing you both over to Cali."

"What?"

"You hurt a Dio. You've created a massive security risk and undone years of Cali's hard work branding herself as a brutal, fearsome leader. You undermined one of the most dangerous women in the world. This isn't about whatever petty squabble drove this foolish behavior. This is about the stability of the Triumvirate. I now need to prove to Cali and Livvie and all our soldiers that I can be trusted. So Cali will deal with you. And whatever she decides, we'll accept as justice."

"But... but she'll kill us!"

"She won't," Noah says in his hard, quiet voice. "That will be too simple. Too painless."

"She'll torture you a little," Eli says.

"Or a lot," Gabriel adds.

"It will be character-building," Mom says.

"You can't do this to us," Juliet wails.

"I'm Claudia August. Unlike you, I've earned the right to do as I choose. You both need to learn that your actions have consequences. We have enemies enough without seeking to make them from our allies. You'll report to Cali tomorrow after school to begin your punishment." Mom turns away. "Take me downstairs, Eli, Noah. I can't bear to look at them any longer."

Eli looks his arm in hers and the two of them float away. Noah flashes me one final, punishing look before he disappears after them. They're going to her rage room. Mom hasn't stepped inside that room for a long time, and I hate that I've been the cause of sending her back into the place.

I reach for my sister, but she shoves my hand away.

"Don't touch me. I can't stand you."

"Jules—"

"No. You could have done something tonight. You could have stopped Fergie. But you did nothing, just stood there like a love-struck puppy while she ruined my show. And you just let Mom hand us over to Cali fucking Dio. What's she going to do? Cut off my fingers? I *need* my fingers. You've ruined everything. I hate you so much."

"Jules, please don't say that. I can't—" I reach for her again, but she ducks around me and runs from the room, nearly hitting Gabriel on the way out.

He watches her bolt down the hallway, then nods to me. "You want a bowl of ice cream?"

"Sure."

We head to the enormous kitchen. I sit at the counter while Gabriel roots around in the freezer and pulls out several containers of Ben and Jerry's ice cream – we keep a steady supply in the house for when he's home from tour. Gabriel's been sober since his late teens – I've never seen a drop of alcohol pass his lips – and I know that when things get intense for him, he reaches for an ice cream tub. I'm surprised he's not five hundred pounds by now, but my dad is just as wiry as he was in his twenties.

Gabriel dumps scoops of ice cream into two bowls, covers them in chocolate drizzle and a handful of candy, and then plops one bowl down in front of me. He straddles one of the barstools, brings the second bowl to his face, flips his long, dark hair over his shoulder, and starts shoveling ice cream into his face.

For a few minutes, we eat in silence. The cold ice cream gives me a headache, but I don't stop. I deserve all the headaches in the universe.

Gabe sets down his bowl and taps his spoon on the counter. "You fucked up, kid."

"Yup. I got that message loud and clear."

"I don't know all that much about running a criminal empire, but even I can see this business has made your mom look weak in front of her soldiers. And Fergie's stunt tonight, as justified as she was, is only going to reinforce that." Gabe picks a red jelly bean from the bottom of his bowl and pops it into his mouth. "As much as the three Imperators put on a show of being the best of friends, the true reason they work so well together is that they cancel each other out. Not one of them is strong enough to take on the others individually. But that all changes if two of them align against the other."

"And you think Cali and Livvie would do that to Mom?" It seems impossible. We spend Christmas with the Dio and Lucian families. We go on vacation together, eat dinner at each other's houses, and share every important family milestone with them. I guess everything is more fucked up than I realized.

Gabe flashes me a sad smile. "I think that if we don't fix things fast, they might not have a choice. Especially if this Fergie girl keeps going after you and your sister publicly."

I slump on the counter. "I really messed up with Fergie."

"You love this girl. I see it in your eyes."

I give him a wobbly smile. "I love her so much that it hurts. Is this what it felt like when you met Mom?"

He holds his hand to his chest. "It *still* feels like that. Every time I have to leave her and you and Juliet, it feels like I'm stabbing myself through the heart. I've fucked up, too, son. You have no idea how many times. But I always come back to something she said to me once. She says that I'm the one who sings the stars and the blood and the pain for her. She needs me to paint the bigger picture of why she does what she does, to be the bright star that keeps her pointing on the right path. She doesn't need me to be her rock, her stable one. She has Eli for that. And she doesn't need me to carry her when she falls, because she has Noah. That sounds like a bad thing, but it's actually wonderful. I don't have to be everything to her. I can be imperfectly in love with her, and that's enough. *I'm* enough. And so are you." He pats my knee. "Maybe that's what this girl of yours is learning now. I heard that this video included appearances from all *three* Poison Ivy boys."

I swallow. I can't bear to think about Saturnalia. It was the happiest night of my life, the night when I realized that I could have what my parents have with Fergie and my two best friends, but then Cas tainted it beyond repair. "It wasn't meant to be."

"Look, if you really love this girl, if she's endgame for you, then you have to show her that you can be what she needs. I know you, son. I know that you'll wait forever for her to come to you. But love is too important to wait."

"I've sent her all kinds of things," I say. "I tried to show her that I'll protect her even if she doesn't want me. But she's made it clear that she can't forgive me, and I don't blame her. She's better off with Torsten."

"Is she now?" Gabe lifts one eyebrow, and I think I see a little of what draws Mom to him. "If she didn't still care about you, she wouldn't have run to the hospital the moment she heard you were in a coma. She's expended all her energy trying to destroy your life. Those aren't the actions of an indifferent person."

"She hates me."

"She does now, but you have to love someone to truly hate them. That's a good song lyric; I should write that down."

"It sounds a little emo, even for you," I tease him with the name of a music genre from decades ago that he loves to hate.

"Says the guy crying into his ice cream bowl about a girl."

Gabe slaps my shoulder. "The Victor August I know doesn't give up so easily. Show her that you've changed. Show her that you see *her*, and not just this perfect vision of her you've created in your mind. Fergie clearly doesn't need your protection, but that isn't the only thing have you to give. Give her your love, and your loyalty, and your kind heart, and I think you might be surprised."

38

FERGIE

I don't know what I expected to happen at school on the Monday following our triumph at the Ribald showcase, but it's not what happens.

Instead, I'm swamped the minute I exit Artie's car and am carried into school on a wave of adulation – like I solved world hunger or won the Super Bowl, when all I did was help a bunch of girls put their bully in her place. Sierra and Drusilla and all their friends lead the crowd, and the minute they set me down in the middle of the courtyard, people press in on me from all sides, congratulating me and talking about the show and sharing videos on their phones and inviting me to parties and to sit with their groups at lunch.

It's strange – all my life I've been on the outside of groups like this, watching the popular kids hanging out with their friends and taking trips to the mall and hosting wild parties. I thought I was missing out on something. Dawson gave me a taste of his world and then made sure I knew my rightful place. I'm the weird blind girl, and that's the way it's always going to be.

And now I'm the center of a group of my own. And all because I took on the Poison Ivy Club.

This should be one of the greatest days of my life, but I'm not really here. I'm not inside my body, enjoying the adulation and triumph. I'm floating somewhere above my body, listening to myself saying all the right things but not feeling them in my bones.

I know I've detached because it feels safer than living with the darkness inside me. When I squeeze Torsten's hand and he squeezes back, the darkness goes away for a bit, but then it comes back stronger than ever. I'm afraid to think about it too much, because if I do I might have to acknowledge that it feels an awful lot like I miss Victor and Cassius, which is fucking ridiculous.

I don't miss them. I don't need them.

I know Torsten senses something's up with me. The bell rings and he drags me to my classes, shoving people aside so I can take a seat in the back row. He doesn't ask me what's wrong, and I'm grateful for it, but I sense him tensing up and shutting down as he feeds off my agitation, and that makes me feel a hundred times worse.

Torsten is amazing. So why isn't he enough? Why am I such a greedy bitch? Why do I hunger after things that are bad for me?

In chemistry class, Torsten and I take our usual seats at the back of the room. He pulls out his sketchbook while I try to pay attention. I pull out my Braille note to start writing in the experiment, but he snatches it out of my hands.

"Hey!"

He taps out a message and hands it back. My fingers fly along the screen as I read what he's written.

YOU ARE NOT OKAY

Yup, Torsten gets me. I sit with the Braille note in front of me, trying to figure out how I can say what I'm feeling in a way he'd understand. Anger wells up inside me. I shouldn't have to say how I feel, because I don't want to feel this way. I don't want those two inside my veins. I want them gone, gone, *gone*.

So I take a deep breath, savoring Torsten's vanilla and honeycomb and orange zest scent, and I flash him my flirtiest smile as I type a message for him.

YOU'RE GETTING GOOD AT BRAILLE

Torsten digs the Braille labeler from the bottom of my bag and fiddles with it. A moment later, he sticks a label onto my Braille note case.

I'VE BEEN PRACTICING

A second label joins it.

OPEN MY TEXTBOOK AND PLACE IT OVER YOUR KNEES.

A lightning bolt shoots through my body. *Is he...?*
He can't be... can he?

I've definitely forgotten about Vic and Cas now. I turn toward Torsten. I can hear his pen scribbling away in his notebook.

"Torsten?" I ask, all sweetness and innocence. "Why am I opening your textbook? I can't read it."

He grabs the labeler and punches out another label.

I SHOULDN'T HAVE TO ASK TWICE. PUT YOUR TEXTBOOK OVER YOUR KNEES AND OPEN YOUR LEGS.

"Goddamn you, you've learned far too much from those two friends of yours." Grinning, I pull the heavy textbook onto my knees and open it. My heart patters in my chest. Heat flares in my cheeks, and between my legs there's a party going on. Slowly, I move my thighs open, reveling in the cool air of the classroom kissing my inner thighs beneath my skirt. I'm wearing a new pair of my favorite scarlet panties, and they're already wet.

Torsten slaps a label on my palm.

GOOD GIRL.

Damn him. He *listens*. For someone who says he doesn't understand people, he can read me like a fucking children's book. He *knows* that those two words *do* things to me.

I hear something drop on the ground. A pencil. It rolls under the desk. Torsten's chair scrapes out, and as he bends down to retrieve it, his hair brushes my arm.

My heart races. I'm aware of the noise in the room – students talking, Mr. Dallas droning on, the click of Bunsen burners being fired up. Surely they must see what's going on? But no one reacts and I... I don't have the willpower to stop this.

I grip the edge of the desk. A hand slides up my thigh.

OMG, he's not doing this *in class*, while Mr. Dallas is up there showing off his diagrams of the endoplasmic reticulum and the Golgi body. It's so wrong, so filthy...

...and so fucking hot.

The warm hands reach behind me, fingers digging into my ass as they pull me forward on the stool. Torsten tugs my lacy scarlet panties down my thigh, using his hands to press my legs even further apart so that my knees hit the wood of the lab bench. I figure that the shelves on three sides of the bench hide most of him from view from the front and sides of the class, and the textbook covers the rest, but surely they know... they must be able to tell...

A dark, hot ache pools in my belly. I keep my face trained

passively on Mr. Dallas, as if I'm hanging off his every word. In reality, every fiber of my being is focused on the gorgeous guy between my legs as he presses his tongue against my swollen clit.

"Aaaah." I can't help the sigh that escapes my throat, because fuck me, he's gotten good at eating me out. I cover my mouth with my hand and try to pretend I was yawning, while all the while Torsten's tongue works in slow, deliberate circles, copying exactly the technique I showed him.

Someone at the next bench giggles. I wonder if it's because they can see what's going on, but I'm so fucking horny I don't care.

They've all seen the video. They all got to watch me fuck three guys at once. If my sexuality is going to be on public display, why not do this on my own terms?

Thinking about everyone around us makes me even fucking hornier. Torsten's tongue thrusts inside me, lapping up the juices that are leaking from me. My nails dig into the edge of the desk, and I know I'm leaving marks.

He pulls back a little, teasing me with light brushes of his tongue, before pounding it into my clit again, drawing out little moans of pleasure that I try to muffle with the back of my sleeve—

"Ms. Munroe," Mr. Dallas' voice penetrates the pleasure. "Where's your lab partner?"

He's between my legs, driving me wild with his tongue.

"He, ah, went to find a pencil," I gasp out as Torsten plunges his tongue inside me again, swirling and dipping before returning to pummel my clit into submission.

"Very well. Then perhaps you can tell the class the name given to the constriction point that divides the chromosome into two sections?"

"Oh, um..." my mind blanks as Torsten's tongue drives faster,

faster. He slides a finger inside me, curling it up to rub against the perfect spot. The harsh fluorescent strip lights of the lab wobble in my vision as he drives me right to the edge—

"Ms. Munroe, I'd hate to think our Harvard-bound star student hasn't been paying attention in my class."

Fuck.

"I listen to every word, I swear. The... ah... the thingie is called... the *centromere*."

"That's correct. And the long and short arms of the chromosome are called?"

"Oh, um... the q arm..." I'm so close. So fucking... "And the p-aaaarrggghh!"

My moan tears through the classroom as my orgasm slams into me. I fall forward on the desk, slamming my head into the Braille note as my legs turn into jelly and my whole body explodes with pleasure. Through the haze of my ecstasy I hear students giggling and Mr. Dallas calling to me, "Fergie, are you okay? What's wrong?"

"Sorry," I grin shyly, raising my head from the Braille note's tactile screen. "I hit my head. I just get really excited about genetics."

All around me, I hear nervous titters and a round of applause from Sierra's bench as Torsten crawls out from under ours and returns to the stool beside me. He picks up his sketchbook and happily resumes his drawings, as if he hadn't just made me scream in the middle of class.

To my absolute shock, Mr. Dallas doesn't press me further. He returns to his lecture. Sierra leans across the aisle and tugs on my sleeve. "Psst, you have a row of Braille dots imprinted on your forehead."

"Oh, fuck." I rub my forehead where I hit myself on the Braille note.

"Don't worry about it." She slaps my shoulder as she leans back in her seat. "You lucky bitch."

Okay, so she definitely saw. But I don't care. I...

Fuck. That was... *fuck*.

I find the note he'd written for me with 'GOOD GIRL' and slap it onto my Braille note case. I want to run my fingers over it all the time and remember how fucking hot this was. The bell rings, and I have to lean against Torsten because my legs won't fucking work.

And people think Torsten is the nice one...

I've created a monster, and I am *here* for it.

"That's interesting," Euri says as the three of us enter the cafeteria to grab a late lunch. We've been working in the Sentinel offices on the article – Euri wants it done before the deadline for her overseas college applications, so she can use it as part of her portfolio.

"What?"

"Drusilla and Sierra and a bunch of their friends are sitting at the Poison Ivy table." Euri leads me to the salad bar and starts piling our plates with food. She doesn't even ask me what I'd like anymore – she has all my favorites committed to memory because that's how fucking awesome she is.

"You're right. That *is* interesting."

Since Saturnalia, Euri and Torsten and I have been eating our lunch in the greenhouse, the art suite, or the Sentinel offices. Euri works on her applications for overseas colleges, Torsten paints, and I think about my revenge plot. Papa Smurf hasn't been at school much, but Victor and Juliet have continued to hold court over the table in the glass room, although I've heard that the number of their friends has dropped. And now...

"Hey, Fergie! Sit with us."

It's Sierra, and I know from the way the entire cafeteria goes dead silent that she's calling me from the Poison Ivy room.

Beside me, Torsten continues to heap his favorite chicken and quinoa salad onto his place, oblivious to the unfolding situation.

I consider my options. On the one hand, sitting at that table after what went down at the showcase feels perfect. But on the other, I don't really want to hang out in a fishbowl with the whole school staring at me. What if I pick my nose or spill food on my shirt? I just want to right Poison Ivy's wrongs – I'm not in this to become queen of the school. And from the way Euri stiffens beside me, I know she's thinking the same thing.

I'm about to say that I'll catch Sierra later when the cafeteria doors bang open and a pissed-off voice says, "What the fuck are you doing, Sierra? That's not your table."

It's Juliet.

And she sounds just as haughty as ever.

"Oh yeah?" Sierra fires back. "And you're going to make us move, are you? You want to sit here all by yourself? Who do you have left at this school who wants to sit with you?"

"Victor!" Juliet screeches. "Xavier, Patrick, Cane, get over here! They're trying to steal our table."

Her words hang in the silent room. Somewhere near the juice bar, a pencil rolls off the edge of a table and hits the tiles.

Not a single person will stand with Juliet.

I don't know where Victor is, but I can feel his presence the way I felt him at the showcase. I expect him to speak up for his sister, but he says nothing. And I hate that I feel a little flicker of pride in him for that.

"It's just a table. It's not owned by anyone," Drusilla's voice joins Sierra. "Poison Ivy has made the rules at Stonehurst Prep for too long. What do you think, Sierra?"

"I think that there's a bar in the back of this room with a

fridge full of Dom Perignon and we should get fucking *sloshed*," Sierra shouts, a wicked grin in her voice.

Chairs scrape. I elbow Euri in the ribs for an update. "A bunch of kids are standing up and joining Sierra and Dru in the glass room," she says.

"This isn't allowed!" Juliet howls. "Victor, you have to stop them—"

"Let them have it, Jules."

Victor sounds closer than I expected. He's at a table just to the left of the salad bar, and the defeated timbre of his voice churns up a maelstrom of conflicted emotions inside me. I hate that I still care about him after everything, but... my coal heart still wishes for what can never be even as I build the wall between us so high and strong that he'll never be able to climb it.

I've done it. I've taken everything Victor August cared about – his popularity, his friends, his little club, his reputation, his house, and his relationship with his sister – and pulverized it to dust.

I won. I should be beyond happy. I should be elated. But I'm still empty inside.

Do you know what helps a feeling of impossible emptiness? Expensive Champagne.

"We'd love to join you." I link arms with Euri and pull her toward the table. "We deserve a celebration."

As the three of us pass behind the glass, the room erupts in cheers. Corks pop and students cheer as the Poison Ivy booze supply is shared out. I squeeze Torsten's hand, knowing that this many people in the small space might be freaking him out. He squeezes back. Outside, I hear Juliet let out a high-pitched shriek and storm from the cafeteria.

Poison Ivy's rule at Stonehurst Prep is over.

40

CASSIUS

I watch through the glass of the cafeteria doors as Fergie laughs with her new friends. She sits at the head of *my* table, in the very seat where Gaius used to sit, where my brother built the very institution she's destroying.

The red mist curls in the corners of my eyes. I know that if I enter the cafeteria now, I'll tear the place to pieces, and that won't help me get back in my mother's good books.

A frustrated growl tears from my lips. My stepsister has taken Torsten and Victor from me. She's turned my mother against me. She's cost me my home and my friends and my future and... and all those rotting feelings I have for her still churn unwanted in my gut.

I feel as though someone has cut open my chest, swung my ribcage open, hollowed out the contents, and draped my organs around me for me to admire before I die. A blood eagle – an old Norse torture so brutal and barbaric that Cali made me wait until I was eighteen before she taught it to me.

That's what Fergie's done to me.

My phone beeps. A text. I read it out of the corner of my eye. Every letter drips with blood.

MEET ME AT YOUR NEW PLACE.

I turn on my heel and storm outside, stalking across the athletic fields toward the woods and the old horticulture building. The lacrosse team is practicing on the field, and one of them can't stop his momentum in time and smashes into me, but I don't feel him. I shove him to the ground, stomp on his arm, and keep walking.

Their coach yells after me, but all I hear is a ringing in my ears.

By the time I hit the woods, the red mist has crept all the way across my vision. I can barely hear a thing except my blood rushing in my ears. When I see the person I've come to meet step out from behind a tree, I lunge at them but manage to pull myself back just in time. I have to remember that they're on my side, the way Gaius was when he was here.

"Hello, Papa Smurf." Juliet flicks her silky hair over her shoulder and fixes me with a steady gaze. She must be the only person in the world who isn't afraid of me. I don't know if that's brave or foolish. "I thought I saw you lurking in the corridor. So you're living here?"

She steps inside the crumbling building. I follow her. She heads down to the basement, into the room where she locked me after Saturnalia. I've spread my sleeping bag and air mattress on some pallets beside the old boiler, and my weapons are lined up against the wall. A rat crawls out from the pile of stinking clothes in the corner. Empty booze bottles roll across the floor. I've drank everything in my brother's expensive collection now. I'd been adding to it over the years, hoping to show him the treasures I found when he got out of jail, but what's the point?

Juliet wrinkles her nose as she picks her way through my belongings. Her eyes light up as she pulls a pair of crumpled scarlet panties from beneath my pillow.

"Are these hers?" She clicks her tongue in disapproval. "Oh, Cas."

The growl starts low in my throat and rumbles through my whole body. Juliet simply smiles indulgently at me.

"Down, boy. You won't hurt me, because you need my brains to get what you truly desire. I assume you saw what happened in the cafeteria."

I don't reply. I can't. I don't have words left. Only blood. Only hate.

"I know that you've heard by now what she did to me at the showcase. And she had the house Victor bought for me demolished. She's not going to stop at painting you blue, and she has the whole school *and* our parents wrapped around her pinkie finger. This can only end one way, Cas. You have to do it. It's the only way to get our life back, to get Victor and Torsten and our parents back. You have to get rid of Fergie Munroe. Permanently."

No.

My soft, squishy heart clenches in horror at what she's asking. But my heart is no longer in my chest cavity. Fergie tore it out and tossed it aside. It screams and pleads with me to spare her, to love her, to give her the grace that no one has ever given me.

But all I hear is a dull, muffled protest that I drown out with blood.

Fergie is mine. Mine mine mine. I can't hurt her. I can't—

But then I realize that Juliet's right. I *have* to kill her. She can't be allowed to live, free as a bird, after carving out my heart and eating it.

If Fergie Munroe never takes another breath then I'll stop feeling this terrible hollow ache inside me.

Her blood will set me free.

"Did you hear me, Cas?" Juliet hisses. "Do you know what you need to do?"

"Yes," I say, the words tasting of blood and freedom. "I'll do it."

It's settled. Fergie Munroe must die.

41

FERGIE

When the final bell rings, it takes a long time for us to make our way outside. We keep being stopped by people who want to talk to us about their run-ins with Poison Ivy or ask us to their parties. Beside me, I can feel Euri rising up to her full height as she sees how she can play this to her advantage.

"Fergie will consider attending social engagements, provided they're messaged to me with all relevant information," she says as she gently pushes people out of our way. "If you want to talk about the Poison Ivy Club, I'm conducting interviews in the new Sentinel offices starting tomorrow. Just email me to arrange a time."

She manages to get us out the front gates and into the pickup zone to wait for Artemis without incident.

"Euri, that was amazing." I touch her shoulder. "If you ever decide to give up on the journalism dream, you could make a living as a bodyguard."

She snorts. "I'm a hundred and ten pounds and I can't even lift a basketball without breaking into a sweat. I think I'll leave the ass-kicking to you, thank you very much."

A car rolls up in front of us. Assuming it's Artemis here to pick us up, I step toward it, but Euri yanks me back.

"That's not Artie's car," she whispers. "It's one of those enormous things that rappers drive. I have no idea whose it is, and the windows are all tinted."

The passenger window rolls down and the driver says, "Fergie Munroe, I've been instructed to collect you from school."

"By who? I didn't order a car," I frown.

"This car is courtesy of Claudia August. She wants to speak to you."

I swallow a lump of fear. Victor's mother can only want to talk to me for one reason – because of the spectacle I made of her daughter at the showcase. I'm not sorry for what I did to Juliet, but I knew when I planned it that I'd be calling out one of the most powerful families in Emerald Beach. I'd been counting on Cali's name to protect me, and I didn't expect the twins to get their mother to fight their battles for them, but this car suggests I may have overplayed my hand.

I'm shitting bricks.

"Hypothetically speaking, what happens if I tell you to fuck off into the sun?" I say to the driver.

"Then I'm instructed to use any force necessary, including the Glock under my seat, to make you comply," he says in a casual tone that succeeds in making a cold trickle of fear run down my spine.

"I thought so." I reach out and run my fingers along the car until I locate the handle. "I guess I'm getting a ride in this tank."

Torsten squeezes my hand. "I'm coming with you."

"No, go with Euri. After what we pulled, she could be a target." I swallow back my fear. "I'm Cali's stepdaughter. Claudia August can't do anything to hurt me without starting a gang war."

She can't. She *wouldn't*.

Would she?

Euri gives me a nudge. "Don't worry about me. Artie's pulled up behind you. Take Torsten with you. This could be a trick."

She's right. I only have this guy's word that he works for the Augusts. This is one of those rare instances where I might need someone with eyes to have my back.

But still, I hesitate. I can't help but wonder if I'm walking into some kind of payback.

My hand flies off the handle as the door swings open.

"Get inside," a dark voice commands from within. That's not the kind of voice you disobey.

It's Claudia August herself.

I get inside.

Torsten climbs in after me. His hand rests on my knee. I welcome the reassuring bulk of his presence as I settle into a leather seat facing the back of the vehicle. The driver doesn't even wait for Torsten to tug the door shut before he tears away.

"Hello, Fergie," Claudia August says. "We haven't spoken since Victor introduced us at Saturnalia. I wish you'd said hello at the fashion showcase; we would have found a place for you at our table."

I can't tell if she's being sarcastic or not. She sits across from us, her voice calm and measured. Meanwhile, I clamp my knees together to stop them from shaking. I can see why this woman runs a criminal empire – just being in her presence is terrifying.

"I'm not sure that would've been a good idea," I mumble. "Victor and I aren't a thing anymore, and Juliet—"

"Yes, I've learned in the most public way possible that my daughter has hurt you deeply in her ignorance, and I can assure you that she and my son are being punished. I've given them to your stepmother to deal to, since it's her family they dishonored."

I dare a smile at that. "After Cali's done with them, will they be returned to you with body and mind intact?"

"If so, then my friend isn't doing her job," Claudia says. "But I'm not here to talk about Victor. My son can line his own coffin and fight his own battles. I do know you've cut him up something terrible. He was quite in love with you. Still is, I believe, for his sins."

"This is about Juliet—"

"It's not about Juliet. At least, not directly. You might know that our whole family was at the showcase. We saw every minute of that performance, and as my daughter collapsed in tears while her victims bared their pain for the world to see, I realized something."

She pauses, and I hold my breath, expecting to feel a bullet tear through my ribcage...

"Did Victor ever tell you about how I came to be the head of the August family?"

I start at the question. "Um... no. I assumed you inherited it."

"Not exactly." I hear glass tinkling as she fiddles with something next to her seat, and a moment later, a crystal glass filled with whisky finds itself in my hand. "I grew up as the daughter of Julian August, the last true blood leader of the August family. He trained me in every aspect of the business. He wanted me to rule after him as Imperator, or if it proved too difficult for our soldiers and the wider community to accept a female leader, he would have me marry someone I could manipulate from the rear. But it never happened like that. My uncle Brutus killed my father in cold blood, buried me alive, and assumed the role of Imperator himself."

"He..." I struggle to catch up. "...buried you alive?"

She laughs. "That is the bit that stands out, yes? If you must know, it was as terrifying and horrible as you can imagine. But with the help of my cousin, Antony, I escaped. Antony helped me to hide in an abandoned house for four years. The family – father, mother, and a teenage girl – who owned the house mysteriously disappeared, leaving their Harrington Hills mansion vacant, and by some eerie coincidence, I looked a lot like the missing daughter. We hid my true identity behind stories of ghosts until the day the cops showed up and informed me that I'd have to attend school or they'd start digging around in my life. They assumed I was the missing daughter – a girl named Mackenzie Malloy. So, I enrolled in Stonehurst Prep under Mackenzie's name. And it was there, during my senior year, where I met Eli, Noah, and Gabriel."

Wow. I lean forward in my seat, entranced by her story and the parallels it has with my own… I mean, aside from the whole buried-alive and assuming-the-identity-of-a-dead-socialite thing.

"Later, I killed my uncle and claimed my birthright as the closest-living blood relative of Julian August, but this meant opening the August family up to challenges for leadership, as many of the soldiers didn't want a woman – much less an eighteen-year-old girl who they'd never met – telling them what to do. We were vulnerable, and the head of the Lucian family, Nero, used my precarious hold on the family to blackmail me into marrying him."

Now there's an arranged marriage? How many mafia romance tropes can one woman's life story contain?

"What happened next?"

"It's all bit of a blur of bloodshed after that, but basically, Mackenzie Malloy came back to Emerald Beach, and she came for my head. In a twist worthy of a soap opera, it turns out that Mackenzie was my twin sister. Her father Howard had sold one of his twin daughters to my father in exchange for a great treasure. My dad got an heir, and Howard got a shipment of rare documents."

Understanding dawns on me. "And are those the Classical scrolls in the museum?"

"Victor said you were clever. Yes, they are. Howard Malloy had hidden them away in the house. His daughter murdered her parents before she disappeared, and then she wanted me gone so she could get back into the house and lay her hands on the treasure. But I found it first. While all this was happening, the entire Triumvirate was falling to pieces. Nero killed Constantine Dio, and Cali took over the Dio family. Sorry," she says with a self-deprecating smirk in her voice. "This is a whole novel."

"Or a series of four novels. With a hot reverse harem thrown in," I say.

"*Exactly*. Mackenzie killed her own parents, and she and my brother planned to take over – because it turns out that she was secretly seeing Antony behind my back. Their plan was to make me do all the hard, dangerous work of getting the Triumvirate off my ass, then swoop in, kill me, and have Mackenzie take over and steal my life. Only I had my three men at my side. We killed Mackenzie and Antony, fed Nero to his pet tiger for good measure, and Cali, Livvie, and I formed a new Triumvirate with our own rules."

"What's different about the new Triumvirate?"

"We did away with the archaic rule that only those who are blood-related can inherit our empires. We did this in part because Cali is not of Dio blood. She was adopted by the last Imperator, Constantine, and although she carries the family name, it is not the name she was born with."

"I didn't know that."

I want to ask about Gaius and his mother, and how they fit in with this story, but I don't want to stop her. This is the most information I've ever gathered about the Triumvirate, and I know it will be valuable.

"You know now. It's probably best you keep that quiet. If Cali wants you to know, she'll tell you and..." Claudia taps her nails against her own glass. "Let's just say that you kids are making things uneasy between us."

"I thought the three of you were friends."

"We are, but our loyalty is to our families and our soldiers first. Usually, our aims are in harmony with each other, but you and Cassius and my twins are playing out this vendetta of yours in public. The soldiers see that, the criminal world sees that, and they think that we can't control our offspring. They don't just see Cas and Juliet trying to hurt you – they see a Dio and an August attacking a Dio. They start to question their own loyalty. And I don't like that."

I consider this. Dad had tried to talk to me about this when we met up for one of our clandestine Italian dinners, but I didn't pay much attention. When Claudia spells it out, I realize that I've been playing an even bigger game than I realized. And I think of how eager Zack Lionel Sommesnay was to help me get that demolition team to Victor's house, even though all I gave him was a lousy name.

"Despite everything we've said about allowing our best soldiers to rise through the ranks and potentially become Imperators themselves, all of us are more attached to the old ways than we like to admit. We want to keep our empires in the family." Claudia pauses to refill our drinks. "Torsten, I know you and your mother rarely agree, but her need to control you and change you comes from her attempts to reconcile your true nature with her desire for you to take over the family trade. Cali's two sons both admire her, but it's Cassius – the son of her blood – who she most cherishes, although she has an assassin's way of showing it. And I..."

I sip my drink as I wait for her to continue.

Claudia swallows. Instead of finishing her thought, she picks up another one. "We return full circle to what I wish to discuss with you. I have always planned for my twins to rule together after I'm gone. Victor has the head for the business, but the Triumvirate has too long been the dominion of men, and so I wanted Juliet to rule at Victor's side, a Queen in all ways but marriage. I wanted to keep it all in the family, nice and neat. This would leave them to fall in love with and marry whoever they chose, and to work with each other's strengths and balance their weaknesses.

"I was lucky enough to fall in love with three men who all wanted to be with me, but only one of them is right for this business. The other two give me other things that I need, and they make me see that I'm so much more than my job and the family name I fought so hard to protect. And I wanted my children to have that same freedom, so I've been determined to bind them together.

"Fergie, you made me see that I'm a fool and a romantic. Victor is strong and just and clever, but he's too easily swayed by love. His heart is too big – his need to protect the people he cares about means he cannot make the hard decisions. He's too easy to manipulate, as you have seen. He cannot rule this family alone. And my daughter has proven that she's ruthless and cunning, and those are admirable qualities if tended by a considered and thoughtful mind, but Juliet possesses neither. She does not see the thousands of people who rely on us for their living, the people who live on the sidelines of society who need a strong hand to guide them. My people are our extended family – they give us their loyalty, and in exchange, we must care for them. Juliet may learn to care for others in time, but... the museum attack has made it clear that I may not have time."

Claudia pauses, letting her words sink in.

"You think you might be killed," I say.

"It's always a danger in our line of work. I'm not afraid of death, Fergie. I've had an intense, beautiful, messy, imperfect life and I have not a single regret. But I *am* afraid of what my legacy may become in the hands of my daughter."

"I don't understand what this has to do with me."

"I'm offering you a job."

I spit whisky all over myself. "Um, excuse me?"

"I want you to work for me. I lost my personal secretary and dear friend Yara in the museum attack, and I think you'd make an excellent replacement. It will be part-time hours and you can fit it in around your schoolwork. I have to move the artifacts we recovered from the museum site to a new secure storage location while we rebuild, and I need to keep it all out of the hands of the city officials because most of those artifacts serve as the currency for my international network. The mayor is making my life difficult enough as it is, and she'll mire the whole project in red tape while she digs for something she can use to put me behind bars. You would oversee this move, as well as other jobs I may require from time to time, and if you wish, you can shadow me and learn about the business side of things."

I don't know what to say. "Is this some kind of power move against Cali?"

"So what if it is? Does it make the offer less appealing to you?"

I'm not sure I like my answer to that question. "Am I... allowed to work for you?"

"You're nineteen years old. You're allowed to do whatever you want. I think for now it would be best to keep this arrangement between the two of us. Cali is not happy with me right now. You are also allowed to say no. I won't hold it against you. You impressed me, Fergie Macintosh. I want to see what you're made of."

Her use of my real name throws me for a moment, but of course she knows. I bet she's known right from the beginning, from when Cali first arranged for me and Dad to have new names. She knew and she never told her son, because the harmony of the Triumvirate was more important to her than his happiness.

"Um... can I think about it?"

"No," she says sharply. "This offer expires the moment you step out of this car. The first thing you learn working for me is that you need to be decisive."

"Then I accept."

Torsten jerks in his seat. He obviously didn't expect me to agree. I press my thumb into his palm – a signal that I'm okay.

"I'm very happy to hear it." Claudia hands me a piece of paper. "This is my private number. Have Torsten put it into your phone for you, and message me. Noah will send you information about your first day of work. And don't forget, this is to remain secret. I place my utmost trust in my staff, and I do not take lightly any abuse of that trust."

"I won't say a word." I glance over. "Torsten, you can't say a word about this to Cas or Victor or Juliet or your mother, do you understand?"

He squeezes my hand. He understands.

"Excellent. Welcome to the August family, Fergie. I look forward to working with you." The car slows as it turns into a driveway. "I hope you don't mind. I've taken the liberty of escorting you home."

"Where are we? This isn't the hotel?"

"We're at your home," she says. "Your *real* home. Your father and Cali need you to come back. I offered to come and make you see reason. Now get inside and prove to your mother that I'm as good as my word."

42

FERGIE

I push the door open and slide out of the car. The tip of my cane hits the driveway, and I'm immediately thrown back to the first day I arrived here, all those months ago now, before I knew about the Triumvirate. Before I helped Poison Ivy feed a teacher to a lion. Before Cassius blew up the best thing that's ever happened to me.

"Fergie?" Dad's voice calls from the front door. A moment later, familiar arms wrap around me, and Dad's cologne invades my nostrils.

"I didn't really believe Claudia could convince you to come back, but I'm so happy you're home."

"I don't know how long I'll stay," I mutter as he drags me and Torsten inside. I feel blindsided by Claudia's proposal. Did she bring me here because she wants to reunite me with my family, or because she wants a spy in Cali's house?

A delicious smell wafts from the kitchen, and Dad's after-shave brings back a rush of childhood memories, and I don't give a fuck about Claudia's intentions. I can't imagine going back to the hotel.

"I promise that you're safe here," Dad leads me through to

the kitchen. "And Torsten too, if he wants to stay. Cassius won't be coming home unless you give the okay. Cali's made sure he knows that he can't go anywhere near you."

"Where's he staying?"

"That's between him and his mother."

I don't care anyway.

But then, why did I even ask?

"Where is Cali?" I change the subject.

"She hasn't been home much since the bombing. There's a lot she has to deal with in her role as Imperator. The best thing we can do to support her is to stay out of the spotlight and not go looking for trouble."

Dad says this last bit pointedly, and I know he's referring to my very public roasting of Juliet August, and the fact that my stepbrother is now permanently blue. I flash him a sweet smile. What he doesn't know about my revenge list won't hurt him. I'm not letting Cassius Dio off the hook that easily.

After we eat our fill of Milo's amazing home cooking, Seymour drives Torsten over to the hotel to pack up my things and deliver them back to my room. Torsten carries Spartacus' cage upstairs. I follow behind, the ball tip on my cane flicking between the steps to help me remember the distance.

I step into my room, and I'm immediately assaulted with memories. It's impossible to be here and not feel my stepbrother in every pore. His scent clings to my things from all those times he snuck into my room while I wasn't looking. My back itches from where his eyes bore into me as he watched me taking a shower, thinking I couldn't tell he was there. My thigh tingles from where his leg pressed against it when we sat on the bed playing with Spartacus, and my ears hum with the softness in his voice as he spoke about his brother...

I run my fingers along the bathroom door, touching the row of various locks I've had installed, every one of which has proved no match for my evil monster of a stepbrother. "I don't know if I'll ever feel safe in here."

"Cali has stepped up security," Dad says from the doorway. "She's got ten of her best up-and-coming assassins on a 24/7 roster outside the gates. No one is getting in or out of this property without their approval."

Cas will find a way.

"I'll stay with you," Torsten adds. "I'll sleep in front of the bathroom door. I'll make sure he can't get in."

I hug Spartacus to my chest, his tiny purr calming the nagging anxiety churning in my gut. "I'd like that very much."

43

VICTOR

"**I** can't believe Mom is making us do this," Juliet wails as I park the car in Cali's driveway.

"Mom doesn't have a choice. We humiliated a Dio in public. We have to give Cali the chance to have justice. If you complain, it's going to make things even worse for us. Just do whatever Cali wants without talking back and we'll make it out of this alive."

"If she wants to cut off our fingers, you're going first, brother," she hisses.

I swallow. *I hope that's not what she wants.*

I have to drag Juliet to the front door. I ring the bell. I glance over my shoulder at the men patrolling outside Cali's gate. Honestly, I want to make a run for it, too. I'm fucking terrified of what's waiting for us inside. But I will stand firm. I deserve this punishment for what I did to Fergie, and I'll bear it as an August should.

Seymour answers the door. "Follow me," he says. "She's expecting you."

We've known Seymour since we were kids. Hearing him be so formal with me stings. As he stands back to let us inside, his gaze falls on me, and it's so riddled with disappointment that I want to sink into the floor.

"Seymour, I—"

"No talking." Seymour leads us downstairs. Cali's house has always felt cold and sterile compared to our busy, messy lives, but today it's downright *frigid*. The bomb has rattled everyone, and I have a sinking feeling that the cracks in the Triumvirate are yawning ever wider.

Cali's in the gym, attacking a punching bag. Her obsidian skin glistens with sweat. She doesn't stop when she sees us, but keeps pummeling the bag, making sure we both see exactly what she can do to us if we don't play by her rules. Finally, she steps back and drops her arms. She's barely even out of breath.

"Thank you, Seymour. I'll take them from here."

Seymour nods and leaves. A few moments later, I hear the distinct click of a lock sliding shut as he locks us in the basement with Cali.

Not a good start.

Cali folds her arms over her chest and studies us. It's the cold, calculating gaze of a hunter surveying her prey. I bite my tongue as a thousand apologies threaten to burst from my lips. Nothing I can say will fix what I helped to destroy.

But that doesn't stop my sister from trying. "You're blowing this whole thing out of proportion. I only took secrets the Poison Ivy Club already gathered. It's their fault for leaving those secrets lying around—"

"Silence," Cali says, her voice hard as stone.

"Why hasn't Cas got into trouble over this?" Juliet whimpers. "He's the one who wanted to release the video. Have you tried saying no to him? He made me do it—"

"Stop talking or I'll sew your lips shut."

Juliet snaps her mouth closed.

Cali continues to study us. I keep still, letting her gaze strip away my arrogance and shrink me down until I'm a foot tall. Beside me, Juliet fidgets, struggling not to talk back. Finally, Cali moves to a closet on the other side of the room. She pulls out a metal bucket and tosses it to me. A shovel nearly hits Juliet in the head, but she catches it just in time. Next comes a roll of garbage bags that punches me in the chest. Hard.

"Follow me," Cali barks.

Juliet shoots me a devilish glare, but she's following Cali's instructions to keep her mouth shut, so we trudge along behind Cali as she leads us down a narrow corridor at the rear of the bar area, outside into the yard, across the pool area and around the back of Milo and Seymour's cottage. She shoves open the door of a pump shed and points to a large sump that's overflowing, covering the floor of the shed in brown liquid and making the ground outside squelchy. The sump reeks so bad that I press the collar of my sweater into my mouth. My eyes water. It smells like... like... rotting meat...

"This is the drain from my chamber," Cali explains. "I've had a lot of business lately, so it gets blocked up with... well, you'll see. You'll need to climb down and unblock it."

"I'm not doing that." Juliet throws down her shovel.

"Fine." Cali slides a knife from her belt. "If you're not gripping a shovel, then you have no use for your fingers."

"*Jules,*" I warn her.

She shudders but picks up the shovel. Cali nods. "Tell Seymour when you're done or if you need more garbage bags. If I'm not satisfied, you'll be doing it again."

Cali walks away, leaving the two of us standing knee-deep in... I don't even want to consider what.

Juliet whimpers and throws her bucket down. It hits the ground, splashing foul-smelling water into my crotch. "Hey," I growl. "We're both on the same team here."

"No, we're not. I can't believe you got us into this," she hisses.

"You didn't stick up for me with Mom or Cali or any of them. You let this happen to us."

"So this is my fault?" I grab the shovel from her and start attacking the hard lump of... *please don't let that be human fat*. "You're the one who took private Poison Ivy information and used it for your own ends. You're the one who ruined Fergie—"

"Oh, *please*, brother. Don't act like you're morally fucking superior. You and Mom make me so sick sometimes with your whole 'we can be the criminals with a conscience,' act. No, you fucking can't. And the sooner you both realize that, the better off we'll be."

The hardness in her voice stops me cold. I stop shoveling and stand up. "What's that supposed to mean?"

"It means, everything Mom does is to protect the Triumvirate, but the Triumvirate makes us *weak*. Why should Cali get to have all the fun and Livvie get all the real estate assets? August takes the risk importing Livvie's fancy designer drugs and exporting her high-end booze, but she keeps the majority of the funds. And don't get me started on Cali fucking Dio. She's no leader – she's a brute, a blunt weapon, just like her shitty sons. Think of what Mom could do if she was in charge of Dio assets." Her eyes narrow at me. "Think of what *we* could do, brother."

"Stop talking like this." I glance over her shoulder, back up at the house, certain that Cali could hear this conversation. "Where are you getting this from? No one is talking about disbanding the Triumvirate."

"Why the fuck not? What's it good for apart from forcing us to make nice with two families who want to stifle our power? It's not working, and we can't just let August be taken over because our mother refuses to give up her monthly tea parties. I think it's time for a new Imperator, and—"

I pick up the bucket and dump it over her head.

"Vic!" she wails, thrashing about as she tries to pull bits of... people... from her hair. "What the fuck did you do that for?"

"I did it so you'd stop talking nonsense. What you just suggested could get you killed, and worse. The Triumvirate protects us. It stops one family, one *person*, from having all the power. I believe in it, and so does Mom, and so do Cali and Livvie. They'll fix this issue between themselves as they've always done and come out stronger than ever, you'll see. And they don't need you meddling in shit when there's a bomber out there. Now hold that bucket for me, and don't force me to stuff the lung that just floated by into your mouth to shut you up, because I'll do it if you utter *one more word* of this bullshit."

Juliet's eyes flash, but she snaps her mouth shut and holds the bucket. As I scoop the foulest slurry I've ever seen out of the sump, I can't help but think about what she's saying. I've lived my whole life with the certainty that the Triumvirate would always exist, but Mom, Cali, and Livvie have never let something come between them as this has.

What will happen if the institution falls? Where will our family end up?

And what will it mean for Fergie?

AFTER WE FINISH CLEARING out the drain, Cali makes us sharpen all her blades. And she has a *lot* of blades. By the time we emerge from the basement, we're sweaty and smelly, and I can no longer feel my fingers. Juliet has bits of... *people*... hanging from her hair. All I can think about is having a shower.

We trudge through the living room, leaving a trail of foulness on the white marble tiles. I circle the sofa and nearly run smack into Fergie.

"Ew. Something smells foul," Fergie says without turning

away. She wrinkles her perfect nose – she knows exactly who's in this room with her, and why we're here, and she's reveling in it.

It's been a long time since I've been this close to Fergie. She's just as beautiful as ever. Her fiery hair falls over her shoulders in glossy waves, and she's wearing a torn heavy metal t-shirt and skintight leather pants with patches sewn on. Spartacus perches on her shoulder, and he glares at me with his huge yellow eyes and swipes a paw at us, as if to warn us not to come any closer.

Good boy.

I'm glad she's got that kitten watching out for her. Fuck knows, he does a better job than me.

"You're going to pay for this, bitch," Juliet growls. She tries to elbow her way around me to get to Fergie, but I hold her back.

Fergie tsks. "Is that any way to talk to the daughter of Cali Dio? You should think before you speak, or you might end up with an even more unpleasant job to do next time. It's been a while since I've waxed. Maybe I'll get you to do it."

Juliet screeches. She turns on her heel and stomps away. "Victor!" she barks, expecting me to follow her.

Instead, I do the only thing I can think of to do. I drop to the floor in front of Fergie. My knees crack on the marble, but I barely feel the pain. I crawl forward on my hands and knees until I'm lying on my stomach, and I lean in and kiss the tops of her pointy boots. I can't help but notice that they're the Fluevogs I bought for her a couple of weeks back. Someone – probably Torsten – has painted little death lilies up the sides.

A faint, impossible flame of hope flickers inside me.

"Duchess, I'm so sorry." I press my lips into the supple leather. "I'm a fucking idiot. I had this whole life planned out for myself, all the chess pieces perfectly in place, and you came along and blew the board to smithereens, and I don't even care. I don't care about the house, or the club, or our family's reputation, or the fact that I just cleared out a sump blocked by globs of human fat. All that matters is you. I want to make you happy, and hear your beautiful, evil laugh, and feel your body melt into mine again. And I know that you don't give a shit what I want, and I respect that, but know that no one will ever love you as fiercely and as imperfectly and loyally as I will."

"Torsten does," she answers, but her voice cracks on the words.

"Yes, and I love him too. If you let me, I will come back and show both of you what it means to be loved by Victor August. I own my mistakes, Fergie, and letting you go was the biggest mistake I ever made. If you let me, I'll spend the rest of my life making up for it."

I suck in a breath as she laces her fingers in my hair. Her soft touch sends an electric jolt straight into my dick. *She's touching me. She's—*

Fergie grabs a handful of hair and jerks me back, bending me painfully to expose my neck. She dips her head toward me, and her sightless eyes burn with a mix of desire, revulsion, and raw, unadulterated *need*. Her lips hover over mine, not touching, but threatening to touch me, to obliterate every last damn part of me that doesn't already belong to her.

"You will spend the rest of your life making up for it, August. I'll make sure of it."

44

TORSTEN

"I'll be fine on my own for one night." Fergie jabs me toward the door. "Go. Duty calls."

I don't care about duty. I don't want to sit around with my sisters for yet *another* family dinner, especially not when Livvie requested my presence at Tombs via email instead of her usual phone call, and specifically outlined that I should attend alone.

I *want* to stay at Cali's house with Fergie, leaning against the bathroom door and watching her sleep, or drawing her while she plays with Spartacus or practices her jiujitsu drills. I've filled almost four notebooks with drawings of Fergie. And drawings of other things, too – drawings for a project I've been thinking about ever since Fergie touched the mural I made in our hotel room.

I haven't told anyone about the project yet. Everyone is too busy shouting at each other. Besides, I probably won't do anything with it. It's probably a terrible idea. There's a reason Victor comes up with the ideas, not me.

But for now, thinking about the project makes me feel good, and thinking about the Triumvirate and Cas and Victor and

Livvie makes me feel not good, so I think about the project, and about Fergie lying in her soft bed, safe from Cas and Juliet and unknown bombers.

I don't want to leave her, but Fergie places her hand over mine in that way she does when she wants to draw me out of myself, and she insists that I go.

"With everything that's going on right now, it would be useful to know what Livvie is thinking," she says.

I tell her that I don't know how useful I'll be at collecting information. I've hacked into emails and government documents for Victor, and I always try to be as thorough and careful as I can, but he often throws his hands up and says, "I don't need any of this stuff, Torsten. Just find me the juicy secrets."

"But all of these things are secrets. Otherwise, I wouldn't have to hack into them," I tell him. And then he laughs and gets to work finding the things he wanted from what I gave him.

Fergie doesn't say any of that. She squeezes my hand again. "You'll be fine. You don't have to doubt yourself all the time. Just try to remember as much of your conversation as possible. Come home and repeat it to me. That's all you have to do."

I'm very good at remembering conversations. I often replay them in my head, over and over, or tell them to Victor and Cassius to get them to explain what I did wrong and why people react the way they do. I used to repeat Livvie's words back to her, but that made her face turn red and lock me in my room, so I don't do that anymore.

Seymour drops me at Tombs. The club is packed with people, and the loud music makes the walls shake. The bouncer points me in the direction of the hidden staircase that leads to one of the upper levels.

All of my mother's clubs have hidden rooms and secret exits where she can conduct her various businesses in secret. The stairs lead to a statue of an Egyptian god in an alcove. I tug on the head of the statue and a door swings open, and I step into a large, perfectly square room containing three long, gilded couches surrounding a low wooden table. I know this room well because I painted all the hieroglyphics on the walls. They're copied from King Tutankhamun's tomb in the Valley of the Kings, and they tell the story of the king's spirit descending into the underworld to be judged. Livvie delivers judgments here, and sends many people to the underworld, so it seemed appropriate.

Livvie rises as I enter. "Torsten, I'm so happy you could make it. Come sit."

I let her seat me on the couch next to her. The other two are occupied by Grace, Shera, and Trudi – my three oldest sisters. The table is covered with food, which doesn't look like it's been touched. Livvie hands me a glass of wine, but I don't drink it. I don't like the taste or the way it makes me feel.

Shera leans over and kisses my cheek. "It's good to see you, brother."

She and I are closest in age, and we've spent the most time together growing up. She doesn't mind being with me, whereas most of my other sisters run away whenever I enter the room. (Except for Isabella, who smiles and runs over whenever she sees me. But I notice she does that to everyone, so I don't think it means anything specific.)

"I'm glad you could join me tonight," Livvie says, gazing at us each in turn. "We have some important family matters to discuss, and I wanted to do that away from the house. I don't want to risk any of the younger children finding out what's going on."

My sisters exchange a meaningful glance that has no meaning to me.

"As you know," Livvie continues, "someone detonated a bomb inside the museum during our annual Saturnalia Council. Both Cali and Victor August sustained moderate injuries. Claudia August's personal secretary, Yara, was killed, and three of our security detail also perished in the blast.

"But more important than their lives has been the impact of this attack within the Triumvirate ranks. With the parcel bomb sent to Victor August, we were able to keep that quiet—"

"What?" Shera leans forward. "Someone sent Victor August a bomb in the mail?"

"Keep up," Livvie snaps. "Yes. And we hushed it up, but the museum bombing has been reported all over the world. Our contemporaries know that someone is targeting us all – not simply the Augusts – and it makes us look weak. The Triumvirate is losing lucrative contracts left, right, and center, and there are rumblings within our network that an unseen enemy is trying to swoop in and take us all out. My spies have even reported that some believe this to be an inside job. After all, getting past the security at the museum is no easy feat."

I don't like this, not when Fergie is so close to all of it. What if someone sends Victor another bomb when she's with him? What if someone sends a bomb to Cassius' house? Fergie's alone there right now.

I stand up.

"Sit down, Torsten."

I stride to the door. I need to get back to Fergie—

Livvie leaps in front of me, throwing her arms across the door frame. "Torsten, *sit down*."

"I have to get back to Fergie. She might be in danger."

"Foolish child – we're *all* in danger. That's what I'm trying to tell you. And if you would allow me to finish, you'd see that I have a plan."

Shera appears at my side. She wraps her arm around mine. "Torsten, please sit down with us. We can't do this without you. We need you."

We need you.

No one in my family has ever wanted or needed me before, except for when Livvie wants me to create a new art forgery for her. My chest burns with the joy of it. That's all I ever wanted, to be useful. To be needed. And if they can save Fergie...

I let my sister lead me back to the table and place a bunch of grapes in my hand. I pull the grapes apart and line them up on the table in sets of six before eating them. I flip open my sketchbook and work on a drawing of Fergie as Gala Dali with her tigers.

"As I was saying before I was *interrupted*," Livvie's eyes narrow at me as she sinks back into the couch, folding her silk dress over her legs. "Cali is working on ferreting out the mastermind. She believes that she's close to finding the mole within the organization, and from there we'll be able to go after this enemy as a united front. The problem is Fergie Munroe. Or Fergie Macintosh, as some of us know her. She's causing a rift between Cali and Claudia."

"Why?" I don't understand. Cali and Claudia barely know Fergie.

"Because of *loyalty*, Torsten – something you don't understand. Alongside Cassius, Victor and Juliet were involved in releasing that video and humiliating Fergie, and Fergie's been working overtime to make them all pay for it, a sentiment I can very much get behind. But this rift between the children is being played out in public, with videos of Cassius being dyed blue and Juliet being humiliated at a fashion show getting millions of hits online. Some people look at these videos and say, 'is everything fine between the parents?' And the answer is no. I can see that Cali and Claudia don't trust each other the way they used to. Unless we can catch the bomber, all of this is going to get ugly, and if we don't want to risk being squeezed out, I need to use their animosity to my advantage."

My sisters perk up at those words.

My mother snatches my journal from my hands. As I watch, my cheeks burning, she flips through the pages, looking at all the drawings of Fergie.

"You're serious about her," she growls, throwing the journal into my lap.

"It's none of your business."

"It *is* my business." Livvie taps her blood-red fingernails on her wine glass. "The two of you have been seen together numerous times. You were holed up in that hotel suite, and now you're back living under Cali's roof. Together. Don't you see what that says to people?"

"No."

"It says that you're a couple."

"We *are* a couple."

Livvie huffs. "Yes, Torsten, I know you're a couple. And I'm very happy for you but—"

"Thank you." She's never said anything like that to me before. *I'm happy for you.* It makes my whole body glow with heat.

Livvie slams her wine glass on the table so hard that wine sloshes over the edge. "You're just as impossible as ever, but for once it might actually work in our favor. You don't live in a happy fuzzy puppy land, Torsten. You're a Lucian, and you can't have a relationship in a vacuum, especially not a relationship with Cali Dio's stepdaughter. Our people still remember when our families used to arrange marriages to solidify alliances. They notice, and they talk, and they say that if Torsten and Fergie are dating, then Lucian and Dio must have an alliance."

My sisters nod along with her. I frown down at my sketchbook, and I clamp my hands together so I don't reach for it and start drawing. I don't understand why any of this matters. Can't they just let me go home to Fergie?

"Torsten, I'm telling you that I'm happy to bless your relationship, and I want you to take it further. I want you and Fergie to get married. This creates a bond between our family and the Dios. We protect each other and back each other up. We're obligated to look out for each other, which will become important as this enemy continues to harass us."

"But what about the Augusts?" Shera asks. "Isn't Claudia your oldest friend? Didn't her husband Eii help you—"

"Yes, yes. But that doesn't change the fact that the August family is weakened, and if they fall, they're not bringing us down with them. It's business." Livvie pats my knee. Her lavender perfume swirls around me, and I want to be sick. "The survival of our family comes first."

45

CASSIUS

I watch through my field binoculars as Torsten gets in Seymour's car and they drive away. I pay his sister Trudi to spy on the Lucians for me, and she informs me that Livvie called all the older siblings together at Tombs for a war council.

My stepsister is unguarded.

It's time to do what I should have done a long time ago.

Get rid of Fergie. Get rid of the landmine that's driving a wedge between our families.

Get rid of this wretched ache in my chest.

I park the car several blocks away and duck around behind the Whitestone mansion, slipping between boundary walls and staying clear of the roaming security patrols. Cali may have added new heavies to her security, but Gaius and I have been honing our skills sneaking around this neighborhood since I could walk. She can't keep me out.

I hoist myself up the large jacaranda tree in the Lovell's yard, swing through the branches until I'm hanging over the edge of Cali's fence, and wait for the next guard to walk past on his patrol. As soon as I see him, I allow myself to drop. He doesn't have a chance to scream. I break his neck with a *snap* and stash his body into the oleander bushes. Cali will be pissed to lose one of her trainees, but if he was dumb enough to ignore an overhanging tree then he'd make a useless assassin. I've done him a favor.

I move quickly and silently through the yard, crushing bushes of pink flowers. Thankfully, Cali doesn't share Claudia's obsession with cacti or Victor's love of poison plants, so I reach the shadows of the house unscathed. I creep around the edge of the house, ducking beneath the view line of the ground-floor windows. I can hear Milo singing along with the radio as he cleans the kitchen, and a TV blares some reality TV makeover show from the living room. I crouch behind a statue of Ares, God of War, and watch my sister's window, counting down the minutes, hoping I'll hit jackpot before the guards notice one of their own has disappeared.

At 11:42PM, the light goes on in Fergie's room.

It's strange to see her do that, turning on lights when I know she's blind. But she can see light sources, and sometimes even different shades and shapes of furniture and people moving around her. That's why Fergie loves clothing with sleek leather and buckles and studs – those things catch the light and she can see them. They make her happy and they look so fucking hot—

My dick goes hard, thinking about the very first time she walked into my brother's room wearing ass-hugging black jeans with a huge, glittery belt buckle and those shattered emerald eyes that seemed to see right through me...

I bet she's having her shower right now, getting herself nice and wet, working the soap into a lather as she washes those glorious tits of hers. I bet she's toweling herself dry, rubbing her hair, maybe even singing a tune to herself...

My dick is so hard now that it's painful, but I don't touch it. My memories aren't enough. Not this time. I need to be there. I *need* to watch her, to draw out the pleasure of tonight's kill. One last time before I kill her, I want to see my stepsister in all her glory.

I creep out from behind the statue and reach for the ash tree beneath her window. It's flimsy, but I think it will hold my weight. I grip a branch above my head and swing myself up. The tree rocks violently, but I'm able to grab the ledge beneath the window and haul myself up. I grip the house by its elaborate stonework, trying not to think about what will happen if I put a step wrong, and slide along to Fergie's window.

It's open.

My stepsister sleeps in Gaius' bed with her window open like she doesn't have a care in the world.

Silly little Sunflower.

I listen, and I can hear the rush of water from the shower. She's in the bathroom. I push the window up all the way, roll myself inside, and drop silently onto the rug.

The room is exactly as I remember it. I gulp in a mouthful of Fergie-scented air, and my dick twitches as it catches her raspberry scent. The lights are all on, including the string of fairy lights she's hung around the bed frame. I remember her saying when she put them up that she can see the little dances of light, that it stimulates what little is left of her vision. Spartacus' cat bed, food dish, and water bowl are on the floor in front of her desk, and the little black kitten is racing around the rug, batting enthusiastically at a tiny mouse toy. Some guard cat he is.

A hard lump rises in my throat as I watch him. I try to force down the memory of Fergie and I waiting nervously for Galen to treat Spartacus, and bringing him home and dangling my shoelaces for him once he got better.

I guess I'm not meant to love anything. I am only a tool for death and destruction.

I step over the spot where Gaius used to keep his drum kit,

my feet sinking into the dents in the carpet. Spartacus looks up at me with his huge kitty eyes.

"Mew?" he asks, bounding over and touching my leg with his little black paw.

Spartacus almost looks like he remembers me, but that's stupid. He's a cat.

I shove him aside and creep to the bathroom door. Fergie has it open, because of course she does. She feels safe here, in this room that should have never been hers.

She's in the shower, dancing around to some song in her head, her wet hair slapping against the bare skin of her back. She runs a sponge over the curve of her ass and...

I lean against the doorframe and watch her, sliding my hand into my shorts to grip my dick. Aaaah, yes. I wrap my hand around myself and squeeze until it hurts.

Yes, I'll jerk off to her one last time before I get rid of her from my life for good.

As I watch, Fergie's dancing becomes more sensuous. She hums to herself as she slides her hands down her body. She smiles that wicked, secretive Fergie smile that makes a knife twist in my gut, and she steps out of the shower for a moment to dig something out of the bottom drawer.

A vibrator.

A hot pink fucking vibrator.

Oh, *fuck yes.*

Fergie steps back under the stream of water. She spreads her legs and slowly slides the vibrator inside her. It's got one of those little wands that stick out and touch her clit. She turns it on, and her lower lip wobbles as it starts to hum and buzz inside her.

She looks so perfect.

For a few moments, she stands still, her hands braced against the tiles, legs spread the way she'd done when Vic and I took her in the shower at the club. She tosses her head back and lets out a low moan. But it's not enough for her. It's too soft, too ordinary for my depraved little stepsister.

Fergie reaches behind her and slaps her own ass, the smack so loud that it startles Spartacus, who rolls across the rug and dives under the bed.

"Oh, Cas," she moans, slapping herself again. "Give it to me rough. I've been so fucking naughty."

She's saying my name.

She's thinking about *me.*

My breath hitches.

My fingers cramp around my dick.

I lean forward, watching as she braces herself against the wall, pressing her cheek into the tiles the way I might've done if I was behind her. With one hand she pinches her nipples – first one, then the other, hard enough so she winces with pain – while the other hand leans around to slap her own ass again.

She's thinking about me, me, me.

Meanwhile, that vibrator goes to town inside her, and she rolls and bucks her hips, forcing it deeper, making it hit just the right spots.

The hum of it reverberates off the bathroom tiles, and Fergie's whimpers of pleasure join it, covering up the slap of my own hand as I jerk myself off.

Fuck, fuck, fuck.

My fist pumps my cock as hot bile rises in my throat. I can see myself in the bathroom mirror – a blue monster jerking himself off watching his unsuspecting stepsister in the shower. I'm so fucking turned on right now, so desperate to run over and fuck her sweet pussy and that tight little ass the way I know she likes it.

But I can't move.

I'm here to kill her, and she's not making it easy.

The urge to call out to her, to drop to my knees and beg for her pussy, overwhelms me. I yank my dick so hard that my head spins, and a low groan escapes my lips.

"What's that?" Fergie cries out. She reaches down and flicks the vibrator off. "Who's there?"

I freeze, my hand stuck down my pants, my dick jerking between my fingers. I can't believe I'm so fucking stupid. That girl has supersonic hearing.

Fergie yanks open the shower door and sticks her head out. Water droplets roll down her chest, pooling on the end of her nipples before dropping onto the floor. The pink vibrator sticks out of her, slick with her juices. I'm fucking *desperate* to come, but I know if I so much as move a hair on my head, she'll figure out I'm here and she'll sound the alarm, and I'll lose my chance.

"Who's there?" Fergie calls again, her voice wavering a little. She tenses her body, moving into a fighting stance.

Spartacus chooses this exact moment to trot up to me, climb up my jeans, dig his claws into my crotch, and meet my gaze with his giant orange eyes. "Mew?"

Fuck off, little dude. I love your little face, but seriously, get lost.

"Spartacus?"

"Mew, mew, *MEW*."

He bats at my hand, whiskers twitching, desperate to get me to play with him. I want to so bad. I've missed him. I've fucking missed a fucking cat.

Who the fuck am I?

Fergie slides the vibe out of her slick pussy and steps toward me. "Come here, boy," she coos, holding her arms out as she shuffles across the bathroom toward him. Toward *me*. "Momma will play with you."

Momma better watch out because I want to play with Momma, and I tend to break my toys.

I freeze in place as Fergie moves toward me, and Spartacus

clings to my jeans and mews at her. It's like he's deliberately leading her right to me...

At the last possible moment, Spartacus leaps off me and bounds over to Fergie. She picks him up and cradles him against her damp skin. He bats at her hair. Her lips curl back into a sweet smile that makes my chest hurt.

I can smell her arousal, and it's driving me fucking crazy. Fergie puts the kitten down and dries herself with a towel. She picks up the vibe and brings it back to bed with her.

My stepsister wraps her hair in the towel and slides her naked body between the sheets. She buries her face in Spartacus' fur. "It's weird," she tells the kitten as she cuddles him close. "It's like I can still smell Cassius. Even when he's gone, he's still inside my head."

My lips move. I think about saying something, about leaping out and wrapping my hands around her throat. How beautiful to see the surprise blossom in her eyes as she realizes it's me, that I've been here all along, and that my name will be the last word her pretty pink lips ever utter.

But I don't. And I tell myself it's because I have a plan. I want to do it while she's sleeping. But I don't know if that's entirely true.

Fergie slides further under the covers and turns the vibrator on again. It's not as good now that I can't see her, nowhere near as good, but it's still fucking heaven watching her face screw up and her pretty lips move, knowing that she has no idea I'm here with her. I don't dare move a muscle, not even to touch myself. I let my dick stay hard, enjoying every twitch of my jeans against the sensitive skin.

She lets out this perfect little squeak as she comes, and I damn near blow my load from the sound.

Fuck, I'll miss this part of her when she's gone – the way she's just so absolutely in the moment.

We could have been amazing together if she hadn't fucked me over.

Fergie sinks back on the pillows and sighs with delight. She pulls out the vibrator and gets up, walks right past me into the bathroom to wash it and put it away. Then she's back in bed, lifting the edge of the blanket so Spartacus can crawl underneath. He curls up in her armpit. She listens to an audiobook for a bit and then she flicks out the light.

"Goodnight, Spartacus," she says. "I love your furry little butt."

I'll have to take the cat with me when I leave. He's going to need someone to look after him once I've done what I came to do.

I lose track of how long I wait in the darkness, but it's a long time after I hear her breathing become slow and regular, after I'm certain that she's sound asleep. I listen to the only home I've ever known winding down for the night – I can hear water running in the pipes somewhere else in the house, and Milo and Seymour talking in quiet voices as they enjoy a nightcap on their little porch, and the tick of the antique clock in the foyer.

Is this what it's like being Fergie, constantly bombarded by auditory information?

When I'm certain everyone has gone to bed, and Fergie must be in a deep sleep, I creep over to the edge of the bed. I slide the knife out from my belt, running my finger along the blade until I draw a cut in my skin. My mother always taught me to care for my tools – the blade is nice and sharp. It will slide in easily, and Fergie will be no more.

And all my problems, all my pain, this rift between me and Cali, me and Victor and Torsten, it'll be gone. Done.

No more Fergie. No one left to hate me.

I dangle the knife over her head, willing myself to plunge it into her flesh, to end this pain right now.

My fingers clench.

You break everything you love, my brother's last words taunt me.

A single tear squeezes from the corner of my eye.

What the fuck?

I haven't cried since...

I don't know if I've ever cried.

I lean back, and the knife falls from my fingers and drops onto the sheets.

Fergie bolts upright, her unseeing eyes flying open. She's instantly awake. I'd be impressed by her reflexes if I wasn't suddenly seized by complete and utter terror.

What if she discovers me? What if she screams and my mother comes running?

What if she doesn't?

What if Fergie goes back to sleep and I pick up my knife and I finish what I came to do?

What if she grabs my hand and *helps* me ease the blade into her heart?

What if she dies in my arms? What if she doesn't? What if she kills herself in front of me because I made her hate me that fucking much?

I go still. I see the knife on the bed, and instinctively I reach for it, just as she thrusts her hand out.

"Cassius."

I jerk away as she reaches for me, her fingers grazing the air inches from my chest.

"I know it's you. I can smell you."

She lunges forward again, her arms flinging wildly at the air. She's panicked, a rare occurrence for my stepsister.

She's so close. I can reach out and touch her. Can she feel my breath on her face?

Her fingers trail across the sheet, brushing the handle of the knife.

"Cassius." Her voice is sharp as my knife, but the edge breaks. She curls her fingers around the handle.

It's that break that undoes me. I don't even realize that tears are falling down my cheeks until one rolls off my chin and drops onto her arm.

Fergie screams and throws the knife. I drop to the floor. The blade whizzes past my face and embeds itself into the wall behind me.

She screams again. Not words, just a wild, inhuman wail of pain that tears something inside me, opening a gaping wound that I don't think will ever close.

I lunge at her, not to hurt her, but because I have to crush her to my chest until that song of pain and terror stops. And then I remember that she's making that noise because of me. Because I shared the sex tape. Because I cut up all her clothes and drove her out of the house and destroyed Euri and Torsten's things and blamed her for all of it.

She cries because I'm the monster, and I came here to kill her.

"I can't," I whisper, but I don't know if she can hear me over her pain. I don't stop to pull the knife from the wall. I throw myself out the window and hurl myself into the tree.

It's a mistake. The branches snap under my weight and I drop to the patio. I land hard on my shoulder. The pain rockets through my body. Fergie leans out the window above me, and she's yelling. Lights in the house flicker on. I bolt for the corner of the yard and haul myself over the wall just as the guards sound the alarm.

I put my head between my legs and fight to get control again. My phone beeps. A text. I claw for it and manage to pull it out of my pocket without dropping it through my trembling fingers.

I need the distraction.

But when I see the message, my already splintered world falls completely to pieces.

It says:

HELLO LITTLE BRO

46

FERGIE

"Sssssh, sweetie, it's all right." Milo strokes my hair. He must've been upstairs doing some late-night chore because he barged into my room the moment I screamed. If only he was fast enough and strong enough to catch—

My door slams against the wall. "There better be a good reason for all this yelling," Cali growls. "I have important business to attend to."

"Fergalish, what happened?" The bed sags as Dad sits beside me, his hand stroking my forehead as if I'm eight years old and have a fever. It's more comforting than I'd like to admit.

"There was an intruder," Milo says. "I saw him run from the window. Seymour's gone after him, but I don't know if he'll catch him in time. He looked kind of... blue..."

"What about the security team?" Cali moves to the window. She smells metallic and tangly, like fresh blood. Was she working in her secret torture chamber? I remember that Dru's weird boyfriend wanted me to find it, and I'm glad I turned him down. He'll have to make do with the little nugget I gave him.

"The guard in the south corner had his neck broken." Milo

slips his arm out of mine and stands. "Fergie, I'll make you some of my chili hot chocolate. Nothing like a hot chocolate to soothe you after a scare."

"Shit." Cali shoves him out of the way and leans out the window. "How did they get close enough to do that without—"

"It was Cas," I blurt out.

Cas.

Cas was in my room.

Cas was holding a knife over me while I slept. And he must've been here earlier, too, when I was in the shower. I kept hearing things, and I had this *sense* that something wasn't right. I thought it was Spartacus playing around but no, it was my stepbrother. I *smelled* him, but I told myself it was just his scent lingering from all those times he'd been in this room before.

How could I be so *blind*? How did I not figure out he was here?

I hug Spartacus to my chest. I hate myself for letting my guard down, for allowing him to get so close and get off on watching me. My stepbrother tried to *kill* me. What could he have done to Spartacus? Or to Dad?

Dad scoops me up into his arms. "I'm sorry, Fergalish. I'm so, so sorry. I thought you'd be safe here."

"It's not your fault," I say, and I think, this time, I mean it. Dad didn't ask to fall in love with a bloodthirsty assassin, and I'm starting to get what he sees in Cali. The life she's made for herself, and her strength in dealing with it – it's *intoxicating*. He's in awe of her, and I don't blame him. I wish I could make men feel like that about me.

I thought I had it. For a few blissful weeks, I knew what it felt like to have something real, but then I lost everything. I can't deny Dad the chance to have what I crave.

"Did my son say anything to you?" Cali snaps. "How did you know it was Cas?"

My cheeks flush with heat. "I know because I can *smell* him. It was Cas. And he did say something. He said..."

I can't.

He said, 'I can't.'

It sounded as if he meant that he couldn't kill me. He came here to kill me in my sleep, only he changed his mind. I'm still alive, and it's not because I woke up and scared him.

Why? Why not finish me off?

I've made it clear that I'm not going to stop, that I'm never going to forgive him.

One of us has to kill the other, or we'll burn this whole town to ashes.

Why did my stepbrother let me live?

47

FERGIE

Torsten returns in the early hours of the morning in a rotten mood, which doesn't improve when he finds out what Cas tried to do to me.

"I'll gut him. I'll peel off his skin and roll it up like a cinnamon roll."

"You do that." I lie back on my bed. "I'd love to see it."

"I can't." He flops down beside me, his hand flapping at his side as he fights to stay calm. "And I don't think you should do anything more to him."

"Stop my revenge plot? *Never.* I have so many devious ideas to go."

"This is bigger than your revenge now. People are noticing. They think that the Triumvirate is growing weak."

I sit up, thinking of the things Claudia has said to me. "Is it?"

"I don't know. Livvie wants us to get married. She wants to align our families against Claudia."

"I can't do that, Torsten."

He stiffens.

"I didn't mean it like that." I take his hand and squeeze it. "I'd like to be married to you very much. But we're both only nineteen. I may be a hard bitch, but I have dreams of a fairy tale wedding to the perfect guy. I want to get married because it's the right person *and* the right time, not to seal some alliance or contract. Does that make sense to you? Do you want to get married because your mother says so?"

"She's not my mother."

I sense I'm tiptoeing on dangerous territory, but I *have* to know. "Torsten, is what Zack said true? How did you come to live with Livvie and have her last name?"

"She won me in a poker game."

He yanks his hand from mine and flaps it in the air by his face. I want to ask so many questions, but I can't think of how to phrase them to get the answers I want without upsetting him. But there is another person who might be able to help me, and it's probably about time I had another chat with her anyway. I reach up and grip his hand, bringing it toward me and placing it over my heart.

"It's okay. I won't talk about Livvie anymore."

"So we won't get married," he says, his fingers curling.

"Not right now," I say. "When the time is right, you can ask me, and I'll say yes."

"When will the time be right?" He sounds worried.

"How about I'll tell you?" I knit my fingers in his. "One day I'll turn to you and say, 'Torsten, the time is right' and you'll know what I mean. Does that work for you?"

I can feel the happiness radiating from his body. He squeezes my hand. "That works."

"Good." I squeeze his back. "And I'm going to have a talk to Livvie. I have a few things I'd like to say to her."

∽

THE NEXT DAY, I have my first shift as Claudia August's personal secretary. She sends a driver to collect me from school and take me somewhere downtown. We park, and my door is flung open. "My new shadow," says Claudia August, helping me out of the car. My boots crunch on loose gravel. "I'm glad you could make it."

I step gingerly over the gravel, feeling larger chunks of loose debris beneath my feet. "Me too. Where are we?"

"At the museum. I thought perhaps we could take a walk. Do you need help?"

"Yes. If you could let me hold your elbow, like this." I show her what to do, and she starts walking slowly, guiding me across the rubble. I only walk a few steps before my lungs start to sting from the dust and ash that we're kicking up. I click my tongue and sense misshapen lumps of marble flanking us on either side as we wander through the ruined building.

Claudia stops. She holds out my hands and drops something heavy into them. I run my fingers along it, feeling the coolness of the stone and the beautifully sculpted feathers curling over in an elegant arc. It's part of a statue.

"This is an ancient Roman copy of a Greek bronze of Nike, the winged goddess of victory," Claudia says. "It was priceless, and it's now in pieces, buried somewhere in this pile of rubble."

I don't know what to say. My fingers trace the delicate lines of the feathers, each one perfectly carved to layer over the other. I can't believe I'm holding something that's thousands of years old. The weight of its history bears down on me, and knowing that it's now gone forever makes a wave of sadness wash over me.

"I wanted you to see it," Claudia says. "I mean, *experience* it. This space, the destruction, all that's been lost."

"I understand – this is more than just a museum to you."

She squeezes my arm. "I don't know how much you know

about our business, and what the boys have told you, but the museum is an innovation of ours that has allowed our families to significantly grow our wealth and influence over the last two decades. Entrepreneurs such as myself who operate in an underground marketplace also need ways to make large monetary transactions without the authorities tracking us. This is where the art and antiquities market comes in. The entire modern art industry supports a shadowy world of money laundering. And in America, the Emerald Beach Museum of Art and Archaeology sits at the heart of that world. When this bastard blew it up, they didn't just destroy these beautiful, priceless objects – they made it much more difficult for Cali, Livvie, and I to move money and assets around unseen. But there's more to it than that... this feels like a personal attack on me.

"To Livvie and Cali, this place is a means to an end. But to me, the museum has always been my father's legacy. And to see it broken like this..." Claudia bends down and I can hear her sifting through the rubble. "Hold out your hand."

I hold out the hand not gripping the marble wing, and she presses something small into my palm. "That's an obol. It's an ancient coin. This one dates from the first century BC. When you died, your family would place an obol in your mouth to take with you to the underworld – and you would use it to bribe the ferryman Charon to grant you passage across the river Styx."

"It's beautiful." I run my fingers over the raised design on the tiny coin. I try to hand it back to her, but she closes my fingers around it.

"Keep it. You're working for me now. You may need it to pay the ferryman sooner than you think." Her voice grows dark. "My men have salvaged what they could from the wreckage, but it's not enough. Many of the artifacts are lost forever, and with them, the money that was stored against their value. There are a lot of dangerous people who are very angry with me right now. I made promises that their money would be safe here, stored in ink and ancient stones. And now..."

She didn't need to finish that sentence. If Claudia August is frightened of who might be coming after her, then they must be fucking *terrifying*. Instead, I say, "So your priority now is to preserve what you have left, especially if you need to trade these treasures for favors."

"Exactly. I don't want to part with anything, but not even the scrolls of ancient knowledge are as important as the safety of the August family. What I need you to do is find me a place to store what remains of my collection. We're currently housing them in the back of one of Livvie's clubs, but that situation is... no longer tenable."

I can imagine. I think about what Torsten told me, that Livvie wants the Lucian and Dio families to form an alliance against the Augusts. I debate telling Claudia, but decide now is not the time. "I have a building already sourced. It's here in the city. The deed is in my name, and Cali and Dad don't know about it. It will require some outfitting with the right equipment, but I think your collection will be safe there."

"I'm intrigued. How does a nineteen-year-old with no assets acquire a piece of real estate?"

"A lady never tells," I say with what I hope is a mysterious smile. "Would you like to see it?"

I FISH the keys Zack Sommesnay gave me from the bottom of my purse and unlock the building, holding the door open to usher Claudia inside. It's the first time I've visited my building. The hairs on the back of my neck stand on end as I climb the stairs behind the Chinese restaurant and step into the huge warehouse.

I'm not even sure what I'm looking at, but Claudia seems impressed.

"This could work," she says. "There's enough room for the sculptures on this floor alongside Cali's weaponry collection. Art will go upstairs. The scrolls require a specific temperature-controlled environment, and with a few adjustments, the fridge behind the Chinese takeout will do the trick nicely. This is very good, Fergie."

I glow under her praise. It occurs to me that I've never actually had a real job before. I used to do some secretarial work at Dad's clinic after school, but a job you get from your dad because he feels sorry no other business in Witchwood Falls will offer work to a blind girl doesn't count. Claudia August didn't give me this job out of guilt or pity. She *recruited* me because she sees something in me, and I want more than I've wanted anything in a long time to make her proud.

Claudia passes me a laptop and informs me that it's hooked into her personal network. "You'll be able to find everything you need on there," she says. "You can come back to the house with me, if you like. I have an office there, and I promise Juliet and Victor won't disturb us—"

"No, that's okay. I should make my base of operations here – there's a lot to do, and I want to be onsite to make sure it all goes smoothly."

"Very well." She gives my shoulder a squeeze. "I have to get back. For now, it's better that we're seen together as little as possible. Call me if you have any problems."

"Will do."

I tuck the laptop under my arm and move around the room, getting to know the corners of the space and the random bits of furniture and office equipment left behind by the previous owners. There's currently no electricity, but that's the first thing I arrange after I find an executive desk and leather chair in the corner and open the laptop.

I'm aware of the presence of two people at the rear of the room, watching my every move. A security detail from Claudia. I can assume that all my keystrokes are logged, as well. Claudia August trusts me, but she's not stupid. She knows I'm Cali's daughter.

In amongst the files for the management of the August empire, I find lists of local contacts – loyal soldiers who'll do any work that needs doing. My first clue that things are strained is that it takes three phone calls before someone will stay on the line after I explain that I'm calling on behalf of Claudia August. Finally, I manage to secure a crew to move the artifacts from Livvie's club to the building, and another company will set up the storage and ventilation and make sure that everything is secure. I plan to ask Claudia what security she can spare for guarding the facility, because who knows what Zack Lionel Sommesnay has planned for her next.

Inspired now, I call up Euri, and get a contact off her for the local paper. I offer the journalist a piece about what Claudia is doing to protect the artifacts after the bombing. She's excited to run it – when that goes out in the papers it will put Claudia back in the media and show that she *alone* is working to preserve the museum collection. I hope that any criminals who see it will be able to read between the lines – Claudia August is one to back. If this battle is going to be fought in public, then Claudia August needs to control her message.

I know I'm playing a dangerous game. If Cali knew I was working for Claudia, actively helping her... I remember when my stepmother entered my room the other night reeking of dried blood...

But no one asked me if I wanted to be part of the Triumvirate. I've been kept in the dark by the people who are supposed to be my family. Hell, my own stepbrother is trying to murder me. I will make up my own mind about where I stand in the grand scheme.

I'm feeling pretty proud of myself and what I've managed to do for Claudia. My phone peeps. The security guard strides toward me, but I hold up my hand. "It's just a text message, man. We're cool."

He doesn't come any closer. I think he's surprised that I know he's there. I lean back in my chair and read the text from an unknown number:

LIVVIE LUCIAN WILL SEE YOU TONIGHT, 11PM, AT TOMBS. DRESS TO IMPRESS.

48

CASSIUS

I lie naked on top of my sleeping bag, which rests on a stack of old pallets in the corner of the damp, ruined basement. I kick aside an empty bottle of Jack Daniels as I stare at the text, reading the words over and over until they blur on the screen.

HELLO LITTLE BRO

It's Gaius' nickname for me. Sure, it's not exactly the most imaginative name – anyone might've guessed that's what he called me – but when I read it my body hums with electric energy.

It's him. I *know* it's him.

Which makes no sense.

Gaius isn't allowed a mobile phone in prison, and he hasn't tried to contact us from inside. He never called the house or answered the letters I sent, and I don't believe he's written to Cali, either.

After he went away he's just been this big, silent void in my life – a hole where his wisecracking jokes and playfights used to be. When Cali was away on jobs I'd wander into his room and sit at his old drumkit and pound and pound away until I broke all the drums. It made me feel close to him, and it made me hate him for leaving me. Because I still don't understand why he did it, why he'd go to jail instead of me, and why Cali didn't get him out.

But then Fergie moved in and Cali packed up his broken drumkit and I fell for the stepsister I was supposed to hate on his behalf.

Why is he contacting me now?

What does he want?

Does he want to talk to me? Does he want my help? Does he want to make me feel guilty for letting him take the fall?

You break everything you love.

My blue-tinged fingers hover over the keypad. I want to write back, but I have no idea what to say, how to begin. If I don't answer, then I never have to watch him type the words that I've dreaded ever since he went away.

I never have to hear him say that he hates me—

This is fucking stupid. I'm not afraid of words on a phone.

I glare at those three words on the screen, and I think about being ignored by him for all these years, and I think about my own mother screaming at me that I'm a thug who doesn't care about my family, and I think about Fergie moving into Gaius' room and being so beautiful and perfect and the way she screamed in terror when I dropped the knife, and I hate myself, I *hate* myself more than it is possible to hate another human being, more than I've hated in my whole life, and I hate Gaius for being the perfect brother that I'll always fail to live up to, and suddenly I'm overcome with rage at the idea of him coming back into my life and taking everything from me again and I—

I fling the phone against the wall. It hits the cinder blocks and smashes into pieces. The moment the shattered screen bounces on the concrete floor, regret slams into me.

"Fuck."

That was my one chance to talk to my brother, the one glimmer of hope in my bleak existence, and I destroyed it.

You break everything you love.

I collect up the broken bits of phone. Maybe the SIM card is still intact. Maybe I'll be able to get it repaired and I can find out what Gaius wanted...

Or maybe... maybe my brother traded his teeth or his asshole for a mobile phone just so he could talk to me, and I've gone and wasted it because I'm a waste of fucking oxygen.

Maybe I don't need to kill Fergie to rid myself of this dark, broken void inside me.

Maybe the world is better off if I don't exist.

49

FERGIE

Seymour drops me and Torsten in front of the club. The place is buzzing, with people milling around outside and heavy bass making the street vibrate beneath my feet. "Torsten, Fergie, over here?" people I don't know call out. Lights flash bright in my face as people snap pictures.

I know exactly why Livvie asked us to meet her at the club when she knew it would be packed – she wants her people to see us together. She wants to play this Dio/Lucian alliance for all its worth.

Inside, we hand our coats to the doorman and descend through the towering pillars into the main dance floor. I know I look fucking fierce – I'm wearing a skintight red dress and matching devil horns sticking out of my head. They're made from chunks of crystal, and sometimes I catch them out of the corner of my eye reflecting prisms of light, and I love them. Torsten must look pretty damn fine, too, because we can hardly move a foot in any direction without some girl draping herself over him.

He shoves them all away. "What are we doing here?"

"I thought your mother wanted to meet us here. Do you see

her anywhere?" I sway my hips as I twirl around. I'd kind of like to stay and dance a bit – this song rocks, and I was rudely kicked out of the last party at this club. Torsten's hand clenches on the small of my back, and I lick my lips at the thought of grinding up against him...

But no, we have to stick to the plan. The crowd is making Torsten anxious. This isn't his scene. Now if I was here with Victor, we'd dance so hot that we'd burn this fucking place down...

Why? Why are you thinking about Victor? You don't want Victor. You have Torsten, and he's all you need—

"She won't be down here with the plebs." Torsten tightens his grip on my hand and yanks me through the crowd with such force I think my left arm is now two inches longer than my right. He helps me climb a winding spiral staircase, and shoves his way through a velvet rope into a VIP area, then down a long hallway and through a narrow door and—

"Torsten, Fergie, it's a pleasure to see you both again."

Livvie's voice sounds as warm and friendly as I remember it, but I know enough about her now to know I can't entirely trust it. The door swings shut behind us, and the pounding music becomes only background noise and a mild vibration in the walls. I click my tongue and listen to the echo in the space. The music dulls my senses, but I get a vague idea of the room – it's not an office, as I expected, but some kind of lounge. It's snug and dark, with only a couple ambient lamps for light, and there's little furniture inside except for some low couches. My heels fall into thick, rich carpet.

"Please, sit with me." Livvie pats the couch where she's sitting. Torsten leads me over and helps me to sit so I'm facing her. He slumps down next to me and pulls out his sketchbook. "May I offer you a drink?"

"No," Torsten growls.

"Yes, thank you." I remember from my brief visit to Tombs that Livvie's club does great cocktails, and I'm feeling the party vibes tonight.

"Certainly. I hope you don't mind, I've already had my bartender mix us something special. I'm hoping we have much to celebrate tonight." Her jewelry tinkles as she leans forward. "Hold out your left hand..."

I obey. Livvie herself places a martini glass in my fingers. She pats my arm as she retreats, and I hear the clink of her glass hitting mine. "To our future."

"To our future." I take a sip. The drink is zesty and a little sour, with a hint of pomegranate. It's delicious.

"I'm delighted you asked to meet me." The fabric on the sofa crinkles and sighs as Livvie leans back into it. I run my fingers along the cushions and feel velvet and silk and little beads. "I trust you have good news for me. I must say, I'm quite excited. I love wedding planning. We'll have it at the house, in the art gallery, and the reception here at the club. I know it's not traditional, but I think you should wear that gold dress I saw you in a few weeks ago—"

"We're not getting married," I say.

"Pardon me?"

"We're not getting married, and I don't want you to use mine and Torsten's relationship as a political tool anymore."

"Who says I'm doing that?" If Livvie is fazed by my rejection, it doesn't show in her voice.

"Aren't you? That's why you wanted us to show up here at this time of night. Every person in the club has seen us arrive together and head up into the VIP area. It's all part of the story you want us to help you tell. Well, we're not playing."

"Mmmm, this is heavenly," Livvie moans with pleasure as she sips her drink. I'm not sure she's even heard me. Beside me, Torsten scribbles away in his book. I'm starting to think he has the right idea about how to deal with this woman. "Drink up, Fergie, there are plenty more where this came from."

"Did you hear me? I said that—"

"Oh, I heard you. And I want you to know that I'm not doing this to further my own agenda. Well, not completely. I've never seen my son so happy before. He might've told you that I'm this horrible witch who treated him terribly during his childhood, that I took him from his true parents and raised him in a crime family and took advantage of his artistic abilities and screamed at him when he didn't fit in with the image I wanted to portray. All of that is true. I didn't know how to handle his mood swings or his different way of being in the world. I had a shaky empire, won with bloodshed and sacrifice, and I had to hold on at all costs, and I let so much slip trying to keep my family safe. And my biggest regret is that I let my relationship with you become this horrible, strained, broken thing." She addresses Torsten, and her voice cracks. I sense she is speaking from her heart.

Torsten stops sketching. He doesn't move, but I sense the atmosphere sparking with light and truth and possibility.

"I'm sorry, son," Livvie says, her words a whisper. "I have my own baggage from my father, and I let that infect our relationship. I didn't know what I was doing, and I couldn't ask for help. I had to be Livvie Lucian, my word is law. I had to show I could control you and... well, we both know how well that worked out. I know you think that because I won you in a poker game, I never wanted you. But the opposite is true. I *demanded* you as the price in that game because I knew what the man who called himself your father planned to force you to do. I knew I could win and save you from that horrid life, and give you something better. But when you were here in America with me and it was just the two of us behind closed doors and I wasn't Livvie Lucian, Imperator, but Livvie Lucian, a young mother with no help and no idea what the fuck she's doing... I got it all so horribly wrong."

I reach across to Torsten, knit my fingers in his, and squeeze. He squeezes back, but his hand trembles a little.

"I tried to encourage your art, remember? I got you all those tutors. I tried to give you a role in the business that wasn't about succeeding me, but I could never get through to you, not the way Fergie can. And I own the mistakes I made, I own the fact that I expected things from you that you couldn't give. That's a Lucian family legacy, you know." Livvie laughs bitterly. "My father had five sons, each stupider than the last. But because I was born a girl, my only use to him was a chattel to be traded among his male associates to further his business. Nero Lucian underestimated me right up until the moment I pushed him into the jaws of his pet lion."

I'm dying to hear more of the story of how Livvie took the Imperatorship from her father, but that's not why I'm here. "Aren't you doing the same thing to Torsten that your father did to you?"

Livvie's chair creaks again. "*Touché,* Fergie. Very well. But no matter what I do or don't say, people will draw their own conclusions, especially when they see the two of you together. The staff at that hotel of yours aren't exactly quiet about what you've been up to. Many of them work at my hotels, too, and they're a chatty bunch. I've heard that you shake the walls when my son makes you scream. It's one of my proudest moments as a mother."

My cheeks flush with heat. Torsten's hand moves across the page again.

"I can't give you a wedding, but if you want us to be more public with our relationship, we can do that," I say. "We'll start by heading down to the VIP area after I finish my drink and making a spectacle of ourselves."

Torsten's hand briefly stops moving. I know he's wondering

what I'm doing. I'm not sure I know myself. Part of me just wants an excuse to drag him onto the dance floor or make out with him in a dark corner while heavy bass pulses in my veins. The rest of me – the sensible part – knows that being in Livvie's good books could come in handy in the future.

Livvie, Claudia, Cali. I know I'm playing a dangerous game with their loyalties. But I'm starting to realize that Torsten's right – this game is bigger than my revenge now, and I need to play it as if my life depends on it.

And if that means hedging my bets with all three Imperators, then that's exactly what I'll do.

FERGIE

Wednesday evening, I flop down on the sofa in the downstairs living room. Dad pauses the show he's watching.

"Hey, Fergalish. Cali's out for the evening on a job. Feel like getting Milo to make us some unhealthy snacks and watching some Battlestar Galactica?"

The job Cali's out on is the one I told Zack about – some Russian Oligarch in the city for business that some other Oligarch wants knocked off. It's a whole vibe to see my dad chilling on the couch while his wife is literally out killing someone.

"Hell yes. Do you still have our DVD?" We got the show with audio descriptions – that's where a voiceover tells me what's happening on the screen so I can follow the actions as well as the dialogue. When I was a kid, lots of shows didn't have audio description, so Dad would make up his own – sometimes it was way more fun than the actual show.

"I sure do." He pats my knee as he slides off the sofa to set it up. "Would Torsten like to watch, too?"

"He's painting in my room. He doesn't really like TV." We've tried to watch shows before, but Torsten doesn't understand a lot of the stories. He often can't see why people react the way they do to the situations, so I have to keep pausing and explaining, and sometimes that's hard when I actually can't see the show. It's so much more fun to just push his head between my legs.

But I don't tell my dad that.

"I like seeing you with Torsten," Dad says as he settles back on the couch. "I know that Livvie has had a lot of stress over that boy, but I think a lot of that is to do with her parenting style. I think he's good for you."

His meaning hangs in the air between us.

I think he's better for you than your stepbrother or Victor August.

I think he's the one you should choose.

But I know Dad's trying hard to mend what's broken between us, so I let this pass with a nod. "Yeah. Torsten's great. Once you understand how his mind works, he's so much fun to be with."

"Were you out with him yesterday after school? You've been away in the evenings a lot lately."

Yesterday I was managing the removal of the remaining museum artifacts from Livvie's club. I think about telling Dad about my job with Claudia, but I can't risk it. Cali *cannot* know. "Yeah. We just went to an art gallery. Torsten likes to explain the paintings to me."

"That's wonderful, but I want you to be careful. Torsten may not have much of a role in Cali's world, but he's still a Lucian. And you're a Dio now. You two being together *means* things to people, and I don't want you to have to deal with that until you're ready, especially not after..."

I know he's thinking about the video. He wants to save me from what I went through last time, what I put him through. But

I'm not the same person I was with Dawson. I'm so much stronger.

I'm trapped in a speeding train hurtling down the rails, and I have no idea what will happen when the track runs out. In the world of the Triumvirate, I can't just have a boyfriend. I'm forming *alliances*. I can't just have a job – I'm using Claudia, and she's using me. Because if people notice Cali Dio's stepdaughter working for you, that says things, too. And as for Cali, she kicked her own son out because of me, and she's punishing the August twins because of me...

It would be nice, just for a while, to believe that Torsten and I exist in a happy bubble. But that's not reality. I change the subject. "How do you like the new clinic?"

"You know, it's not the kind of thing I'm used to doing at all," Dad laughs. "Treating Cali's people is a change from the terrified children and bored soccer moms I used to see, but it *is* interesting. This week I've repaired crowns for two Colosseum fighters and given a woman who Cali wants to hide from the Yakuza a brand new set of teeth. I'm wiped, though. I didn't expect to be pulling so many all-nighters as a dentist."

I've heard him leave the house late at night at least three times this week. No one in Cali's house seems to spend much time in their own beds.

Milo arrives then with platters of candy and home-baked treats, as well as two towering mugs of chili hot chocolate. He and Seymour wave goodbye – Cali gave them the night off, so they're going to the theater. Apart from Torsten, who will stay upstairs in my room painting all night, and the guards outside, Dad and I have the house to ourselves.

We watch a couple of episodes, but we still have piles of food left.

"Do you want to watch another?" Dad asks, his voice hopeful.

"I have a better idea," I say. I escape upstairs and dig out a box I'd hidden at the back of my closet. Thankfully, Cassius' destructive rampage hadn't touched it. I bring it back downstairs and set it out on the table.

"Monopoly?" Dad pulls the box toward him. "I didn't know you still had this."

I got rid of most of my possessions when we moved. I didn't want any reminders of Witchwood Falls. But I hadn't quite been able to bring myself to get rid of my battered old Monopoly set. It's a special version – it has Braille tiles and Braille on all the properties, chance cards, and money, so I can play. As a kid, I was pretty good, although maybe Dad was going easy on me.

"Remember when I used to make you play with me when I was a kid?" I say as I start setting out the pieces. "But I didn't understand the rules so I'd just make random rules of my own, and you'd have to pretend you understood."

"You were always so imaginative," Dad says. "Just like Miranda. I always told her that she should be an artist or an interior designer. She could make something beautiful out of any old trash. Do you remember the mobile she made you? With all the barnyard animals that made noises?"

"How could I forget?" I laugh. "I was *terrified* of that thing. I still have nightmares about that screaming piglet."

We both crack up laughing.

Dad places his hand over mine. "How are you handling all this?" he asks, his voice suddenly sad, pensive. "I mean, really? Between learning about who Cali is, and the video, and those boys..."

"It's... a lot." I gesture to the enormous room. "When you said you knew someone who could help us, I didn't exactly expect to move across the country into a mansion with my new stepmother the assassin. Plus, she hates me—"

"Cali doesn't hate you," Dad says. "Far from it. She admires you, especially when you insisted on going to school here."

I snort. "She has a funny way of showing it."

"Cali's one of those people who are extra hard on anyone she respects. She doesn't waste her time or energy unless she thinks you're worth it—"

He's interrupted by a crash. It came from the front foyer. Dad's on his feet in a moment. I grab my cane from the couch and follow him.

"Cali?" Dad cries, his voice thick with concern. "Is that you? Did the job—"

His words cut off with a cry. I realize the crash is someone falling through the front door. I can see a pale square of moonlight from the open door, and a dark shape wiggling around on the floor.

"John," Cali gasps, lurching toward me. "Fergie. I—"

She collapses into my arms. Her breath burbles in her throat. As I reach around her to steady her, my hands touch something warm and gooey.

Blood.

Blood oozing from a bullet wound in her stomach.

"Cali!" Dad's at my side in moments. "Fergie, she's been shot. Call an ambulance."

"No..." Cali breathes. "No ambulance..."

Her head lolls against my leg.

"We need Galen," I tell Dad. "Do you know how to contact him?"

"No. I'm not... I'm not that involved in the business." Dad's voice rises. I can tell he's rapidly close to panic. I need to give him something to do, something to focus on that's not his wife dying in my arms. As gently as I can, I slide myself out from beneath Cali and lean her against Dad.

"Stay with her. Put pressure on the wound. I'll get Galen."

I run back into the living room where I left my phone. I grab it from between the sofa cushions and dial a number I thought I'd never dial again.

My stepbrother picks up on the first ring. "Don't you—"

"Cali's been shot," I say. "She's lying in the foyer, pissing blood, and Milo and Seymour are at the theater, and I need Galen's number."

"Open the gates. I'll take care of it," he barks.

The phone goes dead.

I race back downstairs and drop down beside Dad. "Help is on the way." (I think.) "But I have to find the button to open the gate. Do you know where it is? Or how do I tell the security guys to do it?"

Dad doesn't hear me. He keeps murmuring to Cali.

"Dad?" I lean down beside him, squeezing his shoulder. "I know this is horrible, but I need to know where that button is."

"Please," he murmurs. "Don't take her away from me, like Miranda. I can't bear to lose another one."

Okay, so he's no help. I think back to other times when I've left the house. I think there's a panel on the right of the front door, near the coat room. I left my cane back in the living room, so I take off in the direction of the front door, arms outstretched. When I hit the wall, I feel along it in wide circles until...

There it is! A panel. But fuck, it's a touchscreen. Fuck, *fuck*.

"Torsten!" I scream at the top of my lungs. But when he's in the middle of painting, he might not be reachable. I have to do this myself.

I mash my fingers over the screen until it beeps at me. Okay, I've found a menu, and these buttons seem to control different functions around the house, so somewhere...

I press at the screen until I hear another beep. Behind me, the lights in the house flicker like a disco. Not that one, then. I hit another and the sprinklers in the front yard turn on. I hit a few more and a whole host of electronic gadgets inside the house beep in protest, but I can hear the sound of the gate swinging open. The intercom cackles as the security detail demand to know who's coming in, and I manage to find the talk button and tell them to override Cali's instructions to keep Cas out and to allow his vehicle through.

I collapse against the wall with relief.

A few minutes later, a car careens into the driveway. Doors

slam and three people barge through the door and rush past me. I hear a familiar voice swear as he takes in the scene.

Cassius.

My body jerks as his plum and carnation scent washes over me. It's a trauma response – my body still remembers waking up in the middle of the night with him looming over me, the knife, *the knife...*

And yet, as he strides across the room to help his mother, the only thing I want to do is fall into his monstrous arms and feel safe there.

"John, you need to let me look at her," Galen says in his steady, authoritative voice. He must've been one of the other people. My dad wails, and there are noises of people moving and Galen shuffling through his medical bag. I don't know what's going on but I have to hope they're saving Cali's life.

"Are you okay?" Cassius growls in my ear, closer than I expect.

I leap in the air, struggling to keep my pounding heart under control. "I'm fine. I wasn't there when this happened. She was out on a job—"

A job that I told Zack Lionel Sommesnay about.

I'm not ready to confront that thought. Not yet. This could be a coincidence. It could be that her mark heard her coming, or she got into a firefight with his security. Zack's a bureaucrat, not a shooter...

But it's hard to tell myself these things when Cas is standing so close, swallowing all my air with plum and musk and carnations.

"Her car's in the driveway, and there's blood smeared down the driver's side door. She drove herself home." Cassius' boots scrape across the floor as he paces wildly. He's agitated. "Fuck. *Fuck.* Galen, can't you work any faster?"

"I'm doing all I can. Help me lay her out on this table." I hear a crash as Galen sweeps an artful arrangement of candleholders onto the floor. Cassius grunts as he picks up his mother and lays her out on the table. I crawl over to my dad and wrap him in my arms. He feels tiny and frail, like I'm holding a child.

"Cali, can you hear me?" Galen calls softly. I can hear him shuffling through his bag. "This is going to hurt like hell, pet. Cassius, hand me that scalpel."

I press Dad's head into my shoulder. Someone else leans over me, mashing me against his torso. At first, I think it's Cas, and I try to struggle, but the scent of vanilla and lemongrass tells me that all the commotion has brought Torsten downstairs. He holds me the way I desperately need to be held, but his hands over my ears can't muffle Cali's scream as Galen does... whatever he does to her.

To hear Cali Dio let down all that wall of ice she's carved around herself and give in to the pain loosens something inside me. A shard of my coal-heart chips off and jabs me in the ribs. I hear Cas murmuring to her, telling her that it will all be okay, that he will protect her, that he will gut whoever did this to her.

Cali's scream goes on and on and on until it's impossible to remember a world where my stepmother wasn't in terrifying pain.

Dad shakes in my arms, and I realize for the first time how he must've felt when I came home and told him about Dawson's video – helpless against the evil in the world. If someone can fell the mighty Cali Do, what hope do the rest of us have?

I don't know how long it is before Cali's screams become moans, and then fade into sobs, and finally into the steady breathing of the sleeping dead. A kind, warm hand tugs my shoulder, pulling me away from my dad so that he can go to her.

"She's alive, John," Galen says as he leads my dad away. "But barely. If Cassius hadn't gotten to me so quickly, we would have lost her. I've put her in one of the downstairs guest rooms, and

I'm taking you to her now. I'll stay here and watch over her for the next twenty-four hours, but she's not out of the woods yet. Whoever shot her intended to kill her, but I don't think they were a professional or they would have succeeded."

Whoever shot her intended to kill her.

Was it Zack? Is this my doing? Has my revenge plan put my own stepmother in danger?

52

FERGIE

Hours later, I'm in bed, tossing for the second straight hour. Torsten is in Cas' library, working on one of his paintings, and Spartacus has long ago given up trying to sleep with my restless ass and stalked off in disgust.

The sheets feel like they're crawling with bugs. No matter how many times I get up to scrub my hands, I can't get the smell of Cali's blood off my fingers. I tried to call Drusilla ten times, but she's not picking up her phone. I need answers. I *need* to know if I did this.

I cover my head with my pillow, but all I can hear are my stepmother's screams roaring in my ears.

I don't think I'll ever feel clean again.

I can't take it anymore. I pull my dressing gown over my naked body and pad downstairs to the kitchen. If I can't sleep, I might as well eat my body weight in junk food.

I feel my way to the refrigerator and start pulling open containers at random, searching for the baklava Milo made the other day. I don't find it, but I do find half a chocolate cake and some Chinese takeout, and a bottle of wine in the cooler. I take my booty to the counter and set it down, then go back to the drawers to hunt for a corkscrew. My fingers close around it and—

"You should be careful with that thing, Sunflower. You might put someone's eye out."

I jump out of my fucking skin.

I hadn't heard him come into the room, and he'd been so still and silent. I guess it's his assassin training, but it's fucking unnerving, especially since the last time we were alone in a room together he tried to stab me.

"How long have you been sitting there?" I growl at Cassius. My heart hammers against my ribs.

"Hours."

He doesn't sound like himself. All the fight has gone out of his voice. I hold up the corkscrew. "Want a glass?"

"Thanks. I'd have drunk most of a bottle of whisky by now but *someone* turned all mine into Jell-O shots."

He sounds totally flat when he says it. Nothing like the unhinged monster I know. Gingerly, I move toward the table. Cas may be wounded, but he's still The Bear, and I've spent the last month poking him in the ribs.

I sit on the very edge of my chair, ready to make a run for it if needed. I feel for the bottle and jab the corkscrew in. It takes me a couple of yanks to get the cork out. I pour myself a generous glass and hand the bottle to Cas.

I hear him gulping wine straight from the bottle. I tear open the Chinese boxes and shove sweet and sour chicken across the counter at him. "You should probably eat," I say. "You need to keep your strength up if you're going to strangle whoever did this to her."

He grunts. I hear him slide the spoon into the gloopy take-out, but I don't hear him chew. My stomach growls, and I unwrap the chocolate cake and slice off a corner.

The guilt gnaws and chews at me, and I can't fucking *stand* it.

"Cassius, are you okay?"

"Why are you asking me that?" he growls.

"Because your mother is in a room down the hall, fighting for her life?"

"You hate me. You dyed me blue, for fuck's sake. So I ask you again, why are you asking me to spill my fucking feelings?"

The edge has crept back into his voice. I slide my foot onto the floor, ready to spring away if he tries to attack me. "You want the honest fucking truth? You know the thing about hatred is that it's only possible where there is love. I know this because when Dawson released that video of me, all that happened was that I became numb. I couldn't hate him because I'd never loved him, so I turned all those awful feelings inward, onto myself. I hated myself for being so open and trusting. I became this zombie, asleep at the wheel of my own life. You and Victor and Torsten woke me up again. You made me *feel*. You made me believe that the world can be bright and beautiful, that we can make our own luck and find our own justice. I *loved* you, Cas. True, wild, limitless fucking love. And so when you did what you did, it couldn't make me numb. It makes me burn with a rage I've never known before, and all because underneath it all, I still feel something for you."

He chokes on his drink. "You... you still have feelings..."

"Yeah. I do. Mostly I feel pity. And a strong wish that I could not be blind for a day so I could see you walking around like Papa Smurf. But if there wasn't something of my love left, then I couldn't hate you. I'm working on getting rid of it," I say with a smile.

The air around us sizzles with tension. I squeeze my thighs together as a sharp, hot ache rises pulses between my legs. My brain and heart may be desperate to rid me of Cassius Dio, but my body remembers how good and safe and special it felt to submit to him.

"So you've got more revenge planned," he says, his voice ragged. If I didn't know better, I'd say he was thinking the exact same thing.

"Oh yes. I'm thinking of going biblical – plagues of locusts and frogs. It'll be epic. But in the meantime, here we are, together, eating Milo's chocolate cake."

I hear Cassius slide out of his chair.

My breath hitches.

My spoon freezes halfway to my mouth.

He moves around the edge of the counter. Every nerve in my body screams at me to run. His bulk sucks all the air from the room. My disobedient pussy howls at me to give myself over to him.

He steps closer.

Closer.

His breath kisses my cheek.

I'm aware of the thin sliver of air that separates our bodies, and how desperately I want to close that space into nothing at all.

I'm drowning in plum and carnations, and it's a very good way to die.

"Go to bed, Fergie," he growls.

That growl reverberates through my body, humming between my legs. My hungry pussy begs for more like a greedy bitch.

I lift my chin. "I'm not tired."

"If you know what's good for you, you'll turn that ass of yours around and go back to bed *right now.*"

"Make me."

Cas swipes my glass off the counter. It smashes on the floor, sloshing wine on my ankles. "I said, *go to bed.* Be a good little sister."

Those words – so obviously meant to bait me, but so cracked

and broken with his own pain – do something inside me. And because apparently I have a death wish, I stand up, my chest pressing against his so I can feel his heart pounding against his ribs. I stand on my tiptoes to get right up in his fucking face. "What if I don't want to? What are you going to do about it, big brother?"

A roar tears from Cas' throat. It's not a human sound, but it does something dark and nasty to my insides. And I fucking *love* it.

His chest presses against mine, hemming me in so I have no escape. His hands fly up and grip my wrists, hard enough to make me yelp. His fingers burn my skin and my pussy... my pussy is on fucking *fire* for him.

How long have I craved the madness that only my step-brother can give?

He pins my hands to my sides and uses his bulk to walk me backward until I'm pressed against the kitchen cabinets. "You asked for this, Sunflower. You could have been a good girl and walked away. But that's not you, is it? You want what only I can give you. You want to be punished for all those horrible things you did to me. Turn around. Put your hands on the counter."

He drops my hands, flings open a drawer, and rummages around inside.

"What are you doing?"

"I said, *turn around*. Don't make me ask twice."

I shoot him a look that I hope screams defiance, but my body is no longer my own. I hate that he's right, but he is. I want this. Some dark, sick part of me knows that my revenge on Cassius is partly about pushing his buttons and seeing what sick thing he'll come up with in return. We're both as twisted and broken as each other.

And this, right now, is what happens when we come together.

I turn, slowly, letting my robe fall down over my shoulder so he can see that I'm not wearing anything underneath. I shove the chocolate cake out of the way and plant my hands on the counter. I wait, my whole body alive in a way it hasn't been since the night of Saturnalia, since the night my stepbrother made me beg for his cock.

Fuck me, and *fuck him*, but I'd beg again. I'd do the most sinful, degrading things right here, right now if he commanded me, if it meant I could have that night and *that* Cas back.

I wait, my knees shaking in fear and anticipation, my pussy aching with need.

I wait while he moves around behind me, collecting things from drawers and cupboards.

What the fuck is he doing? Is he baking a fucking soufflé?

Just as I can't stand another moment, Cas flips up the hem of my robe, exposing my bare ass. His calloused fingers squeeze my cheeks – first one, then the other, squeezing and kneading until I'm in no doubt that he intends to have all of me tonight. Then with a growl that makes my insides tremble, he brings something hard down on my bare skin.

WHACK.

I moan. It's a fucking *wooden spoon,* and it hurts. It hurts so goddamn good.

WHACK.

He hits the other cheek. I jerk away, but he grabs me in his huge, calloused hands and slams me back into the counter, holding me down in the middle of my back so I can't escape. I wriggle and jerk, but he's got me right where he wants me, and he won't show mercy.

"Now, now, good girls don't run away from their punishment," he murmurs, his breath hot on my neck. "And you want to be my good girl, don't you, little sis?"

WHACK. WHACK.

Holy fuckballs it hurts it hurts so good...

"I want you to say it for me, stepsister."

"No," I cry out as he grabs my flesh and squeezes again, making me feel the bruises he's raising on my skin.

"You will say it. Say that you're my good girl. Say that you're sorry for all of the nasty tricks you've played on me. Say that you're mine to do whatever I like."

"No!"

WHACK.

Tears spring in my eyes. Cas plunges his hand between my legs, rubbing roughly at my clit as he slides the spoon along my ass crack, teasing me. I whimper as his fingers find the perfect spot, and he circles and dips and rubs until I'm right on the edge.

"You can deny it all you like, but I have this hot little pussy in my hands and I know exactly what she needs. Now, say it!"

Fucccck.

"I'm... I'm sorry," I whimper.

"For?"

"For making your whisky into Jell-O shots. And turning you blue."

"Good girl. And what else?"

"And... and getting my friend to make a video of you running around like Papa Smurf and putting it on the internet so everyone could see."

And possibly being the reason your mother is fighting for her life right now.

"I must admit, there was poetic justice in that. But tell me, little sister," Cas purrs as he strokes my clit. "Who do you belong to?"

"I belong to you."

"Mmmm, that's right. And who gets to own this sweet pussy tonight?"

"You."

Saying it aloud releases something inside me. All this time, my tricks and revenge plans have been about resisting the magnetic pull of Cassius. And I can't do it anymore. I'm done. He is my drug, and I'm addicted.

He hits me again with the spoon, and I fall apart on his fingers. I flail about on the counter as the orgasm steals my legs from under me.

Cas catches me in his strong arms before I slide off onto the floor. He tuts. "Where do you think you're going, Sunflower? You promised that you're mine tonight – my toy. And I do love to break my toys."

He picks me up like I weigh nothing and slams me back on the counter. More dishes sail off the edge and crash on the tiles. We must've made a hell of a mess, but I don't fucking care. I'll apologize to Milo later. I know exactly what I'm doing. I feel guilty that I told Zack about Cali's job, and right now I need my stepbrother's cruelty and his cock like I need air in my lungs.

Cas kicks my legs apart, keeping his hand on the small of my back while he grabs another of the objects he found.

"You know, I never did learn how to use this fucking coffee machine," he says conversationally. "But every time I watch Milo froth the milk, I always imagine what else it could be used for."

I hear the buzz of the milk frother turn on and off again, and the next moment, something is nudging against my entrance.

"You are not putting a fucking milk frother inside me," I growl.

"I am. And you are going to love it. Now open those legs for your stepbrother, or I'll find a way to *make* you open them."

I let my legs fall open, and he nudges something between them. I'm so wet that it slides inside easily, and I can feel from the size and heft of it that it's the handle of the frother.

Cas turns it on.

Fuck me *dead*.

It's as powerful as one of the higher settings on my vibrator, and it's inside me and it's right up against my G spot and I can't stop *I can't I can't...*

"I saw you had something inside you in the shower the other night, while you were thinking of me," he whispers against my earlobe. "I want to make your depraved little dreams come true."

"You mean, when you snuck in the house to *kill* me," I whisper back, a shiver running through my body as the reality of who I'm letting touch me crashes into me.

"I did, little Sunflower. I did come here to kill you, but when I held that knife over you, I realized how much more fun we have when you're alive. Don't you agree?"

He hits me with that spoon again – not on the ass this time but right on my *fucking clit*.

"Yes," I growl through gritted teeth as the frother works its magic, burrowing deeper inside me. My clit hums with need, desperate for more stimulation, begging for anything my depraved stepbrother will give me.

Cas alternates rubbing the tip of the spoon over my clit with slapping me with it, and all the while that frother buzzes against my G spot, and it's not long before I fall to pieces again, howling and writhing against the counter as wave after wave of pleasure slams into my body.

My stepbrother waits until I'm done flailing to turn off the frother and pull it slowly out of me. He rubs the flat of the wooden spoon over my throbbing clit, and then presses it against my lips. I turn my head away, but he grabs my jaw and yanks my mouth open.

"Didn't you ever lick the spoon as a kid?" he says. "Go on, Sunflower. Taste how I make you feel. Taste your hatred for me."

Fuck. This is so sick.

I grip his arm, digging my nails into my skin. But Cas is not going to let me go until I do it, and I don't know if I even *want* him to let me go.

I stick out my tongue and lick the spoon.

I taste myself, sweet and tart and a little bit like raspberries. Cas' eyes bore into me as he watches me lick the spoon, and the little groan he makes is so fucking hot.

"I've found some more toys in here for us to play with," he says. "Next is a roll of clingfilm. Hands out."

I obey, and he tears off a length of clingfilm and wraps it around my wrists, tying them together. I laugh, expecting to be able to break out of his makeshift cuffs easily, but when I pull on it, I find I'm stuck tight.

He picks me up and spins me around, lifting me under my ass and setting me down on top of the counter. Pots and containers crash against marble as he sweeps everything onto the floor.

"I've been wanting to put something on those huge nipples of yours ever since I first took one in my mouth," he says with a throaty rasp. "I found some chopsticks and rubber bands, which will do nicely."

I'm so stumped by what he's just said that I foolishly don't escape in time. He plants an elbow into my solar plexus, pinning me to the counter. He places two chopsticks on either side of my nipple and wraps a rubber band around them so the chopsticks pinch my nipple between them.

"I'm going to fucking *murder* you," I grit as the pain grows and spreads across my whole chest. It's as if the pain is opening me up, like the petals of a poison flower unfolding.

"I'd like to see you try, Sunflower," Cas grunts as he trails his fingers down my naked thighs. He knows he has me exactly where he wants me, exactly where I want to be. He tugs a little on the chopsticks, sending a fresh wave of pain through my ruined body, and I cry because I don't want to love this, but I do.

He slams my thighs open and plunges his cock inside me. I'm so fucking needy after all he's done that I *howl*. He gave me no time to adjust to his size or catch my breath. He fucks me hard and fast and wild, like an animal, like he's born for one purpose and that's to make me see stars.

I fight against the restraints as his massive cock stretches me and pushes me to the limit of what I can take. I want to rake my nails down his back, slap his face, make him. But all I can do is lie there and take his cock and love every fucking sickening moment of it.

Hate sex is the best sex. My sick, monstrous stepbrother drives deep inside me, pounding me against the kitchen counter, and every insult I can possibly think of to call him falls from my lips as he pounds my pussy into oblivion. He grabs one of the chopsticks and twists it, and I shatter in his arms.

My stepbrother is buried inside me. I will never ever be able to free myself from him. We're tied together. Family.

"I hate you," he whispers as his lips close over mine.

"I hate you more," I whisper back.

Our lips meet in a clash of teeth and tongues. I come around his cock in a tangle of nerve endings and exploded galaxies. My stepbrother breaks me into a million tiny pieces and knits me back together again, more brutal than I was before.

He comes with a sound that's like a great oak tree breaking apart in a lightning storm, charred pieces falling away to reveal fragile new life beneath.

He collapses on top of me, breathing hard. I come back to earth with him still inside me, his cock twitching. What is this? What are we doing? We're supposed to be sworn enemies, not *this*. Not... *us*.

"Cas?"

Hearing his name snaps something inside him. His body

jerks and he slides off me, his breath coming out in ragged gasps.

Without him holding me up, I slide off the edge of the counter onto the floor, ignoring the shards of glass digging into my thigh.

What the fuck am I doing?

I can't feel my legs. My battered pussy will not be able to have sex for a month. I defiled Milo's beautiful kitchen, while my stepmother fights for her life just down the hall, possibly because of something I did. And I slept with the one human being who I hate more than anything in the world.

It's a *great* day.

53

CASSIUS

"Cassius." A sweet voice calls me from the darkness. "Wake up."

I lurch awake, my hand flying to the gun I have tucked into my belt. My brother's face leers at me from my dreams.

"What the fuck?" I growl, swiping at him. He catches my hand and presses my palm into my chest. And that's when the blurry figure of Gaius wobbles and fades into the much more delectable vision of my stepsister.

"Relax, it's me." Fergie leans over the bed. The tips of her fiery hair brush my face, and it takes everything I have not to grab them and press them to my nose to breathe in that sweet raspberry scent. "You're in my room. You slept here last night with me and Torsten, remember? You were having a bad dream, I think. You yelled your brother's name in your sleep."

"No, I didn't."

"You *did*. I heard—"

"I didn't." I grab her ass and squeeze it right over where I spanked her with that wooden spoon. She winces, but the fire of lust dances in her eyes. "Don't make me repeat myself, little sis."

"Fine, you didn't." She crawls off me. I don't see Torsten anywhere – he's still angry with me, so I'm guessing he's run off somewhere to paint in private. "I came to tell you that Cali's awake."

I roll over in her bed, wiping the sleep from my eyes. My dick jerks at the sight of Fergie's skintight skull-covered leggings hugging her ass, obviously still remembering being buried balls deep inside her on the kitchen counter last night. Thankfully, she can't see it, because she'd probably want to jump on it like the thirsty bitch she is, and I have other things to do, like figure out how I'm going to get back in contact with Gaius. The repair people managed to get me a new phone with the same number, but they couldn't salvage the text message or the number of the person who sent it. I could take it to Torsten, but he's not talking to me now—

"Did you hear me?" Fergie waves her hands in front of my face. "Or are you stunned into silence by my beauty? Your mom is awake. She lives to massacre again."

Cali's awake.

Shit. I hadn't even heard Fergie before. I'm so wrapped up in my own shit that I can't even think about the fact that my mother nearly died last night. A million dark thoughts swirl through my head. I'd lain awake most of the night, thinking about Gaius and the fire and Cali, and especially about the woman I dreamed might rule by my side before I messed it all up.

Fergie spins on her heel and stalks away, and I can't help but notice that she's walking a little crooked. Now my dick is jerking with desperate urgency, and I debate slamming my stepsister against the wall and giving her a little morning glory straight into that tight asshole of hers.

But that's not why I'm here. It's not why I risked coming home.

I drag myself to my feet and follow Fergie.

My mother is awake.

Awake.

Awake but not moving? Awake but not standing over me with a knife, ready to slit my throat for what I've done to our family? Awake but no longer Cali Dio?

What if this is it?

What if this is the end of Cali's term as Imperator?

I'm not ready for that.

Not without her blessing.

Not without Gaius.

Not without my Quee—

I don't allow myself to finish the thought.

We descend the staircase in stony silence and turn off into the guest wing. Cali's in the nearest room. Two of our soldiers stand guard at the door, and I know that Seymour has had the detail on the house doubled since I broke in. Galen stands over one of the machines he's hooked up to her, frowning at the readings. John is curled into a chair beside the bed, stroking her hand and whispering lovey-dovey bullshit in her ear.

My mother inclines her head toward me. "You're not rid of me yet, son."

She looks like shit. Her skin's all splotchy, her eyes dull. I stand over the bed, and I realize for the first time that Cali Dio is made of flesh and bone like the rest of us. She can break, just as easily as all those people whose necks I've broken.

Just the way I am broken.

One thought flashes in my mind – it could have been Fergie in that bed with a bullet through her chest, fighting for her life. If someone can get close enough to hurt Cali, then they could get my stepsister.

The irony that only days ago I broke into her room to kill her is not lost on me. But I'm more convinced than ever that Fergie isn't what's broken about our family – I am.

Maybe this crime is my last shot – my final chance at redemption.

"Who did this?" I growl.

"Funny. I was about to ask you the same question," Cali growls right back.

"I had nothing to do with this. I didn't even know you had a job on."

"Why should I believe you? You tried to kill your own sister. I have no clue as to the depths you'll sink to for your shot at my power."

"That was..." I glance behind me. Fergie leans against the back of her father's chair, her shattered emerald eyes focused on a spot behind Cali's head. Her fiery hair is messed up from sleep, and it's piled on one side of her head in messy waves. She's so beautiful, she's like a mythological creature. "That was a mistake."

"Damn right it was a mistake. You betrayed this family. I don't want you in this house—"

"I don't think Cas meant it," Fergie pipes up. "He was trying to scare me for a joke, and he went too far. Isn't that right, Cas?"

I look away from her. Even though she can't see me, I can't meet her gaze while she's lying to save me, not after everything I've done. *I don't deserve her.* "It's true. Fergie and I have had this war going ever since I released that video. It's stupid. I got carried away, you know what I'm like. We'll stop. Catching the dead man who shot you is more important."

"You're sure?" Cali glares at Fergie.

"I'm sure," she replies, her voice loud and clear and certain.

Fuck, I *really* don't deserve her.

I'm not fool enough to believe that fucking her over the kitchen counter last night was enough to mend things between us, or even if she *wants* to mend things. I'm more confused than ever about what to do about my firecracker of a stepsister. But Cali's right about one thing, Fergie is a Dio now. She's family. And family comes first, especially when the Triumvirate is crumbling around us and my mother...

...my mother is shot through the chest. Galen says the bullet missed her heart by a fraction of an inch. She shouldn't still be alive, and it will be a long time before she can enter her secret vault and wield her torture implements again, if she ever can.

Cali sinks back into the cushions. She knows it, too, even if she won't admit it aloud yet. Her eyes meet mine, but they're large and swimming with pain and confusion. Gaius must have her on some killer drugs. "Fine. But I'm not ready to let you back in this house, or into my trust. If you step out of line one more time..."

"Let me prove to you that I can be trusted, that I'm here for this family." I drop to my knee beside her bed. "Let me find the bastard who did this and wrap his spinal cord around his neck and choke him with it."

Her eye twinkle a little at that. "You *have* been excited to practice your blood eagle..."

"Yes." I rub my hands together. "It will be perfect. I'll separate his ribs from his spine, peel back the bones and skin to give him wings, and draw out his lungs from his chest cavity."

"Gross," Fergie says, but there's a hint of fascination in her voice.

"Effective," corrects Cali.

"It will send a message to anyone out there thinking of trying something stupid – the Dio family is united and stronger than ever." As I say the words, I adjust my boxers to hide the massive hard-on I have at the idea of Fergie being turned on by my torture plans.

John looks from Cali to me, and back to Cali again. "Some-times, the two of you terrify me."

"You chose this family—" Cali starts to say as she tries to sit up, but she breaks down into a coughing fit.

John eases her head back against the pillow. "I did choose this family, and I haven't regretted it for a single moment. But I need you to stop trying to be Cali Dio the Imperator for a moment and focus on being Cali Dio, my wife who got shot through the chest and needs to rest up so she doesn't inadver-tently push a broken rib through her lungs. You don't have to send Cas after this guy; you have plenty of soldiers—"

"Cas is the best," she whispers, her eyes fluttering closed.

I am? She thinks I am the best?

I glow under her praise. I don't think I've ever heard Cali say something to me that isn't a barked order. *Cas is the best*. My whole body glows like I've injected sunlight into my veins.

"I will do you proud." I squeeze her hand.

My mother's eyes flutter before falling shut again. For several long moments, she lies as still as a corpse. Fear twists in my gut, and I look over at Fergie, wishing for the first time in my life that I could be capable of having the kind of relationship my mother and John have, that maybe if I got shot, someone would sit by my bedside.

I've never had someone who would cry for me before. But maybe...

...maybe things could be different.

Cali's eyes fly open. She glares at me. She nods her head.

My heart hardens. I won't let her down. Not again. "What do I need to know?"

"I don't think the shooter is connected to my job. They got me before I could even enter the house. I didn't get a look at him, but it doesn't matter. Whoever shot me might not be a professional but they know the way I operate, how I'd try to enter, where my blind spots would be. They knew I'd do this job alone. This was a hit – someone is trying to take me out, and they have inside information." Cali tries to rise from the bed, her whole face crumpling with pain. "I have to warn Livvie. And Claudia..."

"Cassius will do it. You have to rest." John shoves her back down.

"No, you don't understand. Claudia, she did—"

"John's right," I say. "I'll take over the business until you get back on your feet. I'll even give Fergie a role if you want, show you that we really are getting along again and make her truly part of the family—"

"No," Cali snaps. "That's what I'm trying to tell you. The August family is behind the hit, I know it. And you can't give Fergie any of my secrets. She's working for Claudia August."

"She's not," I growl.

I jerk my head toward my stepsister, waiting for her to confirm that Cali's delusional. Fergie's face crumples, her sightless eyes darting away.

No. It can't be true.

But it is.

My stepsister – the girl I have just convinced myself is the one person in the world who sees me for who I am and won't run away in terror – is working for our enemy.

John whirls around. "Fergalish, that isn't true. It can't be true. Tell me—"

"It's not like that," she cries, shifting her weight to her back foot, as if she intends to make a run for it. "Even with all the shit going down because of the video, I thought our families were *friends*. Claudia offered me a job helping her organize storage for the artifacts after the museum. Her secretary died and she—"

"It doesn't matter what fucking lie Claudia spun to get you to agree," Cali snaps. "What matters is that people have seen the two of you together. *Our* people have watched the scorned step-daughter of Cali Dio laughing with the August Imperator, and they *talk*. They come to me with reports that my own step-daughter is working for the Augusts without telling me, and they say that Claudia is making a move against us, that she wants to make a grab for Dio's holdings now that her own position is weakened, and I laugh it off because it's nearly time for Lupercalia and because Claudia August is the closest thing I have to a true friend, but then I get fucking *shot*—"

"That's not true at all," Fergie shoots back. "Claudia's not trying to take Dio's territory – she's just trying to rescue what's left of the artifacts. She wants to get the museum running again so you can all restore trust with your foreign clients. She's trying to save the Triumvirate. She knew nothing about your job. If you blame anyone for this, blame *me*. I'm the one who told Zack where you'd be last night—"

"What?"

I didn't even know I had a heart in my chest until this moment, because it stops fucking beating. I can't breathe. I can't *think*. Fergie's words replay in my mind, over and over, a loop of misery and betrayal.

Fergie throws herself into her dad's arms. "Zack Lionel Sommesnay," she sobs. "He's dating a friend of mine. He helped me get even with Cas and Juliet and Victor for releasing that video, and all he wanted in return was to know when Cali's next job was. He swore that he just wanted to get the authorities involved and make life difficult for you. He's a bureaucrat working with the mayor. He's not a hitman. I'm so sorry. I... I didn't know that this would happen—"

Her words cut off with a cry as I tear her from John's arms and fling her at the wall. She braces herself so she hits without injuring herself, although the impact sends several paintings crashing to the floor. I stalk toward her and instead of cowering, she squares her stance and faces me down.

"You don't get the right to be angry at me, Cassius," she growls. "*You* drove me away. You took the greatest night of my life and turned it into my biggest humiliation. You kept the truth from me so I didn't know what I was doing. You tried to *stab me in my sleep* like the coward you are. Why the fuck would you expect me to have any loyalty to this family? All of you want to wrap me in cotton and keep me out of things. Well, I'm not some poor little blind girl. I've proven myself time and time again, but I'm not going to stand around and wait for you to notice me. I want to graduate high school and get myself a job where I can be the one with power for a change, and if Claudia will help me do that, then sign me the fuck up to the August clan."

No.

You're not an August.

You're mine.

Mine.

I lunge for Fergie, but I'm so angry and so hurt that I can't see through the red, and I miss her by a mile. I try to spin around and grab her, but she sweeps my foot out from under me. I go down hard, my shoulder cracking on the tiles, and she takes the opportunity to duck around me and run for the door. She crashes into the wall, sending more gilded frames flying, before darting into the hallway and far, far away from me.

John looks stunned, his glasses drooping on the end of his nose. And Cali... Cali looks like she's going to throw up. She flops back against the pillow, her eyes fluttering shut again as she thrashes her head against the pain.

"I sent the wrong son to jail," she cries out. "I wish Gaius were here."

54

VICTOR

With Gabriel's help, I make arrangements for the next phase in Operation Grovel. I've sworn to Fergie that I'll spend the rest of my life making up for hurting her. Now I have to show her that Victor August keeps his promises.

When I'm certain everything is ready, I drive around to Fergie's house, humming a Broken Muse song under my breath. I'm feeling good about today. For the first time in a long while, I've done something right – and not out of a sense of duty or to protect someone I love, but because I want to. Because doing this for her has lightened my heart and made the world brighter. Now, if only she likes it—

Hang on, what's this?

I've turned into Cali's driveway and hit the button for the gates, but they haven't opened. There must be a glitch in the system. Cas and I have had access to each other's houses ever since we learned to drive.

A security guard clad in black jogs over and knocks on my window. I roll it down and gesture to the gate. "It's not letting me in."

"That's what it's there for, sir," the guard says without a trace of irony.

I tap the button clipped above the rearview mirror. "This doesn't seem to be working. If you could open the gates for me, I'm sure Seymour can take a look at it and—"

"You're not allowed in, sir."

Huh?

"I think there's been some mistake." I give him my megawatt smile. "You're new, right? Allow me to introduce myself – I'm Victor August. That's *August*. I'm a longtime friend of Cassius. Cassius Dio, perhaps you've heard of him?"

The guard opens the lapel of his jacket and touches his finger to the trigger of his Glock. "No mistake. You're not allowed inside. Please turn around and exit the property before I'm forced to remove you."

"Listen, pal, I'm here to see Fergie. I know she's here so could you just—"

"Sir, don't make me ask twice."

It's then that I notice movement behind him. There's another guard in the bushes up ahead, and another further down the road. Odd. Cali's never had this level of security.

I glare at the guard, but he's not budging. It takes an awkward few tries to turn the Porsche around in the small gap they've left me on the street, but I do it and take off with as much dignity as I can muster. When I'm around the corner and out of the guard's sight, I pull over and dial Torsten.

"Hey, it's Victor," I say as soon as he picks up.

"I know. It says your name on my phone."

"Yes, it does. Listen, I just tried to drive into Cali's place. I want to see Fergie. I have a fun surprise for her. But my gate access has stopped working and the street is swarming with security and they won't let me through. Did something happen?"

"Yes."

I wait, but when no details are forthcoming, I add, "Torsten, can you tell me what happened that's made Cali step up security and lock me out?"

"Cas broke in and tried to stab Fergie in her sleep—"

"What? Is she okay?"

"Yes." Torsten sounds exasperated. He doesn't like being interrupted when he's answering a question. "Then Cali got shot on a job. Cali thinks your mother sent an assassin to take her out, but Fergie says it's because she told Zack Lionel Sommesnay about the job."

Holy fuck. That's a lot to take in.

Cas tried to stab Fergie? *Fucking hell.*

And Cali Dio, shot? I can't imagine it. I mean, people in our world die every day, but usually at the hands of Cali herself. Who could have got the drop on her?

And what's this about my mother?

"This makes no sense. When has Fergie even spoken to Zack Lionel Sommesnay? We still have no clue who he is. Why does Cali think Fergie is betraying the Dios? What is Cas' role in all this? Is he back in the house now? Is Fergie okay with that? Has she forgiven him?"

Has she forgiven Cas, but not me?

Torsten remains silent. I hear his pen scraping in the background. This is Torsten's way of telling me that either he doesn't know the answer to any of my questions, or he's not supposed to tell me and he's overwhelmed and stressed about lying, so he just shuts down.

"Don't worry about it," I say. "I only want to see Fergie. I want to take her somewhere. It's perfectly safe, I promise."

"Fergie's not allowed to leave the house."

"I'm not going to let anything happen to her."

"Cali and Cas think she'll go to your mother."

I sigh. How did everything get even more messed up? "So Fergie's a prisoner?"

"Yes."

"That's not right. I know you agree with me. Can you get Fergie out of the house? I'll take care of the rest."

"If Fergie wants to."

"Okay, you ask her if she wants to. I'll wait here until—"

He hangs up. I stare at the phone, not entirely sure if he's just decided he can't be bothered with me or if he really is going to try and sneak her out.

I should never have doubted him. Five minutes later, Seymour drives around the corner and parks up beside me. Torsten and Fergie climb out from beneath a picnic blanket in the back of the car.

I roll down my window and she leans in, her fiery hair brushing my arm. I suck in a lungful of raspberries. God, she's amazing.

"What do you want, Victor?"

"I've come to whisk you away for an evening of magic. There's something I want to tell you, to show you."

She sighs. "I can't do this now. Everything is fucked up. I can't be seen with you. There's all the shit going down between your mom and Cali—"

"I'm aware of it."

"You don't know everything." I get the feeling she likes the power of having more intel than me. "Your mother hired me to work for her and—"

"I'm sorry, *what?*"

Fergie tosses her hair over her shoulder. "I work for your mother. Can you be any more behind?"

"Apparently not."

"Well, I do. She asked me to help her find a new home for all the artifacts salvaged from the museum wreckage. I think she wants me to replace her last secretary, the one who got blown up."

Yara. My heart hurts to think of her. Yara had a hard life, and she'd made a remarkable success of it. She deserved many more years on this earth to enjoy herself. I pat the seat next to me. "Hop in. You can curl up on the seat so no one will see you. We're going somewhere private, and I promise to have you home before your evil stepmother misses you."

"You're not planning on taking me to get up close and personal with Clarence?" She narrows her eyes.

"Why would you even *think* that?"

"Don't laugh. Cassius tried to kill me the other night."

"I heard. He never would have gone through with it." *I don't think.*

"Don't look so stricken, Vic. You're right – he chickened out like a little bitch." Fergie looks like she's going to burst out laughing. "I'm fine, and Cas and I fucked on the kitchen counter last night so he's too sex-drunk to come after me today. But I don't exactly trust either of you right now."

I stare at her. My mouth opens, but I can't think of what I want to say. Fergie laughs and turns to Seymour, and tells him to return to the house and keep her dad and Cali from noticing they're gone.

"I'll check in with you," she says to the old driver. "You've got the tracker on my phone. You know where to find me. And Torsten's coming with us, so I'll be safe—"

I shake my head, forgetting for a moment that she can't see it. "This is sort of a private thing—"

"Torsten's coming. That's non-negotiable."

"Okay." I unlock the back door so he can slide in. He lies down on the seats, cradling his sketchbook in his ink-stained hands. Fergie walks around the car and gets in the passenger side, folding up her cane and dropping it at her feet, before slouching down and curling up into a ball so no one can see her through the window.

As we speed through the city, Fergie updates me on Cali's condition. She says that Cassius called my mom to tell her, although I gather the conversation was rather tense. Mom hasn't said anything to me about it. Granted, she isn't talking to me or Juliet right now after the mess we made of everything, but you'd think she'd mention Cali – who is practically our aunty, our families are so close – is fighting for her life.

Shit. Things with the Triumvirate are worse than I thought. *Why* would Mom ask Fergie to work for her? She *had* to know Cali would find out and it would cause trouble. Maybe Mom wanted to cause trouble, but that makes no sense, either—

And then, because I haven't had enough, Fergie tells me that Livvie has been pushing for the two of them to be married. It seems that the Lucians are angling for an alliance against our family, and given that Cali currently believes Mom put a hit out on her, I—

And Lupercalia is only a couple of weeks away.

Lupercalia is the second important celebration on the Triumvirate calendar. It's supposed to be a time when the rigid hierarchy of our families is cast aside, and soldiers who have distinguished themselves can petition their Imperator for advancement. Mom and Cali and Livvie throw a huge party at Colosseum with games and fights to promote the spirit of unity between the three families. It's usually one of my favorite nights, not least of all because most regular decision results are in for the Ivy Leagues, so we're celebrating another successful year of the Poison Ivy Club. Cas enters the fights, and Torsten and I bet on him and win a lot of money. We party until the sun rises, and it's wonderful.

But this year...

A sick, heavy feeling settles in my stomach. My head is spinning from all this shit. The Poison Ivy Club may be done, but the repercussions for the shit we did are going to echo in our lives for a long, long time.

I glance back at Torsten in the rearview mirror. He has his head propped up on the door, his sketchbook open on his lap, and he's drawing frantically even though the car's jerking his pencil like crazy. Even from this angle I can tell it's another drawing of Fergie.

He's so much happier because of her. She's good for him, and he's good for her. He protected her where I failed her.

Am I doing the right thing, trying to get her back? Maybe she'd be better off with Torsten?

But then I think of the four of us on the night of Saturnalia and how perfect it was. That's what I want – my friends and my girl. All of us together again, an unstoppable force.

Torsten raises his head and looks me dead in the eye, and for once I can read his thoughts.

He knows exactly what I'm trying to do. And he's afraid. He's afraid that I'll win her away from him. But I'm done competing. I'm done trying to be everything to everyone. And that's what I want to show her tonight.

I pull into my destination and park the car. Fergie peers up at me as I walk around and open her door for her. I take her hand and pull her to her feet, giving her a moment to unfold her cane. I know she doesn't like to be led around.

I pull open the back door for Torsten. "Come with us," I say.

His head snaps up, and his eyes widen as he takes in our location. His hand flaps at his side.

"Please? I think Fergie would feel more comfortable knowing you were watching over her. But you have to promise to stay out of the way until she needs you."

"I understand." He folds up his sketchbook and slides out of the car, falling in step behind us as we cross the parking lot and enter the building through a narrow alley where Cassius blinded Jason for disobeying us.

"Where are we?" Fergie asks as I lead her through the maze of corridors behind the stage.

"We're in Tombs," I say. "It took a lot of sweet talking and an enormous bribe to convince Livvie to give me the key, but I did it. Tonight, the club is just for the two of us. Well, the two of us and Torsten and a few other special guests. Come on, there's someone I want you to meet."

I push open the stage door and we step into the empty, cavernous club. The lights are low, but as per my instructions, the staff has left on the LED lights embedded behind the walls of hieroglyphics. The shapes of eyes, reeds, wiggly lines, and constipated birds illuminate the space, but I don't see any of it. I only have eyes on the woman on my arm.

Fergie gazes all around, her face lighting up with awe, and I know she can make out some of the multi-colored lights. "It's pretty," she says. "I didn't get to appreciate it the first time I came, what with Cassius nearly killing my entourage and all."

"I heard that you and Torsten appreciated it fine the other night."

"That's true. We appreciated the hell out of a dark corner and a velvet-lined chaise lounge in the VIP area," Fergie shoots back, not a blush to be seen on her pretty cheeks.

"So Livvie informed me in lurid detail. Tonight, we have the place almost all to ourselves." I turn her toward the stage, and the shadowy figure there shoots me the thumbs up.

A single spotlight flickers on, illuminating a white-haired, blue-eyed man with a violin pressed to his chin. He lifts his bow and plays a low, mournful note.

Fergie turns to me, her eyes wide. "Vic, what is this..."

"Shhh." I hold my finger over her lips, enjoying the thrill as our bodies touch. "Listen."

The violinist – whose name is Ivan Nicolescu – marches to the middle of the stage, and there he meets a second violinist. A woman this time, with a long mane of dark curls that cascade down her back. Faye de Winter raises her violin, and she and Ivan begin to duel, their notes twining together into a frantic, haunting dance.

Fergie gasps as she recognizes the song, but I don't think she's quite clicked what's going on.

Two more spotlights appear, illuminating a dark-haired man sitting at a grand piano and a hulking giant of a dude with swinging dreadlocks plucking the strings of a cello like it's a bass guitar.

Fergie can't see the figures, but she can hear the music. Her body sways as the song captures her limbs and takes over her body. That's what good music can do – you give yourself over utterly to it and cross over into another world.

And I should know. After all, I'm Gabriel Fallen's son.

Dad strides onstage, tears the microphone from its stand, and lets out a scream that could've issued from hell itself.

I've seen him perform dozens of times, both with Broken Muse and solo, and every time, I get chills. I can't believe that it's my quirky, silly dad up there screaming lyrics that reach into my chest and squeeze my heart. I understand completely why my mom fell hard for him, why she says that he sings the stars.

Fergie's whole body shudders as the music tears through her. I understand what Cas meant when he said that she's always so completely *in the moment*. She feels the music in her body in a way that I don't think I'll ever understand.

I put my arms around her and she sways, her hands curling into fists as the riffs grow in intensity. The song builds in layers and layers until it explodes into a cacophony of sound. Gabriel and his band *own* this atmospheric, gothic mix of dark classical music and heavy metal. No one else in the world sounds quite like them, except possibly the band Blood Lust, who they some-times tour with.

I don't always get this kind of music – it's *intense* – and I've been dragged around too many loud shows with too many badly-dressed teen goths so I'm a little jaded. But I know that I can't listen to the lyrics, 'We've sharpened our steel. We've made our sacrifices. We're unleashing war,' knowing where they come from, without a lump forming in my throat. I've seen Fergie wearing a Broken Muse band shirt a few times, and I know she loves music even more than Cas, so I've been hoping I made the right call arranging this.

"How'd we do, son?" Gabriel calls out as he waits for Titus to change a broken string before the next song.

"Keep it up," I answer back. "Fergie's favorite song of yours is 'The Fall of the House of Usher.' Just FYI."

"Perfect. You have good taste, Fergie." Gabriel whirls back to the microphone, flips his long, dark hair over his shoulder, and growls the opening line.

Beside me, Fergie's mouth hangs open. She's speechless. I've rendered Fergie Macintosh *speechless*.

"How are you doing there, Duchess?" I grin as I throw my arm around her and pull her into me. "You need a drink? Or a defibrillator?"

"Th-th-that's... Gabriel Fallen," Fergie stutters.

"It certainly is."

"And he... he just called you *son*."

"He did. Gabriel Fallen is my dad."

"But..." Fergie screws up her face into this completely adorable confused look. "That's impossible. Gabriel Fallen is... is Gabriel Fallen. He can't be your dad."

"Well, he is," I laugh. "I could've sworn you knew. Everyone in school knows."

"I didn't know. They're my favorite band."

"Yeah, I figured that out when I saw the giant poster on the wall in your old bedroom in Witchwood Falls."

Fergie's body stiffens. "I should have known Victor August wouldn't leave the past alone. You've been looking into Fergie Macintosh."

"Yes. And I think, if you stop hating me for a couple of seconds, you'd understand why." I take her hand in mine and gesture toward the stage. "You don't know what that man up there had to go through to win my mother, to even have the family that we have today. My parents went through hell to be together, and to give me and Juliet everything they missed out on, and I owe them my life for that. And that's why I'm here, fighting for you. Because you're my family, Fergie. You and Torsten and Cas, too. I didn't take over the Poison Ivy Club because of the Triumvirate or the money or the notoriety or any of that. I'm terrified because I love the people in my life so much that it hurts, and I can't stand the idea that I might make some stupid mistake and lose them. Especially after I lost Gemma, and after..."

"After what?"

"Look, I know she's not your favorite person right now – and kudos for the fashion show stunt because you hit her where it hurt – but Juliet is a piece of me. And..." I clutch Fergie tighter as I allow the memories to surface. "I nearly lost her once. Three years ago, she was kidnapped from school. Some scumbag soldier of Mom's who was still loyal to her dead uncle decided he'd use my sister as a bargaining chip to force Claudia August to step down as Imperator. Luckily, he wasn't the brightest bulb in the box. We tracked him down, got Jules back, and Mom and Cali worked together to root out every last one of his loyalists."

"That must've been scary."

"It was. I was supposed to drive her home after school. When she didn't show, I thought she'd gone off with her friends, so I went home," I say. "My sister was being tied up and tortured in some sick fuck's basement, and I was by the pool eating ice cream with Gabriel without a care in the world."

"You can't blame yourself for that, Vic. You didn't plan for that to happen."

"I should have known," I growl. "We're a crime family. I should always expect people to try and take what my mother has built. I should have—"

Titus must've fixed the string, because my words are drowned out by a loud, raging riff. Fergie is drawn back to the stage, to the music, and I let it take her. I accept that although I long to control everything around me, I will never be able to hold this woman tightly enough. I have to let her be free.

This song she loves fills every corner of the empty club. It's a song of hate, a song of rage and manipulation, made more potent by the truth of it. It's written by the pianist, Dorien Valencourt, and Faye de Winter, the violinist, as their fuck-you to a woman who tried to manipulate them out of their fortunes and their talents and their lives. But that's a story for another time.

When the song finishes and Gabriel's voice trembles on that final note, I place my hands over Fergie's and lead her toward the back of the room. "I pride myself on being the one who puts everything back together again. I'm the protector, the *fixer*. But I don't know how to fix what's broken between us. All I know is that I miss you, and that I was listening to Dad sing this song in the shower and it makes my chest hurt with how much I miss you."

She shakes her head. "I still can't believe your dad is Gabriel Fallen."

I glance over my shoulder at Torsten. He's found a spot in a dark corner of the room and has flopped down in a booth, his sketchbook open and his hand moving frantically as he works.

But he draws without looking at the page. Instead, his eyes remain glued on us.

"I want to know how to fix it. How to fix us," I say. "Please, just tell me there's still hope for me. I'll do *anything*."

"I don't need you, Vic. I have Torsten."

It hurts to hear her say it, but I know it's the truth. "I don't think you've ever needed anyone a day in your life, Fergie Macintosh. I don't need you to need me. But I want to be part of your life again. I want to be your family."

"What about Cas? What about the growing feud between our families? What about the fact that I made everything a hundred times worse?"

"I don't care. None of it matters if I have you. If I can make you mine again."

"Victor, you know that being with me will put you in danger. Our people are watching everything we do. They'll see us together and think—"

I squeeze her hand, my heart fluttering with hope. "Does that mean you care what happens to me?"

She screws up her face. "I hate that I care."

"That's a yes!" I hug her.

"Yes, you big silly," she flashes me a sad smile that makes my chest hurt. "I *care*. And after seeing my dad falling to pieces over Cali and not being able to do a thing to help, I realize that I understand what you mean about family. I hate what you did, but I think I understand why you did it, and I can't blame you for that. Well, I can, and I did. But I think demolishing your house and smelling you after you shoveled up minced-up body parts for Cali is punishment enough."

I pull her into me, breathing in her raspberry scent, wishing I could crawl beneath her skin. "How did you destroy the house, anyway?"

Darkness flickers across her face. "You're not going to like it. I asked Drusilla's boyfriend to help me. He's a Bitcoin guy with a lot of money in real estate, and he has a demolition crew on his payroll who weren't going to ask too many questions. But in return he wanted me to tell him the name of Cali's next mark."

She's right, I *don't* like the sound of this. "Why does he care about that?"

Fergie screws up her face. "Because his name is Zack Lionel Sommesnay."

"Hang on, you've *met* Sommesnay?"

"Yes. You have too, actually. He was the German guy were saw at the Olympus Club, while we were playing Juliet's silly game."

"I don't remember."

She sighs. "Of course you don't. But I don't forget a voice, and he was definitely there. He's been going after the Triumvirate for months with the mayor's office, which Torsten tells me that you already know. Apparently, your parents killed his mother, and he's spent his whole life amassing a fortune just so he'd have the resources to bring them down. I didn't know he'd try to hurt Cali. I thought he'd just annoy them with bureaucracy, the way he's been doing for months. I thought maybe he'd just warn the guy that Cali was coming for him, or maybe call the police. Cali will never end up in jail, but it would've made Cas' life difficult for a while, and I wanted that. I hated you all. I wanted to burn everything down. I didn't know—"

"Of course you didn't." I hold her against my chest, stroking her silky hair. It feels so good to have her in my arms again. Already my brain whirs through possibilities, ways I can fix this. "Does Cas know about Zack Lionel Sommesnay?"

"I told him. I had no choice. Cali found out I was working for your mother. They both hate me now. I think my dad loving me and Cali being unable to move from bed are the only reasons I'm still alive."

Accurate.

"Ssssh." I kiss her eyelids, licking away the tears that gather in the corners. I don't want to ever see my Duchess cry again. "It's okay. This is not your fault. Cali wanted to keep you in the dark about the Triumvirate. You only had a day to process it before Cas put out that video. You can only make decisions with the information you have. And trust me, Cas has messed up *way* worse than this. Let me talk to him. I'll make him see sense."

"I think Cas and I are beyond talking." Her jaw clenches.

"Let me try first. *Please.*"

Fergie squeezes me tight, which I take to be a yes. I bury my face in her hair and breathe her in deep, unable to believe how lucky I am. My body feels completely at peace, as if my arms were made for holding her. And my cock...

My cock wants phase two of my surprise to begin.

I wave to Dad and drag Fergie upstairs to the VIP suite. On the way, I grab Torsten's arm and pull him along with me. We're family. I want him to be part of this, too. If it all goes the way I hope...

I plan to take Fergie to the corner of the room where I usually sit with Cas and Torsten, but when we reach the top of the stairs, Torsten tugs on my arm. He nods his head at the wall of hieroglyphics he painted for his mother, and I know he has some secret that he wants to reveal.

"Show us," I say.

Torsten presses the hieroglyphics in a certain configuration, and a secret panel slides open. I help Fergie through the narrow opening while Torsten locates the panel for the lights. We're in a high-ceilinged room painted with floor-to-ceiling murals of Egyptian kings and queens. At one end of the room is a golden throne, a scepter and crown resting on the velvet cushion. Opposite the throne is a gilded sofa as long and wide as a king-size bed, and several deep purple cushions and ottomans. A small hidden bar sits in the corner, and a rack of BDSM equipment hangs on the wall behind us.

"Livvie Lucian, you never fail to surprise me." I stare around the room in awe as I lead Fergie over to the sofa.

I remember all those months ago when she showed up at this same club after Cassius forbid her, dressed in that skintight gold dress and looking every bit the queen I know she is. She's even more queenly now, her chin high and haughty as I lay her down. She reaches up and brushes my cheek with her soft fingers, like a monarch indulging her servant.

All I know is that I want to worship her.

"Tonight is all about you," I say, my fingers tugging on the hem of her ripped black tank.

"Good. Just the way I like it." She licks her lips as she raises her arms. I yank the top over her head and toss it away. I beckon Torsten over. He slides in behind her head, cradling her body in his arms while I drag down her skintight cuffed jeans to reveal a sexy AF crimson thong.

I slide off the end of the sofa and kneel between her legs, pushing her knees apart.

"Please," I beg her. "Please let me worship you."

Fergie lifts her head and smiles. "I like hearing you beg, Victor August. I like having you on your knees for me."

And I think my sister may be right about one thing – Fergie has had a taste of power, and she *loves* it. She is Cleopatra, a ruler in her own right, not a tool or commodity to be traded for favors.

She is my Queen.

My knees crack on the hard floor, and it feels so right. I'm exactly where I want to be.

With reverence, I hook my fingers into the string of her thong and pull it down, revealing that perfect pussy with the landing strip pointing to the happiest place.

I lower my lips to her and take my first taste of that raspberry pink pussy. And it's amazing.

Heavenly.

A religious experience.

It feels as though it's been years without tasting her, instead of weeks. I'm a man who has crawled through the desert, my throat raw and bleeding from thirst, and Fergie is my first drink of sweet water.

Her pussy is life. I stroke her with my tongue, taking it slow, letting her know exactly how much I love being back between her legs.

"Tell me." Her words come out in a choking gasp. "Tell me why you came back to me."

"Because I'm exactly where I belong, Duchess," I nibble on her thigh. "I'll never leave you."

"Good." She wraps those long legs around me and rides my face, taking her pleasure, demanding what's hers. I can do nothing but hold on and fuck her clit with my tongue until she's gasping my name.

"I could die right now buried in your pussy, and I'd die completely happy," I coo, my voice muffled by her legs.

"Don't you dare fucking die on me, Victor August," she grunts out. "Not before I've taken what's mine."

With that, she comes apart in my arms. Her orgasm tears through her, making her legs clamp over my face. Her wetness dribbles over my lips, and I lick up every last morsel.

She's perfect. My Duchess. My Fergie. And she's back where she belongs – in my arms.

Fergie collapses on the sofa, and I disentangle myself from between her legs. Torsten strokes her breasts, his fingers moving over her nipples in a way she definitely likes, judging by the mewling sounds she makes. He peers up at me with his wide, dark eyes, his question dying before it reaches his lips. He doesn't know how to ask if this is real, if I'm here to put our family back together or if I've come on a chariot of fire to burn it all down.

"I want you to understand something," I say. "Both of you. This thing between us might've started as a pissing contest between me and Cas, but I don't give a shit about that anymore. We're family, the three of us, and that's more important to me than the fact that we're August and Lucian and Dio. So Torsten, I want you to choose which of our girl's holes you want, because we're filling Fergie up tonight, and as the one who's protected her alone for so long, you get first dibs on your favorite."

"Um, excuse me?" Fergie lifts an eyebrow. "As much as I admire the sentiment here, I think I get a say in which of my holes are open for business."

"Ass," Torsten says without hesitation.

"As you wish." I grab Fergie's wrist and pull her on top of me as I lay back on the couch. "Come on, Duchess, we all saw you on that tape. We know you love butt stuff."

She rolls her emerald eyes. "Fine, you got me. I love butt stuff, but no spanking. I'm raw enough from what Cas did the other night."

That's right. She slept with Cas. I can't help the little sliver of fear rolling down my spine when she says that. Because as much as he'd try to chalk it up to a temporary moment of insanity over seeing his mother with a bullet hole in her chest, if Cas slept with Fergie then it means something to him, and Cas has an annoying habit of using violence to stamp down his feelings when they get too painful or inconvenient.

Fergie may think they have some kind of truce because he tanned her ass with a wooden spoon, but I know the truth. He may have started to acknowledge that he's wrong about her fake name, but he will see her working for Claudia and giving that information to Zack as a betrayal.

She's backed Cas into a corner, and nothing is more dangerous than a bear who has no way out.

But Cas is tomorrow's problem. Tonight, I have Fergie in my arms. And I'm not going to waste a moment of our time together thinking about her stepbrother. I pull her up so she's straddling me. She trails her hands down my chest, sliding them into the hem of my Calvin Klein jeans, tugging at the zipper like it's Christmas Day and she can't wait to open her present.

My Queen draws me out, stroking me a couple of times, enjoying my groan of pleasure. She bends her mouth toward me, but I push her gently away.

"Tonight is about you," I say. "Go on, my Queen. Take your pleasure."

Fergie doesn't have to be told twice. She straddles me and sinks down on my cock, sheathing me inside her. She's so fucking tight and hot and wet, I almost come right then. I've missed this. I've missed her. How could I have been so stupid? How could I let her slip through my fingers?

I'm never letting that happen again. I grip her hips, holding her against me, working myself even deeper inside her. I'm never letting her go.

"Ride me, my Queen," I growl.

Fergie obeys, tossing her head back and grinding her hips down on me before rising up on her knees to draw me out of her. She slams down again and I see stars behind my eyes. Her muscles clench around me, milking me until the stars I'm seeing go supernova. All I can do is gaze up at her in awe and wonder as she rides me like I'm a fucking stallion.

I have never felt more powerful, more at peace, as I watch my Queen take what's hers. She takes everything I have to give, and she'll never be sated.

Fergie scrapes her nails down my bare chest, and the sting only makes her hot pussy feel even better. She leans over and kisses me, our mouths colliding with harsh breath and dueling tongues.

"Torsten," I choke out. "Get over here *now*. I don't know how much longer I can..."

Ever the obedient one, Torsten leans over us, molding his chest into Fergie's back. I hold Fergie still while he lines himself up and lubes up her ass and his cock.

"Is this okay?" he asks Fergie as he begins. I can feel the pressure change as the head of his cock slides inside her. Her lips form an O of pleasure, and her eyes widen and I have to look away and think about unsexy things (car crashes, airport lines, Noah in the bathtub, babies crying... no, not babies, babies makes me think of Fergie's stomach growing large with my child...) because it's been so long and I'm right on the edge.

"It's better than okay," Fergie gasps. "It's amazing."

With a grunt, he pushes in deeper. I grit my teeth as the pressure of him rubs against me through the thin wall that separates us inside her. "Is this okay?"

"Damnit, Torsten, my love, it's perfect," she growls. "Now fuck me."

He obeys, drawing out and slamming into her with that even, relentless rhythm she taught him. I start to move, too, my head swimming with thoughts I can't control, thoughts of the dynasty we could create right here, right now.

The two of us hold Fergie between us as we take over, moving with Torsten's steady rhythm as she closes her eyes and gives herself over completely to us. She's so perfect. She takes us like a queen, her body damp with sweat and a stream of delicious curses falling from her lips. It's not long until I feel her walls clench around me as she comes.

Feeling her body clamp around me and knowing that I did this, we did this, we made her feel so good, it undoes me. I come with a wave of bliss that's like nothing I ever felt.

I collapse on the sofa, my balls empty, my mind still. I pull out of Fergie, but Torsten keeps going. She grips the edge of the sofa and grinds her ass back against him as he drives himself deep inside her.

I wipe myself off and stagger to my feet. I'm not ready to stop playing with my Queen just yet. I wander over to the throne and pick up the scepter. In typical Livvie Lucian fashion, it's not all it seems. The end of the scepter is a silicone dildo, with a sticker on the side that says it's freshly cleaned and sanitized, and the handle is encrusted with jewels that look as if they might be more than decorative.

I carry the scepter back to the sofa and slide back underneath Fergie.

"You want to be our Queen?" I shove her legs apart.

She murmurs consent as I slide the end of the scepter between her legs. Torsten continues to fuck her from behind in that relentless rhythm. Fergie groans as it stretches her, her whole body shuddering. It takes me a few thrusts to seat it inside her. The jeweled tip rests outside her, one of the jewels perfectly positioned to scrape over her clit every time she moves.

I take her hand and lower it between her legs, letting her feel the present I've given her. "Look how beautiful you are," I say. "You're our Queen. Isn't she, Torsten?"

"Our Queen," he replies. It's so good to watch him with her. Even that night in the library, he wanted as little of her to touch him as possible. Torsten hears and smells and feels *everything*, and the sensations get too much. It can turn a sexy experience into something scary or gross or overwhelming. But now, he digs his nails into her thighs and draws her ass back against him. Being with her has given him a way to feel his way through what he needs to feel.

"Our Queen," I confirm. I cup my hand over Fergie's and help her slide the dildo deeper, so she can feel that little jewel dancing over her clit. A moan of delight tumbles from her crimson lips, followed by another string of expletives as her body shudders through yet another orgasm.

When she recovers enough to move, she arches toward me, her other hand groping for my cock. I didn't want her to worry about me, but I'm only fucking human and I'm already hard again from watching Torsten and that scepter inside her. Fergie's fingers wrap around me, and I close my eyes.

This is what heaven feels like.

This is the family I've sworn to protect.

This is the future of the Triumvirate.

55

FERGIE

I spend the night with Victor and Torsten in the VIP suite. In a hundred inventive ways, Victor shows me how much he misses me, how much he wants this to work, and that he no longer sees me as a prize to be won.

It's intoxicating being in his presence again. Victor August has a way of wrapping you into his arms and making you feel like you're the only thing that matters. It's a nice change after the chaos that Cas has put me through.

As the sun rises over the city, penetrating the high windows of the VIP suite with squares of bright light, Victor hands me a bowl filled with grapes and curls up beside me on the couch.

"I know that I can't make up for how I hurt you," he whispers, pushing my hair away from my shoulder so he can nibble on my neck while I eat. "But I'm going to spend the rest of my life trying to show you how much of a goddess you are to me."

"I'm amenable to that," I grin as I pop a grape into my mouth.

"Okay. Good." His voice turns serious. "As my goddess, can I give you some advice that you might not want to hear?"

"Only if you rub my feet while you tell me."

"You make it sound like it's work, Duchess." Victor nudges my body so that I turn toward him, and he slides my feet into his lap. As he digs his fingers into a spot that has me moaning, he says. "You have to stop poking the bear. Everything you've done to Cas – while completely justified and utterly hilarious – only fuels the rage inside him that says you're his enemy. But the thing is, he still has feelings for you. He hates you so much because he loves you."

I snort. "Cassius Dio is incapable of love."

"I wouldn't be so sure."

I set down the bowl. "I know you're loyal to him because you've been friends for so long, but if you love someone, you don't go out of your way to destroy them."

"Is that so, Duchess?"

I whack him around the head. "I'm not in love with Cassius anymore."

"The welts on your ass would suggest otherwise. The two of you are more alike than you realize, and that means that you're going to keep on playing this game, back and forth, until one of you destroys the other. And the thing about Cas is that he's had a lot more practice than you at destroying people. I'm merely suggesting a different path."

"Which is?"

"That the two of you forgive and forget. I mean, make him grovel. The bastard did think he could kill you. Make him get down on his knees and kiss your feet and crawl through the dirt for your forgiveness. But show him that there's some path to redemption. I know it seems hard to believe, but Cas is doing this because he believes that he's so completely rotten that nothing and no one will ever love him. If you show him that's not true – that he can be loved even if he's fucked up – then he'll be yours forever. He'll go back to being the Cas you fell for."

"I don't want him to be mine."

"Sure, Duchess."

Victor returns to massaging my feet. As I polish off the platter of cheese and grapes, I turn his words over in my head.

Victor's wrong. I don't want Cassius back. I don't. What happened the other day was a mistake brought on by my guilt over Cali. Cas snuck in my window and tried to kill *me. He put a sex video of me on the internet.*

What I want *to do is poke the bear. I want to poke him so hard that he devours his own tail.*

Everything becomes clear. Victor's right – revenge has been fun, so much fun, but I've been going about this all wrong. All I've been doing is aggravating Cassius. I haven't hit him where it hurts the most.

I haven't destroyed him the way he sought to destroy me.

And now I know exactly how to hit that monster where it will hurt him most. Victor has given me what I need to do to bring Cassius to his knees. I just have to hope that when the time comes, I'm strong enough to go through with it.

I lean forward and kiss Victor on the cheek. "Lupercalia is coming up. I want you to take me with you."

"You want to go to Lupercalia?" he says. "Do you think that's a good idea?"

"I think that Cali needs me to be there, for the sake of appearances. People need to see who I'm loyal to."

"Have you decided that?"

"There's no decision to be made. Family is family. I may hate Cas, and Cali's not exactly my favorite person with the whole locking me in the house and blocking me from the family business thing, but she needs to see that I've made a choice. I was playing with fire working for Claudia, and I got burned. Lesson learned. And as for Livvie, I've made it clear to her that Torsten and I aren't going to be part of her play for power. Besides, my dad asked me to go with him. It's a bonding thing, and since I'm in the spotlight anyway, it'll give me a chance to bend some of these rumors to my own ends. I promise I'll stay away from Cas. He'll be down in the ring, anyway, far away from our VIP tables. Our paths won't even cross."

If Victor suspects my lie, he doesn't say a thing. "Okay, We'll take you to Lupercalia. Wear something utterly sinful."

"I plan on it." I grip his hand. "But I'm not ready to let you go yet. Before you take me back to the Dio prison, I want you and Torsten to do something for me."

"Anything."

I tug him toward the door. "Then come with me. You're going to get inked."

56

CASSIUS

Lupercalia.

The one event I look forward to every year. A Triumvirate-sanctioned bloodbath where I get to embrace the red mist and let it carry me where it will. The festival celebrating the unity of the three families culminates in a series of fights – some between professionals from our ranks for the entertainment of the crowd, and some are executions. Soldiers found to be traitors are pitted against each other or put through other imaginative tortures. If I've been a good boy, Cali allows me to help her arrange and carry out these acts of justice.

But this year... I'm on edge. Agitated. I don't know what the fuck is going to go down. The three families and their soldiers are at each other's throats. What's going to happen when we crowd them all into the Colosseum together and scent the air with blood?

And I don't like this feeling. I should be excited about the carnage, but as I make the preparations on Cali's behalf and go through my training regime, I'm more aware than ever that the peace we enjoy balances on a knife edge.

It doesn't help that I have to train on my own. Most fighters at Cali's club are smart enough to refuse to train with me, but there are usually some young naive punks who think they can beat The Bear. Not this year, though. I know it's because of the video. Because my skin is still bright blue, and everyone who sees it knows exactly why. No one wants to be seen with the guy messing with Cali Dio's stepdaughter.

Even if that guy is their next Imperator.

I don't care what Cali says. Gaius might've been the better leader. Gaius might've been the one who'd know exactly what to do. But Gaius isn't here. Gaius shut us both off the day he went to prison, and that text message from the other week was someone's idea of a sick joke.

I'm the Dio family's greatest hope. Which probably means we're doomed.

But I don't go down without a fight.

It's the evening of Lupercalia, a few hours before the fights are due to begin, and I'm in the fighter's area backstage. I run through warmups and drills while Livvie's crew move around above my head, setting up the tables and stringing the lights. I like being the first one here so I can size up each fighter and prisoner as they arrive. I want to smile at them and get them acquainted with the last face they'll see before they get their one-way ticket to hell—

"Cassius Dio, what a surprise to find you here."

My head whips up at the sound of a familiar female voice. Livvie Lucian stands in the doorway, her designer suit clinging to every curve, and a mischievous half-smile playing on her crimson lips.

"What do you want?" I demand.

"I want to talk to you." Livvie's heels click on the cold concrete as she crosses the room, never taking her eyes off me. She perches on the very edge of the wooden bench, as if terrified it might infect her with my pestilence.

"How's your mother?" Livvie says, in a perfectly even tone that might've sounded friendly if I didn't know better.

"She's doing well," I shoot back. "Galen says she'll make a full recovery."

He says nothing of the sort, but I don't want Livvie to know that.

"That's wonderful news. Will we see her tonight?"

"Tell me what you want and get the fuck out," I growl.

She tsks. "Oh, sweet Cassius. You were never one for small talk. Very well. Even as thick as you are, you can't help but notice what's happening. Your little stunt with Fergie's video has destabilized the Triumvirate, something that outside forces have been trying unsuccessfully to do for months. We're at a tipping point now. Everything Claudia, Cali, and I have worked for is piled atop a crate of dynamite. All it will take is a single spark and the Triumvirate will go up in flames, taking all of us with it. I want you to be the spark."

I jerk my head in surprise. "What are you saying? You *want* me to blow shit up?"

"Not literally – I've had quite enough of that, thank you." She shudders, remembering the museum. "I want you to destroy the Triumvirate."

"The fuck? Why?"

"Because I'm nothing if not a pragmatist." Livvie crosses one lean ankle over the other. "The Triumvirate is doomed – it always has been. You can't put that much raw estrogen in a room together without the claws eventually coming out. One of us was always going to make a grab for more power, and it might as well be me. I'll be damned if I lose everything I've built. So I come to you with an offer."

"Which is?"

"My son is in love with your stepsister, and I want them to be married – a Dio/Lucian alliance, the perfect way to ensure my family's security. Claudia August either suspects this, or she knows, because she's making moves on Fergie as well. She has hired your stepsister to be her little errand girl. Did you know that?"

"I know," I growl, my hands balling into fists. The red closes around my vision, squeezing me, taunting me with Fergie's final betrayal.

"Good. Then you know that Fergie is the lynchpin in the coming war. Whoever controls her will have the support of our people. Whoever loses her will lose their family and their seat at the table, and Cali is too stuck in her ways to see that. I want you to step up and take Cali's place. I want you to support this alliance and help me to get rid of the Augusts. Do this, and I'll make you the head of the Dio family. And you'll have Fergie. She can be both yours and Torsten's wife – a symbol of our families coming together. Claudia has set the precedent for this type of marriage, and I've never really seen the benefit until now. Think about it, Cassius. You'll have exactly what you always wanted: You'll be Imperator, and you'll have your stepsister's body for whatever perversions your deviant mind can dream up."

I stand, and it takes every thread of my fraying self-control to keep my fists jammed at my sides. "Leave. *Now.*"

"For once in your life, Cassius, use that pile of mush between your ears." Livvie beams up at me as she sweeps out of the room. "Join with me or lose your stepsister and your family forever. I'll be waiting for your answer."

I REMAIN backstage for the next couple of hours, turning over Livvie's proposal while I do pull-ups and punch holes in the concrete walls to keep my blood warm. Some of the other fighters do light sparring with each other, but they won't let me join them. The last fighter who did 'light sparring' with me still can't see out of his left eye.

After what Livvie proposed and Fergie's revelations, I'm not going easy tonight. I need to drink blood and swallow screams. I need violence humming in my veins to get rid of the raspberry sting of my stepsister.

I slide my hands into my bear claws.

I wait.

Above our heads, the Colosseum fills with the sounds of our people. Lupercalia is the second largest gathering on the Triumvirate calendar, a celebration of the union of our families, and anyone with any position of power within the organization will be here tonight. I know it will be a full house. Now that it's known the three Imperators are at odds, they've come to see blood drawn. All eyes will be on Cali and Claudia and Livvie for a sign of what's to come. If they give the word, it's all-out war in the streets of Emerald Beach.

I can't stop it. Livvie's right – the Triumvirate has always been doomed. Power can't be shared by the powerful. Someone will always crave more than their due. But I can do one thing tonight – my duty as a son. I'll break so many necks tonight that I'll draw the crowd's eye away from my mother and her injuries.

I'll show them all that the Dio family is stronger than ever.

The ceremony begins and the word comes down from above that us fighters should be ready for our cue. Livvie's crew begins to drag the prisoners from their cells. A nervous energy permeates the waiting area. We can all smell the blood in the air. My opponents exchange frightened glances. Some of them are leaving the arena in body bags.

We sit through the first few acts – some warm-up routines to get the crowd in a bloodthirsty mood. Fire dancers, acrobats, a few empty words from Livvie and Claudia. And then, finally, just as the red mist closes over my vision, I'm called into the arena.

Heat courses through my veins as I climb the stairs and step into the ring. The crowd roars their approval. They may be turning against my family, they may clamor to see me fail, but they still remember my name.

"The Bear! The Bear!"

I raise my arms and turn in a slow circle so they can take in the sharp claws glinting from my fingertips and the enormous bear tattoo covering my torso. I fight in shorts, no headgear, no other armor. I don't need it. Sometimes I let my opponent get their weapon into my skin, just to feel the sting of it, the way a bear might watch a mosquito bite its back before flicking it away.

No one calls out 'Papa Smurf' or comments on my still-blue skin. They wouldn't dare, unless they want to be pulled into the arena and made an example of. I stare at my blue arms as I strike another pose. I have to admit, I kind of like the color. Beneath the glaring arena lights, I appear alien, otherworldly. Fucking *terrifying*.

On the Imperator's platform, I see the glitter of the lights reflecting off fine crystal and expensive jewelry. My mother is up there, sitting in her usual chair, her midnight skin making her appear as a shadow in the moonlight. Beside her, Galen and John watch her every move in case she needs attention, and the other seats at her table are filled with her most trusted assassins. On the other side of the platform, Livvie has filled her table with her brood of children and their parents – a show of force if not of strength. And Claudia August stands on the railing, flanked by her three husbands. I can't see Vic or Torsten anywhere.

I can't see *her*.

My first opponent approaches. He's a Sicilian fighter who trained under the Badalamenti family and came to Emerald Beach to prove himself at Cali's school. He's a promising fighter and she won't want me to break him, but he knows what he's getting into by entering the Lupercalia ring. I've been winning at Lupercalia since I was fourteen years old.

Our bout lasts less than twenty seconds before I pound his face into the concrete wall of the arena. He flops to the ground like a wet fish. He does not rise again.

Security drags him away and sends out the next two fighters. This time, I'm not fighting professionals, but two of Livvie's soldiers who were found to be leaking sensitive information about her business. She hasn't been able to figure out where that information is flowing *to*, but we have a pretty good idea anyway. Zack Lionel Sommesnay.

What no one knows is who Sommesnay is, or what it is he wants.

No one, except my fucking stepsister.

It's not my job tonight to wrest information from these two degenerates. They've already been thoroughly probed by my mother. No, tonight I serve only one role, the role I was born to play.

Executioner.

I step toward them and swipe at the air with my claws. The blades make a satisfying whoosh as they slice, missing my prey by inches. One of the men flinches, but the other surges forward, foolishly thinking he has a shot. He barrels toward me in an attempt to knock me off my feet. He intends to go down as a fighter. I admire that.

I draw out their execution, breaking the first guy's legs and stomping on his pelvis until the bone crunches beneath my foot. The second I cut open and wind out his intestines like spaghetti. I drape them around my neck and wear them as a necklace while the crowd rises to their feet, roaring their approval.

After them, I fight two more of Cali's fighters. One walks away with only a broken nose. I nod to my mother in the VIP seats, knowing she'll be giving that guy a spot in her ranks. The other is not so lucky.

But still, I'm not sated. Still the red mist clings to me, choking me with all of the things I cannot feel, all the ways I wish things had worked out differently. My blood pounds in my ears, singing a haunting melody for me alone...

Fergie... Fergie... Fergie...

I drop the severed head I'm holding onto the dusty arena floor. I let the roar of the crowd wash over me, calling on their bloodlust to slough away my need for her. I raise my claws to the heavens and let my gaze search the crowd for her, landing on the spot at my mother's table where she should be sitting.

She isn't even here.

It stings.

Why does it sting?

Why does it hurt so much that she isn't here, after she betrayed me? After she nearly had my mother killed?

"Is there no one else who will fight me?" I roar.

Cowards.

Bastards.

I need this.

I need the blood, or I'm going to go fucking crazy.

I need to smear myself in it. I need to drink it until I can no longer taste raspberries.

"Does no one in this room have a bone to pick with Cassius Dio?" I yell, raising my eyes to the heavens and beating my fists on my bare chest, drawing rivers of my own blood from where the claws dig in.

"I do."

The voice rings clear through the hushed Colosseum. I'd recognize it anywhere.

Fergie.

My blood boils.

How fucking *dare* she?

My eyes are drawn to the edge of the arena, where the crowd parts for Fergie to march through. Her white cane sweeps the ground in front of her. Vic and Torsten run after her. Torsten grabs her wrist and tries to pull her back. She places a hand on his chest and shoves him away. I don't hear what she says to him over the roar of blood in my ears.

He grabs her neck and pulls her in and kisses her. Torsten fucking Lucian kisses my stepsister in front of everyone. He kisses her like he needs her to breathe.

I'm so fucking stunned that by the time I've recovered, Fergie's convinced the guards to open the door to the arena and let her through. Victor pounds on the door, begging them to let him in, but that's against the rules.

One fighter may challenge me.

A suicide pact.

I remember holding her against the wall in Galen's clinic and seeing the moment the fire left her eyes. I remember her taunting me, begging me to end her life, the way her lip trembled when she spoke of loving me. She *loved* me, and now she enters my domain and begs me to tear her to pieces.

My stepsister stands on the sandy floor, facing me. She wears skintight leather pants with thin gold zippers and a leather bralette that shows off her smooth stomach.

Her sightless eyes find mine, and it's as if she *sees* me. Sees every rotten thought and every hopeless wish that twitches like a still-warm corpse inside me.

"Hello, brother."

I *growl*. I can't form words. I'm so fucking beyond words.

Someone yells, "Fergie, get out of the ring."

It's Victor. Of course it is. Victor fucking August has pushed his way to the mesh on the side of the arena. He's torn off his shirt and I see he's sporting a new tattoo – a lily across his pec to match the one Fergie drew on our lockers, rendered in a beautiful black and gray design that I suspect came from Torsten.

Fucking *hell*.

The guards hold Victor back because the rules of this game are sacred – if there's a challenge, there can only be two fighters in the ring at a time, and only one remains standing at the end.

It's me or my blind stepsister.

"Fergie, you have to get out." Victor shakes the mesh. "He'll fucking kill you."

"I'm perfectly aware of what Cassius is capable of." She smiles up at him then, and it's the smile of someone who has thrown their lot in with death. Someone who has nothing left to lose.

It's the sexist fucking smile I've ever seen.

I can't help myself. My dick grows hard. I'm still wearing only my tattered boxers, splattered with blood, and I'm sure everyone in Colosseum can see that I've got a tent for my stepsister.

Everyone except Fergie, who just stands there, silent, accusing.

"Victor, get back. I'm doing this. I'm doing it because this is the only language he understands," she says so calmly, as if I'm not right fucking here.

"We have a challenger!" the announcer screams into the microphone. "We haven't had anything this exciting at a Lupercalia for twenty years. Fighters, take up your positions. Do not engage until my word. Five... four..."

The announcer counts down, and the bell rings. But unlike my previous fights, where the audience howls for blood, this time they remain eerily silent. The only sound is my own blood rushing in my ears and the pounding of my heart against my broken ribs.

It all comes back in a rush of emotion. Everything this woman made me *feel*. I thought she was a gold digger, but it turns out she's even worse than that. She's a fucking black widow. And whether she truly did make a mistake or she's trying to dismantle everything my mother built, it doesn't matter.

She made a fool of me.

She made me feel *bad* for what I did.

She made my stomach hurt.

She put me off my food.

She made me love her. She made it so I can't go a single day, a single minute, without thinking of her.

If she expects mercy because she's a girl, or because she's blind, if she expects me to fall to my knees to worship her the way Vic and Torsten clearly do, it's not going to happen.

I *remember* the way she looked at me like she truly saw me, and I remember the way her glorious pussy tightened around my cock, and I get angrier and angrier and hornier and harder until the red mist closes over me completely, blocking out my pitiable thoughts at last.

I'm ready.

I can do this.

I'm *Cassius fucking Dio*.

I pounce.

Fergie doesn't move a muscle. She just stands there as I come for her.

I raise my hand to swipe at her with my claw, but I can't do it. I'm frozen. But I'm close enough that when she reaches out, she can touch me. She drags her own torso over the claws, raising three deep gashes in the soft skin of her bare stomach, just above her tattoo. Her blood scents the air. She grunts from the pain and leans forward a little. I swipe my arm back, desperate to get away before I...

She grabs my wrist and pulls and twists and—

—I don't know how it happens, but I'm on the ground.

I'm on the ground and I can't move.

What the fuck?

Her knee jams into my neck, pressing my face into the sand. That shouldn't be enough to stop me, but it is. I swallow a mouthful of sand, and it tastes gritty and metallic, stained with the blood I've spilled.

I throw my weight to roll over her, and I feel a pop and a surge of pain.

I try to curl my fingers into a fist, but the message isn't getting to them.

She broke my arm. The bitch *broke my arm*.

I'm dimly aware through the red mist that she's worked the bear claw off my fist. She's taking my weapon from me. She can't do this. I'm Cassius fucking—

Everything goes dark.

FERGIE

Beneath me, Cassius stops moving.

But I don't stop.

I slide my fingers into the bear glove. It's way too big for me, but it doesn't matter. I close my fist, feeling the way the claws retract and extend again when I stretch my fingers.

I lean over my stepbrother, and I slash and punch and hack at him with those claws. This isn't jiujitsu. I have no form, no control. I'm wild, wanton, drowning in grief and rage and love. I hurt and I maim and I hack at my stepbrother's body until his blood splatters across my face, until my arm hurts too much to lift again.

Then, I get to my feet and I kick him – in the head, in the ribs, in the kidneys. I kick until what I'm kicking ceases to feel like a body but is instead a lump of lifeless meat.

And all the while, I expect the triumph to surge through me. In this moment, as Cassius Dio lies in a pool of his own blood and broken teeth in front of every important person in the Triumvirate, I know I have finally won. I've done what he tried to do to me – I've taken that one secret piece of him that was supposed to be just for me, and put it on display for the world to jeer at in all its bloody glory.

I feel nothing. I'm numb. My body doesn't even register the pain I'm putting it through, and my mind is completely blank.

Rough hands grab me and drag me away. I keep kicking, kicking, kicking. I'm vaguely aware that I'm screaming at them to let me kill him, to make certain that I'm finally rid of the poison that is Cassius Dio.

"It's over," Vic coos, pushing my head into his arms. He holds me against his body, rocking, speaking words of comfort that can't penetrate the horror of what I've done.

Slowly, slowly, I breathe in his dark chocolate and hazelnut scent, and I come back to myself – the numbness flees, replaced by a horrible, sickening dread.

"Is he dead?" I ask.

"I don't know, Duchess." Vic strokes my hair. "I don't know."

A GROUP OF FIGHTERS SCOOPS CASSIUS' body from the arena. Cali screams that Lupercalia is over, and the crowd scatters, too afraid of their Imperator to stick around and see Cali punish me.

Because I know that Cali's wrath will descend on me. It's my fault she got shot, and that the Triumvirate is in tatters, and I've just possibly killed her son in front of everyone. She can't allow that to stand.

I killed Cassius.

Why did I do that? How did I do that?

I hate him. I love him. I miss him already.

I sink into Victor's arms, and I don't understand the tears streaming down my cheeks. I never wanted him gone. I wanted to kill the demon that made him hate me. I walked into that arena tonight knowing that the only way to reach him is through violence – the only language he understands.

I had to triumph, or I'd be the one who didn't walk out alive.

But I keep remembering his tiny voice in my room when he told me that he couldn't kill me. Cassius Dio may be a monster. But he had a heart, and it still beat for me.

Until I stopped it.

Torsten comes running over, out of breath. "They're taking him to Galen," he says. "That must mean he's still alive."

"For now," Victor says, his voice impossibly dark.

I fall from Victor's arms. His touch is too much right now, too raw and real and tinged with his own pain. Torsten – who always seems to know exactly what I need – takes my hand and leads me through the crowd.

"Victor will drive us to see him," he says. Torsten doesn't ask if I want to see Cas. He *knows*. He understands better than I do what it means to love and hate someone in equal measure.

I hold onto Torsten and he holds onto Victor, and together we battle our way through the surging crowd. At any moment I expect to feel a bullet tear through my back.

But then again, Cali wouldn't be that merciful.

She'd want my death to be slow.

Painful.

Humiliating.

We make it out of the bottleneck at the entrance, and Victor drags us down a flight of stairs into a room that smells of urine and concrete. The echoes of our footsteps tell me that the room is long and narrow, barely taller than my head height. Although the walls are solid concrete, the ceiling is of wood and steel.

"We're in the maintenance ditches in the old roundhouse," Vic says. "Livvie had them dug deeper so that we could have rooms down here. This is where they hold prisoners before they go into the arena."

He shoves through a wooden door into another section of the ditch. There's furniture in this room, and the urine smell isn't as bad here. Several people are pressed together in the narrow space, and Galen is yelling at everyone to stand back and let him work.

"Fergie, you're okay!"

Arms go around me as Claudia pulls me in for a tight hug. I'm surprised by this public display of affection for me, and I hate that part of me wonders how much is genuine and how much is a pantomime for the people in the room. Victor tightens his grip on my arm.

I'm in shock. I don't know what to do. I let her hug me. It feels good to be hugged right now.

"That was quite spectacular," Claudia says as she pulls back. I sense her studying me, wondering what other surprises I have for her. "I couldn't have plotted it any better if I tried. How did you get one over on Cas like that?"

"I have training," I say, and it's a woefully inadequate explanation of what happened in the ring, but it's all I have right now. "I'm a second-degree black belt in jiujitsu."

"You are *amazing*. You didn't just beat Cas, you *destroyed* him. The Dio family is done."

"That wasn't what I intended," I mutter.

"Mom, please," Victor's voice is strained. "We don't know if Cas is still—"

"Fergie, you marvelous creature," Livvie shoves her way into our tight circle and kisses my cheeks. I start shaking. I can't stop. Livvie turns to Victor and Torsten. "Get her out of here. Cali's going to be here any minute. If she sees you, she'll kill you, and then you'll be no use to me."

I surge forward. "I have to see Cas. I have to know if—"

"Fergie, *let's go*." Victor picks me off the ground like I weigh nothing, tosses me over his shoulder, and runs from the room.

I beat his back with my fists. "Put me down. I have to see him. I have to know that he's okay."

"You're no good to Cas if you're dead," Victor says in that smooth voice of his. "I saw him – he's breathing. He's alive. I'll go in there and find out what's going on. Torsten, you hold her. Make sure she doesn't try to follow me or run outside or do anything stupid. Don't let Cali see her if she comes this way, okay?"

Torsten's arms go around me.

I can't take it anymore. I break down completely.

The horror of our fight blooms in my chest like a poison flower, twisting through my veins, winding around my ribcage, squeezing until I gasp for air. My whole world becomes a haunted, hopeless funeral dirge to the stepbrother I love, the monster I've slain, the broken man who only ever wanted someone to see the truth in his heart.

Cas.

My Cas.

What have I done?

59

FERGIE

I lose track of how long we wait before Vic returns. His voice is grim.

"Cas is alive, but only just. He's in a coma, and it's bad. Worse than mine. Galen's taking him to his clinic where he can monitor him. He says that Cas has swelling in his brain from the beating. They're going to treat him as best they can, but all we can do is wait and see if the swelling goes down. Galen says that even if he wakes up, he's unlikely to regain a hundred percent of his normal brain function."

I did that.

I hurt Cas so bad that he might not ever wake up. And if he does, he won't be the same Cas.

Fuck.

No.

All I wanted was to show him that we're the same – that when he fights me, he fights himself. But I didn't stop to consider that in trying to beat the monster at his own game, I became a monster, too.

"Fergie," Vic's voice is kind, but stern. "We have to leave."

I collapse into his arms and let him carry me out of there. I'm dimly aware of conversations going on around me, plans being made. Torsten goes to the clinic with Livvie, and Vic drives me back to his place. Noah and Eli stayed with Claudia at the club, but Gabriel came back to the house to feed their animals. He ushers us inside and settles me into a comfy chair in their living room, and brings me a bowl of ice cream.

"I can't stop crying," I whisper to Victor, staring at the melting chocolate-cherry crunch in my bowl.

"It's okay," Gabriel says. A pair of arms join Victor's around me, and I feel strands of long, thick hair brushing my face. "Tears are only water – and like every living thing, our souls need water to grow."

Well, fuck. Now I'm being hugged by Gabriel Fallen. This is one of the most surreal experiences of my life, and I'm too messed up to appreciate it.

My phone buzzes. Siri announces that it's my dad calling. I can't talk to him, I can't face him telling me that I've ruined everything. Again. The phone rings and rings as fresh sobs rip through my body. How can one person have so many tears inside them?

Victor sits down beside me. "No one blames you, Fergie. You and Cas have been hurtling toward this end for a long time. One of you was always going to destroy the other. When you stepped into that ring, I thought... I thought I'd lost you."

I try to speak, but all that comes out are loud, wretched hiccups. I can't tell Victor that he has lost me. I died in that arena tonight, my coal-heart bleeding out alongside my step-brother.

How can I go on, knowing that I've broken everything?

60

FERGIE

I
t's eight days later, and Cassius still hasn't woken up.

I'm a mess.

One minute I'm declaring the world is better off without him, the next I'm curled up in a ball, bawling my eyes out. I have no idea what I want or how I feel except that I fucking hate him for putting us all through hell and I love him so much that I can't breathe and I want him to wake the fuck up so I can choke him to death with my bare hands.

No one dares talk to me except Victor and Torsten and Gabriel. They won't let me visit the clinic, so the three of us sleep in Vic's bed, and when they leave to sit with Cas, Gabriel feeds me ice cream, shows me how to water Vic's poison flowers, and lets me sit in the corner and weep while he writes songs.

Vic tells me that as the three leaders of the Triumvirate march in and out of Galen's clinic all day, they shoot each other stony looks but no one says a word. He says this is bad, that it would be better if they shouted at each other, got it all out in the open like a big family argument. But instead, they're all scheming their next move.

Victor doesn't say a word about what's going on in the city, but when he's gone, I listen to the news on my phone. I see soldiers from the three families fighting in the streets. An August warehouse blows up and someone walks into one of Livvie's clubs and starts shooting. The Triumvirate's control over the city is slipping, and they're too caught up in their own personal battles to see it.

And it's all because of me.

Dad sends me a text saying that he's okay and he's happy I won, but that for both our safety, he can't be seen with me right now.

I understand. A tiny part of me is still that little girl who needs her daddy, but mostly, I have all I need in Torsten and Victor's arms.

Almost all I need.

The final broken piece of my coal-heart lies in a hospital bed in the basement of an old asylum, attached to machines that force him to breathe. He's lost to me forever, and it's all my fault.

"FERGIE, WHAT'S UP?" Euri sounds suspicious. I don't blame her. I've been so tied up with Torsten and revenge plans and working for Claudia that I haven't seen her much outside of school. She's been busy too, putting the finishing touches on her college applications, but I haven't been there for her through that process the way I wanted to be, and I hate calling her now to ask her for a favor.

"Euri, hi. I... I need to talk to you. Did you—"

"Did I know that Cas is hurt? And you had something to do with it?" Euri's voice rises with panic. "Rumors are flying all over school, but no one knows anything. I've called and texted you hundreds of times, but you didn't answer. I've been so worried."

"I'm sorry. I... I stepped into the arena at Colosseum and fought Cassius—"

"You what?"

Her voice goes so shrill I have to hold the phone away from my ear.

"It was the only thing I could think to do to get through to him. And I won. I beat him. But he's..." I swallow. I can barely get the words out. "He's in a coma. I put him in a coma."

"Oh, Fergie..." Euri breathes. "I... I don't know what to say."

"Everything is a mess... the Triumvirate is crumbling, and there's all this violence and it's all my fault..."

"You can't blame yourself for what—"

"How far along are you on that article?"

I know I'm a basket case, but I have to get this out before I lose my nerve.

"I'm almost done. I just wanted to get a couple more quotes and check some of my figures. We've done an amazing job. I sent the first half to my contact, and he really thinks we might have a shot at being picked up by the *Atlantic* or *Slate* or maybe even the *Times*. I mean, this is big. It's really big. It's—"

I squeeze my eyes shut. I hate the excitement in Euri's voice because I remember it so well – being on the trail of something big, feeling as though you're contributing something more than another issue of the school newspaper that no one reads. Back in Witchwood Falls, I broke a story about funds being skimmed from the volleyball team by their coach, and it got picked up by the *Boston Herald*.

Euri's been more of a friend to me than anyone, even after I've screwed her over again and again. I can't take this away from her, and yet...

I can't stop thinking about the fight. About the way the crowd went crazy as I brought down Cassius Dio. About the blood dripping from my hands. I've washed and washed them, but they never feel clean. I don't think I'll ever feel clean again.

I won't have Euri's blood on my hands, too.

"We have to pull the story."

"What? No, we can't." Euri lets out a long breath. "It's perfectly normal to get cold feet, especially with these big newspapers involved, and I know you're risking a lot after the video, but you said you didn't care about your Harvard admission—"

"—I don't, but—"

"—and what we're doing is important. Think of all the victims who were hurt by Poison Ivy. Think about my sister. We can't back out now—"

"This isn't cold feet, Euri."

"Is this about Cassius? Did you get back together with him?"

"I have not gotten together with Cassius." I feel his wet, warm blood slide through my fingers again. "I told you that I could guarantee your safety when this thing gets out, and I can't do that anymore. Dangerous people are going to see this article as another attack, and I can't let you put your name on anything that will put you in danger. Right now, this city is on fire – it's a small fire, and there's still a chance of putting it out. But this article will be like throwing kerosene onto that fire – this whole city will burn, and you along with it."

Euri is silent for a long time. Finally, in a quiet, calm voice, she says, "Are you sure?"

"I'm sure."

"Okay. Then I won't publish the article."

"Thank you." My whole body sags in relief. "I know it sucks after all that work we put in, but we've got rid of the Poison Ivy Club, so mission accomplished—"

But she's already hung up.

Cali and I sit on opposite sides of the waiting room. Violence cascades off her like water off a duck's feathers if it was a really fucking terrifying duck.

Victor hovers between us, positioning himself to shield me from any potential bullet or poison dart. I know it's hopeless – if Cali Dio wants me dead, she'll find a way – but I let him do it because it makes him feel useful.

It must be nice to feel useful. Ever since Cas has been in this coma, all I feel is sick to my stomach.

A chair creaks. Cali is getting to her feet. Vic shoots up to guard me, but Cali's voice darkens as she barks, "I want to speak to Fergie."

"I don't think that's a good idea," Vic says.

"Galen had me frisked for weapons at the door," Cali snaps. "If I wanted her dead, you wouldn't be able to stop me, Victor August."

I sigh. "It's fine, Vic. Leave us alone for a few minutes, would you?"

Whatever torture Cali has planned for me, I deserve all of it, and more.

Victor makes a strangled sound in the back of his throat. He doesn't want to leave my side, but he also won't contradict me in front of Cali. I have more power than he does at the moment, and he won't do anything to make me appear weak. He squeezes my shoulder and moves toward the door. "I'll watch through the glass," he promises.

"No, you won't. Go see if your mother needs something to eat. She's been here since this morning."

I hear the waiting room door open and shut again.

"Thank fuck," Cali breathes. "I thought that boy would never leave. All that nervous pacing of his was making me homicidal."

I lift an eyebrow at my stepmother. "Isn't homicidal your usual state?"

Cali snorts. She slumps down in the chair next to me, her body perfectly still. Usually when people sit near me, I"m hyper-aware of every movement they make, all their little shufflings and sighs. But with Cali, it's like she's a statue. She doesn't move a single muscle unless she has a purpose.

"I'd like some coffee," she says, breaking the silence.

"There's a machine in the corner of the room."

"I know that, but what comes out of that contraption doesn't deserve to carry the name of coffee. Want to get out of here?"

"Excuse me?" Is she asking me to leave... with her?

This is a trap. Get the fuck away from her while you still can.

"We're past the point where our proximity is going to wake my son out of his stupor," she says. "And I need proper coffee or I'll drown Galen in a bedpan. You will come with me."

I don't want to go anywhere with my stepmother. We haven't been alone together since the day she found me in the basement looking at the poor workmanship on her gym mirrors, and that wasn't exactly a stellar example of our deep emotional family connection.

But I'm curious.

Why does Cali want to talk to me, alone, without Victor?

She doesn't. She's taking you somewhere to dispose of you, the voice in my head screams.

I don't blame Cali if that were true. I did put her son in a coma. But what she told Victor is also true. Despite what's happened to her over the past couple of weeks, she's still the woman with all the power here. If she wanted me dead, I'd be dead already.

I follow the clack-clack of Cali's heels back out through the passage into my father's clinic, and out to her car. Seymour holds the door open for me. Cali slides into the front seat. "Take us to the gym," she tells Seymour.

Her gym. Not a coffee shop, but the literal place where Cali trains the next generation of assassins.

Oh, this is a brilliant idea.

No one speaks on the short drive. My nails dig into the back of the seat. I wind down the window and allow the California sun to dry my tears and warm my face. If this is the last time I get to feel the sun on my skin, I intend to enjoy it.

We arrive, and Seymour opens the door for me. I step out into a street – it feels a little narrow, with two- and three-story buildings quite close to the street. There's lots of chatter around me – people at the shops talking in different languages – Spanish, Italian, Korean...

"Stairs," Cali barks. I sweep my cane across the threshold of a small foyer, locate the stairs and the handrail, and follow Cali up. We pass the first floor and move on to the second, and I can tell from the way the echoes shrink into the space that this upper floor is heavily soundproofed. We cross a much wider foyer, and I can smell potted plants and sweat. Cali opens a door and gives me a shove into the room.

"Konstantin, I need you," Cali snaps at someone down the hall. A moment later, I'm joined in the room by a guy. He has a huge, menacing presence – the kind of build that bends the air around him, the way Cas does.

The way Cas *used* to do.

Fuck, Cas.

I left him alone in the hospital to come here, and I don't think I'll ever see him again.

Please, please, Cas. Wake up. I don't care what your mother does to me, but I want you to wake up. I want you to keep being your beautiful, monstrous self. I want you to know that I loved you because of everything you are, and I always will.

"Fergie, meet Konstantin," Cali says gruffly. "Konstantin, this is my stepdaughter, Fergie."

"Hi, Konstantin." I shove my hand out quickly, so he can shake.

"It's a pleasure, Fergie." Konstantin's grip crushes my fingers. "Will you be staying to watch me fight?"

"Of course she will," Cali snaps. "Fergie is your opponent."

What?

Konstantin jerks his hand from mine. "I'm not fighting her. She's blind. She's got a cane and everything."

"You'll fight her, and you'll give it one-hundred fucking percent or I'll throw you out of this academy." Cali's voice turns toward me. "Fergie, Konstantin here is ten pounds lighter than Cassius, so you shouldn't have any problems. We'll do three five-minute bouts. No groin attacks, no hair pulling, no gouging, biting, or spitting. Otherwise, it's all fair game."

Wait, what the fuck is going on?

I assume this is Cali's punishment for what I did to Cas – she's going to make me fight dudes way out of my weight class until I make a mistake and get my head staved in. Then she can wash her hands of the guilt when she tells my dad.

Or maybe she doesn't feel guilty at all about killing her step-daughter.

I tilt my head toward Konstantin. "What choice do I have?"

"None whatsoever."

"I thought so." I rip off my hoodie. Underneath I'm wearing a black tank top. Cassius has cut holes all through it, so I know Konstantin is getting a good look at my scarlet bra right now. Maybe I can use boobs to distract him.

"Just give me a second," I tell Cali. I don't want to ask Konstantin to lead me around the ring, because then he's never going to fight me and Cali will just find someone larger and meaner. So I pick up my cane and walk myself around, feeling the edges of the mat, getting a sense of the space – where the walls are, any obstacles like pillars or steps.

"Okay. I'm ready." I kick off my boots and step onto the mat. I'm wearing a pair of designer pants that Cassius also cut up, so my knees hang out.

Konstantin growls a little, but I hear him slide in a mouth guard and take his place opposite me on the mats. I should really be wearing a mouth guard too, but I won't give Cali the satisfaction of hearing me ask for one.

Cali calls the fight. I hear Konstantin's feet shuffle as he debates his move.

I wait.

There's always a moment of blind panic when I begin a bout – when I'm all alone in space and I know my opponent is going to fly at me and I won't be fast enough to stop them. I brace myself for the first attack, for the pain that I have to fight through if I want to win.

The blow hits me in the cheek, sending my head snapping back and rolling my brain around inside my skull. This guy doesn't fuck around. I pivot my body with the force of the movement, gulping down the cry that threatens to escape me. My entire skull pulses with hot pain, but my body remembers what to do next. I swoop low, and before Konstantin knows what's happening, he's on his back and I'm on top of him.

As soon as we're grappling, I know I can win. Konstantin is big and strong, but I can tell from his movement that he's used to winning by brute force and intimidation. But it's hard to intimidate an opponent who can't see you, and here on the floor, I can use his weight against him, forcing him to trap his own limbs so that he can't use any of that power.

Konstantin grunts as he tries to throw me off, but he doesn't know what the fuck he's doing. I love this part of a fight – scrapping for purchase, wriggling my arms into the tight spaces to create the holds that incapacitate him. He laughs, not understanding what I'm doing until my arm goes across his neck and I twist, and he can't laugh anymore. He scratches and scrabbles at my arm, but it only lasts for moments before he drops to the mats, completely passed out.

I slide out from beneath Konstantin and roll to the edge of the mat, fighting to catch my breath. But before I can, Cali calls in another guy and I have to do it all again. I lose the first round when the guy dropkicks me on my ass and pins me before I can get up, but he's not so lucky in the second. In the third round, I force him to break his own finger. Fair's fair.

By the time Cali calls in the next guy, I'm wheezing like crazy, and my whole body screams for mercy. She barks at me to get up, and I drag myself to my feet and step back onto the mat. I know that this time, I'm too tired. Too slow.

To my surprise, she barks at her fighter. "Get out of here."

He scampers. I wish like hell I could follow him. I stand, dripping with sweat, my skin torn and bruised, as Cali steps across the mat and faces me. Her steps are so light they're almost invisible to me, but I know she's there.

She walks in a slow circle around me, a panther closing in on its prey. I feel her eyes burning into me as she inspects me like a pair of Jimmy Choos on the sale rack.

"You're unfit," she scolds. "You don't have the stamina for serious fighting."

"Yes, well, *someone* told me that I wasn't allowed to train in martial arts when I moved to Emerald Beach," I shoot back, because apparently I have a death wish.

Cali makes a strange snorting sound that I *suspect* might be a laugh. "Perhaps that someone can admit that a mistake was made. This gym is available to you whenever you wish to use it. Konstantin will be your training partner, and you are welcome to spar with any of my students to help build your conditioning. See me if you want weapons training. And don't fight my son again – he gets carried away, and I don't want an asset like you broken before you've had a chance in the field."

I blink, not believing the words I'm hearing. "I'm sorry?"

"Don't make me repeat myself," she snaps.

"I heard you. I just don't *understand*. Why are you offering me the chance to train here? Why did you bring me to fight all these dudes? I nearly killed your son."

"Yes," she says. "But you didn't."

"Of course I didn't. I don't want to go to jail."

She snort-laughs again. "You're a Dio now, Fergie. You're untouchable. You could behead the chief of police on TV and you'd still walk away scot-free. That's not why you didn't kill Cassius, and we both know it."

My lip quivers.

Please, if any gods are listening. Please don't let me cry in front of Cali Dio.

"I *did* mean to kill him. I hate him so much for releasing that video, for not believing in me, and for everything he's done since. If I didn't kill him, he would've killed me—"

"No."

"He already tried."

"No, he didn't. Did you wonder why Cassius didn't kill you when he snuck into the house that night?" she says. "It's not because you stopped him. I've watched the security footage. He had every chance to gut you in your sleep. He didn't kill you because he loves you. And you're the only person in the world I think might be strong enough to be loved by Cassius."

"Um, thanks, I guess—"

Cali keeps talking as if I haven't spoken. "But I know you won't be happy as his trophy Queen. You need work, and I have plenty of work to suit your talents, but you'll need to go through the same training as my other soldiers, or they won't respect you—"

I can't help it. I burst out laughing. "I can't be an *assassin*. I'm going to Harvard Law School."

"Sure you are."

"I *am*." I ball my hands into fists. As I say the words, I realize that I mean them. "I earned my place, fair and square. Dawson took it away from me, and Poison Ivy got it back. I don't intend to spit on my hard-won prize."

Now that Euri's not releasing the video, Harvard is back on the cards. Maybe it's the right thing to do after all. I could get far away from Emerald Beach and all the terrible things I've done. I could wash my hands of the Triumvirate and start over again. I could become the Fergie I was always supposed to be.

But Torsten... and Victor... and Cas...

"That's really what you want? You want to spend the rest of your life standing up in courtrooms trying to get justice for 'the little guy'? You should know better than anyone that there's no justice to be had that way."

She grabs my arm and nearly wrenches it out of the socket as she drags me out of the room. I'm pulled down a hallway and through a labyrinth of doors and rooms until we reach a vast, open space where I can hear the sound of children shouting and tiny fists punching backs as feet fight for purchase on gym mats.

"Where are we?" I ask.

"This is a martial arts class for the local kids. Any fighter who trains with me has to donate their time to teach here. We offer free classes for anyone who wants them – self-defense for women and children and members of the LGBT+ community are some of our most popular offerings. Sometimes I fly in promising students from across the country to get specialist training – the kind of training they'd never afford on their own."

I try to say something, but I find myself speechless. Vicious, cold-hearted Cali Dio – the most feared assassin in the world – runs free self-defense classes?

"Don't look at me like that," she snaps. "Claudia has her little museum of old junk and Livvie has her seventeen million children, and this is what I do. These kids didn't ask for their lot in life. They come to me weak and helpless, and I teach them to *fight*. I teach them to honor themselves enough to not allow themselves to become victims in the first place."

I can't help the lump rising in my throat. "Why are you showing me this?"

Cali sighs. "I guess we're doing this."

"Doing what?"

"I think John calls it 'bonding.' Listen carefully, because I'm only going to tell this story once. I was trafficked into this country from Ghana and sold to Nero Lucian."

"Livvie's father?"

"Indeed. Be thankful you never met the man, because he was a piece of work. I was about eight years old when my parents sold me. I was supposed to work backstage in one of Nero's clubs until I was old enough to service his clients out front. I decided instead to make a run for it.

"One night, when I was fifteen, I was to serve drinks at a private party Nero was hosting. I'd been trained to mix the cocktails and left to work unsupervised – a mistake Nero came to regret. I acquired a large amount of cyanide from... well, that's a story for another day. When the chef wasn't looking, I shook a generous amount into every sour cocktail I served. All night I circled that room, being as gregarious as I could, trying to get all the men to have as many cocktails as they liked. One man's eyes kept following me. I knew his name was Constantine Dio, but I knew nothing more than this."

"All night I waited for the men to fall down. Constantine told me later that he'd taken one sniff of his drink, smelt the unmistakable aroma of almonds, and understood what I'd done. He handed his drink to a fellow gangster, went to the bar, and ordered me to make him another. He watched me like a hawk the entire time – he had quite the features of a hawk, down to the beaky nose – and I couldn't place the poison inside. One by one, the men at the party convulsed on the floor, and eventually stopped moving altogether, and Constantine cornered me in the kitchen and told me he knew what I'd done."

"I thought that was the end of me. Constantine commanded me to go with him, and I obeyed. I thought he would lead me into some secret room and shoot me, but instead, he led me outside to his car, and we drove away. He took me to his home and gave me a suite of rooms fit for a princess, and let me eat whatever I wanted and watch TV.

"I don't know if he saw something in me that night that spoke to the demon inside him, but he bought me from Nero for an astronomical sum. He did his best to raise me. He trained me. Everything I know, I got from him. He's the closest thing to a father I never had." Her eyes closed. "Even if his blood doesn't run in my veins, I'm proud to carry his name."

"I understand."

"I tried to raise my sons the same way. I tried to show them that they could find their strength in their fists. Gaius... he takes after his father. He doesn't like to get his hands dirty. He prefers to manipulate things behind the scenes. Manipulate people. That's not the way I do things. He takes after his parents in that regard."

Her words spark a memory inside me, a conversation with Victor about Cassius' and Gaius' paternity. "His parents? You mean, you and—"

"I adopted Gaius. He was born to a British duke with a drug empire and a manipulative cow who tried to destroy Claudia. We took care of them both, but when I saw the little babe..." she sighs. "I can be sentimental too, sometimes."

"And Cassius' father?" Cali seemed like she wasn't used to living with a man before she met Dad, and Cas never spoke of his dad, so I wonder...

"He's in prison," Cali says. "He was an assassin I'd trained, one of our best. But he got too big for his boots and started acting as though I should reward his sperm donation with a place in my family. But I knew he wasn't a Dio, in name or action. His lust for power would have consumed him, or I would get sick of his shit and behead him. And I didn't want either of those outcomes, so I made sure he was intercepted on a job and arrested."

"You sent him to prison?"

"It was either that or put a bullet between his eyes." She laughs a little then, and it almost sounds normal. "And he was quite something to look at. I couldn't stand to ruin that much natural beauty. Cassius looks so like him. Don't tell him this, by the way. He believes his father is dead. It's better that way."

I don't know that it is. I think Cas should have had the chance to know where he came from.

Now it's too late.

We stand in silence, listening to the kids laughing and shouting as they work on their drills.

Cali says. "You know, my son has never cared about anyone the way he does about you."

"He's got a funny way of showing it."

"That's because I trained him well," Cali says. "Caring is a weakness that an assassin can ill-afford, but as much as I try to beat the human out of my sons, Cas' big, stupid heart is too easily broken. He believes I favor Gaius over him, and he couldn't be more wrong. Gaius is clever. He can be a politician as well as a thug, but he doesn't care about this family the way Cas does.

"But something in Cas' brain shuts off when he gets the scent of blood. He reminds me of myself before Constantine Dio taught me to temper my brutality with mercy. That's why I need Claudia and Livvie to calm my violent nature, and I couldn't risk handing the Dio empire over to Cassius when he had no one to do that for him. But then he met you."

A cold lump rises in my throat. "And I put him in a coma."

"If anyone can beat death, it's Cassius Dio," she says simply, and I wish I can believe her.

I sniff back the tears that threaten to spill over again. "Cas doesn't need me. He's always had Victor. And Torsten."

That snort again. "Victor August thinks he controls my son, and that's his problem. Cassius cannot be controlled. He must be *wielded* – like a weapon in the hands of a master. Torsten might be the only person he'd listen to, but when that red mist is over his eyes, Cassius will tear his closest friend's throat out. No, they cannot control him. They cannot cage a monster. But you... you are a mirror to him – you are bloodthirsty, but you're also deliberate, calculating, with a staunch sense of justice. You're the puzzle piece that had to slot into place to make me see that Cassius could do what I wanted him to do."

"I'm not sure what you're saying."

"I'm saying..." she breaks off to cough, and I know that the exertion of today is getting to her. "That someone has a hit out on me. It doesn't matter what you told this Zack Lionel Sommesnay about my job; he would have found me anyway. I'm going to die soon, Fergie. He will not stop until I'm dead. When that happens, I want the two of you to take over this family."

I can't speak. I let her words sink through the layers of grief inside me. It's too much to comprehend right now. The cold, evil stepmother who I thought hated me, believes I have what it takes to rule her empire at Cassius' side.

Who knew that the way to my evil stepmother's heart was by beating her son to within an inch of his life?

CASSIUS

I wake to pain.

White, blazing, *otherworldly* pain.

I open my eyes, but all I see is pain. I'm blinded by it...
...*blinded*...

It all comes back to me. Fergie stepping into the ring to fight me. Me lunging at her, ready to tear her throat out, and then somehow, I'm on the ground, spitting out sand and blood, and she won't stop kicking me...

Through the pain, I see it all again – that blaze of hatred burning in her eyes as she watches me from the other side of the ring, a snake coiling itself in preparation to strike. Once more I peer into those shattered emerald orbs and see they're no longer cold and calculating but burning brighter than the brightest star.

"Careful," a soft voice says. It's Galen. "Don't move, or you'll break another bone. And I have my work cut out with you as it is."

"You can't tell me what to do." And just to show him, I swing my arm to slap him across the face. Only trying to move my arm brings a burst of such crippling pain that I squeal like a fucking pig.

Ow. ow ow ow. What the *fuck?*

I still can't fucking see. My head is filled with cotton and shattered emeralds and the scent of raspberries and blood...

"I told you." Galen sounds a little smug. "You have five broken ribs, Cassius. Bite marks on your shoulders that have become infected. Oh, and you just woke up *from a coma*, you idiot. So maybe cool it with the attitude."

As he lists off the injuries, my mind whirs... *Fergie did this.* My blind little stepsister pummeled me in the ring, in front of everyone in the Triumvirate. She put me in a *coma*.

And that's the last thought I have time for before I'm pulled under again.

SOMETIME LATER, I wake up. This time, the pain feels less like being hit by a freight train and more like being whacked repeatedly with a sledgehammer. So I guess that's an improvement.

"Cas. You're awake."

It's Victor.

"Hello," I croak. I crack my eyes open. This time I can see a little – I'm in Galen's clinic, hooked up to all kinds of machines. Vic leans over the bed, his face lined with concern. Torsten hunches over a chair in the corner, furiously sketching. "How do I look? I bet I'm more handsome than you now."

"That's not possible," Vic says with a tiny quirk of his aristocratic mouth.

"No, it's true. Girls love a cripple." I peer down at the casts and bandages that wrap around my body like an Egyptian mummy.

"You're not crippled, Cas. You had a dislocated shoulder, and you've got several broken ribs that will take time to heal. And your brain... there's a bit of swelling. Galen says you might have some problems with memory and impulse control." Vic rolls his eyes. "As if you weren't unhinged enough already."

He says it lovingly, but a jolt of shame courses through me. He's not wrong. I've flown off the rails ever since I first stuck my dick in my new stepsister. Fergie's got into my head like a blood-sucking parasite, and now she's fused to my spine – I can't separate myself from her without killing us both. "Fergie? Is she—"

"She's not here. She's been staying away in case you woke up and decided to kill her—"

"Kill her?" A slow grin spread across my face. "I want to fucking *marry* her."

Victor chokes. "What did you say?"

I wince as I try to move my foot, and blinding pain shoots through my body. "She did this to me. Don't you see? She never lied to me. She me... me she fee..."

I trail off. I'm trying to say something important, but the words aren't there. It's as if there's a huge blank space inside my brain where they're supposed to be.

Victor leans closer. "Cas, are you..."

Suddenly, the words come. "She loves me, Vic. She loves *me* – Cassius Dio. A man so monstrous that not even his own mother loves him. But I'm loved by Fergie Munroe."

"I think you've gone loopy from all the drugs Galen's got you on. Fergie did this because she hates you. She's at the end of her fucking rope, and frankly, so am I. You climbed in her window and tried to stab her in her sleep."

"She knows I didn't mean it. These are not the marks of a woman who hates me." I manage to move my index finger to indicate my ruined body. "Fergie and I are finally speaking the same language. Go and get her. I want to see my girl."

Realization dawns on Victor's face as he finally gets that I'm serious. "Cas, you may feel like this now, but you could change your mind at any time. I can't go through watching the two of you try to destroy each other again. It's destroying *me*. It's destroying Torsten. So you can't make us do this unless we really believe—"

"I fon't ducking care," I snap, aware that I'm messing up my words. "I mean... I mean... she's the only woman for me. Find her. Bring her to me."

"Cas, she's not going to come." But Victor doesn't sound so sure. He knows deep down that I'm right. Fergie did this to me because she needed me to see her. And I finally do, in full 3D fucking vision, blinking red lights. She's mine. She's always been mine.

She's *ours*.

"Bring her." I lie back in the bed and let the drugs pull me under.

I'm so fucking relieved to see Seymour's car pull up to our house and Fergie get out. I run to her as Seymour speeds off with Cali in the backseat.

When I'd gone back to the waiting room after Cas woke up and found Fergie and Cali weren't there, I went into full-blown panic mode. I got in the car and drove around everywhere I could imagine she'd be, looking for her. Torsten was the one sensible enough to call Fergie's mobile. She answered straight away, her voice amused and very much alive. "I'll be home shortly."

And here she is, definitely alive and smiling. Smiling after spending the afternoon with Cali Dio. I hold Fergie at arm's length, inspecting her for injuries. "You still have all your fingers. What about your toes? You're walking a little funny. Did she hobble you?"

Fergie laughs. "No hobbling, although I definitely need a hot shower and some arnica cream. Cali wanted me to fight."

"She... what?"

"She wanted to see me fight. I'm going to be able to train again. She wants me to use her gym as often as I like. I'll be able to do jiujitsu, and I can learn other martial arts, things I might be able to use on the street where competition rules don't apply." Her whole face lights up with the promise of it. "Vic, she wants me to marry Cas. She thinks I might have what it takes to inherit the Dio empire alongside him. Can you believe it?"

Jesus, this is big.

I can see what Cali is thinking. Fergie is the biggest thorn in her side right now, especially after she brought Cassius down in the ring. Cali could either kill her off and risk a power vacuum, or she could take advantage of Fergie's newfound celebrity and bring her into the fold as her successor. It's a smart move, which is why my mother thought of it first.

"I can believe it." I kiss her, long and slow and deep. I need the kiss to steel me for what I have to tell her next. I pull back and suck in a deep breath. "Cassius is awake."

Her whole face squeezes, like she's in pain.

"He wants to see you. Do you want to see him?"

Fergie thinks for a long time. "Yes," she says. "But I need to shower first."

She leaves me to play with Spartacus while she showers. The water runs and runs, and it takes her even longer to blow dry that mane of fiery hair. She emerges wearing skintight black jeans and a black t-shirt with a low V-neck that shows off the crimson bra beneath.

I grin as she does a twirl. "You look incredible, baby."

"That's the idea. Euri made this shirt for me from one that Cas cut up." She kisses me on the cheek. I know she's left an impression of her lipstick, but I don't want to wipe it away. I think it's better if Cassius sees it.

I drive her back to Galen's clinic. She pushes through the curtain surrounding Cas' bed, and he sits up when he sees her. His eyes are wide and his monstrous face breaks into this grin of such utter joy that it makes me tear up a little.

Trust Cas to need Fergie to beat him nearly to death and give him permanent brain damage to make him realize that he loves her.

"Hello, Cas," she says, sweeping her fiery hair over her shoulder.

Cas' breath hitches. His eyes grow even wider. It's almost comical. He looks like a puppy who's just seen his favorite bone.

"Fergie." His voice cracks as he struggles to find the words. "You..."

"Yes?"

"You look so fuckable right now."

She laughs – a harsh, barking laugh that sets my teeth on edge. I wonder if this was a good idea. "I had your handprint on my ass for *days*."

Cas' whole face lights up. He looks so dopey, it's almost adorable. "You're lucky I'm still attached to these machines, or I'd have you bent over this bed right now. I see you're wearing one of my creations."

I follow his gaze to Fergie's outfit, noticing for the first time that the black tank top she's wearing over a sparkly crimson bra is slashed to ribbons, and that her black jeans have tattered tears down the front of the legs – they're basically held together by threads.

She looks smoking, but I realize that the last few times I've seen her, most of her clothes have been cut and slashed. Did Cassius do that?

"As much as I appreciated you giving me a whole new wardrobe," she shoots back, "I don't think you should quit your day job."

Cas waves his hand in what I can only assume is supposed to be an impression of Tyra Banks, "Make it work, girl."

Fergie's cane rolls over the floor as she walks around the bed. I pull out a plastic chair for her, and she sits down. Cas reaches an arm out to her, but she's not close enough for him to touch, and she makes no move to get closer.

Cas lets his arm drop, his face falling.

"I could have killed you," she whispers. "I wanted to kill you. Do you understand why?"

"Yes," he says. "Because I hurt you. I'm sorry."

The *fuck?*

I have never, *ever* heard those words come out of Cas' mouth before. Not even after the fire, when Gemma told him that what he did drove her to jump. Cassius Dio never has the depth of character to look at his actions and see that he might've been wrong.

I study his face, wondering if it's some manipulation. But it's not. Cas can do many things, but he can't hide behind a mask the way other people can, especially not after he's suffered brain damage.

And he's not hiding now.

His eyes darken, and he truly, with his whole heart, means those words.

Wow. Fergie has changed him. She truly has changed all of us.

She lifts a hand to her ear. "Pardon? I didn't quite catch that."

"I'm sorry," he growls. "I'll say it a thousand times. A million times, if that will make you believe it. When I saw that fake name, I thought... I thought that you'd played me, and you're the first person apart from those two who I've ever been truly myself with, and I thought that you'd made me into a fool. You're the first person who made me believe that I was worth something, that I could be loved, and I wanted to believe it so badly that when I thought it was a lie, I had to become what I already believed I was – the monster who no one can ever love. I said I did it to protect my family, but I think I did it to protect..."

"...your heart?" she finishes.

"That's it. I tried to protect my heart."

"Yes, well." Fergie flips her hair again. He groans and cups his hands over his crotch. "You're not the only one who lashes out when they feel threatened."

"And I've got the blue skin to show it." He pats a blue-stained cheek. "Seriously, though, it's been fun sparring with you, little sis. You're a crafty minx, I'll give you that. But I have to declare defeat. You won. I would physically bow at your feet but Galen's got me hooked up to all this nonsense, so..." he waves around his arm with the IV, and the machines beep in protest.

"So..." she leans a fraction closer.

"I love you, Fergie. I know I'm a monster, but I'm *your* fucking monster. And if you can ever see your way to forgiving me, I will spend every day of my life making you see that you can trust me."

I watch Fergie's face as his words sink in. There's a battle raging behind her eyes. She *wants* to forgive him. She wants so badly to go back to what we had the night of Saturnalia, to be the Poison Ivy Club again – the four of us against the world.

But the club is gone, and we can't go back.

Cassius can't get that video off the internet, and he can't take the knife out of her heart.

Fergie stands up. Her shoulders square, letting her hair cascade down her back in a crimson waterfall. She grips her cane so hard that her knuckles glow white.

She is both terrifying and beautiful.

"I love you, Cassius Dio," she says. "I loved you and I love you still. But you broke my trust, and it's going to take more than words to repair that. I love you, but I can't do this right now."

And she turns on her heel and walks away.

64

CASSIUS

She left.

She fucking *left*.

Victor looks at me with this expression of great unease. He's waiting for me to lose my shit, for the red mist to descend and drag me over the edge. And it's there, pinching at the edges of my eyes, willing me to go apeshit and burn the hospital down.

But that's not going to repair the hurt in Fergie's voice.

She left.

She left because I was a fool to expect that words could repair the damage I did to her. To us.

I believed that saying sorry was enough. I've never said those words before in my life, despite all the times when I probably should have.

She said she loves me.

I cling to those words with everything I have, willing Fergie's love to keep me from giving over to the red mist. I don't even care if I never get her back. Hell, I don't fucking deserve her.

But I *want* to fall at her feet and worship her. I want to make sure that for the rest of her life she never, ever has to question Cassius Dio's loyalty.

I'm no longer just a monster. I'm a phoenix, reborn from the ashes of her love.

I'm *her* fucking monster.

There are plenty of people out there who've wronged my Fergie. Every kid at school who has watched that video or shared it, for a start. I'll pile up the bodies at her feet. I'll give her blood enough that she can bathe in the stuff, like Countess Bathory.

I'll show her how Cassius Dio worships his Queen.

I start pulling the wires out of my arm. The machines go crazy, beeping and buzzing with annoyance. My head swims, but I don't have time to think about that now. I have vengeance to seek, blood to spill in the name of my Queen.

Victor tries to shove me back down. "You probably shouldn't do that—"

"I don't care," I growl as I kick a monitor across the room. It hits the wall and smashes, delicate medical instruments scattering in all directions. I reach for the IV in my arm—

"CASSIUS, STOP."

I freeze.

I freeze because something has just happened that's never happened before.

Torsten's on his feet, facing me, his face red with rage.

He yelled at me.

He told me to stop.

"This isn't how you get her back," he says, his hand flapping at his side. "If you walk out there now and fall over and *die*, you will break her heart. Is that what you want?"

You break everything you love.

I slump onto the bed. "I don't know how to do anything else."

"Yes, you do." Vic sits backward on the plastic chair. His dark eyes search my face. "The kitten."

"That was..." but I can't explain. I can't articulate what went through my head when I held Spartacus in my hands and realized how much I wanted to protect him. "That was a temporary bout of insanity."

"No, it wasn't. Do you want to get Fergie back?" Victor leans forward, as if after all the shit I've put him through, he still cares about the answer.

"More than anything I've ever wanted. But it doesn't matter what I want." My shoulders slump. "You heard her. She can't... what's the word? She can't... forgive me. And I don't blame her—"

Victor's eyes dance. "I think she might forgive you if you grovel enough. If you show her who you truly are."

"And how the fuck do I do that, Dr. Phil?" I snap.

Victor grins, and something of the devious Poison Ivy leader lights up his eyes. "I think I know exactly how."

65

FERGIE

C as spends another week under Galen's careful watch. Victor tells me that he pulled all the life-sustaining machines out of his arms, which is such typical Cas.

The brain scans confirm he has some damage. He'll have trouble with short-term memory for the rest of his life, and it will impact his speech. Whenever I think of it, guilt stabs in my gut.

I don't go back to see him. I know if I do, I'll take another look at his face and I'll relent. I'll break down and I'll forgive him. And I'm not ready.

What he did to me was fucking awful. I can't walk down the hallways at Stonehurst Prep without thinking that everyone I pass has seen me naked, tied into a sex swing, taking three guys at once. It haunts my fucking dreams and it will never ever be gone from the internet.

And what I've done to him is just as bad. I've hurt him so bad that his brain will never recover. We can't go back to what we had on Saturnalia, but...

...but maybe there will be a way forward. In time.

For now, I focus on my classes. I have my Harvard acceptance, my ticket far away from this nightmare, so I don't even give a shit about high school anymore, but I still need to keep my grades up and graduate.

Plus, throwing myself into schoolwork gives me something to think about other than the trouble swirling around me like moths at a flame.

I'm still working for Claudia. Livvie wants me to marry Torsten, and my evil queen stepmother, Cali Dio, has told me that she wants me to be her successor. I've gone from being completely in the dark about the nefarious deeds of the Triumvirate to being the next in line to be one of its Queens, and I have to sort out how I feel about that. Right now, I feel like running as fast as I fucking can to the other side of the country.

I call Euri and spill everything. She seems to have forgiven me for pulling the article. Her applications are probably strong enough without it, anyway. When she hears that I'm considering Cali's offer, she goes berserk. "You can't be serious, Fergie. You're talking about marrying Cassius and training to be an *assassin* so you can take over a crime family? I mean, what about college? What about being a lawyer? I thought you wanted to make people's lives better, not *take* people's lives."

Euri has a point. But as I think about everything I know about Victor, Torsten, and Cassius and their mothers, I start to see that the world isn't as black and white as Euri believes. The three current Queens have their own agendas, their own moral compass, and I have to admit that on some points I agree with them.

Maybe teachers who sexually assault their students should be fed to lions.

Maybe the profits of crime can be used to tip the balance of power.

Maybe people who can't solve their problems with words can lay them to rest in the arena.

Maybe monsters like me deserve to love, and to be loved.

I'M SITTING ALONE in the greenhouse, reading over my history quiz notes on my Braille note, when someone plops down across from me.

"I heard that Cali got shot," Drusilla says. "And that you put Cassius in hospital."

My head jerks up. "How do you know?"

I realize too late that my words have simply confirmed her questions, and I curse myself for being so stupid. I have a lot to learn about being part of the criminal underworld.

"Zack told me," she says.

"So Zack has ears inside the Triumvirate?" I ask as casually as I can.

"Of course."

"Who? I might be able to slip them some information."

"If you have information you want to share, come directly to me. I don't know who he has on the inside. He won't tell me."

"It doesn't sound like he trusts you." I'm taking a risk here, I know. Dru and I have been allies, but when she finds out what I'm doing within the Triumvirate, and what I intend to do to Zack if I ever see him again, she's not going to be happy with me.

"He shares what I need to know," she says. "My beef is with the Poison Ivy boys, and Cassius in particular. As far as I'm concerned, thanks to you, they've learned their lesson. His beef is with Claudia August."

"It is?"

"Oh, yeah. But I don't know why, beyond what he told you about the Triumvirate killing his mother. But I think everything he's doing is to take her down."

He's after Claudia.

That's something we didn't already know, and it might explain why he chose to blow up the museum and send that parcel bomb to Victor. He's trying to destroy the things she cares about most. This isn't about power – it's *personal*.

This means Zack Lionel Sommesnay is far more dangerous than I gave him credit for.

But I can't say that to Dru, so I just say, "He should get in line."

"Mmmm." Drusilla reaches across and breaks off half my carob cake. "Enough about Zack. Tell me all about how you beat Cassius into a bloody pulp. And spare no details."

66

CASSIUS

It takes Torsten all of ten minutes to track the guy down. The bastard hasn't even moved away. He's still at the same address he's lived all his life, still ruling over the school like he doesn't have a care in the world.

As soon as Galen clears me to leave the clinic, we make our plans. My mother still hasn't said I can come home, and I'm not willing to put Fergie through any trauma by moving back there, anyway, so I go back to living in the basement of the old horticulture building, with Fergie's crimson panties tucked under my pillow. Torsten still won't talk to me, but Victor brings me bags of Milo's food.

I feel completely the same as I always have, except that when my heart beats now, it beats for Fergie, and when I open my mouth to speak, sometimes the right words won't come. But we have a plan, and the plan makes me feel hope for the first time in a long time.

When everything is in place, Torsten and I set off first thing in the morning.

The drive from California to Massachusetts is at least forty-five hours, which let me tell you is a long fucking time to be in the car with a guy who refuses to talk to you. I have Fergie's playlist on my phone from when she shared it with me, back when we used to talk, and I blast that all the way, letting heavy metal bleed out of my ears until I can't hear Torsten screaming at me through his silence.

Finally, I can't fucking take it. I pull over on the side of an empty highway and drag Torsten from the car. It's close to midnight and pitch fucking black.

"Punch me," I say.

He glares at me.

"You're mad at me because I furt Hergie. I mean, because I hurt Fergie. I get it. I'm fucking mad at myself. So I want you to punch me."

He looks down at his hand, and then at me. "Why would I do that?"

I sigh. I can't believe I have to explain this. "Because it might make you feel better. Because it—"

WHAM.

His fist connects with my nose.

Something goes crunch. My face explodes with pain, but I don't cry out. I swallow that pain down inside me, because it's what I need to live.

Torsten stares down at his hand. His knuckles are bleeding. He looks up at me and beams that rare Torsten smile.

"Thanks. You were right. I do feel better."

If he was Victor, I'd hug him. But he's Torsten, so I get back in the car, and he follows. We drive on into the night. Blood drips from my nose onto my shirt, but I don't bother to wipe it away. It feels special – a gift from my oldest friend.

We're still silent, but the silence is different. I won't be so arrogant to assume that everything's now fine between us, but it's definitely a lot better.

In the middle of Bumfuck Nowhere, I pull over at a rest stop and we catch a few hours of fitful sleep. I dream of wrapping my fist in Fergie's crimson hair as I bury myself inside her. I dream of her crimson lips around my cock. I dream of her raking her nails down my back as I drive her to orgasm, and her screaming that she forgives me.

After a breakfast of greasy diner food, we hit the road again. Victor calls to say he's at the airport with our cargo. One of us needed to stay behind to watch over Fergie, and we couldn't all get on a flight because Torsten doesn't do well with airports or planes or baggage carousels. Plus, Victor needed time to put the final pieces of our plan in place.

A few hours later, we roll into Witchwood Falls, the birthplace of Fergie Macintosh.

Victor's waiting for us, a neat silver suitcase next to him, his suit looking perfectly pressed. "I hate planes," he grumbles, smoothing down the front of his suit. "Hours cramped in those seats is absolute *hell* on my Armani."

"I punched Cassius," Torsten pipes up, a big smile on his face.

"Good. I bet he deserved it. Can you punch him again so he'll buy me a new suit—"

"There's only one fashion accessory I need," I growl. Victor sighs, but he digs around in his bag and pulls out the Harvard sweatshirt he bought online.

It's so small that when I pull it over my head and tug it over the strapping around my ribs, the shoulder seams tear. "Relax, I brought a backup." He wraps a crimson striped scarf around my neck, hiding the torn seams. "Let's go."

We sit outside the gates of Witchwood Falls High, watching kids arriving and meeting their friends on the steps. I try to imagine Fergie at this school, to remember that here she was an outcast, an honor roll student with perfect attendance, and not the Queen she was always born to be. This place didn't deserve her.

"There he is," Victor says.

I turn to where he's pointing. It's *him,* all right. Dawson Hayward, Fergie's ex-boyfriend. The guy who ruined her life by posting a sex tape of the two of them, who drove her into my arms, who made her into the monster that stole my heart.

He will make a perfect gift, all wrapped up in a pretty bow for my stepsister.

An atonement.

I can't take back the video I put out there, but I can make sure that the first guy who wronged her learns the lesson I've learned.

Dawson's standing around with a big group – lots of guys in letter jackets, a couple of girls in cheerleader skirts. Their school doesn't have a uniform, and I can tell by their clothing and demeanor that this is the popular crowd. And right now they're all entranced by this douchebag and his friend as they mime some viral dance moves.

I cannot *imagine* what Fergie saw in this guy.

I get out of the car and stalk toward him. "Hey, Dawson Hayward."

He looks up at me. His arm is around a pretty blonde freshman, his hand oh-so-casually brushing her breast. I've a mind to snap it off, but I need him to come with us. He tilts his head to the side and frowns at me.

"Look, it's the Blue Man Group," Dawson's friend sniggers. I fix him with a look that implies just how quickly I can snap him in half, and his laughter cuts off as he stares at his shoes.

"Do I know you?" Dawson asks.

"Not sure." I flash him a smile that has a couple of his friends backing away from me. "I'm Craig Dillion from Harvard recruitment. I saw you play the other week, and I want to talk to you about opportunities. Want to grab some coffee?"

I can't even remember what fucking sport Fergie says he played. But it doesn't matter, because at the mention of Harvard, the guy's big, stupid face lights up. He slides his arm from around the girl and steps toward me, his chest puffing out. "Sure. There's a place I know around the corner."

"Dawson, you have class," the blonde tugs on his jacket.

"This is important, baby." He pushes her away. "Sure. You want to follow me?"

"Nah." I point to the car – my Rolls Royce Phantom. Dawson looks like he's going to shit his pants with excitement. "I'll drive us. You just tell me where to go."

WE GET takeout coffee from a little kiosk and drive to a secluded spot on the edge of a park. Dawson sips away happily while he talks about some of the best games of the season, and ten minutes later, just when I'm about ready to pound his face in out of boredom, he's sound asleep. The sedative Victor made from the plants in his greenhouse has worked perfectly.

"Good," Victor purrs as he slides Dawson's drooling face off his shoulder. "I was getting sick of hearing that fucker talk."

Anyone can stop at the park and see us, so we shove Dawson into the car and drive into the woods. We pull over at the Witchwood Falls trailhead, drag Dawson's body out of the car, bind his wrists and ankles, and stuff him into the Phantom's trunk.

At least Victor and I can take turns driving, although Victor drives like a grandpa and he insists on stopping every three hours to do ridiculous calisthenics stretches.

"You look like a... a twirly music box person," I grumble as I stock up on chocolate snacks. I can't remember the word I want.

"A ballet dancer?" Victor guesses as he points his toes in my face.

"Yes. That's the one." I duck under his leg and steal the driver's seat. At least Galen says I'm still allowed to drive.

Dawson wakes up somewhere around Chicago, but I crank the stereo to drown out his thuds and screams.

By the time we drive back into Emerald Beach, I think my body is now made entirely of truck stop hot dogs and Cheetos. Victor drops me off in front of my house and slides into the driver's seat. "Are you sure you don't want me or Torsten to go up and get her?"

"No." I'm adamant that it has to be me. Fergie must know that this is my idea. If I can't get her to come with me, then I'll have to face the fact that it really is over for us. But she's *going* to come with me. "I'll make her come."

Victor winces. "That's what I'm afraid of."

I laugh. "We'll be there. You'll see."

Fergie Munroe can't resist Poison Ivy shenanigans.

Victor pulls away, and I head for the door. The security guards still guard every corner of the house, but my mother must've softened toward me because although they glare at me, they don't stop me as I march through. My memory of the night is mostly blank, but I think I might've killed one of their buddies. But ever since the accident, I've been put back on the, um, security okay list (what's the word? I can't remember the word...), so they have to let me through. Seymour pulls the front door open before I can ring the bell. The security must've warned him I was showing up.

"What are you doing here?" he sounds wary.

"I want to get my sister," I growl.

"I'll ask her if she wants to see you—"

I shove him out of the way and storm inside, just as my

mother hobbles in from the living room on a pair of crutches. The sight of her makes my breath stick in my throat.

I've never, ever seen her so... *weak* before. It doesn't suit her.

"What are you doing here?" She doesn't sound pissed to see me, just surprised.

John comes up and stands beside Cali, one hand resting protectively on her arm.

"I'm here to make things right with Fergie," I say, aware that my words slur a little, but I can't help that.

"You're not going anywhere near her." John moves to the base of the stairs, spreading his arms wide as if those little matchstick limbs could stop me from getting past.

Thanks for confirming that she's upstairs in her room. John has a lot to learn about covert ops.

Cali's eyes fix on mine, and a silent war plays out between us. We're too alike, but if she can find love with a fucking dentist, then surely she can see I need the chance to fix things with my stepsister—

Cali shuffles back and nods at me.

"Let him go," she says to John. "Fergie can fight her own battles."

She certainly can.

After twelve days in a coma, followed by weeks of recovery and four days on the road cramped in a seat in the Phantom, my body is pretty close to utter collapse. I hope my mother can't see how my legs tremble as I start to climb the stairs. I'm not sure I can even make it all the way up that staircase, but if Fergie's there, I'll crawl over hot coals to get to her.

John steps out of my way, although he looks absolutely murderous. If someone could drive a mild-mannered dentist to embrace Cali's lifestyle choices, it would be me.

"Thanks, stepdad," I smirk at him as I waltz past. John shoots out a gangly arm to grab me, but Cali holds him back. She knows who'll win that fight.

I beam down at him as I shuffle up the stairs. I like this new John. We both want the same thing – for Fergie to be happy. The only difference is that I know she can be happy with me.

I reach the top of the staircase and make my way down the hallway toward my stepsister's room. Satyricon's 'Dark Medieval Times' album blasts through the wall – she must be in a *mood*.

There's a shiny new lock on the door, but one swift kick from me and that lock is history. Fergie screams as I barge inside. She leaps up from her bed, and she's wearing only her crimson underwear with her earbuds in. A box of tissues is beside her, most of it gone. Spartacus is batting the used ones around the floor, tearing them with his claws to make tiny tissue snowflakes.

"Put some clothes on and stop crying over me, Sunflower," I say, with more bravado than I really feel. "You're coming with me."

"What the fuck are you doing here?" She plants both her hands on my chest and tries to shove me out the door. "I told you that I needed time. Stay away from me."

I pick her up and throw her over my shoulder.

"Put me down," she screams, twisting in my arms. I smack her ass playfully as I start carrying her.

"I know you haven't forgiven me," I say as I wrap my hand around her ass cheek. I step into the room and rummage one-handed through the pile of clothes on her floor, hunting for something she'd like to wear. "And I'm not here to ask for your forgiveness. I'm here because I have a present for you."

"Funny sort of present that involves kidnapping someone." Fergie pounds at the back with her tiny, adorable fists. I can't help but notice that she's relaxed a little in my arms. She might not have forgiven me, but she trusts me. Sort of.

"You love it. Maybe I'll fuck you over the hood of the Tesla before we go. Now, are you going to be a good girl and put some clothes on, or am I going to carry you downstairs like this so your dad can see what his good little girl likes to wear when she's all alone? We could shove that vibrator you're hiding inside you, make a real show for him."

"I hate you so fucking much," Fergie grumbles, but she's not screaming anymore. I flip her back on the bed and rummage in her closet for a t-shirt, hoodie, and those skintight leather pants of hers.

She grabs the outfit from my hands and fixes me with a glare so icy it could freeze Mars. How can a blind girl have a glare that evil? It's not fucking right.

Fergie pulls on the outfit I picked out. "Fine." She faces me with her hands on her hips. "I've changed now. So what's this surprise—"

Her words dissolve into a shriek as I throw her over my shoulder again. My whole body burns from the exertion, but I like holding her, touching her, feeling her squirm. I carry her downstairs, past Cali and Dad and Seymour and Milo, who all yell at me. I head out to the garage and dump her into the back-seat of the Tesla. Before she has a chance to escape, I leap into the front and speed out of there.

"Okay, I'm in the car. Where are you taking me?" she grumbles.

"It's a surprise."

"I don't like surprises, especially not from you. I want to know what's going on."

"What's going on is that I want to give you a gift. Maybe I want to give you something to say that..." it takes me a few moments to find the words. "That I was wrong."

"You know, most men get down on their knees and grovel."

"I'll do that if you want me to," I growl. "I'll do anything you ask, Sunflower. But right now I'm asking you to trust me."

"You have given me absolutely no reason to trust you."

"It's not just me. Victor and Torsten are in on this, too, and you trust them. We wanted to give you a present. Don't you want your present?"

"I *do* like presents." Fergie brightens. "Hey, are you taking me to see Clarence again? Because we should stop and get him a treat."

"No Clarence this time. He ate something rotten a couple of weeks back and has a bit of a stomach bug. But you're going to like this even better."

I park and lead her between wrecked railway carriages and piles of rotting sleepers, and through the gates to the old round-house. "Do you know where we are?"

She sniffs. "We're at Colosseum. I can tell because it smells like blood and debauchery."

Fergie grips my arm a little tighter as I lead her over the sloped area where the crowd would normally gather, right down to the very edge of the arena. I know she's thinking about what went down here only a few weeks ago, how she beat me – a six-foot-four fighter with rage in my veins – until I nearly died.

I'm thinking about it too, and my dick's already as hard as a fucking rod.

"We've executed many enemies in this ring," I say. "Before my mother's time, the Triumvirate would feed prisoners to wild animals in front of the crowds. Our mothers outlawed this practice. Claudia couldn't deal with the cruelty of forcing animals to dance for our amusement."

Fergie turns to me, a beautiful eyebrow cocked. "What about Coach Franklin?"

I shrug. "Clarence is a practicality. Bodies need to be disposed of, and besides, he loves his special treats. Except when he gets a tummy ache. Torsten and Victor are inside the ring, and they have your gift with them. Do you want to step inside and find out what it is?"

"This is a trick, right? You're going to lure me back into the ring and then you'll kill me..."

"I wouldn't fucking dare."

"He's telling the truth, Duchess," Victor calls out.

Fergie's face twists. "Torsten?" she asks.

"I'm here," he says.

"I need you to tell me the truth about what I'm stepping into."

"Cassius isn't lying. We have a present for you."

Fergie squeezes my hand. "Fine. Let's go."

A grin spreads across my face. "Excellent answer. Right this way, my Queen."

I lead her through the concrete backstage area and through the heavy wooden doors into the ring. The tip of her cane and her heavy boots kick up crescents of dust as we make our way over to where Torsten and Victor are standing.

"Wake him up," I say.

Torsten picks up a bucket of water and tips it over Dawson's head. The little shitstain mumbles and stirs, but he's still pretty out of it. That won't do at all. He needs to be fully awake for this – that's fair. After all, Fergie had to live through what he did to her.

What *I* did to her.

I bend over him and slap his face, pull his hair, pinch his cheeks. It's only when I jab a thumb into his eye that he jerks awake.

"Ow, what the fuck? Where am I?" he gazes all around, his eyes bright with fear. Then they land on my stepsister. "F-F-Fergie?"

"Dawson?"

Fergie's nails dig into my arm.

"Surprise," I say.

"Cassius, why... why would you bring him here?" Fergie's whole body shudders. "I never want to see him again. I can't... I don't..."

She turns away, staggering a few steps with her cane before her knees give out and she collapses to the ground.

Torsten is the first to run to her. He touches her elbow, and I think it's a code the two of them have worked out, because she squeezes his hand and he plants a kiss on her head.

Red welts dot my vision, but they're not from rage this time, but terror. I got it so wrong with Gemma – have I done that again? Am I so fucked in the head from the fight that I don't know my girl any longer? "Sunflower, I'm sorry. I thought you'd like this."

"I..." she grits her teeth as her whole body trembles. "I don't... I can't..."

"She's having a trauma reaction," Victor says. "Remember when Coach Franklin attacked her? Seeing Dawson again has brought that all back."

"Thanks for that diagnosis, Dr. Phil," I snap. "What I want to know is what will snap her out of it. Because she's not going to enjoy torturing him if she can't—"

Fergie's head snaps up, her eyes focused on me. "What did you say?"

I grab her shoulders and hold on, hold on so tight because I never want to let her go again. "He's your gift. I didn't do this to hurt you, Sunflower. I saw how much fun you had getting your revenge on me, and I wanted you to be able to do the same to him. I thought you'd love it. It's okay, we'll hide him away and kill him in private, and Torsten will take you out for ice cream or whatever the fuck you need to make you our Fergie again."

"No." She uses my shoulders to push herself to her feet. Her face is a little pale, her cheeks splotchy, and she's a little unsteady on her feet. She doesn't let go of me as she tilts her head up and regards me with those unseeing, defiant eyes. "No. I want this. You're right, Cassius. You know me better than I know myself sometimes. It hurts to see him again, but not as much as I'm going to make him hurt. This is going to be fun."

"Fergie?" Dawson chooses that moment to plead. "Babe, I don't know what these guys have told you, but they kidnapped me from school. They stuffed me in the trunk of their car and beat me up, and you need to call the police, like *right now*."

"Is that what I need to do, Dawson?" she asks him, her voice honey-sweet. She turns back to me, and those emerald eyes are no longer filled with pain. Instead, they're bright and clear and mischievous. "I agree with doing this here," she says to me. "I wouldn't want him to make Clarence sick from the taste of his bullshit. But Cas, what about Dawson's family? His dad is a big-deal pastor with a lot of political connections. They'll come looking for him and—"

"This right here, Sunflower, is officially sanctioned by the Triumvirate. Cali can arrange things so that any authorities looking into Dawson's death will run up against a dead end, so you don't have to fear this biting you in the ass."

"Gods bless my stepmother." Fergie rubs her hands together with glee. "What's first?"

"First, you choose your means of execution. We have a variety of devices placed here in the arena for your pleasure. We can lock him inside an Iron Maiden filled with spikes. We could impale him, à la Vlad Tepes, or stretch him on a rack until his big football shoulders pop out of their sockets..."

"I like the sound of the Iron Maiden," she says. "Very metal."

"An excellent choice. We also have the strappado, where we

tie his hands behind his back, hoist him up on a rope, and then drop him repeatedly. Or there's the Catherine Wheel – that one's rather messy. Or we can throw him in a bag with a monkey and a poisonous snake and toss him into the Tartarus River..."

"*Or* we could opt for my mother's favorite Ancient Roman method," Victor adds. "Crucifixion."

"It *is* a classic," I agree.

"Dawson always wanted to be such a good Christian," Fergie says, her lip curling back into a beautiful sneer. "And he certainly does think he's God's gift to women. I vote crucifixion. But I want to hammer the nails in myself."

"Fergie, you're kidding, right? This is all a joke?" Dawson glances around at us, his eyes wide with fear. "This is all because of that video, right? Okay, so you've had your fun, and I'm pretty scared. I think you got me back, so if you could let me go now, I promise I won't press charges. We can just pretend this never happened."

"You won't press charges?" I get right up in his face. *Who does this guy think he is?* "You're the one who put a video of a girl on the internet without her consent. You took advantage of our Fergie and got away with it, and now you're telling us that *you* won't press charges?"

With every word I say, I'm getting angrier and angrier. At him. And at myself. I can't believe I did that to Fergie, that I made myself just like this scumbag. All I can hope as the red mist descends is that by giving her this gift, I can go some way toward healing the hurt that I did.

I'll spend every day for the rest of my life making sure Fergie knows she is the Queen and I don't deserve to kiss her feet.

As I gaze down at this scumbag, I see that he has no such regrets. All he's thinking about is saving his own skin.

"Look, buddy," he babbles. "None of us have to get in trouble over this. If it's money you want, I can pay you. My parents have money. I just want to—"

His words dissolve into screams as I sink my teeth into his nose.

67

CASSIUS

Blood spurts in my mouth. I gulp down the bitter tang of it. It tastes fucking *delicious*. Dawson wails like a baby and thrashes about, which only makes my teeth tear deeper into his flesh.

I crunch down and jerk back, spitting a gob of skin and blood and gristle onto the ground.

Dawson is howling now, no longer trying to bargain his way out of this. I watch with glee as raw horror enters his eyes. I've seen this look on many of my victims before – the grim realization that their lives are about to be over in the most painful way imaginable.

Fergie touches my arm. "Let me taste," she whispers.

Whatever my Queen demands.

I bend down and kiss her. Her hot tongue plunges into my mouth, licking and sucking the blood of her old boyfriend like a vampire in heat. I yank her against me and devour her, plunging my tongue deep and tasting that sweet mouth that's been denied to me for so long.

Bending down still hurts my ribs, but I'm used to pain. It's all these other feelings that are new to me.

I kiss my girl with everything I have – with all the fire and fury of my hatred for myself, with all my promises and apologies and broken wishes. Her arms wrap around my neck, pulling me closer as she takes everything I give her and begs for more.

My heart hammers against my chest as her hot lips light a trail of fire through my veins that ends at my dick. Her tongue explores every surface, lapping the scumbag's life from me. She mews in my arms like a little kitten, and it's so fucking hot I almost come in my pants right there.

But there will be plenty of time for that.

We have all night.

Fergie's tongue slides over my teeth, licking up every last drop of blood. She leans back, wiping the edge of her mouth where a little has smeared, and smiles up at me with the happiest smile. I just want to give her the world. I want to lay at her feet every person who's ever wronged her, and watch her stave in their skulls with her stiletto heels.

"Fergie, do you want to see the cross before we string him up?" Victor calls out.

"Hell yes." She pulls away from me and darts toward Victor, her cane kicking up dust. He plants his foot on the brake, securing the portable cross on its heavy skids in the center of the arena, right underneath one of the spotlights, so that Fergie might be able to make out the silhouette of her ex slowly dying. Vic guides her hands onto the wood, letting her stroke every surface of the cross. It's about eight feet high and bears nail holes from several previous victims. Our mothers went through quite the purge during the bloody early years of their reign.

"This feels *amazing*," Fergie purrs. She moves to Vic and wraps her hand around the back of his neck, pulling him in for a kiss. Her body melts into him, but I can tell that she's focused on me, her body tensing as she listens to my reaction. She's testing me, assessing what I do when I see her with Vic. She cups her hand around his crotch, and he moans into her mouth.

"I see this cross isn't the only thing around here that's erect," she murmurs.

For the first time since the three of us started this thing with her, I feel nothing but happiness. All I want to do is see my Queen smile, and if grinding up on Vic makes her happy, then I'm all for it.

Vic's the one who breaks the kiss. "As much as I want to continue this," he growls, stroking his thumb across her cheek, "we need to get this boy up on that cross. He's lost a lot of blood from Cas' bite, and I don't want him to pass out just yet."

Dawson is too weak after his ordeal to put up much of a fight as we untie him and drag him to the cross. Victor and Torsten hold him up while I tie his arms to the horizontal beam. That makes it easier for us to do what comes next. Dawson kicks wildly, and one of his kicks grazes Fergie's leg.

"Tsk, tsk," I click my tongue. "That's not going to do."

With a swift kick, I break both his kneecaps. Problem solved. He hangs like a wet fish, moaning in agony. It's delightful.

I grip Dawson's wrist, holding his hand tight against the wood with one hand. With the other, I hold the large nail in place, right in the center of his wrist. Victor hands Fergie the hammer – it's a big ceremonial thing, like a mallet.

Victor moves Fergie's arm in a graceful arc, showing her exactly where the nail is and how to swing to drive it home.

"Do mind Cas' fingers," Victor says with a grin. "I wouldn't want you to hit him and destroy this good mood he's in."

"She can hit me as many times as she likes if it makes her feel good," I declare.

"Careful, brother." Fergie points the hammer at me. "I might take you up on that."

"You can't do this," Dawson begs. "This is a joke, right? Fergie, you know this isn't—aarrrggh!"

His words give way to wails as Fergie swings. She lands the hit perfectly, driving the point of the nail into his skin. A line of blood trickles from the hole, and I keep his hand pinned and the nail steady, because it hasn't bitten into the wood yet and Dawson's suddenly got a little uppity.

Fergie pulls her arm back for another swing, but this time, she misses by a good few inches, slamming the mallet into Dawson's elbow and, judging by the crunch and his whimpers, shattering the bone.

"Oops," Fergie giggles. "Sorry about that, Dawson. I'm *so* blind."

She steps back and raises her arm to swing again. She's so beautiful. Her hair flies behind her, whipping around her body every time she brings the mallet down. She whacks my fingers twice, but the pain is beautiful because it comes from her.

By the time she drives the first nail in, she's splattered with blood. Dawson has passed out from the pain. I throw a bucket of cold water over him to wake him up again, and we start with the next wrist. Fergie hammers that one in, too, but she lets me do his feet. I take my time, making sure to inflict the maximum pain possible on Dawson's delicate foot bones.

Fergie steps back, her arm resting on Torsten's as she admires our handiwork. "I can see the outline of the cross in the light," she says. "And I can smell it. The blood. His fear. It's beautiful. How long will it take him to die?"

"Please, Fergggggiiieeeeee..." Dawson moans.

"It really depends," I say. "I've had a few last as long as twenty-four hours. Right now, Dawson's legs can't support him, so his weight has transferred to his arms. This will eventually drag his shoulders from their sockets, and then the elbows, and then the wrists, and then all his weight will be on his chest, making it rather difficult for him to breathe. He might die from suffocation, blood loss, organ failure, or a heart attack from the pain. Or we could be merciful and put him out of his misery with a bullet right now."

Fergie pretends to think it over. "Hmmmm, no, I'm not into mercy. We'll just have to wait. However will we pass the time?" She turns to me, a wicked grin spreading across her lips.

"I can think of a few ways."

I sweep her into my arms and *consume* her. I've needed to taste her for so long. Even in the kitchen, when we fucked on the counter, I didn't kiss her. Not like *this*. I didn't kiss her because I didn't deserve to, but maybe here, tonight, drenched in the blood of her enemy, I can begin to claw my way back into her heart.

Behind us, Dawson cries, blood from his nose wound gurgling in his mouth.

"You." I let go of Fergie to cup his cheek in my hand, digging my thumb into the wound on his nose. "You had this beautiful woman, and not only did you not give her the millions of orgasms that she deserved, but you had the audacity to toss her away. I want the last thing you see on this earth to be how you should have treated this woman, this Queen."

I turn back to Fergie. From the backstage area, Victor carries a gilded, velvet-cushioned, high-backed chair – a throne the Imperators sometimes use when they want to make declarations from the arena. This one is my mother's throne, because the cushion is blood red. There are matching thrones, with ice-blue and emerald green cushions, for Claudia and Livvie.

But we only need one.

Victor positions the throne in front of the cross, so Dawson has a perfect view. We wouldn't want him to miss a thing. Torsten helps Fergie into the throne. She looks perfect there, her red-painted nails tap-tap-tapping on the arms, her legs crossed elegantly at the thigh, those leather pants of hers hugging her figure perfectly.

I kneel in front of her. The hard dirt floor of the arena feels so good beneath me. I am where I'm supposed to be.

I peer up into those fathomless emerald eyes.

Slowly, I reach up and grab the waistband of her pants. I tug them down, my fingers grazing her soft skin. My breath catches. I can't believe this is really happening.

After the first time we fucked, when I tricked her with my 'pool boy' charade, I played a game with her. I told her that I'd only fuck her again if she begged for it. I did it because I didn't want to admit how much my stepsister had wormed her way into my soul. The night of Saturnalia, I thought nothing in the world could be better than hearing her beg me to fuck her, to make all her holes mine.

But it's even better to kneel for her now, to know that I'd lay down my life for this woman without a moment's hesitation, to know in my bone and marrow that every moment of my wretched, monstrous life is dedicated to serving her, loving her.

"Please," I moan, my fingers teasing the lacy edge of her crimson panties. "Please let me make you feel good."

"Very well."

Excited to be allowed between Fergie's legs again, I roll down her leather pants, sliding them over her feet. First one, then the other, nice and slow, so Dawson can watch it all. I run my fingers along her thighs, pushing her legs open so that her feet hang over the arms. Her pussy glistens for me, all pink and flushed and already leaking juices. The most beautiful sight I've ever seen.

Mine once more. Mine and Vic's and Torsten's.

And we are *hers*.

As slowly and delicately as I can muster in my excitement, I cradle her feet in my hands. I slide off her boots and kiss the tops of her feet before placing them on my shoulders. I kiss her muscled shins, the insides and backs of her knees, and move up her thighs.

"This is my gift to you," I murmur, staring up into the shattered emeralds. "As penance for the wrongs I've done."

Fergie pats my hair, the way she might pat Spartacus. Her mouth tugs into a delicious smile.

"You're getting closer to forgiveness, Cas," she says.

"Am I just?" I tease her by nibbling the skin on her inner thighs. She tosses her head back and moans.

I can still see some faint bruises from the wooden spoon on her thighs and the backs of her legs, and I run my tongue over them. My marks. She must be remembering, too, because her moans grow deeper and she thrusts her hips toward me, begging for more. Such a hungry queen. Good thing we have all night.

Behind us, Dawson's wail fades into rough, labored heaving as every breath becomes a struggle. I don't turn around to look, but I hear his body sag as his shoulders dislocate and his body slips down the cross. And I know from the delicious shudder through her body that Fergie feels it, too.

"You get off on this, don't you, my filthy little sister." I grin as I slide my finger between her folds. "You get off on a little torture."

"Maybe," she grins in an infuriating tone as I curl my finger around to rub her G spot.

"Maybe? Well, we shall have to see if we can get you to be more specific."

I dive into her pussy and lick and suck, my heart so full and happy to be tasting her again. Her raspberry scent mingles with the blood on my tongue, and it's the most exquisite thing I've ever tasted. I devour her, tugging her clit between my teeth until she gasps.

I'm not Victor. I don't do gentle or kind. If Fergie wants me, if she's going to take me back, it's as all of me. I'm her monster and I won't ever change.

I push a second finger inside her and twist it a little, stroking that rough patch that drives her so wild. Her legs clamp around my head as she squeezes me, dragging me against her. I push a third finger into her ass, feeling her muscles clench around me as I invade her back hole. Oh, I'm going to have so much fun with her tonight.

"Come for me, sister," I coo. "There's a good girl."

With a howl, Fergie topples over the edge, her whole body clenching and spasming around me.

I love seeing my sister come undone for me.

As she collapses back on her throne, I slide her feet off my shoulders. I tear off my shirt and kick off my jeans and boxers and lie down on my back at her feet, down in the dirt and blood, where I belong. Where I'm happiest.

"I'm laid out for you to use as you wish," I say to her.

Fergie growls like a fucking lion as she crawls over me. Her fist curls around my cock and she pumps me, squeezing me so tight that I see stars. I fist her beautiful hair, pulling her closer so she can smell my pre-cum. I want her to know how wild she makes me.

"You want to show that douchebag over there how you eat a real cock?"

"Hell yes." Fergie's lips curl back into a villainous smirk as she bends over me, taking my whole length into her mouth just as Dawson lets out a pained moan. She sucks me deep until I can feel my tip brush the back of her throat. Fuck, such a hot little mouth.

She grips the base with one hand and strokes me, slow and steady. She's so warm and soft and wet, and I won't be able to hold on much longer.

I pull her hair and slam my hips up into her face. "That's it, my little slut," I coo. "You love it when I fuck your face like this. It gets you off knowing how hard you make me. This cock belongs to you and only you. It's yours forever. Use it and abuse it however you wish."

Fergie makes these little moans as she sucks me. Drool drips down her hand. I glance over my shoulder at her disgusting ex hanging on that cross, blood pooling at his feet. "You don't know what you're missing," I cry out gleefully as I slam into her mouth.

Fuck, it feels so good. So right. So *perfect*.

My balls clench, and the tight ball of tension at the base of my spine uncoils and releases. I yank her hair to pull her off me and come in a big white rope right across her face. My jizz drips from the edge of her nose, and she flicks out her long, pink tongue and licks it off.

"That's it," I moan. "You're such a good sister. Lick it all off for me. Show me how much you like it."

Fergie cocks her head and makes a pouty face. "I wanted you to come inside my pussy," she says. "Or my ass."

"Oh, that's happening, don't you worry. With you sitting on me like this I'll be hard again in minutes, and I'll be able to last for a lot longer next time. Tonight is all about giving my Queen as much pleasure as she can handle. Why don't you help me while we listen to your ex slowly die."

Fergie takes my dick in her hands and strokes it slowly, lovingly, while she cranes her head to listen to Dawson's groans of pain. His elbows would have loosened by now. Once I measured a guy's arms at this point and they were five inches longer than they were before.

When I'm hard again, she shuffles up and straddles me. I hold her hips and guide her as she impales herself on me.

Fuck.

Damn, it feels good to be inside her again, all hot and tight and sweet as raspberries.

My balls are completely empty, and I know that with this goddess on top of me I'll be able to stay hard for hours, long enough to fuck her so hard that she won't walk straight for days.

Fergie starts to ride me, rocking back on her heels as she drags her nails down my chest. I notice shadows moving behind her, and Victor appears over her shoulder. He lays a kiss on her cheek.

"Mind if I cut in?" he asks.

"Mmmmmm." Fergie cups his chin and pulls his face to hers. Their tongues tangle together as she continues to bounce up and down on my cock. Watching her kiss my best friend used to make me feel like punching something. I wanted her to choose me. I wanted someone I cared about to actually choose me. And she did, so now when I see her shove her tongue down Vic's throat, all I can think of is how lucky I am that our Queen likes to share us.

Vic runs his hands down Fergie's body, cupping her breasts and rolling her nipples between his fingers. She leans her head back against his shoulder as I grip her hips and thrust up into her. His eyes meet mine, and I can see all the filthy possibilities for tonight simmering in their ice-blue depths.

That's what's so cool about sharing your girl with the person who knows you best in the world. Vic may not be as depraved as I am, but he has an imagination that can bring my every dark fantasy to life.

With a final, lingering kiss, Vic leaves Fergie with me. He drags over the bag of toys he brought with him (such a Boy Scout... always prepared) and squeezes lube onto his cock and down Fergie's ass crack. She moans as he pushes a finger inside her, and I can feel the pressure of him against my cock through that thin wall of flesh.

I want to be the one in her ass, but I'm not about to complain. We have all night to enjoy her in every imaginable position.

"Are you ready, Duchess?" Vic nibbles her neck as he positions himself behind her.

"Fuck, yes."

With a grunt, he pushes the head of his cock inside her. It squeezes against mine as I thrust into Fergie, and she moans and rolls her neck back to claim his lips. I expect him to tilt his hips forward and fully seat himself inside her, but he just waits, taking his time, kissing her languidly, fondling her tits.

"You have to be the gentleman, don't you, August?" I growl.

"There's nothing wrong with making this a bit romantic," he shoots back, one eyebrow raised in a cock.

"You want some scented candles and rose petals, too?" I lean back, hands behind my head as I watch Fergie's tits bounce. "You've already got your head inside her ass, man. Just go for it. Our Queen likes it rough."

"Fergie?" Vic doesn't look convinced.

"He's right. Dammit, Vic, I want both of you inside meeeeeaaarggh," Fergie's words dissolve into a scream of pure joy as Vic pushes his length all the way inside her. Instantly, the pressure against my cock tightens as he rubs against that thin wall. I draw out and thrust inside her, fitting in with Victor's steady rhythm, so that it feels as if there's one long cock sliding through her body, splitting her in two.

I reach up and turn her head a little, so she's facing Dawson. "You're now looking that fuckstain in the eye," I growl to her. "I want you to tell him everything, while Victor and I make you scream."

Fergie nods, her jaw tight. "Hey, Dawson," she calls up cheerfully, even as her nails dig into my chest.

He murmurs something in reply. It might've been "help me"

or "fuck you," but I can't hear him over the sound of my Queen moaning with pleasure as Vic and I fuck both her holes.

"I just want to tell you that you were a lousy fuckkkkkkk..." Fergie struggles to finish her thought as she gives her body over to us. She stills, her eyes fluttering shut, and Vic and I take over completely. I hold her hips in place while Vic bands his arm around her, pressing her back into his chest. We change our rhythm a little, going a little slower, giving her time to breathe through each thrust so she can say what she needs to say.

"All those times you made me get on my knees for you," Fergie continues, "and you refused to go down on me because you claimed you 'didn't like the taste.' I bet you wish you were over here right now, but you'll never get to taste pussy again, Dawson. I've got three guys who worship me, and I don't need you. No woman on earth needs a deadbeat like you. Right now, I'm sitting on Cassius' enormous cock while Victor works himself into my ass. My ass – a place you begged me to let you go because then you wouldn't be breaking your virginity pledge, and a place you'll never get to go now. I am so full of cock, Dawson, and it's wonderful..."

Fergie sags forward, but Victor holds her upright. "I've got you, Duchess," he whispers. "Do you want us to stop?"

"Don't you fucking dare," she whimpers. "I still have so much to say to our friend Dawson. I want to tell you that I see right through you. I know you liked to go after girls like me because it made you feel powerful. You liked convincing me to do things with you and get them on tape so you could laugh about it with your friends. You thought you could get away with what you did to me because you're the quarterback and I'm the poor little blind girl. You actually believed I should be *grateful* to you. Do you think that now? That poor little blind girl is more powerful than you will ever beeeee..."

Her words dissolving into hungry little moans drive me right to the edge. Hearing Fergie take her power back is the hottest thing in the world. I'm so close to coming right now. I—

"Torsten, I want you," Fergie yells. "I want you to shove your cock so far down my throat that I can't waste another word on this shitstain."

Torsten's whole face lights up like a kid at Christmas. He kicks off his jeans and boxers and steps over me, and normally I wouldn't be super keen on having my friend's ass in my face, but as asses go, Torsten's isn't bad to look at. Fergie swallows his cock, and he sighs with happiness.

We worship our Queen until she dissolves in our arms.

The three of us thrust together, impaling her between us as Dawson lets out a wild, keening cry. It's that cry that finally undoes me – knowing that I may be a complete fuckup, but I did this one thing right. I gave my girl a gift that truly demonstrates how I feel about her, and how she should feel about herself. As I spill myself into her and listen to her screaming her way through another mind-bending orgasm, I know that for once in my life, I, Cassius Dio, have done something *right*.

68

FERGIE

It takes Dawson a long time to die. While we wait, the four of us fuck in a variety of imaginative positions. By the time he draws his last breath, I'm completely exhausted. My pussy has been pounded into submission, I can't feel my legs, and I can barely hold my eyes open.

Cassius lifts me off the chair and carries me over to the cross.

"Thus, with a kiss, you die." I misquote Shakespeare as I lick my lips to make them wet and press them to Dawson's parched ones. I kiss him as he fades away, swallowing his last breath.

In his final moments, he belongs to me.

It's hot as fuck.

Cassius draws me back into his strong arms. He pulls strands of my matted hair from my face and kisses my cheeks and the tip of my nose with a tenderness I didn't know he possessed.

"Sunflower," he whispers. "Are you mine again?"

"I don't know," I answer. "Are you mine?"

"I've been yours since the moment you first walked into my brother's room and wrapped those gorgeous legs around me. Will you come home with me? To *our* home? I've missed seeing that beautiful ass shimmying around our bathroom. And I miss

Spartacus and his insistence on climbing up my jeans like an ice climber with tiny little crampon claws."

"I don't know. Will Cali even let the two of us in the same room again? Besides, I was kind of thinking of moving back into the hotel with Torsten – fresh towels delivered daily, room service..."

"You get all that at home," Cas insists. "And you can't tell me that hotel had better food than Milo."

"That's true."

He crushes me to his body until I'm struggling for breath, and still, he doesn't let go. It's as if he can't get close enough to me, he needs to crawl inside me, to become part of me, flesh and bone and marrow.

"Cas, you have to be careful with her." Vic manages to loosen his arms a little. He hands me a bottle of Powerade and a chocolate bar, while Torsten wraps his leather jacket over my shoulders. "Please eat and drink a little. You burned a lot of calories last night."

"Vic's right. Torture is a serious workout," Cas adds with a smirk in his voice. "How do you think I got so ripped?"

I laugh, but as I bite into the chocolate bar and the sugar rush hits my veins, I turn serious. "What are we going to do now?"

Cassius shrugs. "We could fuck again. That was fun."

I punch him in the arm. "I'm serious. We can't just walk back to our old lives and pretend that nothing has changed. Your mothers are fighting for power, there's a war on the streets, and Drusilla's crazy boyfriend is trying to kill us all. We can't just hide away in a fuck-palace and pretend none of that affects us."

"Sounds like a great idea to me," Cas squeezes my tits. "Let's go and buy a fuck-palace."

"I don't care about the Triumvirate," Torsten says.

"I know you don't. And a month ago, I'd have agreed with

you. But now..." I think about how much I've enjoyed working with Claudia, and everything Cali told me and showed me at her club. And Livvie... I'm still not a hundred percent sure about Torsten's mother, but I can see that she does what she does because she loves her family more than herself. "When I came to Emerald Beach, it was just me and my dad against the world. But now I feel like all your families are mine, too. And I don't want anyone to get hurt."

"People are already hurt," Vic says. And I know he's thinking about Cali, and Yara, and the parcel bomb that could have destroyed his entire family.

"We're not in fluffy bunny land anymore, Sunflower," Cas says. "The Triumvirate is toast, even if our mothers don't see it yet. There's going to be a power vacuum in Emerald Beach. More heads are going to roll."

"Maybe it doesn't have to be," Vic says, his voice tinged with that familiar August smugness. He's got an idea.

"Tell us what you're thinking, August?" I growl. "Because if it's another ridiculous scheme—"

"This time, it's remarkably simple," Vic says. "We could save the Triumvirate if Fergie marries us. All three of us."

I glare at him, unable to believe the words came out of his mouth. It's one thing for Livvie to suggest marriage to solidify her power, but from Vic? "You're crazy."

"It's not as crazy as it sounds. My mother told me that at one point, to hold on to her position as Imperator, she agreed to marry Nero Lucian and Constantine Dio. And everyone knows about my three dads. Like it or not, Duchess, you've become the focal point for this power game. If you were to marry all of us, it would show unity between the three families. It might be enough to make our mothers bury their differences and their soldiers to stop killing each other in the streets."

I squeeze my eyes shut. What Vic is saying makes sense. And

I can't pretend that I haven't *occasionally* thought about how amazing it would be to have all three of them in my life, permanently. And when Cali told me that she wants me to rule the Dio family with Cas at my side, I didn't exactly shy away from the idea.

So then why does the idea of this marriage have me wanting to run for the hills?

As soon as I ask the question, I know the answer.

Because it's not my choice.

I can't help but think that he's suggesting it because it's a practical solution. Not because it's what he truly wants. Vic and I are supposed to go to Harvard. We have a future that's wide fucking open. And if we get married and tether ourselves to the Triumvirate, then it just won't be.

I *want* to marry Vic and Torsten and Cas because we love each other and we have a future together, not because it's some last-ditch effort to save an alliance that's fallen apart so easily over a few months that maybe shouldn't even *be* saved.

"Um..."

"Easy there, Sunflower." Cas pries my fingers off his arm, and I realize that I was squeezing him so hard that my nails drew blood.

"Sorry." I turn to each of them in turn – the three beautiful, ruthless, perfect men who I want in my life forever. "This marriage thing... it's a little freaky. I'm only nineteen. Can I think about it?"

"Of course," Vic says. "But don't think too long, or one of our mothers will do something that they won't be able to come back from."

69

FERGIE

The next day, Cas moves back into Cali's house.

Dad isn't happy about it. I can tell from the way he's silent around me and Cas when we're together. He thinks this is another of Cas' tricks, that he's wormed his way back into the house to get close enough to me to finish me off for good. I don't blame Dad for thinking that. It will take a long time and a lot of groveling on Cas' part to get my father back on his side.

I decide not to push it. I'll let them work their shit out in their own time. Dad has enough to worry about. Cali's still barely walking, and even though her injuries aren't terminal, she spends every spare moment showing me and Cas how to manage her empire and all the jobs that need to be done. It's a lot to take on, especially since all her files are handwritten in leatherbound ledgers and therefore not accessible to me, but I like organizing and making lists and seeing projects through. All the study schedules and essay prep I've done over the years are paying off.

Torsten stays at Cali's house with us, too. If Cali is worried about what Livvie thinks of this, she doesn't mention it. I think things are so tense between the Imperators that it plays into Cali's favor to have him here. I'm not complaining. I like falling asleep to his comforting presence beside me, and the constant sound of his charcoal pencils scrapping over paper. He's working on some secret project that he won't tell me about, and I'm happy that in this tense time, he can find something to be excited about.

One morning, we're all sitting around the kitchen island, Torsten, Cas and I finishing off a plate of Milo's *gözleme* while Dad drinks his coffee and reads the paper and Cali argues with Seymour that she doesn't need any help getting to the car. I feel a strange fluttering in my chest, a sense of finally coming home. Look at us, eating breakfast just like a family. This is all I ever wanted. Maybe I can really, truly have a normal life—

"Hmmm," Dad folds over a page of the paper. "Did you hear about this, Fergalish?"

"What?"

"There's a story in here from back home in Witchwood Falls. Apparently, Dawson Hayward has gone missing, and his parents' church is offering a generous reward for information about his disappearance. You wouldn't happen to know anything about that, would you, Cassius?"

"Not a thing," Cas munches away happily.

"At least we know that wherever he is, he's not alone, because he has God," I say. Cassius lets out a high-pitched chortle that he tries to disguise as choking on his water and doesn't quite succeed. I kick him under the table.

Yup. We're a totally normal family.

THE DAY I return to Stonehurst is a strange one – most colleges are posting their regular decisions today, so everyone is too busy refreshing their phones to give a shit that Fergie Munroe is back on the arm of a still blue-tinged Cassius Dio, or that Poison Ivy seems to be back together.

It's weird to watch their excitement from the outside. I didn't apply for any regular decision schools because I'm going to Harvard. I'm going to Harvard because we never published that article. But it doesn't feel like the triumph I expect it to. I keep thinking about Cali's business files that Vic is helping me type into my Braille note, and helping Claudia with the artifacts. Do I want to move to the other side of the country to go to school while my family is still in danger? Can I leave now, in the middle of this mess that I've helped create?

But today isn't just about me. Euri should be hearing from at least some of her schools today. I go to the Sentinel offices to see if she's there. I've hardly seen her at all lately – she doesn't exactly want to hang out with Vic and Cassius, and I respect that. But I still care about her, and I want her to have the future she deserves. I think she'll blow them away at Oxford or Blackfriars.

She's not in the offices, and she's not at her locker, and she doesn't answer the string of texts I send. I sit next to Sierra in class and ask her if she's seen Euri, but Sierra is too distracted refreshing her phone a million times to utter more than a, "Mmmmm."

Later, I'm at my locker stashing my Braille note when someone comes up behind me and throws their arms around me. "I got into Yale!" Drusilla cries. She takes my hands and pumps them in the air in a silly victory dance. "I'm going to Yale, bitch."

"Congrats!" I grin. I asked Vic if he could reverse some of the things Torsten had done to Dru's records. He went one better, using the very last of the favors he's owed in Poison Ivy to get her in front of the Yale admissions, and Dru's sparkling personality must've done the rest. "That's awesome."

"Thank Vic for me. No offense to him, since he pulled some strings for me, but I don't exactly want to talk to him."

"He understands." I squeeze her shoulder. "You deserve this, Dru."

"I fucking know I do." She skips off down the hall. "I got into Yale! Go Bulldogs."

I listen to her excited singing and to other students congratulating her, and feel a little piece of my coal-heart soften. Poison Ivy may be done with for good, but perhaps they leave a legacy of something more than intimidation and broken dreams. Maybe Claudia and Cali and Livvie are right, and power can be used to make good things happen for deserving people.

Maybe there's hope for us all yet.

I'm sitting on the couch, enjoying an audiobook with Spartacus purring on my lap, when Cas comes up behind me and places his hands over my eyes.

"Mew!" Spartacus is not amused at his calm being disturbed. He bats at Cas' forearm.

I whirl around and slap my stepbrother on the nose. "Nice try. I heard you clomping down the stairs and trying to be oh so quiet as you slunk across the room. You have to be stealthier than that to sneak up on a blind girl. And your mother says you're one of her best assassins?"

He laughs. "Stealth is never my best subject."

"Let me guess, you get top marks for sheer pigheaded stubbornness and being a complete psychopath?"

"Babe, I'm the fucking valedictorian of psychopathy." Cas tries to pull me up. "Come with me. I have another surprise for you."

"Let me guess... we're flying to Rome to throw someone off the Tarquin steps?"

He laughs. "No, but I like the way you think. Let's do that."

"I can't." I point to Spartacus, who has settled back into my lap. "I have cat gravity. It's a hundred times the force of normal gravity. I can't moooove."

Cassius scoops up the cat and places him on Cali's favorite chair. "Problem solved. Now, get that damn fine ass into the car or I'll spank it so red you won't sit down for a month. We have an appointment to keep."

I pile into the backseat of the Tesla. Torsten's already there, scribbling away in his book. We drive for a few minutes and then I sense the wheels rolling over the unique pattern of tiles on Victor's driveway as we arrive to pick him up. Cassius honks several times, but Victor still hasn't appeared. I push my door open. "I'll get him."

Cas reaches across and slams the door shut. "No, you don't. It's best you don't go in there now."

Right. Juliet hates me, and Claudia isn't exactly Cali's favorite person anymore.

It's another ten minutes before Victor finally slides into the passenger seat. "Sorry, I didn't mean to take so long. Juliet's on the warpath today. She got rejected from her fashion school."

"Too bad." I can't muster up the energy to feel sympathy for her. After everything she did to manipulate herself into the fashion world, she deserves to learn that she can't control everything.

Even though it's freezing out, I wind down my window and listen to the sounds of the city whizzing by. We cross the river into Tartarus Oaks and pull into one of the narrow streets. I can hear the rumble of engines from the motorcycle garage down the block, and smell the heady, spicy scent of a Chinese takeout. Vic helps me out of the car, waits for me to fold out my cane, and escorts me after the others into a small shop.

"This is Boris," Cas says as he introduces me to the people who work there. "He's an old buddy of mine. He inked the bear on my chest. And this is Scarlett, his apprentice. We thought you might like her to do your ink."

"My ink?" I squeal. We're in a tattoo parlor? Before Lupercalia, Vic and Torsten inked my Death Lily symbol on their chests, but I mainly did it to show Cassius that I had them on my side. I didn't even consider getting one of my own – after all, I'm blind, so it's not as if I can see it – but now that we're here...

"Yeah, Vic and Torsten love the pieces you got them to do for Lupercalia, but we think that since we're a family, you and I should have something, too," Cas says. "And I know you, Sunflower – once you get one tattoo, you won't want to stop."

"Hey." Scarlett takes my hand and shakes it. "I'm so excited to meet you. I saw you kick Cas' ass in the ring at Lupercalia. You're amazing."

"Thanks," I beam. It's nice to have fans.

"Is this your first time being inked?"

"Yes, and to be honest, I'm sort of a bit confused about why I'm here." I turn to my three guys. "You do remember that I'm blind, right? I can't actually see tattoos."

"We know," Vic says with a grin. "Originally, we were just coming so Cas could get his Death Lily done, but then we thought that you should have something to show that you're our Queen. Torsten and Scarlett have worked together to create a special design just for you. It's similar to the stencil you painted on our lockers, just more detailed and prettier. We want to show everyone that we belong to you."

"And I thought that you wouldn't want to be left out," Torsten says.

"You thought right." I reach across to squeeze his hand. "Is this the secret project you've been working on?"

"No," he says. "I'll tell you about that later. I'm not ready."

"Okay." I give his hand another squeeze, then turn back to Scarlett. "Count me in. What do we do?"

"Well, first," Scarlett leads me behind the counter and has me sit down in a special chair. "We're going to decide where your ink will go, and then I'll mix the colors and we'll get started. Don't worry, it doesn't hurt as much as you think."

"I'm not worried," I say, but my voice shakes a little. Vic laughs.

"If you want to be hardcore, Sunflower, you could get what I'm getting," Cas says from across the room. "It's called scarification. Instead of injecting ink into my skin, Boris is going to *cut* your Death Lily into me. If he does it right, and I practice good aftercare, when the cuts heal, they will be raised scars so you'll be able to feel it."

I open my mouth to speak, but I have no words. I think of the scars I can already feel that cover Cas' and Torsten's bodies – they tell the story of their lives. And now I'm part of that story. It blows me away that the three of them want to wear my symbol permanently on their bodies. Everyone will see it. Everyone will know that we're together.

It might not be marriage, which I still haven't agreed to, but it will send a powerful symbol through the Triumvirate.

Victor bends down and kisses me. "I know what you're thinking," he whispers. "You think that we're doing this because of the Triumvirate. But that's not why. We belong to you, Duchess. You're our Queen, and we will give our lives to protect you. We're proud to wear our love for you on our bodies."

"Thank you." I lean up and kiss him, tangling our tongues together until I'm out of breath and Scarlett whistles behind me. I turn to her. "I'm ready now. I think I'll just have a normal ink tattoo, thanks."

I'm intrigued by Cas' scarification, but not intrigued enough to try it.

"You're going to love it," Scarlett says. "The Death Lily your friend drew is pretty stunning. Have you ever considered a career as a tattoo artist?"

"No," Torsten says.

"Well, you should. You're a natural." Scarlett hands me a flat square with a raised design. "And I've solved the problem of you not being able to see it. I have a 3D printer. I already made you a copy."

I run my fingers over it, feeling the petals of the flower and the wreath of ivy around it, forming a frame that incorporates the three families' symbols: The lion, the sword, and the eagle. There's also a tiny bear paw.

Scarlett has made it in different layers so I can get a sense of what lines will be thick and where she'll apply shading and texture.

"This is perfect," I whisper.

"I know, right? I'm glad I could help you see it. I actually tattoo a lot of blind people," Scarlett says. "There are many ways to appreciate art, not just with your eyes."

"I couldn't agree more," I grin as I settle into the chair. My chest flutters with nerves, but I'm excited, too. I love the idea of having Torsten's art on my skin. And after all this time being a pawn torn between the three Triumvirate families, being used by all of them, it feels good to wear my own mark and to claim my own power.

I'm Fergie Macintosh, and no one owns me.

"Do you have any idea where you'd like to wear this design?" Scarlett asks. "It would look awesome on the back of your shoulder, or on your bicep or hip—"

I'm distracted by sounds from the chair next to mine. Boris has started his work on Cas. The scarification must be painful beyond belief because my monstrous stepbrother grunts and twitches.

"Maybe this will make you sit still," I lean over and whisper to him. "I forgive you."

"You do?" His words slur a little. He does that sometimes now, especially when he's happy.

"I do. What you did was awful, Cas. But I understand why you did it. And I think... I think that I'm ready to trust you with my heart again. But you're on thin ice, mister." I shake my finger at him. "You can't fuck up again."

"I won't," he promises, gripping my hand. He crushes my fingers as the blade slices his skin.

Call me crazy, call me a sucker for punishment, call me addicted to the kind of brutal, obsessive love that only my stepbrother can give me, but I believe him.

FERGIE

Days pass, each one happier than the last. I don't go to school, too absorbed in having my guys back and in catching up with the chaos of the world of the Triumvirate. Euri even calls me a few times, but we keep missing each other. She says she has something she wants to tell me, and I know it's that she got into some fabulous overseas college, and I'm glad at least that she doesn't hate me after I pulled the article. With the instability in the city, having that article come out would ignite a gang war that would stain the streets crimson with blood.

We've finally settled on plans for next year, and I'm excited. It seems as if the Imperators are trying to work things out, and Cas, Torsten, and Vic are working on their parents in their own ways, trying to get them talking. We'll help them to see that they're stronger together and as soon as Cali is well enough, she'll take over the family business again.

Victor and I are going to Harvard, and Torsten and Cas are talking about coming with us. Cas would open an East Coast gym – an offshoot of his mother's school – and Torsten has his eye on an elite private art college nearby. He doesn't think he'll be able to pass the interview, but I know with our help, he can do anything.

But just because I've decided to leave the family business in Cali's capable hands, doesn't mean I'm resting on my ass. I want to be ready in case things change. I understand now that the current peace is hard-won and precarious.

With Cali still injured, Seymour drives me to the gym, and each day I spend hours fighting. My muscles scream with pain, but I can feel my conditioning slowly coming back. Cas is with me at every training session with Konstantin – they give me pointers, correct my form, and show me new ways of doing things that counter my years of jiujitsu training. Neither of them goes easy on me, and I appreciate them all the more for that.

One day, we're mid-bout when Cas' phone rings. Usually, nothing breaks through to Cas when he's in the zone, but it's a very distinctive ring that instantly jerks him out of the fight. "It's Cali," he says as he releases the hold on me. I roll away, taking the reprieve to catch my breath and work out the kinks in my aching shoulder.

Cas moves to the corner of the room and talks to his mother in a hushed, urgent voice. He covers the mouthpiece with his hand, and not even I can make out what he's saying.

He hangs up abruptly and returns to me.

"Mom wants us to go to dinner tonight at Livvie's house. The Augusts will be there, too. The Imperators are going to try and work out how to fix this. They want us all there, and that includes you."

"Good. About time."

"Yup. I can't believe I'm saying this, but I'm sick of the... the... um, the fighting." Cas steps off the mats and I hear him zipping up his hoodie. "I should go. Mom will want me at home to brief me on the negotiations. It's not exactly my strongest skill."

"I want to stay a bit later," I say. "Is that okay? Konstantin can help me nail this hold."

"Sure, but only for another hour. No more. Seymour will be downstairs to drive you home. I don't want you alone in this neighborhood with Zack Lionel Sommesnay still on the loose, and I need you to look incredible tonight because everyone in the room will have their eyes on you."

I swallow down that daunting thought as Cas leans in and steals a violent, breathless kiss.

After he leaves, Konstantin and I get into the intricacies of the new hold, and before I know it, an hour is up and it's time for me to leave. I throw on some sweatpants, sling my bag over my shoulder, pick up my cane, and head for the stairs. As I descend, I pull out my phone to check my messages.

I've missed a dozen calls from Euri. As I step outside to wait for Seymour, I hold the phone up to my ear.

"Hey, Euri, what's up?"

"Fergie, hey..." Euri sounds a little frazzled. "I'm so glad you picked up. I really need to see you. Can I come over tonight? I promise to bring some worthy snacks."

"Unfortunately, I have this thing with my parents," I say. That's a woefully inadequate truth, but I don't know how much Euri wants to know about the Triumvirate now. "So no can do. What about tomorrow night? Cas gave me a bottle of top-shelf vodka, and it's got your name on it. We could make Jell-O shots again—"

"I can't tomorrow," she sounds sad. "I don't think you'll want to talk to me tomorrow."

I stop in the doorway, listening for the familiar rumble of Seymour's engine idling, but I don't hear it. He must not be here yet. I lean against the door and prop the phone on my shoulder as I hunt around in my bag for my jacket. "You're being dramatic.

We've been through hell together. I'll never hate you. Why would you say that?"

"Fergie, I've been trying to tell you for d-d-days," Euri's voice stutters. "I know you said that we can't publish that article, but I changed my mind."

Fear sinks in my chest. "What do you mean, you changed your mind?"

"I mean, by the time you told me, I already had the draft out to a couple of people I know. Do you remember Jessie – the tutor at that Young Journalist internship I did last year? Anyway, I got the call from him a few days ago that they want to print the article in the *New York Times*."

"Euri, no. You *can't*. We have to stop it—"

"It's too late. It's already happened. The edition came out this morning. Fergie, it was the. *New. York. Times*. I can't say no to that. And it's an important story, you know? I never liked that we pulled it just because it was a little inconvenient for Victor August and his friends. And I put your name back in the credits – you said it didn't bother you if you lost your place at Harvard, but Jessie doesn't even think you will. He thinks they'll like the story of the blind girl taking down the cheating ring."

My head buzzes. This can't be real. It can't be happening. "Euri, please tell me you're kidding."

"I am not kidding. The article came out today in the Sentinel. And in the *New York Times*. Fergie, I can't believe it! The *New York Times*! I am just—"

No. Nonoonononono. This isn't real.

I'm asleep. I'm asleep and this is a nightmare.

Any moment now I'm going to wake up with Cas slapping my cheek with his cock...

I slide down the wall as the weight of what she's done crushes my chest. "Shit."

"—and their parents will protect them from whatever fallout they'll face, so it's not like it's even a big deal—"

"Excuse me, ma'am?"

I turn to the sound of a voice, closer than I'd like. A guy grabs my arm and tries to yank me out of the doorway.

I wrench my hand and break his grip and turn away. There are some freaks in this neighborhood. Shouldn't they know better than to attack anyone in Cali Dio's doorway?

"Get lost, jerk," I mutter, pressing the phone back against my ear so I can talk some sense into Euri, but the guy comes back and tries to grab me again. It's a hold they teach in cop school, for disarming suspects. So it's a cop. I slam the back of his hand against the wall, and he curses.

"Euri, I have to go. Some cop is harassing me." I turn in the direction of the voice. "What the fuck is your problem? Touch me again and I'll break your fucking arm."

"Ma'am, you're going to come with me."

"Why? I'm just standing in a doorway, not breaking any laws. Besides, you're supposed to identify yourself. I'm blind, so I'd like you to hand me your badge."

The voice turns cold, dangerous. "What makes you think I'm a police officer?"

A chill settles in my heart.

In a split second, it all makes sense. Seymour would never be late and he'd never leave me waiting by myself in this neighborhood in Tartarus Oaks.

This guy has hurt Seymour.

I'm in deep fucking shit.

I can tell from the direction of the guy's voice that he's big, and I can only assume that he has friends with him. I only have a moment to surprise him. He expects me to run back up the stairs and into Cali's gym, but I can't guarantee that all the guys up there are loyal. I could be walking straight into a trap.

Instead, I crouch low and run at him. My brain rattles as my skull smashes into his crotch, and I use the momentum to roll him over my shoulder, his body flying over mine. He crashes into the wall in the stairwell, and I make a run for the street.

I don't make it far. More hands grab me, slamming my wrists up against the brick wall. "Restrain her hands," the guy says, his voice tight with pain. "The little filly has spirit."

My attackers hold my hands and feet while someone presses a damp, chemical-smelling cloth over my mouth, pressing it tightly over my nostrils and lips. I struggle against them, and I manage to get one wrist free and elbow a guy in the solar plexus, but another hand reaches up and stuffs the cloth over my nostrils. I try to stop breathing in the stuff, but it's too late, too late, I can feel my limbs go numb and...

"Victor." My mother closes the door to my room and sits down on the bed. "Do you know where your sister is?"

I shake my head. Juliet and I haven't exactly been talking lately. She's been spending as little time at our house as possible, especially now that she didn't get into college.

"Can you find her, please? Try her friends, school, anywhere. She has to be at this meeting tonight. This is the last thing I need right now." Mom wrings her hands through her hair. "I swear, it's like someone's out to get me. And it doesn't help that your dad's gone AWOL."

That's odd. "Gabe's missing?"

"Yeah. I mean, it's fine. He's not exactly going to be useful in a gang shootout, although I was hoping for a show of strength against Cali and Livvie. But it's not like him not to check in with me. He got a phone call this morning from a new producer who's interested in doing some film score work, and you know how much your father has always wanted a project like that." Mom frowns. "He left for the meeting five hours ago. I just didn't expect it to go on so long, but I guess that's a good thing."

"Yeah. He's probably taken the whole film crew out for ice cream," I grin, because that's exactly the kind of thing Dad would do.

"You're right. What about Fergie? She's going to be there tonight, right?" Claudia paces the length of my room again, wringing her hands with agitation. "Will she sit with us?"

"I don't know, Mom. Cas told her about it, so I assume she'll be with the Dios. I haven't talked to her all day." I frown at her. "Don't look at me like that. She's at Cali's gym beating a bunch of assassins to a bloody pulp. She's hardly going to stop having fun to shoot me a smiley emoji."

"I don't trust Cassius."

"You should. The three of us want what you want – to keep this city and avoid a gang war." My phone buzzes on the bed. I pat Mom's knee. "That's probably one of them now."

But the screen flashes UNKNOWN NUMBER, and when I pick it up, I'm greeted by a digitally altered voice that chills the blood in my veins.

"Hello, Victor. You don't know me, but I know all about you. There's a lovely article about you in the paper today."

"Who is this? I'm hanging up now," I snap. "I'm not in the mood for jokes."

"But if you hang up, then you won't see your girlfriend and your father alive again, and they're *dying* to talk to you."

My blood freezes. Beside me, my mother makes a frantic series of mimes. I click on the RECORD button.

"What are you talking about?"

The creepy voice chuckles. "A picture speaks a thousand words, don't you think?"

My phone beeps. UNKNOWN NUMBER has sent me a text. My heart plummets as I load an image of Fergie bound to a chair, her mouth gagged with electrical tape, her eyes wide, frightened. Beside her is another figure, also taped to a chair.

He's cloaked in shadows, but I'd recognize that shimmering head of dark hair anywhere.

Gabriel.

This bastard has Fergie and Gabriel. But how...

The movie score was obviously fake, a ruse to lure my father into a trap. But Fergie's with Cassius – how did they get her away from him? And what did he mean about an article in the paper about me?

Unless... unless Cas is in on it...

Mom's cheek brushes mine as she leans in to listen.

"Okay," I say into the phone. "You have my attention. What do you want?"

"That's the Victor August I know and love," the voice coos. "You may think you're a future king, but you'll dance like a marionette for me. If you want to see them both alive again, you'll do exactly as I say."

CASSIUS

"What the fuck?"

I'm sitting on the sofa, wearing an uncomfortable suit because Cali wants me to look smart for the meeting, and she comes in and tosses her phone at my head. It bounces off my chest and lands on the sofa, the screen pointing toward me.

"What was that for?"

"What do you fucking think?" she screams. "Just once, I'd like someone in this family to not be a complete screw-up."

My stone heart plummets straight into my boots as I read the headline on the news site.

THE POISON IVY CLUB: WHAT RICH KIDS WILL DO TO GET IN.

I scan the first paragraph, and it's enough – I know what I'm looking at.

It's an article about us. About Victor and Torsten and me, and all the kids we helped into top schools. In it are the secrets and favors we demanded as payment, the stunts we pulled, and all the filthy, nefarious things that we helped to orchestrate. These are secrets that could only be found on the pages of our ledger.

Secrets that only me, Torsten, Victor, and Fergie could possibly know.

And they're splashed all over the front page of the New York Times. Under a byline that reads:

article by Eurydice Jones and Fergus Macintosh

"Fergie wouldn't do this," I say.

"Wouldn't she? Or maybe she's been playing you all this time. Maybe she wanted you to think you kissed and made up so she had time to pull this stunt when it could do maximum damage," Cali says. "Where is she now? She's supposed to be here for the meeting. Why is she conveniently not around when this article dropped?"

Cali has a point. "She wanted to stay back and practice some more. I said it was fine as long as it was only an hour. I sent Seymour to get her."

"Seymour left two hours ago," Milo says. Now he sounds worried.

"So where the fuck are they?" Cali towers over me. Only my mother can make her five-foot-eleven statuesque figure appear like a brick wall of rage.

"This isn't her. I know it."

"Where did the author, this Eurydice Jones, get these details about our lives?"

"I don't know yet, but I know that Fergie—"

The doorbell rings. Milo slinks off to answer it, no doubt happy to escape the room because my mother is about to explode.

"That'll be the fucking Feds," Cali screams, whacking me on

the side of my face. "They're coming to take you away, and you deserve it. I can't believe you'd be so stupid—"

She turns toward the doorway just as Milo enters.

Cali's mouth falls open. I wave my hand in front of her face, an action that would be liable to get my hand chopped off, but she doesn't blink, doesn't move a muscle.

"Wh—what are you doing here?" she stammers out.

I whirl around, taking in the two people standing with Milo. Both are tall and broad, and both are completely familiar.

One I've never seen before in my life. Except that's not true, because I've seen his face in my mirror every time I shave – he has my eyes, my slightly flat nose.

The other familiar figure stands beside Milo, a shit-eating grin plastered across his face.

"How about a hug?" he says to me.

"How about you fuck off into the sun."

"Now, now, little bro," Gaius chuckles as he comes at me, his arms spread wide. "Is that any way to treat your big brother and your dear old dad? How about a proper welcome for the prodigal son's return?"

TO BE CONTINUED

What will happen to Fergie and Gabe? Will the Triumvirate's shaky truce survive a full-blown war? Find out in the explosive final book in the Stonehurst Prep: Elite series, *Poison Kiss* – http://books2read.com/elite3

Victor, Cas, and Torsten think they know everything that goes on in Emerald Beach, but do they? Find out when you sign up to Steffanie Holmes' newsletter and get a bonus scene from *Poison*

Ivy, along with a collection of other bonus material from Steffanie's worlds. Sign up here: https://www.steffanieholmes. com/newsletter

"I was baptized in bloodshed. To the bloodshed, I return."

Discover how the three women of the Triumvirate became who they are in the complete Stonehurst Prep dark contemporary reverse harem series. Start with book 1, *My Stolen Life*: http:// books2read.com/mystolenlife

Turn the page for a sizzling excerpt.

FROM THE AUTHOR

Whew! Hello.

How are you doing after that? You okay? Do you need a hug? Or some heart medication?

Things might seem bad for Fergie now, but trust me, our girl doesn't take shit lying down. Sound the fucktrumpets, because war is coming to Emerald Beach and she and her harem are right in the heart of it. You'll have to read the final book, *Poison Kiss*, to find out what happens next.

It's been so much fun to return to Stonehurst Prep with a new leading lady. Fergie is one of my favourite heroines that I've ever written. She's bold and sassy and she acts before she thinks and she's not defined by what she can't see.

Too often in books, blindness is conflated with weakness. As a blind reader myself, I'm always desperate to see more women like me in books, having adventures and doing normal things and getting our happily ever afters. I wrote Fergie for a teenage Steff who desperately needed a heroine and to believe that life gets better.

But Fergie's also not superhuman. Everything she does – the echolocation, her martial arts skills – is a normal part of the lives of many blind people, including me. (I have a brown belt in Gojo Ryu karate and I've done a bit of Jiujitsu, but now I pole dance instead). She's fallible and way too headstrong and stubborn for her own good. In short, she's a person, with all the traits and foibles and hopes and dreams that we all experience. I wanted you to see her, because too often, women like her are never seen.

Also, my health & safety conscious husband wants to warn everyone that Methylene blue is toxic and getting it on your skin or in your eyes or mouth could make you seriously sick...or worse. Artie carefully gives Fergie only enough to dye Cassius blue without seriously hurting him, but this is NOT a trick to try at home.

Thanks as always to my husband James, and to Meg for the epically helpful editing job, and to Acacia for the stunning covers. To my crew of Badass Author friends – Bea, Danielle, Kim, Erin, Selena, Victoria, Angel Lawson, and Rachel, who have cheered me on while I've torn my hair out writing this doorstopper of a book.

And to you, the reader, for going on this journey with me, even though it's led to some dark places. Warning: if you thought book 2 was tough, book 3 is going to knock your socks off. Grab *Poison Kiss* here: http://books2read.com/elite3.

If you're curious about Claudia, Cali, and Livvie and how they became who they are, then you *need* the complete Stonehurst Prep dark contemporary reverse harem series. Start with book 1, *My Stolen Life*: http://books2read.com/mystolenlife

If you want to keep up with my bookish news and get weekly stories about the real life true crimes and ghost stories that inspire my books, you can join my newsletter at https://www.stefanieholmes.com/newsletter. When you join you'll get a free copy of *Cabinet of Curiosities*, a compendium of bonus and deleted scenes and stories. It includes a fun bonus scene from *Poison Ivy* where you'll learn a little more about the Triumvirate.

I'm so happy you enjoyed Fergie's story! I'd love it if you wanted to leave a review on Amazon or Goodreads. It will help other readers to find their next read.

Thank you, thank you! I love you heaps! Until next time.

Steff

ENJOY THIS EXCERPT FROM MY STOLEN LIFE

PROLOGUE: MACKENZIE

I roll over in bed and slam against a wall.

Huh? Odd.

My bed isn't pushed against a wall. I must've twisted around in my sleep and hit the headboard. I do thrash around a lot, especially when I have bad dreams, and tonights was particularly gruesome. My mind stretches into the silence, searching for the tendrils of my nightmare. *I'm lying in bed and some dark shadow comes and lifts me up, pinning my arms so they hurt. He drags me downstairs to my mother, slumped in her favorite chair. At first, I think she passed out drunk after a night at the club, but then I see the dark pool expanding around her feet, staining the designer rug.*

I see the knife handle sticking out of her neck.

I see her glassy eyes rolled toward the ceiling.

I see the window behind her head, and my own reflection in the glass, my face streaked with blood, my eyes dark voids of pain and hatred.

But it's okay now. It was just a dream. It's—

OW.

I hit the headboard again. I reach down to rub my elbow, and my hand grazes a solid wall of satin. On my other side.

What the hell?

I open my eyes into a darkness that is oppressive and complete, the kind of darkness I'd never see inside my princess bedroom with its flimsy purple curtains letting in the glittering skyline of the city. The kind of darkness that folds in on me, pressing me against the hard, un-bedlike surface I lie on.

Now the panic hits.

I throw out my arms, kick with my legs. I hit walls. Walls all around me, lined with satin, dense with an immense weight pressing from all sides. Walls so close I can't sit up or bend my knees. I scream, and my scream bounces back at me, hollow and weak.

I'm in a coffin. I'm in a motherfucking coffin, and I'm *still alive*.

I scream and scream and scream. The sound fills my head and stabs at my brain. I know all I'm doing is using up my precious oxygen, but I can't make myself stop. In that scream I lose myself, and every memory of who I am dissolves into a puddle of terror.

When I do stop, finally, I gasp and pant, and I taste blood and stale air on my tongue. A cold fear seeps into my bones. Am I dying? My throat crawls with invisible bugs. Is this what it feels like to die?

I hunt around in my pockets, but I'm wearing purple pajamas, and the only thing inside is a bookmark Daddy gave me. I can't see it of course, but I know it has a quote from Julius Caesar on it. *Alea iacta est. The die is cast.*

Like fuck it is.

I think of Daddy, of everything he taught me – memories too dark to be obliterated by fear. Bile rises in my throat. I swallow, choke it back. Daddy always told me our world is forged in blood. I might be only thirteen, but I know who he is, what he's capable of. I've heard the whispers. I've seen the way people hurry to appease him whenever he enters a room. I've had the lessons from Antony in what to do if I find myself alone with one of Daddy's enemies.

Of course, they never taught me what to do if one of those enemies *buries me alive.*

I can't give up.

I claw at the satin on the lid. It tears under my fingers, and I pull out puffs of stuffing to reach the wood beneath. I claw at the surface, digging splinters under my nails. Cramps arc along my arm from the awkward angle. I know it's hopeless; I know I'll never be able to scratch my way through the wood. Even if I can, I *feel* the weight of several feet of dirt above me. I'd be crushed in moments. But I have to try.

I'm my father's daughter, and this is not how I die.

I claw and scratch and tear. I lose track of how much time passes in the tiny space. My ears buzz. My skin weeps with cold sweat.

A noise reaches my ears. A faint shifting. A scuffle. A scrape and thud above my head. Muffled and far away.

Someone piling the dirt in my grave.

Or maybe...

...maybe someone digging it out again.

Fuck, fuck, please.

"Help." My throat is hoarse from screaming. I bang the lid with my fists, not even feeling the splinters piercing my skin. "Help me!"

THUD. Something hits the lid. The coffin groans. My veins burn with fear and hope and terror.

The wood cracks. The lid is flung away. Dirt rains down on me, but I don't care. I suck in lungfuls of fresh, crisp air. A circle of light blinds me. I fling my body up, up into the unknown. Warm arms catch me, hold me close.

"I found you, Claws." Only Antony calls me by that nickname. Of course, it would be my cousin who saves me. Antony drags me over the lip of the grave, *my* grave, and we fall into crackling leaves and damp grass.

I sob into his shoulder. Antony rolls me over, his fingers pressing all over my body, checking if I'm hurt. He rests my back against cold stone. "I have to take care of this," he says. I watch through tear-filled eyes as he pushes the dirt back into the hole – into what was supposed to be my grave – and brushes dead leaves on top. When he's done, it's impossible to tell the ground's been disturbed at all.

I tremble all over. I can't make myself stop shaking. Antony comes back to me and wraps me in his arms. He staggers to his feet, holding me like I'm weightless. He's only just turned eighteen, but already he's built like a tank.

I let out a terrified sob. Antony glances over his shoulder, and there's panic in his eyes. "You've got to be quiet, Claws," he whispers. "They might be nearby. I'm going to get you out of here."

I can't speak. My voice is gone, left in the coffin with my screams. Antony hoists me up and darts into the shadows. He runs with ease, ducking between rows of crumbling gravestones and beneath bent and gnarled trees. Dimly, I recognize this place – the old Emerald Beach cemetery, on the edge of Beaumont Hills overlooking the bay, where the original families of Emerald Beach buried their dead.

Where someone tried to bury me.

Antony bursts from the trees onto a narrow road. His car is parked in the shadows. He opens the passenger door and settles me inside before diving behind the wheel and gunning the engine.

We tear off down the road. Antony rips around the deadly corners like he's on a racetrack. Steep cliffs and crumbling old mansions pass by in a blur.

"My parents..." I gasp out. "Where are my parents?"

"I'm sorry, Claws. I didn't get to them in time. I only found you."

I wait for this to sink in, for the fact I'm now an orphan to hit me in a rush of grief. But I'm numb. My body won't stop shaking, and I left my brain and my heart buried in the silence of that coffin.

"Who?" I ask, and I fancy I catch a hint of my dad's cold savagery in my voice. "Who did this?"

"I don't know yet, but if I had to guess, it was Brutus. I warned your dad that he was making alliances and building up to a challenge. I think he's just made his move."

I try to digest this information. Brutus – who was once my father's trusted friend, who'd eaten dinner at our house and played Chutes and Ladders with me – killed my parents and buried me alive. But it bounces off the edge of my skull and doesn't stick. The life I had before, my old life, it's gone, and as I twist and grasp for memories, all I grab is stale coffin air.

"What now?" I ask.

Antony tosses his phone into my lap. "Look at the headlines."

I read the news app he's got open, but the words and images blur together. "This... this doesn't make any sense..."

"They think you're dead, Claws," Antony says. "That means you have to *stay* dead until we're strong enough to move against him. Until then, you have to be a ghost. But don't worry, I'll protect you. I've got a plan. We'll hide you where they'll never think to look."

Start reading:
http://books2read.com/mystolenlife

MORE FROM THE AUTHOR

From the author of *Poison Ivy* and *Shunned* comes this dark contemporary high school reverse harem romance.

Psst. I have a secret.

Are you ready?

I'm Mackenzie Malloy, and everyone thinks they know who I am.

Five years ago, I disappeared.

No one has seen me or my family outside the walls of Malloy Manor since.
But now I'm coming to reclaim my throne:
The Ice Queen of Stonehurst Prep is back.

Standing between me and my everything?
Three things can bring me down:
The sweet guy who wants answers from his former friend.
The rock god who wants to f*ck me.
The king who'll crush me before giving up his crown.

They think they can ruin me, wreck it all, but I won't let them.
I'm not the Mackenzie Eli used to know.
Hot boys and rock gods like Gabriel won't win me over.
And just like Noah, I'll kill to keep my crown.

I'm just a poor little rich girl with the stolen life.
I'm here to tear down three princes,
before they destroy me.

Read now:
http://books2read.com/mystolenlife

OTHER BOOKS BY STEFFANIE HOLMES

Nevermore Bookshop Mysteries

A Dead and Stormy Night

Of Mice and Murder

Pride and Premeditation

How Heathcliff Stole Christmas

Memoirs of a Garroter

Prose and Cons

A Novel Way to Die

Much Ado About Murder

Crime and Publishing

Plot and Bothered

Kings of Miskatonic Prep

Shunned

Initiated

Possessed

Ignited

Stonehurst Prep

My Stolen Life

My Secret Heart

My Broken Crown

My Savage Kingdom

Stonehurst Prep Elite

Poison Ivy

Poison Flower

Poison Kiss

Dark Academia

Pretty Girls Make Graves

Brutal Boys Cry Blood

Manderley Academy

Ghosted

Haunted

Spirited

Briarwood Witches

Earth and Embers

Fire and Fable

Water and Woe

Wind and Whispers

Spirit and Sorrow

Crookshollow Gothic Romance

Art of Cunning (Alex & Ryan)

Art of the Hunt (Alex & Ryan)

Art of Temptation (Alex & Ryan)

The Man in Black (Elinor & Eric)

Watcher (Belinda & Cole)

Reaper (Belinda & Cole)

Wolves of Crookshollow

Digging the Wolf (Anna & Luke)

Writing the Wolf (Rosa & Caleb)

Inking the Wolf (Bianca & Robbie)

Wedding the Wolf (Willow & Irvine)

Want to be informed when the next Steffanie Holmes paranormal romance story goes live? Sign up for the newsletter at www.steffanieholmes.com/ newsletter to get the scoop, and score a free collection of bonus scenes and stories to enjoy!

ABOUT THE AUTHOR

Steffanie Holmes is the *USA Today* bestselling author of the paranormal, gothic, dark, and fantastical. Her books feature clever, witty heroines, secret societies, creepy old mansions and alpha males who *always* get what they want.

Legally-blind since birth, Steffanie received the 2017 Attitude Award for Artistic Achievement. She was also a finalist for a 2018 Women of Influence award.

Steff is the creator of <u>Rage Against the Manuscript</u> – a resource of free content, books, and courses to help writers tell their story, find their readers, and build a badass writing career.

Steffanie lives in New Zealand with her husband, a horde of cantankerous cats, and their medieval sword collection.

Steffanie Holmes newsletter

Grab a free copy *Cabinet of Curiosities* – a compendium of short stories and bonus scenes, including a bonus scene from *Poison Ivy* – when you sign up for updates with the Steffanie Holmes newsletter.

http://www.steffanieholmes.com/newsletter

Come hang with Steffanie
www.steffanieholmes.com
hello@steffanieholmes.com